The Knight Of Gwynne
Vol. 2

by

Charles James Lever

The Knight Of Gwynne
Vol. 2
by Charles James Lever

Copyright © 2024

All Rights reserved.

ISBN: 978-93-62761-22-4

Published by

DOUBLE 9 BOOKS
2/13-B, Ansari Road
Daryaganj, New Delhi – 110002
info@double9books.com
www.double9books.com
Tel. 011-40042856

This book is under public domain

ABOUT THE AUTHOR

Charles James Lever was an Irish author and storyteller who lived from August 31, 1806 to June 1, 1872. Anthony Trollope said that Lever's books were like his conversations. Lever was born on Amiens Street in Dublin. He was the second son of architect and builder James Lever and went to special schools. He had many adventures at Trinity College, Dublin, from 1823 to 1828. It was there that he got his medical degree in 1831. Some of the stories of his books are based on these experiences. The character of Frank Webber in the book Charles O'Malley was based on Robert Boyle, a friend from college who later became a priest. Lever and Boyle made extra money by singing original songs in the streets of Dublin. They also pulled off a lot of other jokes, which Lever wrote about in more detail in his books O'Malley, Con Cregan, and Lord Kilgobbin. Before he really started studying medicine, Lever went to Canada on an emigrant ship as an untrained surgeon. He has used some of what he learned in Con Cregan, Arthur O'Leary, and Roland Cashel. When he got to Canada, he went into the woods and joined a Native American group. But he had to leave because his life was in danger, just like his character Bagenal Daly did in his book The Knight of Gwynne.

CONTENTS

CHAPTER I
SOME CHARACTERS NEW TO THE
KNIGHT AND THE READER

Soon after breakfast the following morning the Knight set out to pay his promised visit to Miss Daly, who had taken up her abode at a little village on the coast, about three miles distant. Had Darcy known that her removal thither had been in consequence of his own arrival at "The Corvy," the fact would have greatly added to an embarrassment sufficiently great on other grounds. Of this, however, he was not aware; her brother Bagenal accounting for her not inhabiting "The Corvy" as being lonely and desolate, whereas the village of Ballintray was, after its fashion, a little watering-place much frequented in the season by visitors from Coleraine, and other towns still more inland.

Thither now the Knight bent his steps by a little footpath across the fields which, from time to time, approached the seaside, and wound again through the gently undulating surface of that ever-changing tract.

Not a human habitation was in sight; not a living thing was seen to move over that wide expanse; it was solitude the very deepest, and well suited the habit of his mind who now wandered there alone. Deeply lost in thought, he moved onward, his arms folded on his breast, and his eyes downcast; he neither bestowed a glance upon the gloomy desolation of the land prospect, nor one look of admiring wonder at the giant cliffs, which, straight as a wall, formed the barriers against the ocean.

"What a strange turn of fortune!" said he, at length, as relieving his overburdened brain by speech. "I remember well the last day I ever saw her; it was just before my departure for England for my marriage. I remember well driving over to Castle Daly to say good-bye! Perhaps, too, I had some lurking vanity in exhibiting that splendid team of four grays, with two outriders. How perfect it all was! and a proud fellow I was that day! Maria was looking very handsome; she was dressed for riding, but ordered the horses back as I drove up. What spirits she had!—with what zest she seized upon the enjoyments her youth, her beauty, and her fortune gave her!—how ardently she indulged every costly caprice and every whim, as if revelling in the pleasure of extravagance even for its own sake! Fearless in everything, she did indeed seem like a native princess, surrounded by all that barbaric splendor of her father's house, the troops of servants, the equipages without number, the guests that came and went unceasingly, all rendering homage to her beauty. 'T was a gorgeous dream of life, and well she understood how to realize all its enchantment. We scarcely parted good friends on that same last day," said he, after a pause; "her manner was almost mordant. I can recall the cutting sarcasms she dealt around her,—strange exuberance of high spirits carried away to the wildest flights of fancy; and after all, when, having dropped my glove, I returned to the luncheon-room to seek it, I saw her in a window, bathed in tears; she did not perceive me, and we never met after. Poor girl! were those outpourings of sorrow the compensation nature exacted for the exercise of such brilliant powers of wit and imagination? or had she really, as some believed, a secret attachment somewhere? Who knows? And now we are to meet again, after years of absence,—so fallen too! If it were not for these gray hairs and this wrinkled brow, I could believe it all a dream;—and what is it but a dream, if we are not fashioned to act differently because of our calamities? Events are but shadows if they move us not."

From thoughts like these he passed on to others,—as to how he should be received, and what changes time might have wrought in her.

"She was so lovely, and might have been so much more so, had she but curbed that ever-rising spirit of mockery that made the sparkling lustre of her eyes seem like the scathing flash of lightning rather than the soft beam of tranquil beauty. How we quarrelled and made up again! what everlasting treaties ratified and broken! and now to look back on this with a heart and a spirit weary, how sad it seems! Poor Maria! her destiny has been less happy than mine. She is alone in the world; I have affectionate hearts around me to make a home beneath the humble roof of a cabin."

The Knight was aroused from his musings by suddenly finding himself on the brow of a hill, from which the gorge descended abruptly into a little cove, around which the village of Ballintray was built. A row of whitewashed cottages, in winter inhabited by the fishermen and their families, became in the summer season the residence of the visitors, many of whom deserted spacious and well-furnished mansions to pass their days in the squalid discomfort of a cabin. If beauty of situation and picturesque charms of scenery could ever atone for so many inconveniences incurred, this little village might certainly have done so. Landlocked by two jutting promontories, the bay was sheltered both east and westward, while the rising ground behind defended it from the sweeping storms which the south brings in its seasons of rain; in front the distant island of Isla could be seen, and the Scottish coast was always discernible in the clear atmosphere of the evening.

While Darcy stood admiring the well-chosen spot, his eye rested upon a semicircular panel of wood, which, covering over a short and gravelled avenue, displayed in very striking capitals the words "Fumbally's Boarding-House." The edifice itself, more pretentious in extent and character than the cabins around, was ornamented with green jalousies to the windows, and a dazzling brass knocker surmounting a plate of the same metal, whereupon the name "Mrs. Jones Fumbally" was legible, even from the road. Some efforts at planting had been made in the two square plots of yellowish grass in front, but they had been lamentable failures; and, as if to show that the demerit was of the soil and not of the proprietors, the dead shrubs were suffered to stand where they had been stuck down, while, in default of leaves or buds, they put forth a plentiful covering of stockings, nightcaps, and other wearables, which flaunted as gayly in the breeze as the owners were doing on the beach.

Across the high-road and on the beach, which was scarcely more than fifty yards distant, stood a large wooden edifice on wheels, whose make suggested some secret of its original destination, had not that fact been otherwise revealed, since, from beneath the significant name of "Fumbally," an acute decipherer might read the still unerased inscription of "A Panther with only two spots from the head to the tail," an unhappy collocation which fixed upon the estimable lady the epithet of the animal in question.

Various garden-seats and rustic benches were scattered about, some of which were occupied by lounging figures of gentlemen, in costumes ingeniously a cross between the sporting world and the naval service; while the ladies displayed a no less elegant neglige, half sea-nymph, half shepherdess.

So much for the prospect landward, while towards the waves themselves there was a party of bathers, whose flowing hair and lengthened drapery indicated their sex. These maintained through all their sprightly gambols an animated conversation with a party of gentlemen on the rocks, who seemed, by the telescopes and spy-glasses which lay around them, to be equally prepared for the inspection of near and distant objects, and alternately turned from the criticism of a fair naiad beneath to a Scotch collier working "north about" in the distance.

Darcy could not help feeling that if the cockneyism of a boarding-house and the blinds and the brass knocker were sadly repugnant to the sense of admiration the scene itself would excite, there was an ample compensation in the primitive simplicity of the worthy inhabitants, who seemed to revel in all the unsuspecting freedom of our first parents themselves; for while some stood on little promontories of the rocks in most Canova-like drapery, little frescos of naked children flitted around and about, without concern to themselves or astonishment to the beholders.

Never was the good Knight more convinced of his own prudence in paying his first visit alone, and he stood for some time in patient admiration of the scene, until his eye rested on a figure who, seated at some distance off on a little eminence of the rocky coast, was as coolly surveying Darcy through his telescope. The mutual inspection continued for several minutes, when the stranger, deliberately shutting up his glass, advanced towards the Knight.

The gentleman was short, but stoutly knit, with a walk and a carriage of his head that, to Darcy's observant eye, bespoke an innate sense of self-importance; his dress was a greatcoat, cut jockey fashion, and ornamented with very large buttons, displaying heads of stags, foxes, and badgers, and other emblems of the chase, short Russia duck trousers, a wide-leaved straw hat, and a very loose cravat, knotted sailor-fashion on his breast. As he approached the Knight, he came to a full stop about half a dozen paces in front, and putting his hand to his hat, held it straight above his head, pretty much in the way stage imitators of Napoleon were wont to perform the salutation.

"A stranger, sir, I presume?" said he, with an insinuating smile and an air of dignity at the same moment. Darcy bowed a courteous assent, and the other went on: "Sweet scene, sir,—lovely nature,—animated and grand."

"Most impressive, I confess," said Darcy, with difficulty repressing a smile.

"Never here before, I take it?"

"Never, sir."

"Came from Coleraine, possibly? Walked all the way, eh?"

"I came on foot, as you have divined," said Darcy, dryly.

"Not going to make any stay, probably; a mere glance, and go on again. Is n't that so?"

"I believe you are quite correct; but may I, in return for your considerate inquiries, ask one question on my own part? You are, perhaps, sufficiently acquainted with the locality to inform me if a Miss Daly resides in this village, and where."

"Miss Daly, sir, did inhabit that cottage yonder, where you see the oars on the thatch, but it has been let to the Moors of Ballymena; they pay two-ten a week for the three rooms and the use of the kitchen; smart that, ain't it?"

"And Miss Daly resides at present—"

"She's one of us," said the little man, with a significant jerk of his thumb to the blue board with the gilt letters; "not much of that, after all; but she lives under the sway of 'Mother Fum,' though, from one caprice or another, she don't mix with the other boarders. Do you know her yourself?"

"I had that honor some years ago."

"Much altered, I take it, since that; down in the world too! She was an heiress in those days, I've heard, and a beauty. Has some of the good looks still, but lost all the shiners."

"Am I likely to find her at home at this hour?" said Darcy, moving away, and anxious for an opportunity to escape his communicative friend.

"No, not now; never shows in the morning. Just comes down to dinner, and disappears again. Never takes a hand at whist—penny points tell up, you know—seem a trifle at first, but hang me if they don't make a figure in the budget afterwards. There, do you see that fat lady with the black bathing-cap?—no, I mean the one with the blue baize patched on the shoulder, the Widow Mackie,—she makes a nice thing of it,—won twelve and fourpence since the first of the month. Pretty creature that yonder, with one stocking on,—Miss Boyle, of Carrick-maclash."

"I must own," said Darcy, dryly, "that, not having the privilege of knowing these ladies, I do not conceive myself at liberty to regard them with due attention."

"Oh! they never mind that here; no secrets among us."

"Very primitive, and doubtless very delightful; but I have trespassed too long on your politeness. Permit me to wish you a very good morning."

"Not at all; having nothing in the world to do. Paul Dempsey—that's my name—was always an idle man; Paul Dempsey, sir, nephew of old Paul Dempsey, of Dempsey Grove, in the county of Kilkenny; a snug place, that I wish the proprietor felt he had enjoyed sufficiently long. And your name, if I might make bold, is—"

"I call myself Gwynne," said Darcy, after a slight hesitation.

"Gwynne—Gwynne—there was a Gwynne, a tailor, in Ballyragget; a connection, probably?"

"I 'm not aware of any relationship," said Darcy, smiling.

"I 'm glad of it; I owe your brother or your cousin there—that is, if he was either—a sum of seven-and-nine for these ducks. There are Gwynnes in Ross besides, and Quins; are you sure it is not Quin? Very common name Quin."

Mr. Paul Dempsey does the honours of Ballintray

"I believe we spell our name as I have pronounced it." "Well, if you come to spend a little time here, I 'll give you a hint or two. Don't join Leonard—that blue-nosed fellow, yonder, in whiskey. He 'll be asking you, but don't—at it all day." Here Mr. Dempsey pantomimed the action of tossing off a dram. "No whist with the widow; if you were younger, I 'd say no small plays with Bess Boyle,—has a brother in the Antrim militia, a very quarrelsome fellow."

"I thank you sincerely for your kind counsel, although not destined to profit by it. I have one favor to ask: could you procure me the means to enclose my card for Miss Daly, as I must relinquish the hope of seeing her on this occasion?"

"No, no,—stop and dine. Capital cod and oysters,—always good. The mutton *rayther* scraggy, but with a good will and good teeth manageable enough; and excellent malt-"

"I thank you for your hospitable proposal, but cannot accept it."

"Well, I 'll take care of your card; you 'll probably come over again soon. You 're at M'Grotty's, ain't you?"

"Not at present; and as to the card, with your permission I'll enclose it." This Darcy was obliged to insist upon; as, if he left his name as Gwynne, Miss Daly might have failed to recognize him, while he desired to avoid being known as Mr. Darcy.

"Well, come in here; I 'll find you the requisites. But I wish you 'd stop and see the 'Panther.'"

Had the Knight overheard this latter portion of Mr.

Dempsey's invitation, he might have been somewhat surprised; but it chanced that the words were lost, and, preceded by honest Paul, he entered the little garden in front of the house.

When Darcy had enclosed his card and committed it to the hands of Mr. Dempsey, that gentleman was far too deeply impressed with the importance of his mission to delay a moment in executing it, and then the Knight was at last left at liberty to retrace his steps unmolested towards home. If he had smiled at the persevering curiosity and eccentric communicativeness of Mr. Dempsey, Darcy sorrowed deeply over the fallen fortunes which condemned one he had known so courted and so flattered once, to companionship like this. The words of the classic satirist came full upon his memory, and never did a sentiment meet more ready acceptance than the bitter, heart-wrung confession, "Unhappy poverty! you have no heavier misery in your train than that you make men seem ridiculous." A hundred times he wished he had never made the excursion; he would have given anything to be able to think of her as she had been, without the detracting influence of these vulgar associations. "And yet," said he, half aloud, "a year or so more, if I am still living, I shall probably have forgotten my former position, and shall have conformed myself to the new and narrow limits of my lot, doubtless as she does."

The quick tramp of feet on the heather behind him roused him, and, in turning, he saw a person coming towards and evidently endeavouring to overtake him. As he came nearer, the Knight perceived it was the gentleman already alluded to by Dempsey as one disposed to certain little traits of conviviality,—a fact which a nose of a deep copper color, and two bloodshot, bleary eyes, corroborated. His dress was a blue frock with a standing collar, military fashion, and dark trousers; and, although bearing palpable marks of long wear, were still neat and clean-looking. His age, as well as appearances might be trusted, was probably between fifty and sixty.

"Mr. Gwynne, I believe, sir," said the stranger, touching his cap as he spoke. "Miss Daly begged of me to say that she has just received your card, and will be happy to see you."

Darcy stared at the speaker fixedly, and appeared, while unmindful of his words, to be occupied with some deep emotion within him. The other, who had delivered his message in a tone of easy unconcern, now fixed his eyes on the Knight, and they continued for some seconds to regard each other. Gradually, however, the stranger's face changed; a sickly pallor crept over the features stained by long intemperance, his lip trembled, and two heavy tears gushed out and rolled down his seared cheeks.

"My G—d! can it be? It surely is not!" said Darcy, with almost tremulous earnestness.

"Yes, Colonel, it is the man you once remembered in your regiment as Jack Leonard; the same who led a forlorn hope at Quebec,—the man broke with disgrace and dismissed the service for cowardice at Trois Rivières."

"Poor fellow!" said Darcy, taking his hand; "I heard you were dead."

"No, sir, it's very hard to kill a man by mere shame: though if suffering could do it, I might have died."

"I have often doubted about that sentence, Leonard," said Darcy, eagerly. "I wrote to the commander-in-chief to have inquiry made, suspecting that nothing short of some affection of the mind or some serious derangement of health could make a brave man behave badly."

"You were right, sir; I was a drunkard, not a coward. I was unworthy of the service; I merited my disgrace, but not on the grounds for which I met it."

"Good Heaven! then I was right," said Darcy, in a burst of passionate grief; "my letter to the War Office was unanswered. I wrote again, and received for reply that an example was necessary, and Lieutenant Leonard's conduct pointed him out as the most suitable case for heavy punishment."

"It was but just, Colonel; I was a poltroon when I took more than half a bottle of wine. If I were not sober now, I could not have the courage to face you here where I stand."

"Poor Jack!" said Darcy, wringing his hand cordially; "and what have you done since?"

Leonard threw his eyes down upon his threadbare garments, his patched boots, and the white-worn seams of his old frock, but not a word escaped his lips. They walked on for some time side by side without speaking, when Leonard said,—

"They know nothing of me here, Colonel. I need not ask you to be— cautious." There was a hesitation before he uttered the last word.

"I do not desire to be recognized, either," said Darcy, "and prefer being called Mr. Gwynne to the name of my family; and here, if I mistake not, comes a gentleman most eager to learn anything of anybody."

Mr. Dempsey came up at this moment with a lady leaning on each of his arms.

"Glad to see you again, sir; hope you 've thought better of your plans, and are going to try Mother Fum's fare. Mrs. M'Quirk, Mr. Gwynne—Mr. Gwynne, Miss Drew. Leonard will do the honors till we come back." So saying, and with a princely wave of his straw hat, Mr. Dempsey resumed his walk with the step of a conqueror.

"That fellow must be a confounded annoyance to you," said Darcy, as he looked after him.

"Not now, sir," said the other, submissively; "I 'm used to him; besides, since Miss Daly's arrival he is far quieter than he used to be, he seems afraid of her. But I 'll leave you now, Colonel." He touched his cap respectfully, and was about to move away, when Darcy, pitying the confusion which overwhelmed him, caught his hand cordially, and said,—

"Well, Jack, for the moment, good-bye; but come over and see me. I live at the little cottage called 'The Corvy.'"

"Good Heaven, sir! and it is true what I read in the newspaper about your misfortunes?"

"I conclude it is, Jack, though I have not read it; they could scarcely have exaggerated."

"And you bear it like this!" said the other, with a stare of amazement; then added, in a broken voice, "Though, to be sure, there 's a wide difference between loss of fortune and ruined character."

"Come, Jack, I see you are not so good a philosopher as I thought you. Come and dine with me to-morrow at five."

"Dine with *you*, Colonel!" said Leonard, blushing deeply.

"And why not, man? I see you have not forgotten the injustice I once did you, and I am happier this day to know it was I was in the wrong than that a British officer was a coward."

"Oh, Colonel Darcy, I did not think this poor broken heart could ever throb again with gratitude, but you have made it do so; you have kindled the flame of pride where the ashes were almost cold." And with a burning blush upon his face he turned away. Darcy looked after him for a second, and then entered the house.

Darcy had barely time to throw one glance around the scanty furniture of the modest parlor into which he was ushered, when Miss Daly entered. She stopped suddenly short, and for a few seconds each regarded the other without speaking. Time had, indeed, worked many changes in the appearance of each for which they were unprepared; but no less were they unprepared for the emotions this sudden meeting was to call up.

Miss Daly was plainly but handsomely dressed, and wore her silvery hair beneath a cap in two long bands on either cheek, with something of an imitation of a mode she followed in youth; the tones of her voice, too, were wonderfully little changed, and fell upon Darcy's ears with a strange, melancholy meaning.

"We little thought, Knight," said she, "when we parted last, that our next meeting would have been as this, so many years and many sorrows have passed over us since that day!"

"And a large measure of happiness, too, Maria," said Darcy, as, taking her hand, he led her to a seat; "let us never forget, amid all our troubles, how many blessings we have enjoyed."

Whether it was the words themselves that agitated her, or something in his manner of uttering them, Miss Daly blushed deeply and was silent. Darcy was not slow to see her confusion, and suddenly remembering how inapplicable his remark was to her fortunes, though not to his own, added hastily, "I, at least, would be very ungrateful if I could not look back with thankfulness to a long life of prosperity and happiness; and if I bear my present reverses with less repining, it is, I hope and trust, from the sincerity of this feeling."

"You have enjoyed the sunny path in life," said Miss Daly, in a low, faint voice, "and it is, perhaps, as you say, reason for enduring altered fortunes better." She paused, and then, with a more hurried voice, added: "One does not bear calamity better from habit; that is all a mistake. When the temper is soured by disappointment, the spirit of endurance loses its firmest ally. Your misfortunes will, however, be short-lived, I hope; my brother writes me he has great confidence in some legal opinions, and certain steps he has already taken in chancery."

"The warm-hearted and the generous are always sanguine," said Darcy, with a sad smile; "Bagenal would not be your brother if he could see a friend in difficulty without venturing on everything to rescue him. What an old friendship ours has been! class fellows at school, companions in youth, we have run our race together, to end with fortune how similar! I was thinking, Maria, as I came along, of Castle Daly, and remembering how I passed my holidays with you there. Is your memory as good as mine?"

"I scarcely like to think of Castle Daly," said she, almost pettishly, "it reminds me so much of that wasteful, reckless life which laid the foundation of our ruin. Tell me how Lady Eleanor Darcy bears up, and your daughter, of whom I have heard so much, and desire so ardently to see; is she more English or Irish?"

"A thorough Darcy," said the Knight, smiling, "but yet with traits of soft submission and patient trust our family has been but rarely gifted with; her virtues are all the mother's, every blemish of her character has come from the other side."

"Is she rash and headstrong? for those are Darcy failings."

"Not more daring or courageous than I love her to be," said Darcy, proudly, "not a whit more impetuous in sustaining the right or denouncing the wrong than I glory to see her; but too ardent, perhaps, too easily carried away by first impressions, than is either fashionable or frequent in the colder world."

"It is a dangerous temper," said Miss Daly, thoughtfully.

"You are right, Maria; such people are for the most part like the gamester who has but one throw for his fortune, if he loses which, all is lost with it."

"Too true, too true!" said she, in an accent whose melancholy sadness seemed to come from the heart. "You must guard her carefully from any rash attachment; a character like hers is strong to endure, but not less certain to sink under calamity."

"I know it, I feel it," said Darcy; "but my dear child is still too young to have mixed in that world which is already closed against her; her affections could never have strayed beyond the limits of our little home circle; she has kept all her love for those who need it most."

"And Lady Eleanor?" said Miss Daly, as if suddenly desirous to change the theme: "Bagenal tells me her health has been but indifferent; how does she bear our less genial climate here?"

"She 's better than for many years past; I could even say she 's happier. Strange it is, Maria, but the course of prosperity, like the calms in the ocean, too frequently steep the faculties in an apathy that becomes weariness; but when the clouds are drifted along faster, and the waves rustle at the prow, the energies of life are again excited, and the very occasion of danger begets the courage to confront it. We cannot be happy when devoid of self-esteem, and there is but little opportunity to indulge this honest pride when the world goes fairly with us, without any effort of our own; reverses of fortune—"

"Oh, reverses of fortune!" interrupted Miss Daly, rapidly, "people think much more about them than they merit; it is the world itself makes them so difficult to bear; one can think and act as freely beneath the thatch of a cabin as the gilded roof of a palace. It is the mock sympathy, the affected condolence for your fallen estate, that tortures you; the never-ending recurrence to what you once were, contrasted with what you are; the cruelty of that friendship that is never content save when reminding you of a station lost forever, and seeking to unfit you for your humble path in the valley because your step was once proudly on the mountain-top."

"I will not concede all this," said the Knight, mildly; "my fall has been too recent not to remind me of many kindnesses."

"I hate pity," said Miss Daly; "it is like a recommendation to mercy after the sentence of an unjust judge. Now tell me of Lionel."

"A fine, high-spirited soldier, as little affected by his loss as though it touched him not; and yet, poor boy! to all appearance a bright career was about to open before him,—well received by the world, honored by the personal notice of his Prince."

"Ha! now I think of it, why did you not vote against the Minister?"

"It was on that evening," said Darcy, sorrowfully,—"on that very evening—I heard of Gleeson's flight."

"Well,"—then suddenly correcting herself, and restraining the question that almost trembled on her lip, she added, "And you were, doubtless, too much shocked to appear in the House?"

"I was ill," said Darcy, faintly; "indeed, I believe I can say with truth, my own ruin preyed less upon my mind than the perfidy of one so long confided in."

"And they made this accidental illness the ground of a great attack against your character, and sought to discover in your absence the secret of your corruption. How basely minded men must be, when they will invent not only actions, but motives to calumniate!" She paused, and then muttered to herself, "I wish you had voted against that Bill."

"It would have done little good," said the Knight, answering her soliloquy; "my vote could neither retard nor prevent the measure, and as for myself, personally, I am proud enough to think I have given sufficient guarantees by a long life of independent action, not to need this crowning test of honesty. Now to matters nearer to us both: when will you come and visit my wife and daughter? or shall I bring them here to you?"

"No, no, not here. I am not ashamed of this place for myself, though I should be so if they were once to see it."

"But you feel less lonely," said Darcy, in a gentle tone, as if anticipating the reason of her choice of residence.

"Less lonely!" replied she, with a haughty laugh; "what companionship or society have I with people like these? It is not that,—it is my poverty compels me to live here. Of them and of their habits I know nothing; from me and from mine they take good care to keep aloof. No, with your leave I will visit Lady Eleanor at your cottage,—that is, if she has no objection to receive me."

"She will be but too happy," said Darcy, "to know and value one of her husband's oldest and warmest friends."

"You must not expect me soon, however," said she, hastily; "I have grown capricious in everything, and never can answer for performing a pledge at any stated time, and therefore never make one."

Abrupt and sudden as had been the changes of her voice and manner through this interview, there was a tone of unusual harshness in the way this speech was uttered; and as Darcy rose to take his leave, a feeling of sadness came over him to think that this frame of mind must have been the slow result of years of heart-consuming sorrow.

"Whenever you come, Maria," said he, as he took her hand in his, "you will be most welcome to us."

"Have you heard any tidings of Forester?" said Miss Daly, as if suddenly recalling a subject she wished to speak on.

"Forester of the Guards? Lionel's friend, do you mean?"

"Yes; you know that he has left the army, thrown up his commission, and gone no one knows where?"

"I did not know of that before. I am sincerely sorry for it. Is the cause surmised?"

Miss Daly made no answer, but stood with her eyes bent on the ground, and apparently in deep thought; then looking up suddenly, she said, with more composure than ordinary, "Make my compliments to Lady Eleanor, and say that at the first favorable moment I will pay my personal respects to her—kiss Helen for me—good-bye." And, without waiting for Darcy to take his leave, she walked hastily by, and closed the door after her.

"This wayward manner," said Darcy, sorrowfully, to himself, "has a deeper root than mere capriciousness; the heart has suffered so long that the mind begins to partake of the decay." And with this sad reflection he left the village, and turned his solitary steps towards home.

If Darcy was grieved to find Miss Daly surrounded by such unsuitable companionship, he was more thau recompensed at finding that her taste rejected nearer intimacy with Mrs. Fumbally's household. More than once the fear crossed his mind that, with diminished circumstances, she might have lapsed into habits so different from her former life, and he could better look upon her struggling as she did against her adverse fortune than assimilating herself to those as much below her in sentiment as in station. He was happy to have seen his old friend once more, he was glad to refresh his memory of long-forgotten scenes by the sight of her who had been his playfellow and his companion, but he was not free of a certain dread that Miss Daly would scarcely be acceptable to his wife, while her wayward, uncertain temper would form no safe companionship for his daughter. As he pondered on these things, he began to feel how altered circumstances beget suspicion, and how he, who had never known the feeling of distrust, now found himself hesitating and doubting, where formerly he had acted without fear or reserve.

"Yes," said he, aloud, "when wealth and station were mine, the consciousness of power gave energy to my thoughts, but now I am to learn how narrow means can fetter a man's courage."

"Some truth in that," said a voice behind him; "would cut a very different figure myself if old Bob Dempsey, of Dempsey Grove, were to betake himself to a better world."

Darcy's cheek reddened between shame and anger to find himself overheard by his obtrusive companion, and, with a cold salute, he passed on. Mr. Dempsey, however, was not a man to be so easily got rid of; he possessed that happy temper that renders its owner insensible to shame and unconscious of rebuke; besides that, he was always "going your way," quite content to submit to any amount of rebuff rather than be alone. If you talked, it was well; if you listened, it was better; but if you affected open indifference to him, and neither exchanged a word nor vouchsafed the slightest attention, even that was supportable, for he could give the conversation a character of monologue or anecdote, which occupied himself at least.

CHAPTER II
A TALE OF MR. DEMPSEY'S GRANDFATHER

The Knight of Gwynne was far too much occupied in his own reflections to attend to his companion, and exhibited a total unconcern to several piquant little narratives of Mrs. Mackie's dexterity in dealing the cards, of Mrs. Fumbally's parsimony in domestic arrangements, of Miss Boyle's effrontery, of Leonard's intemperance, and even of Miss Daly's assumed superiority.

"You 're taking the wrong path," said Mr. Dempsey, suddenly interrupting one of his own narratives, at a spot where the two roads diverged,—one proceeding inland, while the other followed the line of the coast.

"With your leave, sir," said Darcy, coldly, "I will take this way, and if you 'll kindly permit it, I will do so alone."

"Oh, certainly!" said Dempsey, without the slightest sign of umbrage; "would never have thought of joining you had it not been from overhearing an expression so exactly pat to my own condition, that I thought we were brothers in misfortune; you scarcely bear up as well as I do, though."

Darcy turned abruptly round, as the fear flashed across him, and he muttered to himself, "This fellow knows me; if so, the whole county will soon be as wise as himself, and the place become intolerable." Oppressed with this unpleasant reflection, the Knight moved on, nor was it till after a considerable interval that he was conscious of his companion's presence; for Mr. Dempsey still accompanied him, though at the distance of several paces, and as if following a path of his own choosing.

Darcy laughed good-humoredly at the pertinacity of his tormentor; and half amused by the man, and half ashamed of his own rudeness to him, he made some casual observation on the scenery to open a reconciliation.

"The coast is much finer," said Dempsey, "close to your cottage."

This was a home-thrust for the Knight, to show him that concealment was of no use against so subtle an adversary.

"'The Corvy' is, as you observe, very happily situated," replied Darcy, calmly; "I scarcely know which to prefer,—the coast-line towards Dunluce, or the bold cliffs that stretch away to Bengore."

"When the wind comes north-by-west," said Dempsey, with a shrewd glance of his greenish gray eyes, "there 's always a wreck or two between the Skerries and Portrush."

"Indeed! Is the shore so unsafe as that?"

"Oh, yes. You may expect a very busy winter here when the homeward-bound Americans are coming northward."

"D——n the fellow! does he take me for a wrecker?" said Darcy to himself, not knowing whether to laugh or be angry.

"Such a curiosity that old 'Corvy' is, they tell me," said Dempsey, emboldened by his success; "every species of weapon and arm in the world, they say, gathered together there."

"A few swords and muskets," said the Knight, carelessly; "a stray dirk or two, and some harpoons, furnish the greater part of the armory."

"Oh, perhaps so! The story goes, however, that old Daly—brother, I believe, of our friend at Mother Fum's—could arm twenty fellows at a moment's warning, and did so on more than one occasion too."

"With what object, in Heaven's name?"

"Buccaneering, piracy, wrecking, and so on," said Dempsey, with all the unconcern with which he would have enumerated so many pursuits of the chase.

A hearty roar of laughter broke from the Knight; and when it ceased he said, "I would be sincerely sorry to stand in your shoes, Mr. Dempsey, so near to yonder cliff, if you made that same remark in Mr. Daly's hearing."

"He 'd gain very little by me," said Mr. Dempsey; "one and eightpence, an old watch, an oyster-knife, and my spectacles, are all the property in my possession—except, when, indeed," added he, after a pause, "Bob remits the quarter's allowance."

"It is only just," said Darcy, gravely, "to a gentleman who takes such pains to inform himself on the affairs of his neighbors, that I should tell you that Mr. Bagenal Daly is not a pirate, nor am I a wrecker. I am sure you will be generous enough for this unasked information not to require of me a more lengthened account either of my friend or myself."

"You 're in the Revenue, perhaps?" interrupted the undaunted Dempsey; "I thought so when I saw you first."

Darcy shook his head in dissent.

"Wrong again. Ah! I see it all; the old story. Saw better days—you have just come down here to lie snug and quiet, out of the way of writs and latitats—went too fast—by Jove, that touches myself too! If I hadn't happened to have a grandfather, I'd have been a rich man this day. Did you ever chance to hear of Dodd and Dempsey, the great wine-merchants? My father was son of Dodd and Dempsey,—that is Dempsey, you know; and it was his father-Sam Dempsey—ruined him."

"No very uncommon circumstance," said the Knight, sorrowfully, "for an Irish father."

"You've heard the story, I suppose?—of course you have; every one knows it."

"I rather think not," said the Knight, who was by no means sorry to turn Mr. Dempsey from cross-examination into mere narrative.

"I'll tell it to you; I am sure I ought to know it well, I've heard my father relate it something like a hundred times."

"I fear I must decline so pleasant a proposal," said Darcy, smiling. "At this moment I have an engagement."

"Never mind. To-morrow will do just as well," interrupted the inexorable Dempsey. "Come over and take your mutton-chop with me at five, and you shall have the story into the bargain."

"I regret that I cannot accept so very tempting an invitation," said Darcy, struggling between his sense of pride and a feeling of astonishment at his companion's coolness.

"Not come to dinner!" exclaimed Dempsey, as if the thing was scarcely credible. "Oh, very well, only remember"—and here he put an unusual gravity into his words—"only remember the *onus* is now on you."

The Knight burst into a hearty laugh at this subtle retort, and, willing as he ever was to go with the humor of the moment, replied,—

"I am ready to accept it, sir, and beg that you will dine with me."

"When and where?" said Dempsey.

"To-morrow, at that cottage yonder: five is your hour, I believe—we shall say five."

"Booked!" exclaimed Dempsey, with an air of triumph; while he muttered, with a scarcely subdued voice, "Knew I'd do it!—never failed in my life!"

"Till then, Mr. Dempsey," said Darcy, removing his hat courteously, as he bowed to him, — "till then—"

"Your most obedient," replied Dempsey, returning the salute; and so they parted.

"The Corvy," on the day after the Knight's visit to Port Ballintray, was a scene of rather amusing bustle; the Knight's dinner-party, as Helen quizzingly called it, affording occupation for every member of the household. In former times, the only difficult details of an entertainment were in the selection of the guests, — bringing together a company likely to be suitable to each other, and endowed with those various qualities which make up the success of society; now, however, the question was the more material one, — the dinner itself.

It is always a fortunate thing when whatever absurdity our calamities in life excite should be apparent only to ourselves. The laugh which is so difficult to bear from the world is then an actual relief from our troubles. The Darcys felt this truth, as each little embarrassment that arose was food for mirth; and Lady Eleanor, who least of all could adapt herself to such contingencies, became as eager as the rest about the little preparations of the day.

While the Knight hurried hither and thither, giving directions here and instructions there, he explained to Lady Eleanor some few circumstances respecting the character of his guests. It was, indeed, a new kind of company he was about to present to his wife and daughter; but while conscious of the disparity in every respect, he was not the less eager to do the hospitalities of his humble house with all becoming honor. It is true his invitation to Mr. Dempsey was rather forced from him than willingly accorded; he was about the very last kind of person Darcy would have asked to his table, if perfectly free to choose; but, of all men living, the Knight knew least how to escape from a difficulty the outlet to which should cost him any sacrifice of feeling.

"Well, well, it is but once and away; and, after all, the talkativeness of our little friend Dempsey will be so far a relief to poor Leonard, that he will be brought less prominently forward himself, and be suffered to escape unremarked, — a circumstance which, from all that I can see, will afford him sincere pleasure."

At length all the preparations were happily accomplished: the emissary despatched to Kilrush at daybreak had returned with a much-coveted turkey; the fisherman had succeeded in capturing a lordly salmon; oysters and lobsters poured in abundantly; and Mrs. M'Kerrigan, who had been left as a fixture at "The Corvy," found her only embarrassment in selection from that profusion of "God's gifts," as she phrased it, that now surrounded her. The hour of five drew near, and the ladies were seated in the hall, the doors of which lay open, as the two guests were seen making their way towards the cottage.

"Here they come, papa," said Helen; "and now for a guess. Is not the short man with the straw hat Mr. Dempsey, and his tall companion Mr. Leonard?"

"Of course it is," said Lady Eleanor; "who could mistake the garrulous pertinacity of that little thing that gesticulates at every step, or the plodding patience of his melancholy associate?"

The next moment the Knight was welcoming them in front of the cottage. The ceremony of introduction to the ladies being over, Mr. Dempsey, who probably was aware that the demands upon his descriptive powers would not be inconsiderable when he returned to "Mother Fum's," put his glass to his eye, and commenced a very close scrutiny of the apartment and its contents.

"Quite a show-box, by Jove!" said he, at last, as he peered through a glass cabinet, where Chinese slippers, with models in ivory and carvings in box, were heaped promiscuously together; "upon my word, sir, you have a very remarkable collection. And who may be our friend in the boat here?" added he, turning to the grim visage of Bagenal Daly himself, who stared with a bold effrontery that would not have disgraced the original.

"The gentleman you see there," said the Knight, "is the collector himself, and the other is his servant. They are represented in the costumes in which they made their escape from a captivity among the red men."

"Begad!" said Dempsey, "that fellow with the tortoise painted on his forehead has a look of our old friend, Miss Daly; should n't wonder if he was a member of her family."

"You have well guessed it; he is the lady's brother."

"Ah, ah!" muttered Dempsey to himself, "always thought there was something odd about her,—never suspected Indian blood, however. How Mother Fum will stare when I tell her she's a Squaw! Didn't they show these things at the Rooms in Mary's Street? I think I saw them advertised in the papers."

"I think you must mistake," said the Knight; "they are the private collection of my friend."

"And where may Woc-woc—confound his name!—the 'Howling Wind,' as he is pleased to call himself, be passing his leisure hours just now?"

"He is at present in Dublin, sir; and if you desire, he shall be made aware of your polite inquiries."

"No, no—hang it, no!—don't like the look of him. Should have no objection, though, if he 'd pay old Bob Dempsey a visit, and frighten him out of this world for me."

"Dinner, my lady," said old Tate, as he threw open the doors into the dining-room, and bowed with all his accustomed solemnity.

"Hum!" muttered Dempsey, "my lady won't go down with me,-too old a soldier for that!"

"Will you give my daughter your arm?" said the Knight to the little man, for already Lady Eleanor had passed on with Mr. Leonard.

As Mr. Dempsey arranged his napkin on his knee, he endeavored to catch Leonard's eye, and telegraph to him his astonishment at the elegance of the table equipage which graced the board. Poor Leonard, however, seldom looked up; a deep sense of shame, the agonizing memory of what he once was, recalled vividly by the sight of those objects, and the appearance of persons which reminded him of his past condition, almost stunned him. The whole seemed like a dream; even though intemperance had degraded him, there were intervals in which his mind, clear to see and reflect, sorrowed deeply over his fallen state. Had the Knight met him with a cold and repulsive deportment, or had he refused to acknowledge him altogether, he could better have borne it than all the kindness of his present manner. It was evident, too, from Lady Eleanor's tone to him, that she knew nothing of his unhappy fortune, or that if she did, the delicacy with which she treated him was only the more benevolent. Oppressed by such emotions, he sat endeavoring to eat, and trying to listen and interest himself in the conversation around him; but the effort was too much for his strength, and a vague, half-whispered assent, or a dull, unmeaning smile, were about as much as he could contribute to what was passing.

The Knight, whose tact was rarely at fault, saw every straggle that was passing in Leonard's mind, and adroitly contrived that the conversation should be carried on without any demand upon him, either as talker or listener. If Lady Eleanor and Helen contributed their aid to this end, Mr. Dempsey was not backward on his part, for he talked unceasingly. The good things of the table, to which he did ample justice, afforded an opportunity for catechizing the ladies in their skill in household matters; and Miss Darcy, who seemed immensely amused by the novelty of such a character, sustained her part to admiration, entering deeply into culinary details, and communicating receipts invented for the occasion. At another time, perhaps, the Knight would have checked the spirit of *persiflage* in which his daughter indulged; but he suffered it now to take its course, well pleased that the mark of her ridicule was not only worthy of the sarcasm, but insensible to its arrow.

"Quite right,-quite right not to try Mother Fum's when you can get up a little thing like this,-and such capital sherry; look how Tom takes it in,-slips like oil over his lip!"

Leonard looked up. An expression of rebuking severity for a moment crossed his features; but his eyes fell the next instant, and a low, faint sigh escaped him.

"I ought to know what sherry is, — 'Dodd and Dempsey's' was the great house for sherry."

"By the way," said the Knight, "did not you promise me a little narrative of Dodd and Dempsey, when we parted yesterday?"

"To be sure, I did. Will you have it now?"

Lady Eleanor and Helen rose to withdraw; but Mr. Dempsey, who took the movement as significant, immediately interposed, by saying,—

"Don't stir, ma'am,-sit down, ladies, I beg; there's nothing broad in the story,—it might be told before the maids of honor."

Lady Eleanor and Helen were thunderstruck at the explanation, and the Knight laughed till the tears came.

"My dear Eleanor," said he, "you really must accept Mr. Dempsey's assurance, and listen to his story now."

The ladies took their seats once more, and Mr. Dempsey, having filled his glass, drank off a bumper; but whether it was that the narrative itself demanded a greater exertion at his hands, or that the cold quietude of Lady Eleanor's manner abashed him, but he found a second bumper necessary before he commenced his task.

"I say," whispered he to the Knight, "couldn't you get that decanter out of Leonard's reach before I begin? He'll not leave a drop in it while I am talking."

As if he felt that, after his explanation, the tale should be more particularly addressed to Lady Eleanor, he turned his chair round so as to face her, and thus began:—

"There was once upon a time, ma'am, a Lord-Lieutenant of Ireland who was a Duke. Whether he was Duke of Rutland, or Bedford, or Portland, or any other title it was he had, my memory does n't serve me; it is enough, however, if I say he was immensely rich, and, like many other people in the same way, immensely in debt. The story goes that he never travelled through England, and caught sight of a handsome place, or fine domain, or a beautiful cottage, that he did n't go straightway to the owner and buy it down out of the face, as a body might say, whether he would or no. And so in time it came to pass that there was scarcely a county in England without some magnificent house belonging to him. In many parts of Scotland he had them too, and in all probability he would have done the same in Ireland, if he could. Well, ma'am, there never was such rejoicings as Dublin saw the night his Grace arrived to be our Viceroy. To know that we had got a man with one hundred and fifty thousand a year, and a spirit to spend double the money, was a downright blessing from Providence, and there was no saying what might not be the prosperity of Ireland under so auspicious a ruler.

"To do him justice, he did n't balk public expectation. Open house at the Castle, ditto at the Lodge in the Park, a mansion full of guests in the county Wicklow, a pack of hounds in Kildare, twelve horses training at the Curragh, a yacht like a little man-of-war in Dunleary harbor, large subscriptions to everything like sport, and a pension for life to every man that could sing a jolly song, or write a witty bit of poetry. Well, ma'am, they say, who remember those days, that they saw the best of Ireland; and surely I believe, if his Grace had only lived, and had his own way, the peerage would have been as pleasant, and the bench of bishops as droll, and the ladies of honor as—Well, never mind, I 'll pass on." Here Mr. Dempsey, to console himself for the abruptness of his pause, poured out and drank another bumper of sherry. "Pleasant times they were." said he, smacking his lips; "and faith, if Tom Leonard himself was alive then, the color of his nose might have made him Commander of the Forces; but, to continue, it was Dodd and Dempsey's house supplied the sherry,-only the sherry, ma'am; old Stewart, of Belfast, had the port, and Kinnahan the claret and lighter liquors. I may mention, by the way, that my grandfather's contract included brandy, and that he would n't have given it up for either of the other two. It was just about this time that Dodd died, and my grandfather was left alone in the firm; but whether it was out of respect for his late partner, or that he might have felt himself lonely, but he always kept up the name of Dodd on the brass plate, and signed the name along with his own; indeed, they say that he once saluted his wife by the name of Mrs. Dodd and Dempsey. But, as I was saying, it was one of those days when my grandfather was seated on a high stool in the back office of his house in Abbey Street, that a fine, tall young fellow, with a blue frock-coat, all braided with gold, and an elegant cocked-hat, with a plume of feathers in it, came tramping into the room, his spurs jingling, and his brass sabre clinking, and his sabretash banging at his legs.

"'Mr. Dempsey?' said he.

"'D. and D.,' said my grandfather,—'that is, Dodd and Dempsey, your Grace,' for he half suspected it was the Duke himself.

"'I am Captain M'Claverty, of the Scots Greys,' said he, 'first aide-de-camp to his Excellency.'

"'I hope you may live to be colonel of the regiment,' said my grandfather, for he was as polite and well-bred as any man in Ireland.

"'That's too good a sentiment,' said the captain, 'not to be pledged in a glass of your own sherry.'

"'And we'll do it too,' said old Dempsey. And he opened the desk, and took out a bottle he had for his own private drinking, and uncorked it with a little pocket corkscrew he always carried about with him, and he produced two glasses, and he and the captain hobnobbed and drank to each other.

"'Begad!' said the captain, 'his Grace sent me to thank you for the delicious wine you supplied him with, but it's nothing to this,—-not to be compared to it.'

"'I 've better again,' said my grandfather. 'I 've wine that would bring the tears into your eyes when you saw the decanter getting low.'

"The captain stared at him, and maybe it was that the speech was too much for his nerves, but he drank off two glasses one after the other as quick as he could fill them out.

"'Dempsey,' said he, looking round cautiously, 'are we alone?'

"'We are,' said my grandfather.

"'Tell me, then,' said M'Claverty, 'how could his Grace get a taste of this real sherry—for himself alone, I mean? Of course, I never thought of his giving it to the Judges, and old Lord Dunboyne, and such like.'

"'Does he ever take a little sup in his own room, of an evening?'

"'I am afraid not, but I 'll tell you how I think it might be managed. You 're a snug fellow, Dempsey, you 've plenty of money muddling away in the bank at three-and-a-half per cent; could n't you contrive, some way or other, to get into his Excellency's confidence, and lend him ten or fifteen thousand or so?'

"'Ay, or twenty,' said my grandfather,—'or twenty, if he likes it'

"'I doubt if he would accept such a sum,' said the captain, shaking his head; 'he has bags of money rolling in upon him every week or fortnight; sometimes we don't know where to put them.'

"'Oh, of course,' said my grandfather; 'I meant no offence, I only said twenty, because, if his Grace would condescend, it is n't twenty, but a fifty thousand I could give him, and on the nail too.'

"'You're a fine fellow, Dempsey, a devilish fine fellow; you 're the very kind of fellow the Duke likes,—open-handed, frank, and generous.'

"'Do you really think he'd like me?' said my grandfather; and he rocked on the high stool, so that it nearly came down.

"'Like you! I'll tell you what it is,' said he, laying his hand on my grandfather's knee, 'before one week was over, he could n't do without you. You 'd be there morning, noon, and night; your knife and fork always ready for you, just like one of the family.'

"'Blood alive!' said my grandfather, 'do you tell me so?'

"'I 'll bet you a hundred pounds on it, sir.'

"'Done,' said my grandfather, 'and you must hold the stakes;' and with that he opened his black pocket-book, and put a note for the amount into the captain's hand.

"'This is the 31st of March,' said the captain, taking out his pencil and tablets. 'I 'll just book the bet.'

"And, indeed," added Mr. Dempsey, "for that matter, if it was a day later it would have been only more suitable.

"Well, ma'am, what passed between them afterwards I never heard said; but the captain took his leave, and left my grandfather so delighted and overjoyed that he finished all the sherry in the drawer, and when the head clerk came in to ask for an invoice, or a thing of the kind, he found old Mr. Dempsey with his wig on the high stool, and he bowing round it, and calling it your Grace. There 's no denying it, ma'am, he was blind drunk.

"About ten days or a fortnight after this time, my grandfather received a note from Teesum and Twist, the solicitors, stating that the draft or the bond was already drawn up for the loan he was about to make his Grace, and begging to know to whom it was to be submitted.

"'The captain will win his bet, devil a lie in it,' said my grandfather; 'he's going to bring the Duke and myself together.'

"Well, ma'am, I won't bother you with the law business, though if my father was telling the story he would not spare you one item of it all,—who read this, and who signed the other, and the objections that was made by them thieving attorneys! and how the Solicitor-General struck out this and put in that clause; but to tell you the truth, ma'am, I think that all the details spoil, what we may call, the poetry of the narrative; it is finer to say he paid the money, and the Duke pocketed it.

"Well, weeks went over and months long, and not a bit of the Duke did my grandfather see, nor M'Claverty either; he never came near him. To be sure, his Grace drank as much sherry as ever; indeed, I believe out of love to my grandfather they drank little else. From the bishops and the chaplain, down to the battle-axe guards, it was sherry, morning, noon, and night; and though this was very pleasing to my grandfather, he was always wishing for the time when he was to be presented to his Grace, and their friendship was to begin. My grandfather could think of nothing else, daylight and dark. When he walked, he was always repeating to himself what his Grace might say to him, and what he would say to his Grace; and he was perpetually going up at eleven o'clock, when the guard was relieved in the Castle-yard, suspecting that every now and then a footman in blue and silver would come out, and, touching his elbow, whisper in his ear, 'Mr. Dempsey, the Duke 's waiting for you.' But, my dear ma'am, he might have waited till now, if Providence had spared him, and the devil a taste of the same message would ever have come near him, or a sight of the same footman in blue! It was neither more nor less than a delusion, or an illusion, or a confusion, or whatever the name of it is. At last, ma'am, in one of his prowlings about the Phoenix Park, who does he come on but M'Claverty? He was riding past in a great hurry; but he pulled up when he saw my grandfather, and called out, 'Hang it! who's this? I ought to know *you*.'

"'Indeed you ought,' said my grandfather. 'I 'm Dodd and Dempsey, and by the same token there's a little bet between us, and I 'd like to know who won and who lost.'

"'I think there's small doubt about that,' said the captain. 'Did n't his Grace borrow twenty thousand of you?'

"'He did, no doubt of it.'

"'And was n't it *my* doing?'

"'Upon my conscience, I can't deny it.'

"'Well, then, I won the wager, that's clear.'

"'Oh! I see now,' said my grandfather; 'that was the wager, was it? Oh, bedad! I think you might have given me odds, if that was our bet.'

"'Why, what did you think it was?'

"'Oh, nothing at all, sir. It's no matter now; it was another thing was passing in my mind. I was hoping to have the honor of making his acquaintance, nattered as I was by all you told me about him.'

"'Ah! that's difficult, I confess,' said the captain; 'but still one might do something. He wants a little money just now. If you could make interest to be the lender, I would n't say that what you suggest is impossible.'

"Well, ma'am, it was just as it happened before; the old story,—more parchment, more comparing of deeds, a heavy check on the bank for the amount.

"When it was all done, M'Claverty came in one morning and in plain clothes to my grandfather's back office.

"'Dodd and Dempsey,' said he, 'I 've been thinking over your business, and I'll tell you what my plan is. Old Vereker, the chamberlain, is little better than a beast, thinks nothing of anybody that is n't a lord or a viscount, and, in fact, if he had his will, the Lodge in the Phoenix would be more like Pekin in Tartary than anything else? but I 'll tell you, if he won't present you at the levee, which he flatly refuses at present, I 'll do the thing in a way of my own. His Grace is going to spend a week up at Ballyriggan House, in the county of Wicklow, and I 'll contrive it, when he 's taking his morning walk through the shrubbery, to present you. All you 've to do is to be ready at a turn of the walk. I 'll show you the place, you 'll hear his foot on the gravel, and you 'll slip out, just this way. Leave the rest to me.'

"'It's beautiful,' said my grandfather. 'Begad, that's elegant.'

"'There 's one difficulty,' said M'Claverty,—'one infernal difficulty.'

"'What's that?' asked my grandfather.

"'I may be obliged to be out of the way. I lost five fifties at Daly's the other night, and I may have to cross the water for a few weeks.'

"'Don't let that trouble you,' said my grandfather; 'there's the paper.' And he put the little bit of music into his hand; and sure enough a pleasanter sound than the same crisp squeak of a new note no man ever listened to.

"'It's agreed upon now?' said my grandfather.

"'All right,' said M'Claverty; and with a jolly slap on the shoulder, he said, 'Good-morning, D. and D. and away he went.

"He was true to his word. That day three weeks my grandfather received a note in pencil; it was signed J. M'C, and ran thus: 'Be up at Ballyriggan at eleven o'clock on Wednesday, and wait at the foot of the hill, near the birch copse, beside the wooden bridge. Keep the left of the path, and lie still.' Begad, ma'am, it's well nobody saw it but himself, or they might have thought that Dodd and Dempsey was turned highwayman.

"My grandfather was prouder of the same note, and happier that morning, than if it was an order for fifty butts of sherry. He read it over and over, and he walked up and down the little back office, picturing out the whole scene, settling the chairs till he made a little avenue between them, and practising the way he'd slip out slyly and surprise his Grace. No doubt, it would have been as good as a play to have looked at him.

"One difficulty preyed upon his mind,—what dress ought he to wear? Should he be in a court suit, or ought he rather to go in his robes as an alderman? It would never do to appear in a black coat, a light gray spencer, punch-colored shorts and gaiters, white hat with a strip of black crape on it,—mere Dodd and Dempsey! That wasn't to be thought of. If he could only ask his friend M'Hale, the fishmonger, who was knighted last year, he could tell all about it. M'Hale, however, would blab. He'd tell it to the whole livery; every alderman of Skinner's Alley would know it in a week. No, no, the whole must be managed discreetly; it was a mutual confidence between the Duke and 'D. and D.' 'At all events,' said my grandfather, 'a court dress is a safe thing;' and out he went and bespoke one, to be sent home that evening, for he could n't rest till he tried it on, and felt how he could move his head in the straight collar, and bow, without the sword tripping him up and pitching him into the Duke. I 've heard my father say that in the days that elapsed till the time mentioned for the interview, my grandfather lost two stone in weight. He walked half over the county Dublin, lying in ambush in every little wood he could see, and jumping out whenever he could see or hear any one coming,—little surprises which were sometimes taken as practical jokes, very unbecoming a man of his age and appearance.

"Well, ma'am, Wednesday morning came, and at six o'clock my grandfather was on the way to Ballyriggan, and at nine he was in the wood, posted at the very spot M'Claverty told him, as happy as any man could be whose expectations were so overwhelming. A long hour passed over, and another; nobody passed but a baker's boy with a bull-dog after him, and an old woman that was stealing brushwood in the shrubbery. My grandfather remarked her well, and determined to tell his Grace of it; but his own business soon drove that out of his head, for eleven o'clock came, and now there was no knowing the moment the Duke might appear. With his watch in his hand, he counted the minutes, ay, even the seconds; if he was a thief going to be hanged, and looking out over the heads of the crowd for a fellow to gallop in with a reprieve, he could n't have suffered more: his heart was in his mouth. At last, it might be about half-past eleven, he heard a footstep on the gravel, and then a loud, deep cough, — 'a fine kind of cough,' my grandfather afterwards called it. He peeped out; and there, sure enough, at about sixty paces, coming down the walk, was a large, grand-looking man, — not that he was dressed as became him, for, strange as you may think it, the Lord-Lieutenant had on a shooting-jacket, and a pair of plaid trousers, and cloth boots, and a big lump of a stick in his hand, — and lucky it was that my grandfather knew him, for he bought a picture of him. On he came nearer and nearer; every step on the gravel-walk drove out of my grandfather's head half a dozen of the fine things he had got off by heart to say during the interview, until at last he was so overcome by joy, anxiety, and a kind of terror, that he could n't tell where he was, or what was going to happen to him, but he had a kind of instinct that reminded him he was to jump out when the Duke was near him; and 'pon my conscience so he did, clean and clever, into the middle of the walk, right in front of his Grace. My grandfather used to say, in telling the story, that he verily believed his feelings at that moment would have made him burst a blood-vessel if it wasn't that the Duke put his hands to his sides and laughed till the woods rang again; but, between shame and fright, my grandfather did n't join in the laugh.

"'In Heaven's name!' said his Grace, 'who or what are you? — this isn't May-day.'

"My grandfather took this speech as a rebuke for standing so bold in his Grace's presence; and being a shrewd man, and never deficient in tact, what does he do but drops down on his two knees before him? 'My Lord,' said he, 'I am only Dodd and Dempsey.'

"Whatever there was droll about the same house of Dodd and Dempsey I never heard, but his Grace laughed now till he had to lean against a tree. 'Well, Dodd and Dempsey, if that's your name, get up. I don't mean you any harm. Take courage, man; I am not going to knight you. By the way, are you not the worthy gentleman who lent me a trifle of twenty thousand more than once?'

"My grandfather could n't speak, but he moved his lips, and he moved his bands, this way, as though to say the honor was too great for him, but it was all true.

"'Well, Dodd and Dempsey, I 've a very high respect for you,' said his Grace; 'I intend, some of these fine days, when business permits, to go over and eat an oyster at your villa on the coast.'

"My grandfather remembers no more; indeed, ma'am, I believe that at that instant his Grace's condescension had so much overwhelmed him that he had a kind of vision before his eyes of a whole wood full of Lord-Lieutenants, with about thirty thousand people opening oysters for them as fast as they could eat, and he himself running about with a pepper-caster, pressing them to eat another 'black fin.' It was something of that kind; for when he got on his legs a considerable time must have elapsed, as he found all silent around him, and a smart rheumatic pain in his knee-joints from the cold of the ground.

"The first thing my grandfather did when he got back to town was to remember that he had no villa on the sea-coast, nor any more suitable place to eat an oyster than his house in Abbey Street, for he could n't ask his Grace to go to 'Killeen's.' Accordingly he set out the next day in search of a villa, and before a week was over he had as beautiful a place about a mile below Howth as ever was looked at; and that he mightn't be taken short, he took a lease of two oyster-beds, and made every preparation in life for the Duke's visit. He might have spared himself the trouble. Whether it was that somebody had said something of him behind his back, or that politics were weighing on the Duke's mind,—the Catholics were mighty troublesome then,—or, indeed, that he forgot it altogether, clean, but so it was, my grandfather never heard more of the visit, and if the oysters waited for his Grace to come and eat them, they might have filled up Howth harbor.

"A year passed over, and my grandfather was taking his solitary walk in the Park, very nearly in the same place as before,—for you see, ma'am, he could n't bear the sight of the seacoast, and the very smell of shell-fish made him ill,—when somebody called out his name. He looked up, and there was M'Claverty in a gig.

"'Well, D. and D., how goes the world with you?'

"'Very badly indeed,' says my grandfather; his heart was full, and he just told him the whole story.

"'I'll settle it all,' said the captain; 'leave it to me. There's to be a review to-morrow in the Park; get on the back of the best horse you can find,—the Duke is a capital judge of a nag,—ride him briskly about the field; he'll notice you, never fear; the whole thing will come up before his memory, and you'll have him to breakfast before the week's over.'

"'Do you think so?—do you really think so?'

"'I'll take my oath of it. I say, D. and D., could you do a little thing at a short date just now?'

"'If it wasn't too heavy,' said my grandfather, with a faint sigh.

"'Only a hundred.'

"'Well,' said he, 'you may send it down to the office. Good-bye.' And with that he turned back towards town again; not to go home, however, for he knew well there was no time to lose, but straight he goes to Dycer's,—it was old Tom was alive in those days, and a shrewder man than Tom Dycer there never lived. They tell you, ma'am, there's chaps in London that if you send them your height, and your width, and your girth round the waist, they 'll make you a suit of clothes that will fit you like your own skin; but, 'pon my conscience, I believe if you 'd give your age and the color of your hair to old Tom Dycer, he could provide you a horse the very thing to carry you. Whenever a stranger used to come into the yard, Tom would throw a look at him, out of the corner of his eye,—for he had only one, there was a feather on the other,—Tom would throw a look at him, and he'd shout out, 'Bring out 42; take out that brown mare with the white fetlocks.' That's the way he had of doing business, and the odds were five to one but the gentleman rode out half an hour after on the beast Tom intended for him. This suited my grandfather's knuckle well; for when he told him that it was a horse to ride before the Lord-Lieutenant he wanted, 'Bedad,' says Tom, 'I'll give you one you might ride before the Emperor of Chaney.—Here, Dennis, trot out 176.' To all appearance, ma'am, 176 was no common beast, for every man in the yard, big and little, set off, when they heard the order, down to the stall where he stood, and at last two doors were flung wide open, and out he came with a man leading him. He was seventeen hands two if he was an inch, bright gray, with flea-bitten marks all over him; he held his head up so high at one end, and his tail at the other, that my grandfather said he'd have frightened the stoutest fox-hunter to look at him; besides, my dear, he went with his knees in his mouth when he trotted, and gave a skelp of his hind legs at every stride, that it wasn't safe to be within four yards of him.

"'There's action!' says Tom,—'there's bone and figure! Quiet as a lamb, without stain or blemish, warranted in every harness, and to carry a lady.'

"'I wish he 'd carry a wine-merchant safe for about one hour and a half,' said my grandfather to himself. 'What's his price?'

"But Tom would n't mind him, for he was going on reciting the animal's perfections, and telling him how he was bred out of Kick the Moon, by Moll Flanders, and that Lord Dunraile himself only parted with him because he did n't think him showy enough for a charger. 'Though, to be sure,' said Tom, 'he's greatly improved since that. Will you try him in the school, Mr. Dempsey?' said he; 'not but I tell you that you 'll find him a little mettlesome or so there; take him on the grass, and he's gentleness itself,—he's a kid, that's what he is.'

"'And his price?' said my grandfather.

"Dycer whispered something in his ear.

"'Blood alive!' said my grandfather.

"'Devil a farthing less. Do you think you 're to get beauty and action, ay, and gentle temper, for nothing?'

"My dear, the last words, 'gentle temper,' wasn't well out of his mouth when 'the kid' put his two hind-legs into the little pulpit where the auctioneer was sitting, and sent him flying through the window behind him into the stall.

"'That comes of tickling him,' said Tom; 'them blackguards never will let a horse alone.'

"'I hope you don't let any of them go out to the reviews in the Park, for I declare to Heaven, if I was on his back then, Dodd and Dempsey would be D. D. sure enough.'

"'With a large snaffle, and the saddle well back,' says Tom, 'he's a lamb.'

"'God grant it,' says my grandfather; 'send him over to me to-morrow, about eleven.' He gave a check for the money,—we never heard how much it was,—and away he went.

"That must have been a melancholy evening for him, for he sent for old Rogers, the attorney, and after he was measured for breeches and boots, he made his will and disposed of his effects, 'For there's no knowing,' said he, 'what 176 may do for me.' Rogers did his best to persuade him off the excursion,—

"'Dress up one of Dycer's fellows like you; let him go by the Lord-Lieutenant prancing and rearing, and then you yourself can appear on the ground, all splashed and spurred, half an hour after.'

"'No,' says my grandfather, 'I 'll go myself.'

"For so it is, there 's no denying, when a man has got ambition in his heart it puts pluck there. Well, eleven o'clock came, and the whole of Abbey Street was on foot to see my grandfather; there was n't a window had n't five or six faces in it, and every blackguard in the town was there to see him go off, just as if it was a show.

"'Bad luck to them,' says my grandfather; 'I wish they had brought the horse round to the stable-yard, and let me get up in peace.'

"And he was right there,—for the stirrup, when my grandfather stood beside the horse, was exactly even with his chin; but somehow, with the help of the two clerks and the book-keeper and the office stool, he got up on his back with as merry a cheer as ever rung out to welcome him, while a dirty blackguard, with two old pocket-handkerchiefs for a pair of breeches, shouted out, 'Old Dempsey's going to get an appetite for the oysters!'

"Considering everything, 176 behaved very well; he did n't plunge, and he did n't kick, and my grandfather said, 'Providence was kind enough not to let him rear!' but somehow he wouldn't go straight but sideways, and kept lashing his long tail on my grandfather's legs and sometimes round his body, in a way that terrified him greatly, till he became used to it.

"'Well, if riding be a pleasure,' says my grandfather, 'people must be made different from me.'

"For, saving your favor, ma'am, he was as raw as a griskin, and there was n't a bit of him the size of a half-crown he could sit on without a cry-out; and no other pace would the beast go but this little jig-jig, from side to side, while he was tossing his head and flinging his mane about, just as if to say, 'Could n't I pitch you sky-high if I liked? Could n't I make a Congreve-rocket of you, Dodd and Dempsey?'

"When he got on the 'Fifteen Acres,' it was only the position he found himself in that destroyed the grandeur of the scene; for there were fifty thousand people assembled at least, and there was a line of infantry of two miles long, and the artillery was drawn up at one end, and the cavalry stood beyond them, stretching away towards Knockmaroon.

"My grandfather was now getting accustomed to his sufferings, and he felt that, if 176 did no more, with God's help he could bear it for one day; and so he rode on quietly outside the crowd, attracting, of course, a fair share of observation, for he wasn't always in the saddle, but sometimes a little behind or before it. Well, at last there came a cloud of dust, rising at the far end of the field, and it got thicker and thicker, and then it broke, and there were white plumes dancing, and gold glittering, and horses all shaking their gorgeous trappings, for it was the staff was galloping up, and then there burst out a great cheer, so loud that nothing seemed possible to be louder, until bang—bang—bang, eighteen large guns went thundering together, and the whole line of infantry let off a clattering volley, till you 'd think the earth was crashing open.

"'Devil's luck to ye all! couldn't you be quiet a little longer?' says D. and D., for he was trying to get an easy posture to sit in; but just at this moment 176 pricked up his ears, made three bounds in the air, as if something lifted him up, shook his head like a fish, and away he went: wasn't it wonderful that my grandfather kept his seat? He remembers, he says, that at each bound he was a yard over his back; but as he was a heavy man, and kept his legs open, he had the luck to come down in the same place, and a sore place it must have been! for he let a screech out of him each time that would have pierced the heart of a stone. He knew very little more what happened, except that he was galloping away somewhere, until at last he found himself in a crowd of people, half dead with fatigue and fright, and the horse thick with foam.

"'Where am I?' says my grandfather.

"'You 're in Lucan, sir,' says a man.

"'And where 's the review?' says my grandfather.

"'Five miles behind you, sir.'

"'Blessed Heaven!' says he; 'and where 's the Duke?'

"'God knows,' said the man, giving a wink to the crowd, for they thought he was mad.

"'Won't you get off and take some refreshment?' says the man, for he was the owner of a little public.

"'Get off!' says my grandfather; 'it's easy talking! I found it hard enough to get on. Bring me a pint of porter where I am.' And so he drained off the liquor, and he wiped his face, and he turned the beast's head once more towards town.

"When my grandfather reached the Park again, he was, as you may well believe, a tired and a weary man; and, indeed, for that matter, the beast did n't seem much fresher than himself, for he lashed his sides more rarely, and he condescended to go straight, and he didn't carry his head higher than his rider's. At last they wound their way up through the fir copse at the end of the field, and caught sight of the review, and, to be sure, if poor D. and D. left the ground before under a grand salute of artillery and small arms, another of the same kind welcomed him back again. It was an honor he 'd have been right glad to have dispensed with, for when 176 heard it, he looked about him to see which way he 'd take, gave a loud neigh, and, with a shake that my grandfather said he 'd never forget, he plunged forward, and went straight at the thick of the crowd; it must have been a cruel sight to have seen the people running for their lives. The soldiers that kept the line laughed heartily at the mob; but they hadn't the joke long to themselves, for my grandfather went slap at them into the middle of the field; and he did that day what I hear has been very seldom done by cavalry,—he broke a square of the Seventy-ninth Highlanders, and scattered them over the field.

In truth, the beast must have been the devil himself; for wherever he saw most people, it was there he always went. There were at this time three heavy dragoons and four of the horse-police, with drawn swords, in pursuit of my grandfather; and if he were the enemy of the human race, the cries of the multitude could not have been louder, as one universal shout arose of 'Cut him down! Cleave him in two!' And, do you know, he said, afterwards, he 'd have taken it as a mercy of Providence if they had. Well, my dear, when he had broke through the Highlanders, scattered the mob, dispersed the band, and left a hole in the big drum you could have put your head through, 176 made for the staff, who, I may remark, were all this time enjoying the confusion immensely. When, however, they saw my grandfather heading towards them, there was a general cry of 'Here he comes! here he comes! Take care, your Grace!' And there arose among the group around the Duke a scene of plunging, kicking, and rearing, in the midst of which in dashed my grandfather. Down went an aide-de-camp on one side; 176 plunged, and off went the town-major at the other; while a stroke of a sabre, kindly intended for my grandfather's skull, came down on the horse's back and made him give plunge the third, which shot his rider out of the saddle, and sent him flying through the air like a shell, till he alighted under the leaders of a carriage where the Duchess and the Ladies of Honor were seated.

"Twenty people jumped from their horses now to finish him; if they were bunting a rat, they could not have been more venomous.

"'Stop! stop!' said the Duke; 'he's a capital fellow, don't hurt him. Who are you, my brave little man? You ride like Chifney for the Derby.'

"'God knows who I am!' says my grandfather, creeping out, and wiping his face. 'I was Dodd and Dempsey when I left home this morning; but I 'm bewitched, devil a lie in it.'

"'Dempsey, my Lord Duke,' said M'Claverty, coming up at the moment. 'Don't you know him?' And he whispered a few words in his Grace's ear.

"'Oh, yes, to be sure,' said the Viceroy. 'They tell me you have a capital pack of hounds, Dempsey. What do you hunt?'

"'Horse, foot, and dragoons, my Lord,' said my grandfather; and, to be sure, there was a jolly roar of laughter after the words, for poor D. and D. was just telling his mind, without meaning anything more.

"'Well, then,' said the Duke, 'if you 've always as good sport as to-day, you 've capital fun of it.'

"'Oh, delightful, indeed!' said my grandfather; 'never enjoyed myself more in my life.'

"'Where 's his horse?' said his Grace.

"'He jumped down into the sand-quarry and broke his neck, my Lord Duke.'

"'The heavens be praised!' said my grandfather; 'if it's true, I am as glad as if I got fifty pounds.'

"The trumpets now sounded for the cavalry to march past, and the Duke was about to move away, when M'Claverty again whispered something in his ear.

"'Very true,' said he; 'well thought of. I say, Dempsey, I 'll go over some of these mornings and have a run with your hounds.'

"My grandfather rubbed his eyes and looked up, but all he saw was about twenty staff-officers with their hats off; for every man of them saluted my father as they passed, and the crowd made way for him with as much respect as if it was the Duke himself. He soon got a car to bring him home, and notwithstanding all his sufferings that day, and the great escape he had of his life, there wasn't as proud a man in Dublin as himself.

"'He's coming to hunt with my hounds!' said he; ''t is n't to take an oyster and a glass of wine, and be off again!—no, he's coming down to spend the whole day with me.'

"The thought was ecstasy; it only had one drawback. Dodd and Dempsey's house had never kept hounds. Well, ma'am, I needn't detain you long about what happened; it's enough if I say that in less than six weeks my grandfather had bought up Lord Tyrawley's pack, and his hunting-box and horses, and I believe his grooms; and though he never ventured on the back of a beast himself, he did nothing from morning to night but listen and talk about hunting, and try to get the names of the dogs by heart, and practise to cry 'Tally-ho!' and 'Stole away!' and 'Ho-ith! ho-ith!' with which, indeed, he used to start out of his sleep at night, so full he was of the sport. From the 1st of September he never had a red coat off his back. 'Pon my conscience, I believe he went to bed in his spurs, for he did n't know what moment the Duke might be on him, and that's the way the time went on till spring; but not a sign of his Grace, not a word, not a hint that he ever thought more of his promise! Well, one morning my grandfather was walking very sorrowfully down near the Curragh, where his hunting-lodge was, when he saw them roping-in the course for the races, and he heard the men talking of the magnificent cup the Duke was to give for the winner of the three-year-old stakes, and the thought flashed on him, 'I'll bring myself to his memory that way.' And what does he do, but he goes back to the house and tells his trainer to go over to the racing-stables, and buy, not one, nor two, but the three best horses that were entered for the race. Well, ma'am, their engagements were very heavy, and he had to take them all on himself, and it cost him a sight of money. It happened that this time he was on the right scent, for down comes M'Claverty the same day with orders from the Duke to take the odds, right and left, on one of the three, a little mare called Let-Me-Alone-Before-the-People; she was one of his own breeding, and he had a conceit out of her. Well, M'Claverty laid on the money here and there, till he stood what between the Duke's bets and all the officers of the staff and his own the heaviest winner or loser on that race.

"'She's Martin's mare, is n't she?' said M'Claverty.

"'No, sir, she was bought this morning by Mr. Dempsey, of Tear Fox Lodge.'

"'The devil she is,' said M'Claverty; and he jumped on his horse, and he cantered over to the Lodge.

"'Mr. Dempsey at home?' says he.

"'Yes, sir.'

"'Give him this card, and say, I beg the favor of seeing him for a few moments.'

"The man went off, and came back in a few minutes, with the answer, 'Mr. Dempsey is very sorry, but he 's engaged.'

"'Oh, oh! that's it!' says M'Claverty to himself; 'I see how the wind blows. I say, my man, tell him I 've a message from his Grace the Lord-Lieutenant.'

"Well, the answer came for the captain to send the message in, for my grandfather could n't come out.

"'Say, it's impossible,' said M'Claverty; 'it's for his own private ear.'

"Dodd and Dempsey was strong in my grandfather that day: he would listen to no terms.

"'No,' says he, 'if the goods are worth anything, they never come without an invoice. I 'll have nothing to say to him.'

"But the captain wasn't to be balked; for, in spite of everything, he passed the servant, and came at once into the room where my grandfather was sitting,—ay, and before he could help it, was shaking him by both hands as if he was his brother.

"'Why the devil didn't you let me in?' said he; 'I came from the Duke with a message for you.'

"'Bother!' says my grandfather.

"'I did, though,' says he; 'he's got a heavy book on your little mare, and he wants you to make your boy ride a waiting race, and not win the first beat,—you understand?'

"'I do,' says my grandfather, 'perfectly; and he's got a deal of money on her, has he?'

"'He has,' said the captain; 'and every one at the Castle, too, high and low, from the chief secretary down to the second coachman,—we are all backing her.'

"'I am glad of it,—I am sincerely glad of it,' said my grandfather, rubbing his hands.

"'I knew you would be, old boy!' cried the captain, joyfully.

"'Ah, but you don't know why; you 'd never guess.'

"M'Claverty stared at him, but said nothing.

"'Well, I'll tell you,' resumed my grandfather; 'the reason is this: I 'll not let her run,—no, divil a step! I 'll bring her up to the ground, and you may look at her, and see that she 's all sound and safe, in top condition, and with a skin like a looking-glass, and then I 'll walk her back again! And do you know why I 'll do this?' said he, while his eyes flashed fire, and his lip trembled; 'just because I won't suffer the house of Dodd and Dempsey to be humbugged as if we were greengrocers! Two years ago, it was to "eat an oyster with me;" last year it was a "day with my hounds;" maybe now his Grace would join the race dinner; but that's all past and gone,—I 'll stand it no longer.'

"'Confound it, man,' said the captain, 'the Duke must have forgotten it. You never reminded him of his engagement. He 'd have been delighted to have come to you if he only recollected.'

"'I am sorry my memory was better than his,' said my grandfather, 'and I wish you a very good morning.'

"'Oh, don't go; wait a moment; let us see if we can't put this matter straight. You want the Duke to dine with you?'

"'No, I don't; I tell you I 've given it up.'

"'Well, well, perhaps so; will it do if you dine with him?'

"My grandfather had his hand on the lock,—he was just going,—he turned round, and fixed his eyes on the captain.

"'Are you in earnest, or is this only more of the same game?' said he, sternly.

"'I'll make that very easy to you,' said the captain; 'I 'll bring the invitation to you this night; the mare doesn't run till to-morrow; if you don't receive the card, the rest is in your own power.'

"Well, ma'am, my story is now soon told; that night, about nine o'clock, there comes a footman, all splashed and muddy, in a Castle livery, up to the door of the Lodge, and he gave a violent pull at the bell, and when the servant opened the door, he called out in a loud voice, 'From his Excellency the Lord-Lieutenant,' and into the saddle he jumped, and away he was like lightning; and, sure enough, it was a large card, all printed, except a word here and there, and it went something this way:—

"'I am commanded by his Excellency the Lord-Lieutenant to request the pleasure of Mr. Dempsey's company at dinner on Friday, the 23d instant, at the Lodge, Phoenix Park, at seven o'clock.

"'Granville Vereker, *Chamberlain*.

"'Swords and Bags.'

"'At last!' said my grandfather, and he wiped the tears from his eyes; for to say the truth, ma'am, it was a long chase without ever getting once a 'good view.' I must hurry on; the remainder is easy told. Let-Me-Alone-Before-the-People won the cup, my grandfather was chaired home from the course in the evening, and kept open house at the Lodge for all comers while the races lasted; and at length the eventful day drew near on which he was to realize all his long-coveted ambition. It was on the very morning before, however, that he put on his Court suit for about the twentieth time, and the tailor was standing trembling before him while my grandfather complained of a wrinkle here or a pucker there.

"'You see,' said he, 'you've run yourself so close that you 've no time now to alter these things before the dinner.'

"'I 'll have time enough, sir,' says the man, 'if the news is true.'

"'What news?' says my grandfather, with a choking in his throat, for a sudden fear came over him.

"'The news they have in town this morning.'

"'What is it?—speak it out, man!'

"'They say— But sure you 've heard it, sir?'

"'Go on!' says my grandfather; and he got him by the shoulders and shook him. 'Go on, or I'll strangle you!'

"'They say, sir, that the Ministry is out, and—'

"'And, well—'

"'And that the Lord-Lieutenant has resigned, and the yacht is coming round to Dunleary to take him away this evening, for he won't stay longer than the time to swear in the Lords Justices,—he's so glad to be out of Ireland.'

"My grandfather sat down on the chair, and began to cry, and well he might, for not only was the news true, but he was ruined besides. Every farthing of the great fortune that Dodd and Dempsey made was lost and gone,—scattered to the winds; and when his affairs were wound up, he that was thought one of the richest men in Dublin was found to be something like nine thousand pounds worse than nothing. Happily for him, his mind was gone too, and though he lived a few years after, near Finglass, he was always an innocent, didn't remember anybody, nor who he was, but used to go about asking the people if they knew whether his Grace the Lord-Lieutenant had put off his dinner-party for the 23d; and then he 'd pull out the old card to show them, for he kept it in a little case, and put it under his pillow every night till he died."

While Mr. Dempsey's narrative continued, Tom Leonard indulged freely and without restraint in the delights of the Knight's sherry, forgetting not only all his griefs, but the very circumstances and people around him. Had the party maintained a conversational tone, it is probable that he would have been able to adhere to the wise resolutions he had planned for his guidance on leaving home; unhappily, the length of the tale, the prosy monotony of the speaker's voice, the deepening twilight which stole on ere the story drew to a close, were influences too strong for prudence so frail; an instinct told him that the decanter was close by, and every glass he drained either drowned a care or stifled a compunction.

The pleasant buzz of voices which succeeded to the anecdote of Dodd and Dempsey aroused Leonard from his dreary stupor. Wine and laughter and merry voices were adjuncts he had not met for many a day before; and, strangely enough, the only emotions they could call up were some vague, visionary sorrowings over his fallen and degraded condition.

"By Jove!" said Dempsey, in a whisper to Darcy, "the lieutenant has more sympathy for my grandfather than I have myself, — I 'll be hanged if he is n't wiping his eyes! So you see, ma'am," added he, aloud, "it was a taste for grandeur ruined the Dempseys; the same ambition that has destroyed states and kingdoms has brought your humble servant to a trifle of thirty-eight pounds four and nine per annum for all worldly comforts and virtuous enjoyments; but, as the old ballad says, —

> 'Though classic 't is to show one's grief,
> And cry like Carthaginian Marius,
> I 'll not do this, nor ask relief,
> Like that ould beggar Belisarius.'

No, ma'am, 'Never give in-while there's a score behind the door,' — that's the motto of the Dempseys. If it's not on their coat-of-arms, it's written in their hearts."

"Your grandfather, however, did not seem to possess the family courage," said the Knight, slyly.

"Well, and what would you have? Wasn't he brave enough for a wine-merchant?"

"The ladies will give us some tea, Leonard," said the Knight, as Lady Eleanor and her daughter had, some time before, slipped unobserved from the room.

"Yes, Colonel, always ready."

"That's the way with him," whispered Dempsey; "he'd swear black and blue this minute that you commanded the regiment he served in. He very often calls me the quartermaster."

The party rose to join the ladies; and while Leonard maintained his former silence, Dempsey once more took on himself the burden of the conversation by various little anecdotes of the Fumbally household, and sketches of life and manners at Port Ballintray.

So perfectly at ease did he find himself, so inspired by the happy impression he felt convinced he was making, that he volunteered a song, "if the young lady would only vouchsafe few chords on the piano" by way of accompaniment,—a proposition Helen acceded to.

Thus passed the evening,—a period in which Lady

Eleanor more than once doubted if the whole were not a dream, and the persons before her the mere creations of disordered fancy; an impression certainly not lessened as Mr. Dempsey's last words at parting conveyed a pressing invitation to a "little thing he 'd get up for them at Mother Finn's."

CHAPTER III
SOME VISITORS AT GWYNNE ABBEY

It is a fact not only well worthy of mention, but pregnant with its own instruction, that persons who have long enjoyed all the advantages of an elevated social position better support the reverses which condemned them to humble and narrow fortunes, than do the vulgar-minded, when, by any sudden caprice of the goddess, they are raised to a conspicuous and distinguished elevation.

There is in the gentleman, and still more in the gentlewoman,—as the very word itself announces,—an element of placidity and quietude that suggests a spirit of accommodation to whatever may arise to ruffle the temper or disturb the equanimity. Self-respect and consideration for others are a combination not inconsistent or unfrequent, and there are few who have not seen, some time or other, a reduced gentleman dispensing in a lowly station the mild graces and accomplishments of his order, and, while elevating others, sustaining himself.

The upstart, on the other hand, like a mariner in some unknown sea without chart or compass, has nothing to guide him; impelled hither or thither as caprice or passion dictate, he is neither restrained by a due sense of decorum, nor admonished by a conscientious feeling of good breeding. With the power that rank and wealth bestow he becomes not distinguished, but eccentric; unsustained by the companionship of his equals, he tries to assimilate himself to them rather by their follies than their virtues, and thus presents to the world that mockery of rank and station which makes good men sad, and bad men triumphant.

To these observations we have been led by the altered fortunes of those two families of whom our story treats. If the Darcys suddenly found themselves brought down to a close acquaintanceship with poverty and its fellows, they bore the change with that noble resignation that springs from true regard for others at the sacrifice of ourselves. The little shifts and straits of narrowed means were ever treated jestingly, the trials that a gloomy spirit had converted into sorrows made matters of merriment and laughter; and as the traveller sees the Arab tent in the desert spread beside the ruined temple of ancient grandeur, and happy faces and kind looks beneath the shade of ever-vanished splendor, so did this little group maintain in their fall the kindly affection and the high-souled courage that made of that humble cottage a home of happiness and enjoyment.

Let us now turn to the west, where another and very different picture presented itself. Although certain weighty questions remained to be tried at law between the Darcys and the Hickmans, Bicknell could not advise the Knight to contest the mortgage under which the Hickmans had now taken possession of the abbey.

The reputation for patriotism and independence so fortunately acquired by that family came at a most opportune moment. In no country of Europe are the associations connected with the proprietorship of land more regarded than in Ireland; this feeling, like most others truly Irish, has the double property of being either a great blessing or a great curse, for while it can suggest a noble attachment to country, it can also, as we see it in our own day, be the fertile source of the most atrocious crime.

Had Hickman O'Reilly succeeded to the estate of the Darcys at any other moment than when popular opinion called the one a "patriot" and the other a "traitor," the consequences would have been serious; all the disposable force, civil and military, would scarcely have been sufficient to secure possession. The thought of the "ould ancient family" deposed and exiled by the men of yesterday, would have excited a depth of feeling enough to stir the country far and near. Every trait that adorned the one, for generations, would be remembered, while the humble origin of the other would be offered as the bitterest reproach, by those who thought in embodying the picture of themselves and their fortune they were actually summing up the largest amount of obloquy and disgrace. Such is mob principle in everything! Aristocracy has no such admirers as the lowly born, just as the liberty of the press is inexpressibly dear to that part of the population who know not how to read.

When last we saw Gwynne Abbey, the scene was one of mourning, the parting hour of those whose affections clung to the old walls, and who were to leave it forever. We must now return there for a brief space under different auspices, and when Mr. Hickman O'Reilly, the high sheriff of the county, was entertaining a large and distinguished company in his new and princely residence.

It was the assize week, and the judges, as well as the leading officers of the Crown, were his guests; many of the gentry were also there,—some from indifference to whom their host might be, others from curiosity to see how the upstart, Bob Hickman, would do the honors; and there were many who felt far more at their ease in the abbey now than when they had the fears of Lady Eleanor Darcy's quietude and coldness of manner before them.

No expense was spared to rival the style and retinue of the abbey under its former owners. O'Reilly well knew the value of first impressions in such matters, and how the report that would soon gain currency would decide the matter for or against him. So profusely, and with such disregard to money, was everything done, that, as a mere question of cost, there was no doubt that never in the Knight's palmiest days had anything been seen more magnificent than the preparations. Luxuries, brought at an immense cost, and by contraband, from abroad; wines, of the rarest excellence, abounded at every entertainment; equipages, more splendid than any ever seen there before, appeared each morning; and troops of servants without number moved hither and thither, displaying the gorgeous liveries of the O'Reillys.

The guests were for the most part the neighboring gentry, the military, and the members of the bar; but there were others also, selected with peculiar care, and whose presence was secured at no inconsiderable pains. These were the leading "diners-out" of Dublin, and recognized "men about town," whose names were seen on club committees, and whose word was law on all questions of society. Among them, the chief was Con Heffernan; and he now saw himself for the first time a guest at Gwynne Abbey. The invitation was made and accepted with a certain coquetting that gave it the character of a reconciliation; there were political differences to be got over, mutual recriminations to be forgotten; but as each felt, for his own reasons, not indisposed to renew friendly relations, the matter presented little difficulty, and when Mr. O'Reilly received his guest, on his arrival, with a shake of both hands, the action was meant and taken as a receipt in full for all past misunderstanding, and both had too much tact ever to go back on "bygones."

There had been a little correspondence between the parties, the early portions of which were marked "Confidential," and the latter "Strictly confidential and private." This related to a request made by O'Reilly to Heffernan to entreat his influence in behalf of Lionel Darcy. Nothing could exceed the delicacy of the negotiation; for after professing that the friendship which had subsisted between his own son and young Darcy was the active motive for the request, he went on to say that in the course of certain necessary legal investigations it was discovered that young Lionel, in the unguarded carelessness of a young and extravagant man, had put his name to bills of a large amount, and even hinted that he had not stopped there, but had actually gone the length of signing his father's name to documents for the sale of property. To obtain an appointment for him in some regiment serving in India would at once withdraw him from the likelihood of any exposure in these matters. To interest Heffernan in the affair was the object of O'Reilly's correspondence; and Heffernan was only too glad, at so ready an opportunity, to renew their raptured relations.

Lions were not as fashionable in those days as at present; but still the party had its share in the person of Counsellor O'Halloran, the great orator of the bar, and the great speaker at public meetings, the rising patriot, who, not being deemed of importance enough to be bought, was looked on as incorruptible. He had come down special to defend O'Reilly in a record of Darcy *versus* Hickman,—the first case submitted for trial by Bicknell, and one which, small in itself, would yet, if determined in the Knight's favor, form a rule of great importance respecting those that were to follow.

It was in the first burst of Hickman O'Reilly's indignation against Government that he had secured O'Halloran as his counsel, never anticipating that any conjuncture would bring him once more into relations with the Ministry. His appointment of high sheriff, however, and his subsequent correspondence with Heffernan, ending with the invitation to the abbey, had greatly altered his sentiments, and he more than once regretted the precipitancy with which he had selected his advocate.

Whether "the Counsellor" did or did not perceive that his reception was one of less cordiality and more embarrassment than might be expected, it is not easy to say, for he was one of those persons who live too much out of themselves to betray their own feelings to the world. He was a large and well-looking man, but whose features would have been coarse in their expression were it not for the animated intelligence of his eye, and the quaint humor that played about the angles of his mouth, and added to the peculiar drollery of an accent to which Kerry had lent all its native archness. His gestures were bold, striking, and original; his manner of speaking, even in private, impressive,—from the deliberate slowness of his utterance, and the air of truthfulness sustained by every agency of look, voice, and expression. The least observant could not fail to remark in him a conscious power, a sense of his own great gifts either in argument or invective; for he was no less skilful in unravelling the tangled tissue of a knotted statement than in overwhelming his adversary with a torrent of abusive eloquence. The habits of his profession, but in particular the practice of cross-examination, had given him an immense insight into the darker recesses of the human heart, and made him master of all the subtleties and evasions of inferior capacities. This knowledge he brought with him into society, where his powers of conversation had already established for him a high repute. He abounded in anecdote, which he introduced so easily and naturally that the *à propos* had as much merit as the story itself. Yet with all these qualities, and in a time when the members of his profession were more than ever esteemed and courted, he himself was not received, save on sufferance, into the better society of the capital. The stamp of a "low tone," and the assertion of democratic opinions, were two insurmountable obstacles to his social acceptance; and he was rarely, if ever, seen in those circles which arrogated to themselves the title of best. Whether it was a conscious sense of what was "in him" powerful enough to break down such barriers as these, and that, like Nelson, he felt the day would come when he would have a *"Gazette of his own,"* but his manner at times displayed a spirit of haughty daring and effrontery that formed a singular contrast with the slippery and insinuating softness of his *nisi prius* tone and gesture.

If we seem to dwell longer on this picture than the place the original occupies in our story would warrant, it is because the character is not fictitious, and there is always an interest to those who have seen the broad current of a mighty river rolling onward in its mighty strength, to stand beside the little streamlet which, first rising from the mountain, gave it origin, — to mark the first obstacles that opposed its course, — and to watch the strong impulses that moulded its destiny to overcome them.

Whatever fears Hickman O'Reilly might have felt as to how his counsel, learned in the law, would be received by the Government agent, Mr. Heffernan, were speedily allayed. The gentlemen had never met before, and yet, ere the first day went over, they were as intimate as old acquaintances, each, apparently, well pleased with the strong good sense and natural humor of the other. And so, indeed, it may be remarked in the world, that when two shrewd, far-reaching individuals are brought together, the attraction of quick intelligence and craft is sufficient to draw them into intimate relations at once. There is something wonderfully fraternal in roguery.

This was the only social difficulty O'Reilly dreaded, and happily it was soon dispelled, and the general enjoyment was unclouded by even the slightest accident. The judges were *bon vivants*, who enjoyed good living and good wine; he of the Common Pleas, too, was an excellent shot, and always exchanged his robes for a shooting-jacket on entering the park, and despatched hares and woodcocks as he walked along, with as much unconcern as he had done Whiteboys half an hour before. The Solicitor-General was passionately fond of hunting, and would rather any day have drawn a cover than an indictment; and so with the rest, — they seemed all of them sporting-gentlemen of wit and pleasure, who did a little business at law by way of "distraction." Nor did O'Halloran form an exception; he was as ready as the others to snatch an interval of pleasure amid the fatigues of his laborious day. But, somehow, he contrived that no amount of business should be too much for him; and while his ruddy cheek and bright eye bespoke perfect health and renewed enjoyment, it was remarked that the lamp burned the whole night long unextinguished in his chamber, and that no morning found him ever unprepared to defend the interest of his client.

There was, as we have said, nothing to throw a damper on the general joy. Fortune was bent on dealing kindly with Mr. O'Reilly; for while he was surrounded with distinguished and delighted guests, his father, the doctor, the only one whose presence could have brought a blush to his cheek, was confined to his room by a severe cold, and unable to join the party.

The assize calendar was a long one, and the town the last in the circuit, so that the judges were in no hurry to move on; besides, Gwynne Abbey was a quarter which it was very unlikely would soon be equalled in style of living and resources. For all these several reasons the business of the law went on with an easy and measured pace, the Court opening each day at ten, and closing about three or four, when a magnificent procession of carriages and saddle-horses drew up in the main street to convey the guests back to the abbey.

While the other trials formed the daily subject of table-talk, suggesting those stories of fun, anecdote, and incident with which no other profession can enter into rivalry, the case of Darcy *versus* Hickman was never alluded to, and, being adroitly left last on the list for trial, could not possibly interfere with the freedom so essential to pleasant intercourse.

The day fixed on for this record was a Saturday. It was positively the last day the judges could remain, and having accepted an engagement to a distant part of the country for that very day at dinner, the Court was to sit early, and there being no other cause for trial, it was supposed the cause would be concluded in time to permit their departure. Up to this morning the high sheriff had never omitted, as in duty bound, to accompany the judges to the court-house, displaying in the number and splendor of his equipages a costliness and magnificence that excited the wonder of the assembled gentry. On this day, however, he deemed it would be more delicate on his part to be absent, as the matter in litigation so nearly concerned himself. And half seriously and half in jest he made his apologies to the learned baron who was to try the cause, and begged for permission to remain at the abbey. The request was most natural, and at once acceded to; and although Heffernan had expressed the greatest desire to hear the Counsellor, he determined to pass the morning, at least, with O'Reilly, and endeavor afterwards to be in time for the address to the jury.

At last the procession moved off; several country gentlemen, who had come over to breakfast, joining the party, and making the cavalcade, as it entered the town, a very imposing body. It was the market-day, too; and thus the square in front of the court-house was crowded with a frieze-coated and red-cloaked population, earnestly gesticulating and discussing the approaching trial, for to the Irish peasant the excitement of a law process has the most intense and fascinating interest. All the ordinary traffic of the day was either neglected or carelessly performed, in the anxiety to see those who dispensed the dread forms of justice, but more particularly to obtain a sight of the young "Counsellor," who for the first time had appeared on this circuit, but whose name as a patriot and an orator was widely renowned.

"Here he comes! Here he comes! Make way there!" went from mouth to mouth, as O'Halloran, who had entered the inn for a moment, now issued forth in wig and gown, and carrying a heavily laden bag in his hand. The crowd opened for him respectfully and in dead silence, and then a hearty cheer burst forth, that echoed through the wide square, and was taken up by hundreds of voices in the neighboring streets.

It needed not the reverend companionship of Father John M'Enerty, the parish priest of Curraghglass, who walked at his side, to secure him this hearty burst of welcome, although of a truth the circumstance had its merit also, and many favorable comments were passed upon O'Halloran for the familiar way he leaned on the priest's arm, and the kindly intelligence that subsisted between them.

If anything could have added to the pleasure of the assembled crowd at the instant, it was an announcement by Father John, who, turning round on the steps of the courthouse, informed them in a kind of confidential whisper that was heard over the square, that "if they were good boys, and did n't make any disturbance in the town," the Counsellor would give them a speech when the trial was over.

The most deafening shout of applause followed this declaration, and whatever interest the questions of law had possessed for them before was now merged in the higher anxiety to hear the great Counsellor himself discuss the "veto," that long-agitated question each had taught himself to believe of nearest importance to himself.

"When last I visited this town," said Bicknell to the senior counsel employed in the Knight's behalf, "I witnessed a very different scene. Then we had triumphal arches, and bonfire illuminations, and addresses. It was young Darcy's birthday, and a more enthusiastic reception it is impossible to conceive than he met in these very streets from these very people."

"There is only one species of interest felt for dethroned monarchs," said the other, caustically, — "how they bear their misfortunes."

"The man you see yonder waving his hat to young O'Reilly was one of a deputation to congratulate the heir of Gwynne Abbey! I remember him well, — his name is Mitchell."

"I hope not the same I see upon our jury-list here," said the Counsellor, as he unfolded a written paper, and perused it attentively.

"The same man; he holds his house under the Darcys, and has received many and deep favors at their hands."

"So much the worse, if we should find him in the jury-box. But have we any chance of young Darcy yet? Do you give up all hope of his arrival?"

"The last tidings I received from my clerk were, that he was to follow him down to Plymouth by that night's mail, and still hoped to be in time to catch him ere the transport sailed."

"What a rash and reckless fellow he must be, that would leave a country where he has such interests at stake!"

"If he felt that a point of honor or duty was involved, I don't believe he 'd sacrifice a jot of either to gain this cause, and I 'm certain that some such plea has been made use of on the present occasion."

"How they cheer! What's the source of their enthusiasm at this moment? There it goes, that carriage with the green liveries and the Irish motto round the crest. Look at O'Halloran, too! how he shakes hands with the townsfolk; canvassing for a verdict already! Now, Bicknell, let us move on; but, for my part, I feel our cause is decided outside the court-house. If I 'm not very much mistaken, we are about to have an era of 'popular justice' in Ireland, and our enemies could not wish us worse luck."

CHAPTER IV
A SCENE AT THE ASSIZES

Although Mr. Hickman O'Reilly affected an easy unconcern regarding the issue of the trial, he received during the morning more than one despatch from the court-house narrating its progress. They were brief but significant; and when Hefferuan, with his own tact, inquired if the news were satisfactory, the reply was made by putting into his hands a slip of paper with a few words written in pencil: "They are beaten,-the verdict is certain."

"I concluded," said Heffernan, as he handed back the paper, "that the case was not deemed by you a very doubtful matter."

"Neither doubtful nor important," said Hickman, calmly; "it was an effort, in all probability suggested by some crafty lawyer, to break several leases on the ground of forgery in the signatures. I am sure nothing short of Mr. Darcy's great difficulties would ever have permitted him to approve of such a proceeding."

"The shipwrecked sailor will cling to a hen-coop," said Heffernan. "By the way, where are these Darcys? What has become of them?"

"Living in Wales, or in Scotland, some say."

"Are they utterly ruined?"

"Utterly, irretrievably. A course of extravagance maintained for years at a rate of about double his income, loans obtained at any sacrifice, sales of property effected without regard to loss, have overwhelmed him; and the worst of it is, the little remnant of fortune left is likely to be squandered in vain attempts to recover at law what he has lost by recklessness."

Heffernan walked on for some moments in silence, and, as if pondering over Hickman's words, repeated several times, half aloud: "No doubt of it,—no doubt of it." Then added, in a louder tone: "The whole history of this family, Mr. O'Reilly, is a striking confirmation of a remark I heard made, a few days since, by a distinguished individual,—to *you* I may say it was Lord Cornwallis. 'Heffernan,' said he, 'this country is in a state of rapid transition; everything progresses but the old gentry of the land; they alone seem rooted to ancient prejudices, and fast confirmed in bygone barbarisms.' I ventured to ask him if he could suggest a remedy for the evil, and I 'll never forget the tone with which he whispered in my ear, 'Yes; supersede them!' And that, sir," said Heffernan, laying his hand confidentially on O'Reilly's arm,— "that is and must be the future policy regarding Ireland."

Mr. Heffernan did not permit himself to risk the success of his stroke by a word more, nor did he even dare to cast a look at his companion and watch how his spell was working. As the marksman feels when he has shot his bolt that no after-thought can amend the aim, so did he wait quietly for the result, without a single effort on his part. "The remark is a new one to me," said O'Reilly, at length; "but so completely does it accord with my own sentiments, I feel as if I either had or might have made it myself. The old school you speak of were little calculated to advance the prosperity of the country; the attachment of the people to them was fast wearing out."

"Nay," interposed Heffernan, "it was that very same attachment, that rude remnant of feudalism, made the greatest barrier against improvement. The law of the land was powerless in comparison with the obligations of this clanship. It is time, full time, that the people should become English in feeling, as they are in law and in language; and to make them so, the first step is, to work the reformation in the gentry. Now, at the hazard of a liberty which you may deem an impertinence, I will tell you frankly, Mr. O'Reilly, that you, you yourself, are admirably calculated to lead the van of this great movement. It is all very natural, and perhaps very just, that in a moment of chagrin with a minister or his party, a man should feel indignant, and, although acting under a misconception, throw himself into a direct opposition; yet a little reflection will show that such a line involves a false position. Popularity with the masses could never recompense a man like you for the loss of that higher esteem you must sacrifice for it; the *devoirs* of your station impose a very different class of duties from what this false patriotism suggests; besides, if from indignation—a causeless indignation I am ready to prove it—you separate yourself from the Government, you are virtually suffering your own momentary anger to decide the whole question of your son's career. You are shutting the door of advancement against a young man with every adventitious aid of fortune in his favor; handsome, accomplished, wealthy,-what limit need there be to his ambition? And finally, some fellow, like our friend the Counsellor, without family, friends, or fortune, but with lungs of leather and a ready tongue, will beat you hollow in the race, and secure a wider influence over the mass of the people than a hundred gentlemen like you. You will deem it, probably, enough to spend ten or fifteen thousand on a contested election, and to give a vote for your party in Parliament; he, on the other hand, will write letters, draw up petitions, frame societies, meetings, resolutions, and make speeches, every word of which will sink deeply into the hearts of men whose feelings are his own. You, and others in your station, will be little better than tools in his hands; and powerful as you think yourselves to-day, with your broad acres and your cottier freeholders, the time may come when these men will be less at *your* bidding than *his*, and for this simple reason,—the man of nothing will always be ready to bid higher for mob support than he who has a fortune to lose."

"You have put a very strong case," said O'Reilly; "perhaps I should think it stronger, if I had not heard most of the arguments before, from yourself, and know by this time how their application to me has not sustained your prophecy."

"I am ready to discuss that with you, too," said Heffer-nan. "I know how it all happened: had I been with you the day you dined with Castlereagh, the misunderstanding never could have occurred; but there was a fatality in it all. Come," said he, familiarly, and he slipped his arm, as he spoke, within O'Reilly's, "I am the worst diplomatist in the world, and I fear I never should have risen to high rank in the distinguished corps of engineers if such had been my destination. I can lay down the parallels and the trenches patiently enough, I can even bring up my artillery and my battering-train, but, hang it! somehow, I never can wait for a breach to storm through. The truth is, if it were not for a very strong feeling on the subject I have just spoken of, you never would have seen me here this day. No man is happier or prouder to enjoy your hospitality than I am, but I acknowledge it was a higher sentiment induced me to accept your invitation. When your note reached me, I showed it to Castlereagh.

"'What answer have you sent?' said he.

"'Declined, of course,' said I.

"'You are wrong, Heffernan,' said his Lordship, as he took from me the note which I held ready sealed in my hand; 'in my opinion, Heffernan, you are quite wrong.'

"'I may be so, my Lord; but I confess to you I always act from the first impulse, and if it suggests regret afterwards, it at least saves trouble at the time.'

"'Heffernan,' said the Secretary, as he calmly read over the lines of your letter, 'there are many reasons why you should go: in the first place, O'Reilly has really a fair grudge against us, and this note shows that he has the manliness to forget it. Every line of it bespeaks the gentleman, and I 'll not feel contented with myself until you convey to him my own sorrow for what is past, and the high sense I entertain of his character and conduct.'

"He said a great deal more; enough, if I tell you he induced me to rescind my first intention, and to become your guest; and I may say that I never followed advice the consequences of which have so thoroughly sustained my expectations."

"This is very flattering," said O'Reilly; "it is, indeed, more than I looked for; but, as you have been candid with me, I will be as open with you: I had already made up my mind to retire, for a season at least, from politics. My father, you know, is a very old man, and not without the prejudices that attach to his age; he was always averse to those ambitious views a public career would open, and a degree of coldness had begun to grow up between us in consequence. This estrangement is now happily at an end; and in his consenting to our present mode of life and its expenditure, he is, in reality, paying the recompense of his former opposition. I will not say what changes time may work in my opinion or my line of acting; but I will pledge myself that, if I do resume the path of public life, you are the very first man I will apprise of the intention."

A cordial shake-hands ratified this compact; and Heffer-nan, who now saw that the fortress had capitulated, only stipulating for the honors of war, was about to add something very complimentary, when Beecham O'Reilly galloped up, with his horse splashed and covered with foam.

"Don't you want to hear O'Halloran, Mr. Heffernan?" cried he.

"Yes, by all means."

"Come along, then; don't lose a moment; there's a phaeton ready for you at the door, and if we make haste, we'll be in good time."

O'Reilly whispered a few words in his son's ear, to which the other replied, aloud, —

"Oh! quite safe, perfectly safe. He was obliged to join his regiment, and sail at a moment's notice."

"Young Darcy, I presume?" said Heffernan, with a look of malicious intelligence. But no answer was returned, and O'Reilly continued to converse eagerly in Beecham's ear.

"Here comes the carriage, Mr. Heffernan," said the young man; "so slip in, and let's be off." And, giving his horse to a servant, he took his seat beside Heffernan, and drove off at a rapid pace towards the town.

After a quick drive of some miles, they entered the town, and had no necessity to ask if O'Halloran had begun his address to the jury. The streets which led to the square before the court-house, and the square itself, was actually crammed with country-people, of all sexes and ages; some standing with hats off, or holding their hands close to their ears, but all, in breathless silence, listening to the words of the Counsellor, which were not less audible to those without than within the building.

Nothing short of Beecham O'Reilly's present position in the county, and the fact that the gratification they were then deriving was of his family's procuring for them, could have enabled him to force a passage through that dense crowd, which wedged up all the approaches. As it was, he could only advance step by step, the horses and even the pole of the carriage actually forcing the way through the throng.

As they went thus slowly, the rich tones of the speaker swelled on the air with a clear, distinct, and yet so soft and even musical intonation that they fell deeply into the hearts of the listeners. He was evidently bent as much on appealing to those outside the court as to the jury, for his speech was less addressed to the legal question at issue than to the social condition of the peasantry; the all but absolutism of a landlord,—the serf-like slavery of a tenantry, dependent on the will or the caprice of the owners of the soil! With the consummate art of a rhetorician, he first drew the picture of an estate happily circumstanced, a benevolent landlord surrounded by a contented tenantry, the blessings of the poor man, "rising like the dews of the earth, and descending again in rain to refresh and fertilize the source it sprang from." Not vaguely nor unskilfully, but with thorough knowledge, of his subject, he descanted on the condition of the peasant, his toils, his struggles against poverty and sickness borne with long-suffering and patience, from the firm trust that, even in this world, his destinies were committed to no cruel or unfeeling taskmaster. Although generally a studied plainness and even homeliness of language pervaded all he said, yet at times some bold figure, some striking and brilliant metaphor, would escape him, and then, far from soaring—as it might be suspected he had—above the comprehension of the hearers, a subdued murmur of delight would follow the words, and swelling louder and louder, burst forth at last into one great roar of applause. If a critical ear might cavil at the incompleteness or inaptitude of his similes, to the warm imagination and excited fancy of the Irish peasant they had no such blemishes.

It was at the close of a brilliant peroration on this theme, that Heffernan and Beecham O'Reilly reached the courthouse, and with difficulty forcing their way, obtained standing-room near the bar.

The orator had paused, and turning round he caught Beecham's eye: the glance exchanged was but of a second's duration, but, brief as it was, it did not escape Heffernan's notice, and with a readiness he knew well how to profit by, he assumed a quiet smile, as though to say that he, too, had read its meaning. The young man blushed deeply; whatever his secret thoughts were, he felt ashamed that another should seem to know them, and in a hesitating whisper, said,—

"Perhaps my father has told you—"

A short nod from Heffernan—a gesture to imply anything or nothing—was all his reply, and Beecham went on,—

"He's going to do it, now."

Heffernan made no answer, but, leaning forward on the rail, settled himself to listen attentively to the speaker.

"Gentlemen of the jury," said O'Halloran, in a low and deliberate tone, "if the only question I was interested in bringing before you this day was the cause you sit there to try, I would conclude here. Assured as I feel what your verdict will and must be, I would not add a word more, nor weaken the honest merit of your convictions by anything like an appeal to your feelings. But I cannot do this. The law of the land, in the plenitude of its liberty, throws wide the door of justice, that all may enter and seek redress for wrong, and with such evident anxiety that he who believes himself aggrieved should find no obstacle to his right, and that even he who frivolously and maliciously advances a charge against another suffers no heavier penalty for his offence than the costs of the suit. No, my Lords, for the valuable moments lost in a vexatious cause, for the public time consumed, for insult and outrage cast upon the immutable principles of right and wrong, you have nothing more severe to inflict than the costs of the action!—a pecuniary fine, seldom a heavy one, and not unfrequently to be levied upon insolvency! What encouragement to the spirit of revengeful litigation! How suggestive of injury is the system! How deplorable would it be if the temple could not be opened without the risk of its altar being desecrated! But, happily, there is a remedy—a great and noble remedy—for an evil like this. The same glorious institutions that have built up for our protection the bulwark of the law, have created another barrier against wrong,—grander, more expansive, and more enduring still; one neither founded on the variable basis of nationality or of language, nor propped by the artifices of learned, or the subtleties of crafty men; not following the changeful fortunes of a political condition, or tempered by the tone of the judgment-seat, but of all lands, of every tongue and nation and people, great, enduring, and immutable,—the law of Public Opinion. To the bar of this judgment-seat, one higher and greater than even your Lordships, I would now summon the plaintiff in this action. There is no need that I should detail the charge against him; the accusation he has brought this day is our indictment,—his allegation is his crime."

The reader, by this time, may partake of Mr. Heffernan's prescience, and divine what the secret intelligence between the Counsellor and Beecham portended, and that a long-meditated attack on the Knight of Gwynne, in all the relations of his public and private life, was the chief duty of Mr. O'Halloran in the action. Taking a lesson from the great and illustrious chief of a neighboring state, O'Reilly felt that Usurpation can never be successful till Legitimacy becomes odious. The "prestige" of the "old family" clung too powerfully to every class in the county to make his succession respected. His low origin was too recent, his moneyed dealings too notorious, to gain him acceptance, except on the ruins of the Darcys. The new edifice of his own fame must be erected out of the scattered and broken materials of his rival's house. If any one was well calculated to assist in such an emergency, it was O'Halloran.

It was by—to use his own expression—"weeding the country of such men" that the field would be opened for that new class of politicians who were to issue their edicts in newspapers, and hold their parliaments in public meetings. Against exclusive or exaggerated loyalty the struggle would be violent, but not difficult; while against moderation, sound sense and character, the Counsellor well knew the victory was not so easy of attainment. He himself, therefore, had a direct personal object in this attack on the Knight of Gwynne, and gladly accepted the special retainer that secured his services.

By a series of artful devices, he so arranged his case that the Knight of Gwynne did not appear as an injured individual seeking redress against the collusive guilt of his agent and his tenantry, but as a ruined gambler, endeavoring to break the leases he had himself granted and guaranteed, and, by an act of perfidy, involve hundreds of innocent families in hopeless beggary. To the succor of these unprotected people Mr. Hickman O'Reilly was represented as coming forward, this noble act of devotion being the first pledge he had offered of what might be expected from him as the future leader of a great county.

He sketched with a masterly but diabolical ingenuity the whole career of the Knight, representing him at every stage of life as the pampered voluptuary seeking means for fresh enjoyment without a thought of the consequences; he exhibited him dispensing, not the graceful duties of hospitality, but the reckless waste of a tasteless household, to counterbalance by profusion the insolent hauteur of his wife, "that same Lady Eleanor who would not deign to associate with the wives and daughters of his neighbors!" "I know not," cried the orator, "whether you were more crushed by *his* gold or by *her* insolence: it was time that you should weary of both. You took the wealth on trust, and the rank on guess,—what now remains of either?"

He drew a frightful picture of a suffering and poverty-enslaved tenantry, sinking fast into barbarism from hopelessness,—unhappily, no Irishman need depend upon his imagination for the sketch. He contrasted the hours of toil and sickness with the wanton spendthrift in his pleasures,— the gambler setting the fate of families on the die, reserving for his last hope the consolation that he might still betray those whom he had ruined, land that when he had dissipated the last shilling of his fortune, he still had the resource of putting his honor up to auction! "And who is there will deny that he did this?" cried O'Halloran. "Is there any man in the kingdom has not heard of his conduct in Parliament—that foul act of treachery which the justice of Heaven stigmatized by his ruin! How on the very night of the debate he was actually on his way to inflict the last wound upon his country, when the news came of his own overwhelming destruction! And, like as you have seen sometime in our unhappy land the hired informer transferred from the witness-table to the dock, this man stands now forth to answer for his own offences!

"It was full time that the rotten edifice of this feudalist gentry should fall; honor to you on whom the duty devolves to roll away the first stone!"

A slight movement in the crowd behind the bar disturbed the silence in which the Court listened to the speaker, and a murmur of disapprobation was heard, when a hand, stretched forth, threw a little slip of paper on the table before O'Halloran. It was addressed to him; and believing it came from the attorney in the cause, he paused to read it. Suddenly his features became of an ashy paleness, his lip trembled convulsively, and in a voice scarcely audible from emotion, he addressed the bench,—

"My Lords, I ask the protection of this Court. I implore your Lordships to see that an advocate, in the discharge of his duty, is not the mark of an assassin. I have just received this note—" He attempted to read it, but after a pause of a second or two, unable to utter a word, he handed the paper to the bench.

The judge perused the paper, and immediately whispered an order that the writer, or at least the bearer, of the note should be taken into custody.

"You may rest assured, sir," said the senior judge, addressing O'Halloran, "that we will punish the offender, if he be discovered, with the utmost penalty the law permits. Mr. Sheriff, let the court be searched."

The sub-sheriff was already, with the aid of a strong police force, engaged in the effort to discover the individual who had thus dared to interfere with the administration of justice; but all in vain. The court and the galleries were searched without eliciting anything that could lead to detection; and although several were taken up on suspicion, they were immediately afterwards liberated on being recognized as persons well known and in repute. Meanwhile the business of the trial stood still, and O'Halloran, with his arms folded, and his brows bent in a sullen frown, sat without speaking, or noticing any one around him.

The curiosity to know the exact words the paper contained was meanwhile extreme, and a thousand absurd versions gained currency; for, in the absence of all fact, invention was had recourse to. "Young Darcy is here,—he was seen this morning on the mail,—it was he himself gave the letter." Such were among the rumors around; while Con Heffernan, coolly tapping his snuff-box, asked one of the lawyers near him, but in a voice plainly audible on either side, "I hope our friend Bagenal Daly is well; have you seen him lately?"

From that moment an indistinct murmur ran through the crowd that it was Daly had come back to "the West" to challenge the bar, and the whole bench, if necessary. Many added that there could no longer be any doubt of the fact, as Mr. Heffernan had seen and spoken to him.

Order was at last restored; but so completely had this new incident absorbed all the interest of the trial, that already the galleries began to thin, and of the great crowd that filled the body of the court, many had taken their departure. The Counsellor arose, agitated and evidently disconcerted, to finish his task: he spoke, indeed, indignantly of the late attempt to coerce the free expression of the advocate "by a brutal threat;" but the theme seemed one he felt no pleasure in dwelling upon, and he once more addressed himself to the facts of the case.

The judge charged briefly; and the jury, without retiring from the box, brought in a verdict for Hickman O'Reilly.

When the judges retired to unrobe, a messenger of the court summoned O'Halloran to their chamber. His absence was very brief; but when he returned his face was paler, and his manner more disturbed than ever, notwithstanding an evident effort to seem at ease and unconcerned. By this time Hickman O'Reilly had arrived in the town, and Heffernan was complimenting the Counsellor on the admirable display of his speech.

"I regret sincerely that the delicate nature of the position in which I stood prevented my hearing you," said O'Reilly, shaking his hand.

"You have indeed had a great loss," said Heffernan; "a more brilliant display I never listened to."

"Well, sir," interposed the little priest of Curraghglass, who, not altogether to the Counsellor's satisfaction, had now slipped an arm inside of his, "I hope the evil admits of remedy; Mr. O'Halloran intends to address a few words to the people before he leaves the town."

Whether it was the blank look that suddenly O'Reilly's features assumed, or the sly malice that twinkled in Heffernan's gray eyes, or that his own feelings suggested the course, but the Counsellor hastily whispered a few words in the priest's ear, the only audible portion of which was the conclusion: "Be that as it may, I 'll not do it."

"I 'm ready now, Mr. O'Reilly," said he, turning abruptly round.

"My father has gone over to say good-bye to the judges," said Beecham; "but I'll drive you back to the abbey,—the carriage is now at the door."

With a few more words in a whisper to the priest, O'Halloran moved on with young O'Reilly towards the door.

"Only think, sir," said Father John, dropping behind with Heffernan, from whose apparent intimacy with O'Halloran he augured a similarity of politics, "it is the first time the Counsellor was ever in our town, the people have been waiting since two o'clock to hear him on the 'veto,'—sorra one of them knows what the same 'veto' is,—but it will be a cruel disappointment to see him leave the place without so much as saying a word."

"Do you think a short address from *me* would do instead?" said Heffernan, slyly; "I know pretty well what's doing up in Dublin."

"Nothing could be better, sir," said Father John, in ecstasy; "if the Counsellor would just introduce you in a few words, and say that, from great fatigue, or a sore throat, or anything that way, he deputed his friend Mr.—"

"Heffernan's my name."

"His friend Mr. Heffernan to state his views about the 'veto,'—mind, it must be the 'veto,'-you can touch on the reform in Parliament, the oppression of the penal laws, but the 'veto' will bring a cheer that will beat them all."

"You had better hint the thing to the Counsellor," said Heffernan; "I am ready whenever you want me."

As the priest stepped forward to make the communication to O'Halloran, that gentleman, leaning on Beecham O'Reilly's arm, had just reached the steps of the courthouse, where now a considerable police-force was stationed,—a measure possibly suggested by O'Reilly himself.

The crowd, on catching sight of the Counsellor, cheered vociferously; and, although they were not without fears that he intended to depart without speaking, many averred that he would address them from the carriage. Before Father John could make known his request, a young man, dressed in a riding-costume, burst through the line of police, and, springing up the steps, seized O'Halloran by the collar.

"I gave you a choice, sir," said he, "and you made it;" and at the same instant, with a heavy horsewhip, struck him several times across the shoulders, and even the face. So sudden was the movement, and so violent the assault, that, although a man of great personal strength, O'Halloran had received several blows almost before he could defend himself, and when he had rallied, his adversary, though much lighter and less muscular, showed in skill, at least, he was his superior. The struggle, however, was not to end here; for the mob, now seeing their favorite champion attacked, with a savage howl of vengeance dashed forward, and the police, well aware that the youth would be torn limb from limb, formed a line in front of him with fixed bayonets. For a few moments the result was doubtful; nor was it until more than one retired into the crowd bleeding and wounded, that the mob desisted, or limited their rage to yells of vengeance.

Meanwhile the Counsellor was pulled back within the court-house by his companions, and the young man secured by two policemen,—a circumstance which went far to allay the angry tempest of the people without.

As, pale and powerless from passion, his livid cheek marked with a deep blue welt, O'Halloran sat in one of the waiting-rooms of the court, O'Reilly and his son endeavored, as well as they could, to calm down his rage; expressing, from time to time, their abhorrence of the indignity offered, and the certain penalty that awaited the offender. O'Halloran never spoke; he tried twice to utter something, but the words died away without sound, and he could only point to his cheek with a trembling finger, while his eyes glared like the red orbs of a tiger.

As they stood thus, Heffernan slipped noiselessly behind O'Reilly, and said in his ear,—

"Get him off to the abbey; your son will take care of him. I have something for yourself to hear."

O'Reilly nodded significantly, and then, turning, said a few words in a low, persuasive tone to O'Halloran, concluding thus: "Yes, by all means, leave the whole affair in my hands. I 'll have no difficulty in making a bench. The town is full of my brother magistrates."

"On every account I would recommend this course, sir," said Heffernan, with one of those peculiarly meaning looks by which he so well knew how to assume a further insight into any circumstance than his neighbors possessed.

"I will address the people," cried O'Halloran, breaking his long silence with a deep and passionate utterance of the words; "they shall see in me the strong evidence of the insolent oppression of that faction that rules this country; I 'll make the land ring with the tyranny that would stifle the voice of justice, and make the profession of the bar a forlorn hope to every man of independent feeling."

"The people have dispersed already," said Beecham, as he came back from the door of the court; "the square is quite empty."

"Yes, I did that," whispered Heffernan in O'Reilly's ear; "I made the servant put on the Counsellor's greatcoat, and drive rapidly off towards the abbey. The carriage is now, however, at the back entrance to the court-house; so, by all means, persuade him to return."

"When do you propose bringing the fellow up for examination, Mr. O'Reilly?" said O'Halloran, as he arose from his seat.

"To-morrow morning. I have given orders to summon a full bench of magistrates, and the affair shall be sifted to the bottom."

"You may depend upon that, sir," said the Counsellor, sternly. "Now I 'll go back with you, Mr. Beecham O'Reilly." So saying, he moved towards a private door of the building, where the phaeton was in waiting, and, before any attention was drawn to the spot, he was seated in the carriage, and the horses stepping out at a fast pace towards home.

"It's not Bagenal Daly?" said O'Reilly, the very moment he saw the carriage drive off.

"No, no!" said Heffernan, smiling.

"Nor the young Darcy,—the captain?"

"Nor him either. It's a young fellow we have been seeking for in vain the last month. His name is Forester."

"Not Lord Castlereagh's Forester?"

"The very man. You may have met him here as Darcy's guest?"

O'Reilly nodded.

"What makes the affair worse is that the relationship with Castlereagh will be taken up as a party matter by O'Halloran's friends in the press; they will see a Castle plot, where, in reality, there is nothing to blame save the rash folly of a hot-headed boy."

"What is to be done?" said O'Reilly, putting his hand to his forehead, in his embarrassment to think of some escape from the difficulty.

"I see but one safe issue,—always enough to any question, if men have resolution to adopt it."

"Let me hear what you counsel," said O'Reilly, as he cast a searching glance at his astute companion.

"Get him off as fast as you can."

"O'Halloran! You mistake him, Mr. Heffernan; he'll prosecute the business to the end."

"I'm speaking of Forester," said Heffernan, dryly; "it is *his* absence is the important matter at this moment."

"I confess I am myself unable to appreciate your view of the case," said O'Reilly, with a cunning smile; "the policy is a new one to me which teaches that a magistrate should favor the escape of a prisoner who has just insulted one of his own friends."

"I may be able to explain my meaning to your satisfaction," said Heffernan, as, taking O'Reilly's arm, he spoke for some time in a low but earnest manner. "Yes," said he, aloud, "your son Beecham was the object of this young man's vengeance; chance alone turned his anger on the Counsellor. His sole purpose in 'the West' was to provoke your son to a duel, and I know well what the result of your proceedings to-morrow would effect. Forester would not accept of his liberty on bail, nor would he enter into a security on his part to keep the peace. You will be forced, actually forced, to commit a young man of family and high position to a gaol; and what will the world say? That in seeking satisfaction for a very gross outrage on the character of his friend, a young Englishman of high family was sent to prison! In Ireland, the tale will tell badly; *we* always have more sympathy than censure for such offenders. In England, how many will know of his friends and connections, who never heard of your respectable bench of magistrates,—will it be very wonderful if they side with their countryman against the stranger?"

"How am I to face O'Halloran if I follow this counsel?" said O'Reilly, with a thoughtful but embarrassed air. "Then, as to Lord Castlereagh," continued Heffernan, not heeding the question, "he will take your interference as a personal and particular favor. There never was a more favorable opportunity for you to disconnect yourself with the whole affair. The hired advocate may calumniate as he will, but he can show no collusion or connivance on your part. I may tell you, in confidence, that a more indecent and gross attack was never uttered than this same speech. I heard it, and from the beginning to the end it was a tissue of vulgarity and falsehood. Oh! I know what you would say: I complimented the speaker on his success, and all that; so I did, perfectly true, and he understood me, too,—there is no greater impertinence, perhaps, than in telling a man that you mistook his bad cider for champagne! But enough of him. You may have all the benefit, if there be such, of the treason, and yet never rub shoulders with the traitor. You see I am eager on this point, and I confess I am very much so. Your son Beecham could not have a worse enemy in the world of Club and Fashion than this same Forester; he knows and is known to everybody."

"But I cannot perceive how the thing is to be done," broke in O'Reilly, pettishly; "you seem to forget that O'Halloran is not the man to be put off with any lame, disjointed story."

"Easily enough," said Heffernan, coolly; "there is no difficulty whatever. You can blunder in the warrant of his committal; you can designate him by a wrong Christian name; call him Robert, not Richard; he may be admitted to bail, and the sum a low one. The rest follows naturally; or, better than all, let some other magistrate-you surely know more than one to aid in such a pinch—take the case upon himself, and make all the necessary errors; that's the best plan."

"Conolly, perhaps," said O'Reilly, musingly; "he is a great friend of Darcy's, and would risk something to assist this young fellow."

"Well thought of," cried Heffernan, slapping him on the shoulder; "just give me a line of introduction to Mr. Conolly on one of your visiting-cards, and leave the rest to me."

"If I yield to you in this business, Mr. Heffernan," said O'Reilly, as he sat down to write, "I assure you it is far more from my implicit confidence in your skill to conduct it safely to the end, than from any power of persuasion in your arguments. O'Halloran is a formidable enemy."

"You never were more mistaken in your life," said Heffernan, laughing, "such men are only noxious by the terror they inspire; they are the rattlesnakes of the world of mankind, always giving notice of their approach, and never dangerous to the prudent. He alone is to be dreaded who, tiger-like, utters no cry till his victim is in his fangs."

There was a savage malignity in the way these words were uttered that made O'Reilly almost shudder. Heffernan saw the emotion he had unguardedly evoked, and, laughing, said,—

"Well, am I to hold over the remainder of my visit to the abbey as a debt unpaid? for I really have no fancy to let you off so cheaply."

"But you are coming back with me, are you not?"

"Impossible! I must take charge of this foolish boy, and bring him up to Dublin; I only trust I have a vested right to come back and see you at a future day."

O'Reilly responded to the proposition with courteous warmth; and with mutual pledges, perhaps of not dissimilar sincerity, they parted,—the one to his own home, the other to negotiate in a different quarter and in a very different spirit of diplomacy.

CHAPTER V
MR. HEFFERNAN'S COUNSELS

Mr. Heffernan possessed many worldly gifts and excellences, but upon none did he so much pride himself, in the secret recesses of his heart,—he was too cunning to indulge in more public vauntings,—as in the power he wielded over the passions of men much younger than himself. Thoroughly versed in their habits of life, tastes, and predilections, he knew how much always to concede to the warm and generous temperament of their age, and to maintain his influence over them less by the ascendancy of ability than by a more intimate acquaintance with all the follies and extravagances of fashionable existence.

Whether he had or had not been a principal actor in the scenes he related with so much humor, it was difficult to say; for he would gloss over his own personal adventures so artfully that it was not easy to discover whether the motive were cunning or delicacy. He seemed, at least, to have done everything that wildness and eccentricity had ever devised, to have known intimately every man renowned for such exploits, and to have gone through a career of extravagance and dissipation quite sufficient to make him an unimpeachable authority in every similar case. The reserve which young men feel with regard to those older than themselves was never experienced in Con Heffernan's company; they would venture to tell him anything, well aware that, however absurd the story or embarrassing the scrape, Hefferuan was certain to cap it by another twice as extravagant in every respect.

Although Forester was by no means free from the faults of his age and class, the better principles of his nature had received no severe or lasting injury, and his estimation for Heffernan proceeded from a very different view of his character from that which we have just alluded to. He knew him to be the tried and trusted agent of his cousin, Lord Castlereagh, one for whose abilities he entertained the greatest respect; he saw him consulted and advised with on every question of difficulty, his opinions asked, his suggestions followed; and if, occasionally, the policy was somewhat tortuous, he was taught to believe that the course of politics, like that "of true love, never did run smooth." In this way, then, did he learn to look up to Heffernan, who was too shrewd a judge of motives to risk a greater ascendancy by any hazardous appeal to the weaker points of his character.

Fortune could not have presented a more welcome visitor to Forester's eyes than Heffernau, as he entered the room of the inn where the youth had been conducted by the sergeant of police, and where he sat bewildered by the difficulties in which his own rashness had involved him. The first moments of meeting were occupied by a perfect shower of questions, as to how Heffernan came to be in that quarter of the world, when he had arrived, and with whom he was staying. All questions which Heffernan answered by the laughing subterfuge of saying, "Your good genius, I suppose, sent me to get you out of your scrape; and fortunately I am able to do so. But what in the name of everything ridiculous could have induced you to insult this man, O'Halloran? You ought to have known that men like him cannot fight; they would be made riddles of if they once consented to back by personal daring the insolence of their tongues. They set out by establishing for themselves a kind of outlawry from honor, they acknowledge no debts within the jurisdiction of that court, otherwise they would soon be bankrupt."

"They should be treated like all others without the pale of law, then," said Forester, indignantly.

"Or, like Sackville," added Heffernan, laughing, "when they put their swords 'on the peace establishment,' they should put their tongues on the 'civil list.' Well, well, there are new discoveries made every day; some men succeed better in life by the practice of cowardice than others ever did, or ever will do, by the exercise of valor."

"What can I do here? Is there anything serious in the difficulty?" said Forester, hurriedly; for he was in no humor to enjoy the abstract speculations in which Heffernan indulged.

"It might have been a very troublesome business," replied Heffernan, quietly: "the judge might have issued a bench warrant against you, if he did not want your cousin to make him chief baron; and Justice Conolly might have been much more technically accurate, if he was not desirous of seeing his son in an infantry regiment. It's all arranged now, however; there is only one point for your compliance,—you must get out of Ireland as fast as may be. O'Halloran will apply for a rule in the King's Bench, but the proceedings will not extend to England."

"I am indifferent where I go to," said Forester, turning away; "and provided this foolish affair does not get abroad, I am well content."

"Oh! as to that, you must expect your share of notoriety. O'Halloran will take care to display his martyrdom for the people! It will bring him briefs now; Heaven knows what greater rewards the future may have in store from it!"

"You heard the provocation," said Forester, with an unsuccessful attempt to speak calmly,—"the gross and most unpardonable provocation?"

"I was present," replied Heffernan, quietly.

"Well, what say you? Was there ever uttered an attack more false and foul? Was there ever conceived a more fiendish and malignant slander?"

"I never heard anything worse."

"Not anything worse! No, nor ever one half so bad."

"Well, if you like it, I will agree with you; not one half so bad. It was untrue in all its details, unmanly in spirit. But, let me add, that such philippics have no lasting effect,—they are like unskilful mines, that in their explosion only damage the contrivers. O'Reilly, who was the real deviser of this same attack, whose heart suggested, whose head invented, and whose coffers paid for it, will reap all the obloquy he hoped to heap upon another. Take myself, for instance, an old time-worn man of the world, who has lived long enough never to be sudden in my friendships or my resentments, who thinks that liking and disliking are slow processes,—well, even I was shocked, outraged at this affair; and although having no more intimacy with Darcy than the ordinary intercourse of social life, confess I could not avoid acting promptly and decisively on the subject. It was a question, perhaps, more of feeling than actual judgment,—a case in which the first impulse may generally be deemed the right one." Here Heffernan paused, and drew himself up with an air that seemed to say, "If I am confessing to a weakness in my character, it is at least one that leans to virtue's side."

Forester awaited with impatience for the explanation, and, not perceiving it to come, said, "Well, what did you do in the affair?"

"My part was a very simple one," said Heffernan; "I was Mr. O'Reilly's guest, one of a large party, asked to meet the judges and the Attorney-General. I came in, with many others, to hear O'Halloran; but if I did, I took the liberty of not returning again. I told Mr. O'Reilly frankly that, in point of fact, the thing was false, and, as policy, it was a mistake. Party contests are all very well, they are necessary, because without them there is no banner to fight under; and the man of mock liberality to either side would take precedence of those more honest but less cautious than himself; but these things are great evils when they enlist libellous attacks on character in their train. If the courtesies of life are left at the door of our popular assemblies, they ought at least to be resumed when passing out again into the world."

"And so you actually refused to go back to his house?" said Forester, who felt far more interested in this simple fact than in all the abstract speculation that accompanied it.

"I did so: I even begged of him to send my servant and my carriage after me; and, had it not been for your business, before this time I had been some miles on my way towards Dublin."

Forester never spoke, but he grasped Heffernan's hand, and shook it with earnest cordiality.

"Yes, yes," said Heffernan, as he returned the pressure; "men can be strong partisans, anxious and eager for their own side, but there is something higher and nobler than party." He arose as he spoke, and walked towards the window, and then, suddenly turning round, and with an apparent desire to change the theme, asked, "But how came you here? What good or evil fortune prompted you to be present at this scene?"

"I fear you must allow me to keep that a secret," said Forester, in some confusion.

"Scarcely fair, that, my young friend," said Heffernan, laughing, "after hearing my confession in full."

Forester seemed to feel the force of the observation, but, uncertain how to act, he maintained a silence for several minutes.

"If the affair were altogether my own, I should not hesitate," said he at length, "but it is not so. However, we are in confidence here, and so I will tell you. I came to this part of the country at the earnest desire of Lionel Darcy. I don't know whether you are aware of his sudden departure for India. He had asked for leave of absence to give evidence on this trial; the application was made a few days after a memorial he sent in for a change of regiment. The demand for leave was unheeded, but he received a peremptory order to repair to Portsmouth, and take charge of a detachment under sailing-orders for India; they consisted of men belonging to the Eleventh Light Dragoons, of which he was gazetted to a troop. I was with him at Chatham when the letter reached him, and he explained the entire difficulty to me, showing that he had no alternative, save neglecting the interest of his family, on the one hand, or refusing that offer of active service he had so urgently solicited on the other. We talked the thing over one entire night through, and at last, right or wrong, persuaded ourselves that any evidence he could give would be of comparatively little value; and that the refusal to join would be deemed a stain upon him as an officer, and probably be the cause of greater grief to the Knight himself than his absence at the trial. Poor fellow! he felt for more deeply for quitting England without saying good-bye to his family than for all the rest."

"And so he actually sailed in the transport?" said Heffernan.

"Yes, and without time for more than a few lines to his father, and a parting request to me to come over to Ireland and be present at the trial. Whether he anticipated any attack of this kind or not, I cannot say, but he expressed the desire so strongly I half suspect as much."

"Very cleverly done, faith!" muttered Heffernan, who seemed far more occupied with his own reflections than attending to Forester's words; "a deep and subtle stroke, Master O'Reilly, ably planned and as ably executed."

"I am rejoiced that Lionel escaped this scene, at all events," said Forester.

"I must say, it was neatly done," continued Heffernan, still following out his own train of thought; "'Non contigit cuique,' as the Roman says; it is not every man can take in Con Heffernan,—I did not expect Hickman O'Reilly would try it." He leaned his head on his hand for some minutes, then said aloud, "The best thing for you will be to join your regiment."

"I have left the army," said Forester, with a flush, half of shame, half of anger.

"I think you were right," replied Heffernan, calmly, while he avoided noticing the confusion in the young man's manner. "Soldiering is no career for any man of abilities like yours; the lounging life of a barrack-yard, the mock duties of parade, the tiresome dissipations of the mess, suit small capacities and minds of mere routine. But you have better stuff in you, and, with your connections and family interest, there are higher prizes to strive for in the wheel of fortune."

"You mistake me," said Forester, hastily; "it was with no disparaging opinion of the service I left it. My reasons had nothing in common with such an estimate of the army."

"There's diplomacy, for instance," said Heffernan, not minding the youth's remark; "your brother has influence with the Foreign Office."

"I have no fancy for the career."

"Well, there are Government situations in abundance. A man must do something in our work-a-day world, if only to be companionable to those who do. Idleness begets ennui and falling in love; and although the first only wearies for the time, the latter lays its impress on all a man's after-life, fills him with false notions of happiness, instils wrong motives for exertion, and limits the exercise of capacity to the small and valueless accomplishments that find favor beside the work-table and the piano."

Forester received somewhat haughtily the unasked counsels of Mr. Heffernan respecting his future mode of life, nor was it improbable that he might himself have conveyed his opinion thereupon in words, had not the appearance of the waiter to prepare the table for dinner interposed a barrier.

"At what hour shall I order the horses, sir?" asked the man of Heffernan.

"Shall we say eight o'clock, or is that too early?"

"Not a minute too early for me," said Forester; "I am longing to leave this place, where I hope never again to set foot."

"At eight, then, let them be at the door; and whenever your cook is ready, we dine."

CHAPTER VI
AN UNLOOKED-FOR PROMOTION

The same post that brought the Knight the tidings of his lost suit conveyed the intelligence of his son's departure for India; and although the latter event was one over which, if in his power, he would have exercised no control, yet was it by far the more saddening of the two announcements.

Unable to apply any more consolatory counsels, his invariable reply to Lady Eleanor was, "It was a point of duty; the boy could not have done otherwise; I have too often expressed my opinion to him about the *devoirs* of a soldier to permit of his hesitating here. And as for our suit, Mr. Bicknell says the jury did not deliberate ten minutes on their verdict; whatever right we might have on our side, it was pretty clear we had no law. Poor Lionel is spared the pain of knowing this, at least." He sighed heavily, and was silent. Lady Eleanor and Helen spoke not either; and except their long-drawn breathings nothing was heard in the room.

Lady Eleanor was the first to speak. "Might not Lionel's evidence have given a very different coloring to our cause if he had been there?"

"It is hard to say. I am not aware whether we failed upon a point of fact or law. Mr. Bicknell writes like a man who felt his words were costly matters, and that he should not put his client to unnecessary expense. He limits himself to the simple announcement of the result, and that the charge of the bench was very pointedly unfavorable. He says something about a motion for a new trial, and regrets Daly's having prevented his engaging Mr. O'Halloran, and refers us to the newspapers for detail."

"I never heard a question of this O'Halloran," said Lady Eleanor, "nor of Mr. Daly's opposition to him before."

"Nor did I, either; though, in all likelihood, if I had, I should have been of Bagenal's mind myself. Employing such men has always appeared to me on a par with the barbarism of engaging the services of savage nations in a war against civilized ones; and the practice is defended by the very same arguments,—if they are not with you, they are against you."

"You are right, my dear father," said Helen, while her countenance glowed with unusual animation; "leave such allies to the enemy if he will, no good cause shall be stained by the scalping-knife and the tomahawk."

"Quite right, my dearest child," said he, fondly; "no defeat is so bad as such a victory."

"And where was Mr. Daly? He does not seem to have been at the trial?"

"No; it would appear as if he were detained by some pressing necessity in Dublin. This letter is in his handwriting; let us see what he says."

Before the Knight could execute his intention, old Tate appeared at the door, and announced the name of Mr. Dempsey.

"You must present our compliments," said Darcy, hastily, "and say that a very particular engagement will prevent our having the pleasure of receiving his visit this evening."

"This is really intolerable," said Lady Eleanor, who, never much disposed to look favorably on that gentleman, felt his present appearance anything but agreeable.

"You hear what your master says," said Helen to the old man, who, never having in his whole life received a similar order, felt proportionately astonished and confused.

"Tell Mr. Dempsey we are very sorry; but—"

"For all that, he won't be denied," said Paul, himself finishing the sentence, while, passing unceremoniously in front of Tate, he walked boldly into the middle of the room. His face was flushed, his forehead covered with perspiration, and his clothes, stained with dust, showed that he had come off a very long and fast walk. He wiped his forehead with a flaring cotton handkerchief, and then, with a long-drawn puff, threw himself back into an arm-chair.

There was something so actually comic in the cool assurance of the little man, that Darcy lost all sense of annoyance at the interruption, while he surveyed him and enjoyed the dignified coolness of Lady Eleanor's reception.

"That's the devil's own bit of a road," said Paul, as he fanned himself with a music-book, "between this and Coleraine. Whenever it 's not going up a hill, it's down one. Do you ever walk that way, ma'am?"

"Very seldom indeed, sir."

"Faith, and I 'd wager, when you do, that it gives you a pain just here below the calf of the leg, and a stitch in the small of the back."

Lady Eleanor took no notice of this remark, but addressed some observation to Helen, at which the young girl smiled, and said, in a whisper,—

"Oh, he will not stay long."

"I am afraid, Mr. Dempsey," said the Knight, "that. I must be uncourteous enough to say that we are unprepared for a visitor this evening. Some letters of importance have just arrived; and as they will demand all our attention, you will, I am sure, excuse the frankness of my telling you that we desire to be alone."

"So you shall in a few minutes more," said Paul, coolly. "Let me have a glass of sherry and water, or, if wine is not convenient, ditto of brandy, and I 'm off. I did n't come to stop. It was a letter that you forgot at the post-office, marked 'with speed,' on the outside, that brought me here; for I was spending a few days at Coleraine with old Hewson."

The kindness of this thoughtful act at once eradicated every memory of the vulgarity that accompanied it; and as the Knight took the letter from his hands, he hastened to apologize for what he said by adding his thanks for the service.

"I offered a fellow a shilling to bring it, but being harvest-time he wouldn't come," said Dempsey. "Phew! what a state the roads are in! dust up to your ankles!"

"Come now, pray help yourself to some wine and water," said the Knight; "and while you do so, I 'll ask permission to open my letter."

"There 's a short cut down by Port-na-happle mill, they tell me, ma'am," said Dempsey, who now found a much more complaisant listener than at first; "but, to tell you the truth, I don't think it would suit you or me; there are stone walls to climb over and ditches to cross. Miss Helen, there, might get over them, she has a kind of a thoroughbred stride of her own, but fencing destroys me outright."

"It was a very great politeness to think of bringing us the letter, and I trust your fatigues will not be injurious to you," said Lady Eleanor, smiling faintly.

"Worse than the damage to a pair of very old shoes, ma'am, I don't anticipate; I begin to suspect they've taken their last walk this evening."

While Mr. Dempsey contemplated the coverings of his feet with a very sad expression, the Knight continued to read the letter he held in his hand with an air of extreme intentness.

"Eleanor, my dear," said he, as he retired into the deep recess of a window, "come here for a moment."

"I guessed there would be something of consequence in that," said Dempsey, with a sly glance from Helen to the two figures beside the window. "The envelope was a thin one, and I read 'War Office' in the corner of the inside cover."

Not heeding the delicacy of this announcement, but only thinking of the fact, which she at once connected with Lionel's fortunes, Helen turned an anxious and searching glance towards the window; but the Knight and Lady Eleanor had entered a small room adjoining, and were already concealed from view.

"Was he ever in the militia, miss?" asked Dempsey, with a gesture of his thumb to indicate of whom he spoke.

"I believe not," said Helen, smiling at the pertinacity of his curiosity.

"Well, well," resumed Dempsey, with a sigh, "I would not wish him a hotter march than I had this day, and little notion I had of the same tramp only ten minutes before. I was reading the 'Saunders' of Tuesday last, with an account of that business done at Mayo between O'Halloran and the young officer-you know what I mean?"

"No, I have not heard it; pray tell me," said she, with an eagerness very different from her former manner.

"It was a horsewhipping, miss, that a young fellow in the Guards gave O'Halloran, just as he was coming out of court; something the Counsellor said about somebody in the trial,—names never stay in my head, but I remember it was a great trial at the Westport assizes, and that O'Halloran came down special, and faith, so did the young captain too; and if the lawyer laid it on very heavily within the court, the red-coat made up for it outside. But I believe I have the paper in my pocket, and, if you like, I'll read it out for you."

"Pray do," said Helen, whose anxiety was now intense.

"Well, here goes," said Mr. Dempsey; "but with your permission I 'll just wet my lips again. That 's elegant sherry!"

Having sipped and tasted often enough to try the young lady's patience to its last limit, he unfolded the paper, and read aloud,—

"'When Counsellor O'Halloran had concluded his eloquent speech in the trial of Darcy v. Hickman,—for a full report of which see our early columns,—a young gentleman, pushing his way through the circle of congratulating friends, accosted him with the most insulting and opprobrious epithets, and failing to elicit from the learned gentleman a reciprocity,'-that means, miss, that O'Halloran did n't show fight,—'struck him repeatedly across the shoulders, and even the face, with a horsewhip. He was immediately committed under a bench warrant, but was liberated almost at once. Perhaps our readers may understand these proceedings more clearly when we inform them that Captain Forester, the aggressor in this case, is a near relative of our Irish Secretary, Lord Castlereagh.' That 's very neatly put, miss, isn't it?" said Mr. Dempsey, with a sly twinkle of the eye; "it's as much as to say that the Castle chaps may do what they please. But it won't end there, depend upon it; the Counsellor will see it out."

Helen paid little attention to the observation, for, having taken up the paper as Mr. Dempsey laid it down, she was deeply engaged in the report of the trial and O'Halloran's speech.

"Wasn't that a touching-up the old Knight of Gwynne got?" said Dempsey, as, with his glass to his eye, he peered over her shoulder at the newspaper. "Faith, O'Halloran flayed him alive! He 's the boy can do it!"

Helen scarce seemed to breathe, as, with a heart almost bursting with indignant anger, she read the lines before her.

"Strike him!" cried she, at length, unable longer to control the passion that worked within her; "had he trampled him beneath his feet, it had not been too much?"

The little man started, and stared with amazement at the young girl, as, with flashing eyes and flushed cheek, she arose from her seat, and, tearing the paper into fragments, stamped upon them with her foot.

"Blood alive, miss, don't destroy the paper! I only got a loan of it from Mrs. Kennedy, of the Post-office; she slipped it out of the cover, though it was addressed to Lord O'Neil. Oh dear! oh dear! it's a nice article now!"

These words were uttered in the very depth of despair, as, kneeling down on the carpet, Mr. Dempsey attempted to collect and arrange the scattered fragments.

"It's no use in life! Here's the Widow Wallace's pills in the middle of the Counsellor's speech! and the last day's drawing of the lottery mixed up with that elegant account of old Darcy's—"

A hand which, if of the gentlest mould, now made a gesture to enforce silence, arrested Mr. Dempsey's words, and at the same moment the Knight entered with Lady Eleanor. Darcy started as he gazed on the excited looks and the air of defiance of his daughter, and for a second a deep flush suffused his features, as with an angry frown he asked of Dempsey, "What does this mean, sir?"

"D-n me if I know what it means!" exclaimed Paul, in utter despair at the confusion of his own faculties. "My brain is in a whirl."

"It was a little political dispute between Mr. Dempsey and myself, sir," said Helen, with a faint smile. "He was reading for me an article from the newspaper, whose views were so very opposite to mine, and his advocacy of them so very animated, that—in short, we both became warm."

"Yes, that's it," cried Dempsey, glad to accept any explanation of a case in which he had no precise idea wherein lay the difficulty,—"that's it; I'll take my oath it was."

"He is a fierce Unionist," said Helen, speaking rapidly to cover her increasing confusion, "and has all the conventional cant by heart, 'old-fashioned opinions,' 'musty prejudices,' and so on."

"I did not suspect you were so eager a politician, my dear Helen," said the Knight, as, half chidingly, he threw his eyes towards the scattered fragments of the torn newspaper.

The young girl blushed till her neck became crimson: shame, at the imputation of having so far given way to passion; sorrow, at the reproof, whose injustice she did not dare to expose; and regret, at the necessity of dissimulation, all overwhelming her at the same moment.

"I am not angry, my sweet girl," said the Knight, as he drew his arm around her, and spoke in a low, fond accent. "I may be sorry—sincerely sorry—at the social condition that has suffered political feeling to approach our homes and our firesides, and thus agitate hearts as gentle as yours by these rude themes. For your sentiments on these subjects I can scarcely be a severe critic, for I believe they are all my own."

"Let us forget it all," said Helen, eagerly; for she saw-that Mr. Dempsey, having collected once more the torn scraps, was busy in arranging them into something like order. In fact, his senses were gradually recovering from the mystification into which they had been thrown, and he was anxious to vindicate himself before the party. "All the magnanimity, however, must not be mine," continued she; "and until that odious paper is consumed, I 'll sign no treaty of peace." So saying, and before Dempsey could interfere to prevent it, she snatched up the fragments, and threw them into the fire. "Now, Mr. Dempsey, we are friends again," said she, laughing.

"The Lord grant it!" ejaculated Paul, who really felt no ambition for so energetic an enemy. "I 'll never tell a bit of news in your company again, so long as my name is Paul Dempsey. Every officer of the Guards may horsewhip the Irish bar—I was forgetting—not a syllable more."

The Knight, fortunately, did not hear the last few words, for he was busily engaged in reading the letter he still held in his hands; at length he said,—

"Mr. Dempsey has conferred one great favor on us by bringing us this letter; and as its contents are of a nature not to admit of any delay—"

"He will increase the obligation by taking his leave," added Paul, rising, and, for once in his life, really well pleased at an opportunity of retiring.

"I did not say that," said Darcy, smiling.

"No, no, Mr. Dempsey," added Lady Eleanor, with more than her wonted cordiality; "you will, I hope, remain for tea."

"No, ma'am, I thank you; I have a little engagement,—I made a promise. If I get safe out of the house without some infernal blunder or other, it 's only the mercy of Providence." And with this burst of honest feeling, Paul snatched up his hat, and without waiting for the ceremony of leave-taking, rushed out of the room, and was soon seen crossing the wide common at a brisk pace.

"Our little friend has lost his reason," said the Knight, laughing. "What have you been doing to him, Helen?"

A gesture to express innocence of all interference was the only reply, and the party became suddenly silent.

"Has Helen seen that letter?" said Lady Eleanor, faintly, and Darcy handed the epistle to his daughter. "Read it aloud, my dear," continued Lady Eleanor; "for, up to this, my impressions are so confused, I know not which is reality, which mere apprehension."

Helen's eyes glanced to the top of the letter, and saw the words "War Office;" she then proceeded to read:—

"'Sir,—In reply to the application made to the Commander-in-Chief of the forces in your behalf, expressing your desire for an active employment, I have the honor to inform you that his Royal Highness, having graciously taken into consideration the eminent services rendered by you in former years, and the distinguished character of that corps which, raised by your exertions, still bears your name, has desired me to convey his approval of your claim, and his desire, should a favorable opportunity present itself, of complying with your wish. I have the honor to remain, your most humble and obedient servant,

"'Harry Greville,

"*Private Secretary.*"

On an enclosed slip of paper was the single line in pencil:—

"H. G. begs to intimate to Colonel Darcy the propriety of attending the next levee of H. R. H., which will take place on the 14th."

"Now, you, who read riddles, my dearest Helen, explain this one to us. I made no application of the kind alluded to, nor am I aware of any one having ever done so for me. The thought never once occurred to me, that his Majesty or his Royal Highness would accept the services of an old and shattered hulk, while many a glorious three-decker lies ready to be launched from the stocks. I could not have presumed to ask such a favor, nor do I well know how to acknowledge it."

"But is there anything so very strange," said Helen, proudly, "that those highly placed by station should be as highly gifted by nature, and that his Royal Highness, having heard of your unmerited calumnies, should have seen that this was the fitting moment to remember the services you have rendered the Crown? I have heard that there are several posts of high trust and honor conferred on those who, like yourself, have won distinction in the service."

"Helen is right," said Lady Eleanor, drawing a long breath, and as if released of a weighty load of doubt and uncertainty; "this is the real explanation; the phrases of official life may give it another coloring to our eyes, but such, I feel assured, is the true solution."

"I should like to think it so," said Darcy, feelingly; "it would be a great source of pride to me at this moment, when my fortunes are lower than ever they were,—lower than ever I anticipated they might be,—to know that my benefactor was the Monarch. In any case I must lose no time in acknowledging this mark of favor. It is now the 4th of the month; to be in London by the 14th, I should leave this to-morrow."

"It is better to do so," said Lady Eleanor, with an utterance from which a great effort had banished all agitation; "Helen and I are safe and well here, and as happy as we can be when away from you and Lionel."

"Poor Lionel!" said the Knight, tenderly; "what good news for him it would be were they to give me some staff appointment,—I might have him near us. Come, Eleanor," added he, with more gayety of manner, "I feel a kind of presentiment of good tidings. But we are forgetting Bagenal Daly all this time; perhaps this letter of his may throw some light on the matter."

Darcy now broke the seal of Daly's note, which, even for him, was one of the briefest. This was so far fortunate, since his writing was in his very worst style, blotted and half erased in many places, scarcely legible anywhere. It was only by assembling a "committee of the whole house" that the Darcys were enabled to decipher even a portion of this unhappy document. As well as it could be rendered, it ran somewhat thus:—

"The verdict is against us; old Bretson never forgave you carrying away the medal from him in Trinity some fifty years back; he charged dead against you; I always said he would. *Summum jus, summa injuria*—The Chief Justice—the greatest wrong! and the jury the fellows who lived under you, in your own town, and their fathers and grandfathers! at least, as many of the rascals as had such.—Never mind, Bicknell has moved for a new trial; they have gained the 'Habere' this time, and so has O'Halloran—you heard of the thrashing—"

Here two tremendous patches of ink left some words that followed quite unreadable.

"What can this mean?" said Darcy, repeating the passage over three or four times, while Helen made no effort to enlighten him in the difficulty. Battled in all his attempts, he read on: "'I saw him in his way through Dublin last night,' Who can he possibly mean?" said Darcy, laying down the letter, and pondering for several minutes.

"O'Halloran, perhaps," said Lady Eleanor, in vain seeking a better elucidation.

"Oh, not him, of course!" cried Darcy; "he goes on to say, that 'he is a devilish high-spirited young fellow, and for an Englishman a warm-blooded animal.' Really this is too provoking; at such a time as this he might have taken pains to be a little clearer," exclaimed Darcy.

The letter concluded with some mysterious hints about intelligence that a few days might disclose, but from what quarter or on what subject nothing was said, and it was actually with a sense of relief Darcy read the words, "Yours ever, Bagenal Daly," at the foot of the letter, and thus spared himself the torment of further doubts and guesses.

Helen was restrained from at once conveying the solution of the mystery by recollecting the energy she had displayed in her scene with Mr. Dempsey, and of which the shame still lingered on her flushed cheek.

"He adds something here about writing by the next post," said Lady Eleanor.

"But before that arrives I shall be away," said the Knight; and the train of thought thus evoked soon erased all memory of other matters. And now the little group gathered together to discuss the coming journey, and talk over all the plans by which anxiety was to be beguiled and hope cherished till they met again.

"Miss Daly will not be a very importunate visitor," said Lady Eleanor, dryly, "judging at least from the past; she has made one call here since we came, and then only to leave her card."

"And if Helen does not cultivate a more conciliating manner, I scarce think that Mr. Dempsey will venture on coming either," said the Knight, laughing.

"I can readily forgive all the neglect," said Helen, haughtily, "in compensation for the tranquillity."

"And yet, my dear Helen," said Darcy, "there is a danger in that same compact. We should watch carefully to see whether, in the isolation of a life apart from others, we are not really indulging the most refined selfishness, and dignifying with the name of philosophy a solitude we love for the indulgence of our own egotism. If we are to have our hearts stirred and our sympathies strongly moved, let the themes be great ones, but above all things let us avoid magnifying the petty incidents of daily occurrence into much consequence: this is what the life of monasteries and convents teaches, and a worse lesson there need not be."

Darcy spoke with more than usual seriousness, for he had observed some time past how Helen had imbibed much of Lady Eleanor's distance towards her humble neighbors, and was disposed to retain a stronger memory of their failings in manner than of their better and heartier traits of character.

The young girl felt the remark less as a reproof than a warning, and said,—

"I will not forget it."

CHAPTER VII
A PARTING INTERVIEW

When Heffernan, with his charge, Forester, reached Dublin, he drove straight to Castlereagh's house, affectedly to place the young man under the protection of his distinguished relative, but in reality burning with eager impatience to recount his last stroke of address, and to display the cunning artifice by which he had embroiled O'Reilly with the great popular leader. Mr. Heffernan had a more than ordinary desire to exhibit his skill on this occasion; he was still smarting under the conscious sense of having been duped by O'Reilly, and could not rest tranquilly until revenged. Under the mask of a most benevolent purpose, O'Reilly had induced Heffernan to procure Lionel Darcy an appointment to a regiment in India. Heffernan undertook the task, not, indeed, moved by any kindliness of feeling towards the youth, but as a means of reopening once more negotiations with O'Reilly; and now to discover that he had interested himself simply to withdraw a troublesome witness in a suit—that he had been, in his own phrase, "jockeyed"—was an insult to his cleverness he could not endure.

As Heffernan and Forester drove up to the door, they perceived that a travelling-carriage, ready packed and loaded, stood in waiting, while the bustle and movement of servants indicated a hurried departure.

"What's the matter, Hutton?" asked Heffernan of the valet who appeared at the moment; "is his Lordship at home?"

"Yes, sir, in the drawing-room; but my Lord is just leaving for England. He is now a Cabinet Minister."

Heffernan smiled, and affected to hear the tidings with delight, while he hastily desired the servant to announce him.

The drawing-room was crowded by a strange and anomalous-looking assemblage, whose loud talking and laughing entirely prevented the announcement of Con Heffernan's name from reaching Lord Castlereagh's ears. Groups of personal friends come to say good-bye, deputations eager to have the last word in the ear of the departing Secretary, tradesmen begging recommendations to his successor, with here and there a disappointed suitor, earnestly imploring future consideration, were mixed up with hurrying servants, collecting the various minor articles which lay scattered through the apartment.

The time which it cost Heffernan to wedge his way through the dense crowd was not wholly profitless, since it enabled him to assume that look of cordial satisfaction at the noble Secretary's promotion which he was so very far from really feeling. Like most men who cultivate mere cunning, he underrated all who do not place the greatest reliance upon it, and in this way conceived a very depreciating estimate of Lord Castlereagh's ability. Knowing how deeply he had himself been trusted, and how much employed in state transactions, he speculated on a long career of political influence, and that, while his Lordship remained as Secretary, his own skill and dexterity would never be dispensed with. This pleasant illusion was now suddenly dispelled, and he saw all his speculations scattered to the wind at once; in fact, to borrow his own sagacious illustration, "he had to submit to a new deal with his hand full of trumps."

He was still endeavoring to disentangle himself from the throng, when Lord Castlereagh's quick eye discovered him.

"And here comes Heffernan," cried he, laughingly; "the only man wanting to fill up the measure of congratulations. Pray, my Lord, move one step and rescue our poor friend from suffocation."

"By Jove! my Lord, one would imagine you were the rising and not the setting sun, from all this adulating assemblage," said Heffernan, as he shook the proffered hand of the Secretary, and held it most ostentatiously in his cordial pressure. "This was a complete surprise for me," added he. "I only arrived this evening with Forester."

"With Dick? Indeed! I'm very glad the truant has turned up again. Where is he?"

"He passed me on the stairs, I fancy to his room, for he muttered something about going over in the packet along with you."

"And where have you been, Heffernan, and what doing?" asked Lord Castlereagh, with that easy smile that so well became his features.

"That I can scarcely tell you here," said Heffernan, dropping his voice to a whisper, "though I fancy the news would interest you." He made a motion towards the recess of a window, and Lord Castlereagh accepted the suggestion, but with an indolence and half-apathy which did not escape Heffernan's shrewd perception. Partly piqued by this, and partly stimulated by his own personal interest in the matter, Heffernan related, with unwonted eagerness, the details of his visit to the West, narrating with all his own skill the most striking characteristics of the O'Reilly household, and endeavoring to interest his hearer by those little touches of native archness in description of which he was no mean master.

But often as they had before sufficed to amuse his Lordship, they seemed a failure now; for he listened, if not with impatience, yet with actual indifference, and seemed more than once as if about to stop the narrative by the abrupt question, "How can this possibly interest *me?*"

Heffernan read the expression, and felt it as plainly as though it were spoken.

"I am tedious, my Lord," said he, whilst a slight flush colored the middle of his cheek; "perhaps I only weary you."

"He must be a fastidious hearer who could weary of Mr. Heffernan's company," said his Lordship, with a smile so ambiguous that Heffernan resumed with even greater embarrassment, —

"I was about to observe, my Lord, that this same member for Mayo has become much more tractable. He evidently sees the necessity of confirming his new position, and, I am confident, with very little notice, might be converted into a stanch Government supporter."

"Your old favorite theory, Heffernan," said the Secretary, laughing; "to warm these Popish grubs into Protestant butterflies by the sunshine of kingly favor, forgetting the while that 'the winter of their discontent' is never far distant. But please to remember, besides, that gold mines will not last forever, — the fountain of honor will at last run dry; and if —"

"I ask pardon, my Lord," interrupted Heffernan. "I only alluded to those favors which cost the Minister little, and the Crown still less, — that social acceptance from the Court here upon which some of your Irish friends set great store. If you could find an opportunity of suggesting something of this kind, or if your Lordship's successor —"

"Heaven pity him!" exclaimed Lord Castlereagh. "He will have enough on his hands, without petty embarrassments of this sort. Without you have promised, Heffernan," added he, hastily. "If you have already made any pledge, of course we must sustain your credit."

"I, my Lord! I trust you know my discretion better than to suspect me. I merely threw out the suggestion from supposing that your Lordship's interest in our poor concerns here might outlive your translation to a more distinguished position."

There was a tone of covert impertinence in the accent, as well as the words, which, while Lord Castlereagh was quick enough to perceive, he was too shrewd to mark by any notice.

"And so," said he, abruptly changing the topic, "this affair of Forester's shortened your visit?"

"Of course. Having cut the knot, I left O'Reilly and Conolly to the tender mercies of O'Halloran, who, I perceive by to-day's paper, has denounced his late client in round terms. Another reason, my Lord, for looking after O'Reilly at this moment. It is so easy to secure a prize deserted by her crew."

"I wish Dick had waited a day or two," said Lord Castlereagh, not heeding Heffernan's concluding remark, "and then I should have been off. As it is, he would have done better to adjourn the horse-whipping sine die, His lady-mother will scarcely distinguish between the two parties in such a conflict, and probably deem the indignity pretty equally shared by both parties."

"A very English judgment on an Irish quarrel," observed Heffernan.

"And you yourself, Heffernan,—when are we to see you in London?"

"Heaven knows, my Lord. Sometimes I fancy that I ought not to quit my post here, even for a day; then again I begin to fear lest the new officials may see things in a different light, and that I may be thrown aside as the propagator of antiquated notions."

"Mere modesty, Heffernan," said Lord Castlereagh, with a look of the most comic gravity. "You ought to know by this time that no government can go on without you. You are the fly-wheel that regulates motion and perpetuates impulse to the entire machine. I 'd venture almost to declare that you stand in the inventory of articles transmitted from one viceroy to another; and as we read of 'one throne covered with crimson velvet, and one state couch with gilt supporters,' so we might chance to fall upon the item of 'one Con Heffernan, Kildare Place.'"

"In what capacity, my Lord?" said Heffernan, endeavoring to conceal his anger by a smile.

"Your gifts are too numerous for mention. They might better be summed up under the title of 'State Judas.'"

"You forget, my Lord, that he carried the bag. Now I was never purse-bearer even to the Lord Chancellor. But I can pardon the simile, coming, as I see it does, from certain home convictions. Your Lordship was doubtless assimilating yourself to another historical character of the same period, and, would, like him, accept the iniquity, but 'wash your hands' of its consequences."

"Do you hear that, my Lord?" said Lord Castlereagh, turning round, and addressing the Bishop of Kilmore. "Mr. Heffernan has discovered a parallel between my character and that of Pontius Pilate." A look of rebuking severity from the prelate was directed towards Heffernan, who meekly said, —

"I was only reproving his Lordship for permitting me to discharge *all* the duties of Secretary for Ireland, and yet receive none of the emoluments."

"But you refused office in every shape and form," said Lord Castlereagh, hastily. "Yes, gentlemen, as the last act of my official life amongst you," — here he raised his voice, and moved into the centre of the room, — "I desire to make this public declaration, that as often as I have solicited Mr. Heffernan to accept some situation of trust and profit under the Crown, he has as uniformly declined; not, it is needless to say, from any discrepancy in our political views, for I believe we are agreed on every point, but upon the ground of maintaining his own freedom of acting and judging."

The declamatory tone in which he spoke these words, and the glances of quiet intelligence that were exchanged through the assembly, were in strong contrast with the forced calmness of Heffernan, who, pale and red by turns, could barely suppress the rage that worked within him; nor was it without an immense effort he could mutter a feigned expression of gratitude for his Lordship's panegyric, while he muttered to himself, —

"You shall rue this yet!"

CHAPTER VIII
THE FIRE

It was late in the evening as the Knight of Gwynne entered Dublin, and took up his abode for the night in an obscure inn at the north side of the city. However occupied his thoughts up to that time by the approaching event in his own fortune, he could not help feeling a sudden pang as he saw once more the well-known landmarks that reminded him of former days of happiness and triumph. Strange as it may now sound, there was a time when Irish gentlemen were proud of their native city; when they regarded its University with feelings of affectionate memory, as the scene of early efforts and ambitions, and could look on its Parliament House as the proud evidence of their national independence! Socially, too, they considered Dublin—and with reason—second to no city of Europe; for there was a period, brief but glorious, when the highest breeding of the courtier mingled with the most polished wit and refined conversation, and when the splendor of wealth, freely displayed as it was, was only inferior to the more brilliant lustre of a society richer in genius and in beauty than any capital of the world.

None had been a more favored participator in these scenes than Darcy himself: his personal gifts, added to the claims of his family and fortune, secured him early acceptance in the highest circles; and if his abilities had not won the very highest distinctions, it seemed rather from his own indifference than from their deficiency.

In those days his arrival in town was the signal for a throng of visitors to call, all eagerly asking on what day they might secure him to dine or sup, to meet this one or that. The thousand flatteries society stores up for her favorites, all awaited him. Parties whose fulfilment hung listlessly in doubt were now hastily determined on, as "Darcy has come" got whispered abroad; and many a scheme of pleasure but half planned found a ready advocacy when the prospect of obtaining him as a guest presented itself.

The consciousness of social success is a great element in the victory. Darcy had this, but without the slightest taint of vain boastfulness or egotism; his sense of his own distinction was merely sufficient to heighten his enjoyment of the world, without detracting ever so little from the manly and unassuming features of his character. It is true he endeavored, and even gave himself pains, to be an agreeable companion; but he belonged to a school and a time when conversation was cultivated as an art, and when men preferred making the dinner-table and the drawing-room the arena of their powers, to indicting verses for an "Annual," or composing tales for a fashionable "Miscellany."

We have said enough, perhaps, to show what Dublin was to him once. How very different it seemed to his eyes now! The season was late summer, and the city dusty and deserted,—few persons in the streets, scarcely a carriage to be seen; an air of listlessness and apathy was over everything, for it was the period when the country was just awakening after the intoxicating excitement of the Parliamentary straggle,—awakening to discover that it had been betrayed and deserted!

As soon as Darcy had taken some slight refreshment, he set out in search of Daly. His first visit was to Henrietta Street, to his own house, or rather what had been his, for it was already let, and a flaring brass-plate on the door proclaimed it the office of a fashionable solicitor. He knocked, and inquired if any one "knew where Mr. Bagenal Daly now resided;" but the name seemed perfectly unknown. He next tried Bicknell's; but that gentleman had not returned since the circuit: he was repairing the fatigues of his profession by a week or two's relaxation at a watering-place.

He did not like himself to call at the club, but he despatched a messenger from the inn, who brought word back that Mr. Daly had not been there for several weeks, and that his present address was unknown. Worried and annoyed, Darcy tried in turn each place where Daly had been wont to frequent, but all in vain. Some had seen him, but not lately; others suggested that he did not appear much in public on account of his moneyed difficulties; and one or two limited themselves to a cautious declaration of ignorance, with a certain assumed shrewdness, as though to say that they could tell more if they would.

It was near midnight when Darcy returned to the inn, tired and worn out by his unsuccessful search. The packet in which he was to sail for England was to leave the port early in the morning, and he sat down in the travellers' room, exhausted and fatigued, till his chamber should be got ready for him.

The inn stood in one of the narrow streets leading out of Smithfield, and was generally resorted to by small farmers and cattle-dealers repairing to the weekly market. Of these, three or four still lingered in the public room, conning over their accounts and discussing the prices of "short-horns and black faces" with much interest, and anticipating all the possible changes the new political condition of the country might be likely to induce.

Darcy could scarcely avoid smiling as he overheard some of these speculations, wherein the prospect of a greater export trade was deemed the most certain indication of national misfortune. His attention was, however, suddenly withdrawn from the conversation by a confused murmur of voices, and the tramp of many feet in the street without The noise gradually increased, and attracted the notice of the others, and suddenly the words "Fire! fire!" repeated from mouth to mouth, explained the tumult.

As the tide of men was borne onward, the din grew louder, and at length the narrow street in front of the inn became densely crowded by a mob hurrying eagerly forward, and talking in loud, excited voices.

"They say that Newgate is on fire, sir," said the landlord, as, hastily entering, he addressed Darcy; "but if you 'll come with me to the top of the house, we 'll soon see for ourselves."

Darcy followed the man to the upper story, whence, by a small ladder, they obtained an exit on the roof. The night was calm and starlight, and the air was still. What a contrast—that spangled heaven in all its tranquil beauty—to the dark streets below, where, in tumultuous uproar, the commingled mass was seen by the uncertain glimmer of the lamps, few and dim as they were. Darcy could mark that the crowd consisted of the very lowest and most miserable-looking class of the capital, the dwellers in the dark alleys and purlieus of the ill-favored region. By their excited gestures and wild accents, it was clear to see how much more of pleasure than of sorrow they felt at the occasion that now roused them from their dreary garrets and damp cellars. Shouts of mad triumph and cries of menace burst from them as they went. The Knight was roused from a moody contemplation of the throng by the landlord saying aloud,—

"True enough, the jail is on fire: see, yonder, where the dark smoke is rolling up, that is Newgate."

"But the building is of stone, almost entirely of stone, with little or no wood in its construction," said Darcy; "I cannot imagine how it could take fire."

"The floors, the window-frames, the rafters are of wood, sir," said the other; "and then," added he, with a cunning leer, "remember what the inhabitants are!"

The Knight little minded the remark, for his whole gaze was fixed on the cloud of smoke, dense and black as night, that rolled forth, as if from the ground, and soon enveloped the jail and all the surrounding buildings in darkness.

"What can that mean?" said he, in amazement.

"It means that this is no accident, sir," said the man, shrewdly; "it's only damp straw and soot can produce the effect you see yonder; it is done by the prisoners—see, it is increasing! and here come the fire-engines!"

As he spoke, a heavy, cavernous sound was heard rising from the street, where now a body of horse-police were seen escorting the fire-engines. The service was not without difficulty, for the mob offered every obstacle short of open resistance; and once it was discovered that the traces were cut, and considerable delay thereby occasioned.

"The smoke is spreading; see, sir, how it rolls this way, blacker and heavier than before!"

"It is but smoke, after all," said Darcy; but although the words were uttered half contemptuously, his heart beat anxiously as the dense volume hung suspended in the air, growing each moment blacker as fresh masses arose. The cries and yells of the excited mob were now wilder and more frantic, and seemed to issue from the black, ill-omened mass that filled the atmosphere.

"That's not smoke, sir; look yonder!" said the man, seizing Darcy's arm, and pointing to a reddish glare that seemed trying to force a passage through the smoke, and came not from the jail, but from some building at the side or in front of it.

"There again!" cried he, "that is fire!"

The words were scarcely uttered, when a cheer burst from the mob beneath. A yell more dissonant and appalling could not have broken from demons than was that shout of exultation, as the red flame leaped up and flashed towards the sky. As the strong host of a battle will rout and scatter the weaker enemy, so did the fierce element dispel the less powerful; and now the lurid glow of a great fire lit up the air, and marked out with terrible distinctness the waving crowd that jammed up the streets,—the windows filled with terrified faces, and the very house-tops crowded by terror-stricken and distracted groups.

The scene was truly an awful one; the fire raged in some houses exactly in front of the jail, pouring with unceasing violence its flood of flame through every door and window, and now sending bright jets through the roofs, which, rent with a report like thunder, soon became one undistinguish-able mass of flame. The cries for succor, the shouts of the firemen, the screams of those not yet rescued, and the still increasing excitement of the mob, mingling their hellish yells of triumph through all the dread disaster, made up a discord the most horrible; while, ever and anon, the police and the crowd were in collision, vain efforts being made to keep the mob back from the front of the jail, whither they had fled as a refuge from the heat of the burning houses.

The fire seemed to spread, defying all the efforts of the engines. From house to house the lazy smoke was seen to issue for a moment, and then, almost immediately after, a new cry would announce that another building was in flames. Meanwhile the smoke, which in the commencement had spread from the courtyard and windows of the jail, was again perceived to thicken in the same quarter, and suddenly, as if from a preconcerted signal, it rolled out from every barred casement and loopholed aperture,—from every narrow and deep cell within the lofty walls; and the agonized yell of the prisoners burst forth at the same moment, and the air seemed to vibrate with shrieks and cries.

"Break open the jail!" resounded on every side. "Don't let the prisoners be burned alive!" was uttered in accents whose humanity was far inferior to their menace; and, as if with one accord, a rush was made at the strongly barred gates of the dark building. The movement, although made with the full force of a mighty multitude, was in vain. In vain the stones resounded upon the thickly studded door, in vain the strength of hundreds pressed down upon the oaken barrier. They might as well have tried to force the strong masonry at either side of it!

"Climb the walls!" was now the cry; and the prisoners re-echoed the call in tones of shrieking entreaty. The mob, savage from their recent repulse at the gate, now seized the ladders employed by the firemen, and planted them against the great enclosure-wall of the jail. The police endeavored to charge, but, jammed up by the crowd, their bridles in many instances cut, their weapons wrested from them, they were almost at the mercy of the mob. Orders had been despatched for troops; but as yet they had not appeared, and the narrow streets, being actually choked up with people, would necessarily delay their progress. If there were any persons in that vast mass disposed to repel the violence of the mob, they did not dare to avow it, the odds were so fearfully on the side of the multitude.

The sentry who guarded the gate was trampled down. Some averred he was killed in the first rush upon the gate; certain it was his cap and coat were paraded on a pole, as a warning of what awaited his comrades within the jail, should they dare to fire on the people. This horrible banner was waved to and fro above the stormy multitude. Darcy had but time to mark it, when he saw the crowd open, as if cleft asunder by some giant band, and at the same instant a man rode through the open space, and, tearing down the pole, felled him who carried it to the earth by a stroke of his whip. The red glare of the burning houses made the scene distinct as daylight; but the next moment a rolling cloud of black smoke hid all from view, and left him to doubt the evidence of his eyesight.

"Did you see the horseman?" asked Darcy, in eager curiosity, for he did not dare to trust his uncorroborated sense.

"There he is!" cried the other. "I know him by a white band on his arm. See, he mounts one of the ladders!—there!—he is near the top!"

A cheer that seemed to shake the very atmosphere now rent the air, as, pressing on like soldiers to a breach, the mob approached the walls. Some shots were fired by the guard, and their effect might be noted by the more savage yells of the mob, whose exasperation was now like madness.

"The shots have told,—see!" cried the man. "Now the people are gathering in close groups, here and there."

But Darcy's eyes were fixed on the walls, which were already crowded with the mob, the dark figures looking like spectres as they passed and repassed through the dense canopy of smoke.

"The soldiers! the soldiers!" screamed the populace from below; and at the instant a heavy lumbering sound crept on, and the head of a cavalry squadron wheeled into the square before the jail. The remainder of the troop soon defiled; but instead of advancing, as was expected, they opened their ranks, and displayed the formidable appearance of two eight-pounders, from which the limbers were removed with lightning speed, and their mouths turned full upon the crowd. Meanwhile an infantry force was seen entering the opposite side of the square, thus showing the mob that they were taken in front and rear, no escape being open save by the small alleys which led off from the street before the prison. The military preparations took scarcely more time to effect than we have employed to relate; and now began a scene of tumult and terror the most dreadful to witness. The order to prime and load, followed by the clanking crash of four hundred muskets; the close ranks of the cavalry, as if with difficulty restrained from charging down upon them; and the lighted fuses of the artillery,—all combined to augment the momentary dread, and the shouts of vengeance so lately heard were at once changed into piercing cries for mercy. The blazing houses, from which the red fire shot up unrestrained, no longer attracted notice,—the jail itself had no interest for those whose danger was become so imminent.

An indiscriminate rush was made towards the narrow lanes for escape, and from these arose the most piercing and agonizing cries,—for while pressed down and trampled, many were trodden under foot never again to rise; others were wounded or burned by the falling timbers of the blazing buildings; and the fearful cry of "The soldiers! the soldiers!" still goaded them on by those behind.

"Look yonder," cried Darcy's companion, seizing him by the arm,— "look there,—near the corner of the market! See, the troops have not perceived that ladder, and there are two fellows now descending it."

True enough. At a remote angle of the jail, not concealed from view by the smoke, stood the ladder in question.

"How slowly they move!" cried Darcy, his eyes fixed upon the figures with that strange anxiety so inseparable from the fate of all who are engaged in hazardous enterprise. "They will certainly be taken."

"They must be wounded," cried the other; "they seem to creep rather than step—I know the reason, they are in fetters."

Scarcely was the explanation uttered when the ladder was seen to be violently moved as if from above, and the next moment was hurled back from the wall, on which several soldiers were now perceived firing on those below.

"They are lost!" said the Knight; "they are either captured or cut down by this time."

"The square is cleared already," said the other; "how quietly the troops have done their work! And the fire begins to yield to the engines."

The square was indeed cleared; save the groups beside the fire-engines, and here and there a knot gathered around some wounded man, the space was empty, the troops having drawn off to the sides, around which they stood in double file. A dark cloud rested over the jail itself, but no longer did any smoke issue from the windows; and already the fire, its rage in part expended, in part subdued, showed signs of decline.

"If the wind was from the west," said the landlord, "there 's no saying where that might have stopped this night!"

"It is a strange occurrence altogether," said the Knight, musingly.

"Not a bit strange, sir," replied the other, whose neighborhood made him acquainted with classes and varieties of men of whom Darcy knew nothing; "it was an attempt by the prisoners."

"Do you think so?" asked Darcy.

"Ay, to be sure, sir; there's scarcely a year goes over without one contrivance or another for escape. Last autumn two fellows got away by following the course of the sewers and gaining the Liffey; they must have passed two days underground, and up to their necks in water a great part of the time."

"Ay, and besides that," observed another,-for already some ten or twelve persons were assembled on the roof as well as Darcy and the landlord, — "they had to wade the river at the ebb-tide, when the mud is at least eight or ten feet deep."

"How that was done, I cannot guess," said Darcy.

"A man will do many a thing for liberty, sir," remarked another, who was buttoned up in a frieze coat, although the night was hot and sultry; "these poor devils there were willing to risk being roasted alive for the chance of it."

"Quite true," said Darcy; "fellows that have a taste for breaking the law need not be supposed desirous of observing it as to their mode of death; and yet they must have been daring rascals to have made such an attempt as this."

"Maybe you know the old song, sir," said the other, laughing, —

> "There s many a man no bolts can keep,
> No chains be made to bind them,
> And tho' the fetters be heavy, and cells be deep,
> He 'll fling them far behind them."

"I have heard the ditty," answered the Knight; "and if my memory serves me, the last lines run thus, —

> "Though iron bolts may rust and rot,
> And stone and mortar crumble,
> Freney, beware! for well I wot
> Your pride may have a tumble."

"Devil a lie in that, anyhow, sir," said the other, laughing heartily; "and an uglier tumble a man needn't have than to slip through Tom Galvin's fingers. But I see the fire is out now; so I 'll be jogging homeward. Good-night, sir."

"Good-night," said Darcy; and then, as the other moved away, turning to the landlord, he asked if he knew the stranger.

"No, sir," was the reply; "he came up with some others to have a look at the fire."

"Well, I 'll to my bed," said Darcy; "let me be awakened at four o'clock. I see I shall have but a short sleep; the day is breaking already."

CHAPTER IX
BOARDING-HOUSE CRITICISM

It was not until after the lapse of several days that Darcy's departure was made known to the denizens of Port Ballintray.

If the event was slow of announcement, they endeavored to compensate for the tardiness of the tidings by the freedom of their commentary on all its possible and impossible reasons. There was not a casualty, in the whole catalogue of human vicissitudes, unquoted; deaths, births, and marriages were ransacked in newspapers; all sudden and unexpected turns of fortune were well weighed, accidents and offences scanned with cunning eyes, and the various paragraphs to which editorial mysteriousness gave an equivocal interpretation were commented on with a perseverance and an ingenuity worthy of a higher theme.

It may be remarked that no class of persons are viewed more suspiciously, or excite more sharp criticism from their neighbors, than those who, with evidently narrow means, prefer retirement and estrangement from the world to mixing in the small circle of some petty locality. A hundred schemes are put in motion to ascertain by what right such superiority is asserted,—why, and on what grounds, they affect to be better than their neighbors, and so on; the only offence all the while consisting of an isolation which cannot with truth imply any such imputation.

When the Knight of Gwynne found himself by an unexpected turn of fortune condemned to a station so different from his previous life, he addressed himself at once to the difficulties of his lot; and, well aware that all reserve on his part would be set down as the cloak of some deep mystery, he affected an air of easy cordiality with such of the boarding-house party as he ever met, and endeavored, by a tone of well-assumed familiarity, to avoid all detection of the difference between him and his new associates.

It was in this spirit that he admitted Mr. Dempsey to his acquaintance, and even asked him to his cottage. In this diplomacy he met with little assistance from Lady Eleanor and his daughter; the former, from a natural coldness of manner and an instinctive horror of everything low and underbred. Helen's perceptions of such things were just as acute, but, inheriting the gay and lively temperament of her father's house, she better liked to laugh at the absurdities of vulgar people than indulge a mere sense of dislike to their society. Such allies were too dangerous to depend on, and hence the Knight conducted his plans unaided and unsupported.

Whether Mr. Dempsey was bought off by the flattering exception made in his favor, and that he felt an implied superiority on being deemed their advocate, he certainly assumed that position in the circle of Mrs. Fumbally's household, and on the present occasion sustained his part with a certain mysterious demeanor that imposed on many.

"Well, he's gone, at all events!" said a thin old lady with a green shade over a pair of greener eyes; "that can't be denied, I hope! Went off like a shot on Tuesday morning. Sandy M'Shane brought him into Coleraine, for the Dublin coach; and, by the same token, it was an outside place he took—"

"I beg your pardon, ma'am," interposed a fat little woman, with a choleric red face and a tremulous underlip,—she was an authoress in the provincial papers, and occasionally invented her English as well as her incidents,—"it was the Derry mail he went by. Archy M'Clure trod on his toe, and asked pardon for it, just to get him into conversation; but he seemed very much dejected, and wouldn't interlocute."

"Very strange indeed!" rejoined the lady of the shade, "because I had my information from Williams, the guard of the coach."

"And I mine from Archy M'Clure himself."

"And both were wrong," interposed Paul Dempsey, triumphantly.

"It's not very polite to tell us so, Mr. Dempsey," said the thin old lady, bridling.

"Perhaps the politeness may equal the voracity," said the fat lady, who was almost boiling over with wrath.

"This Gwynne wasn't all right, depend upon it," interposed a certain little man in powder; "I have my own suspicions about him."

"Well, now, Mr. Dunlop, what's your opinion? I'd like to hear it."

"What does Mrs. M'Caudlish say?" rejoined the little gentleman, turning to the authoress,—for in the boarding-house they both presided judicially in all domestic inquisitions regarding conduct and character,—"what does Mrs. M'Caudlish say?"

"I prefer letting Mr. Dunlop expose himself before me."

"The case is doubtful—dark—mysterious," said Dunlop, with a solemn pause after each word.

"The more beyond my conjunctions," said the lady. "You remember what the young gentleman says in the Latin poet, 'Sum Davy, non sum Euripides.'"

"I 'll tell you my opinion, then," said Mr. Dunlop, who was evidently mollified by the classical allusion; and with firm and solemn gesture he crossed over to where she sat, and whispered a few words in her ear.

A slight scream, and a long-drawn "Oh!" was all the answer.

"Upon my soul, I believe so," said Mr. Dunlop, thrusting both hands into the furthest depths of his coat-pockets; "nay, more, I'll maintain it!"

"I know what you are driving at," said Dempsey, laughing; "you think he's the gauger that went off with Mrs. Murdoch of Ballyquirk—"

"Mr. Dempsey! Mr. Dempsey! the ladies, sir! the ladies!" called out two or three reproving voices from the male portion of the assembly; while, as if to corroborate the justice of the appeal, the thin lady drew her shade down two inches lower, and Mr. Dunlop's face became what painters call "of a warm tint."

"Oh! never talk of a rope where a man's father was hanged," muttered Paul to himself, for he felt all the severity of his condemnation, though he knew that the point of law was against him.

"There 's a rule in this establishment, Mr. Dempsey," said Mr. Dunlop, with all the gravity of a judge delivering a charge, — "a rule devised to protect the purity, the innocence,"—here the ladies held down their heads,—"the beauty—"

"Yes, sir, and I will add, the helplessness of that sex—"

"Paul 's right, by Jove!" hiccuped Jack Leonard, whose faculties, far immersed in the effects of strong whiskey-and-water, suddenly flashed out into momentary intelligence,—"I say he's right! Who says the reverse?"

"Oh, Captain Leonard! oh dear, Mr. Dunlop!" screamed three or four female voices in concert, "don't let it proceed further."

A faint and an anxious group were gathered around the little gentleman, whose warlike indications grew stronger as pacific entreaties increased.

"He shall explain his words," said he, with a cautious glance to see that his observation was not overheard; then, seeing that his adversary had relapsed into oblivion, he added, "he shall withdraw them;" and finally, emboldened by success, he vociferated, "or' he shall eat them. I 'll teach him," said the now triumphant victor, "that it is not in Mark Dunlop's presence ladies are to be insulted with impunity. Let the attempt be made by whom it will,—he may be a lieutenant on half pay or on full pay!—I tell him, I don't care a rush."

"Of course not!" "Why would you?" and so on, were uttered in ready chorus around him; and he resumed,—

"And as for this Gwynne, or Quin, who lives up at 'The Corvy' yonder, for all the airs he gives himself, and his fine ladies too, my simple belief is he 's a Government spy!"

"Is that your opinion, sir?" said a deep and almost solemn voice; and at the same instant Miss Daly appeared at the open window. She leaned her arm on the sill, and calmly stared at the now terrified speaker, while she repeated the words, "Is that your opinion, sir?"

Before the surprise her words had excited subsided, she stood at the door of the apartment. She was dressed in her riding-habit, for she had that moment returned from an excursion along the coast.

"Mr. Dunlop," said the lady, advancing towards him, "I never play the eavesdropper; but you spoke so loud, doubtless purposely, that nothing short of deafness could escape hearing you. You were pleased to express a belief respecting the position of a gentleman with whom I have the honor to claim some friendship."

"I always hold myself ready, madam, to render an account to any individual of whom I express an opinion,—to himself, personally, I mean."

"Of course you do, sir. It is a very laudable habit," said she, dryly; "but in this case—don't interrupt me—in the present case it cannot apply, because the person traduced is absent. Yes, sir, I said traduced."

"Oh, madam, I must say the word would better suit one more able to sustain it. I shall take the liberty to withdraw." And so saying, he moved towards the door; but Miss Daly interposed, and, by a gesture of her hand, in which she held a formidable horsewhip, gave a very unmistakable sign that the passage was not free.

"You 'll not go yet, sir. I have not done with you," said she, in a voice every accent of which vibrated in the little man's heart. "You affect to regret, sir, that I am not of the sex that exacts satisfaction, as it is called; but I tell you, I come of a family that never gave long scores to a debt of honor. You have presumed—in a company, certainly, where the hazard of contradiction was small—to asperse a gentleman of whom you know nothing,—not one single fact,—not one iota of his life, character, or fortune. You have dared to call him by words every letter of which would have left a welt on your shoulders if uttered in his hearing. Now, as I am certain he would pay any little debts I might have perchance forgotten in leaving a place where I had resided, so will I do likewise by him; and here, on this spot, and in this fair company, I call upon you to unsay your falsehood, or—" Here she made one step forward, with an air and gesture that made Mr. Dunlop retire with a most comic alacrity. "Don't be afraid, sir," continued she, laughing. "My brother, Mr. Bagenal Daly, will arrive here soon. He's no new name to your ears. In any case, I promise you that whatever you find objectionable in my proceedings towards you he will be most happy to sustain. Now, sir, the hand wants four minutes to six. If the hour strike before you call yourself a wanton, gratuitous calumniator, I'll flog you round the room."

A cry of horror burst from the female portion of the assembly at a threat the utterance of which was really not less terrific than the meaning.

"Such a spectacle," continued Miss Daly, sarcastically, "I should scruple to inflict on this fair company; but the taste that could find pleasure in witless, pointless slander may not, it is possible, dislike to see a little castigation. Now, sir, you have just one minute and a quarter."

"I protest against this conduct, madam. I here declare—"

"Declare nothing, sir, till you have avowed yourself by your real name and character. If you cannot restrain your tongue, I'll very soon convince you that its consequences are far from agreeable. Is what you have spoken false?"

"There may come a heavy reckoning for all this, madam," said Dunlop, trembling between fear and passion.

"I ask you again, and for the last time, are your words untrue? Very well, sir. You held a commission in Germany, they say; and probably, as a military man, you may think it undignified to surrender, except on compulsion."

With these words Miss Daly advanced towards him with a firm and determined air, while a cry of horror arose through the room, and the fairer portion intrepidly threw themselves in front of their champion, while Dempsey and the others only restrained their laughter for fear of personal consequences. Pushing fiercely on, Miss Daly was almost at his side, when the door of the room was opened, and a deep and well-known voice called out to her, —

"Maria, what the devil is all this?"

"Oh, Bagenal," cried she, as she held out her hand, "I scarcely expected you before eight o'clock."

"But in the name of everything ridiculous, what has happened? Were you about to horsewhip this pleasant company?"

"Only one of its members," said Miss Daly, coolly, —"a little gentleman who has thought proper to be more lavish of his calumny than his courage. I hand him over to you now; and, faith, though I don't think that he had any fancy for me, he 'll gain by the exchange! You 'll find him yonder," said she, pointing to a corner where already the majority of the party were gathered together.

Miss Daly was mistaken, however, for Mr. Dunlop had made his escape during the brief interchange of greetings between the brother and sister. "Come, Bagenal," said she, smiling, "it's all for the best. I have given him a lesson he 'll not readily forget, —had you been the teacher, he might not have lived to remember it.'"

"What a place for *you!*" said Bagenal, as he threw his eye superciliously around the apartment and its occupants; then taking her arm within his own, he led her forth, and closed the door after them.

Once more alone, Daly learned with surprise, not unmixed with sorrow, that his sister had never seen the Darcys, and save by a single call, when she left her name, had made no advances towards their acquaintance. She showed a degree of repugnance, too, to allude to the subject, and rather endeavored to dismiss it by saying shortly, —"Lady Eleanor is a fine lady, and her daughter a wit What could there be in common between us?"

"But for Darcy's sake?"

"For *his* sake I stayed away," rejoined she, hastily; "they would have thought me a bore, and perhaps have told him as much. In a word, Bagenal, I did n't like it, and that's enough. Neither of us were trained to put much constraint on our inclinations. I doubt if the lesson would be easily learned at our present time of life."

Daly muttered some half-intelligible bitterness about female obstinacy and wrong-headedness, and walked slowly to and fro. "I must see Maurice at once," said he, at length.

"That will be no easy task; he left this for Dublin on Tuesday last."

"And has not returned? When does he come back?"

"His old butler, who brought me the news, says not for some weeks."

"Confusion and misery!" exclaimed Daly, "was there ever anything so ill-timed! And he's in Dublin?"

"He went thither, but there would seem some mystery about his ultimate destination; the old man binted at London."

"London!" said he, with a heavy sigh. "It's now the 18th, and on Saturday she sails."

"Who sails?" asked Miss Daly, with more of eagerness than she yet exhibited.

"Oh, I forgot, Molly, I had n't told you, I 'm about to take a voyage,—not a very long one, but still distant enough to make me wish to say good-bye ere we separate. If God wills it, I shall be back early in the spring."

"What new freak is this, Bagenal?" said she, almost sternly; "I thought that time and the world's crosses might have taught you to care for quietness, if not for home."

"Home!" repeated he, in an accent the sorrow of which sank into her very heart; "when had I ever a home? I had a house and lands, and equipages, horses, and liveried servants,—all that wealth could command, or, my own reckless vanity could prompt,—but these did not make a home!"

"You often promised we should have such one day, Bagenal," said she, tenderly, while she stole her hand within his; "you often told me that the time would come when we should enjoy poverty with a better grace than ever we dispensed riches."

"We surely are poor enough to make the trial now," said he, with a bitterness of almost savage energy.

"And if we are, Bagenal," replied she, "there is the more need to draw more closely to each other; let us begin at once."

"Not yet, Molly, not yet," said he, passing his hand across his eyes. "I would grasp such a refuge as eagerly as yourself, for," added he, with deep emotion, "I am to the full as weary; but I cannot do it yet."

Miss Daly knew her brother's temper too long and too well either to offer a continued opposition to any strongly expressed resolve, or to question him about a subject on which he showed any desire of reserve.

"Have you no Dublin news for me?" she said, as if willing to suggest some less touching subject for conversation.

"No, Molly; Dublin is deserted. The few who still linger in town seem only half awake to the new condition of events. The Government party are away to England; they feel, doubtless, bound in honor to dispense their gold in the land it came from; and the Patriots—Heaven bless the mark!—they look as rueful as if they began to suspect that Patriotism was too dear a luxury after all."

"And this burning of Newgate,-what did it mean? Was there, as the newspaper makes out, anything like a political plot connected with it?"

"Nothing of the kind, Molly. The whole affair was contrived among the prisoners. Freney, the well-known highwayman, was in the jail, and, although not tried, his conviction was certain."

"And they say he has escaped. Can it be possible that some persons of influence, as the journals hint, actually interested themselves for the escape of a man like this?"

"Everything is possible in a state of society like ours, Molly."

"But a highwayman—a robber—a fellow that made the roads unsafe to travel!"

"All true," said Daly, laughing. "Nobody ever kept a hawk for a singing-bird; but he 's a bold villain to pounce upon another."

"I like not such appliances; they scarcely serve a good name, and they make a bad one worse."

"I'm quite of your mind, Molly," said Daly, thoughtfully; "and if honest men were plenty, he would be but a fool who held any dealings with the knaves. But here comes the car to convey me to 'The Corvy.' I will make a hasty visit to Lady Eleanor, and be back with you by supper-time."

CHAPTER X
DALY'S FAREWELL

Neither of the ladies were at home when Bagenal Daly, followed by his servant Sandy, reached "The Corvy," and sat down in the porch to await their return. Busied with his own reflections, which, to judge from the deep abstraction of his manner, seemed weighty and important, Daly never looked up from the ground, while Sandy leisurely walked round the building to note the changes made in his absence, and comment, in no flattering sense, on the art by which the builder had concealed so many traits of "The Corvy's" origin.

"Ye 'd no ken she was a ship ava!" said he to himself, as he examined the walls over which the trellised creepers were trained, and the latticed windows festooned by the honeysuckle and the clematis, and gazed in sadness over the altered building. "She's no a bit like the auld Corvy!"

"Of course she 's not!" said Daly, testily, for the remark had suddenly aroused him from his musings. "What the devil would you have? Are *you* like the raw and ragged fellow I took from this bleak coast, and led over more than half the world?"

"Troth, I am no the same man noo that I was sax-and-forty years agane, and sorry I am to say it."

"Sorry,—sorry! not to be half-starved and less than half-clad; hauling a net one day, and being dragged for yourself the next—sorry!"

"Even sae, sore sorry. Eight-and-sixty may be aye sorry not to be twa-and-twenty. I ken nae rise in life can pay off that score. It 's na ower pleasant to think on, but I'm no the man I was then. No, nor, for that matter, yersell neither."

Daly was too long accustomed to the familiarity of Sandy's manner to feel offended at the remark, though he did not seem by any means to relish its application. Without making any reply, he arose and entered the hall. On every side were objects reminding him of the past, strange and sad commentary on the words of his servant. Sandy appeared to feel the force of such allies, and, as he stood near, watched the effect the various articles produced on his master's countenance.

"A bonnie rifle she is," said he, as if interpreting the admiring look Daly bestowed upon a richly ornamented gun. "Do you mind the day yer honor shot the corbie at the Tegern See?"

"Where the Tyrol fellows set on us, on the road to Innspruck, and I brought down the bird to show them that they had to deal with a marksman as good at least as themselves."

"Just sae; it was a bra' shot; your hand was as firm, and your eye as steady then as any man's."

"I could do the feat this minute," said Daly, angrily, as turning away he detached a heavy broadsword from the wall.

"She was aye over weighty in the hilt," said Sandy, with a dry malice.

"You used to draw that bowstring to your ear," said Daly, sternly, as he pointed to a Swiss bow of portentous size.

"I had twa hands in those days," said the other, calmly, and without the slightest change of either voice or manner.

Not so with him to whom they were addressed. A flood of feelings seemed to pour across his memory, and, laying his hand on Sandy's shoulder, he said, in an accent of very unusual emotion, "You are right, Sandy, I must be changed from what I used to be."

"Let us awa to the auld life we led in those days," said the other, impetuously, "and we 'll soon be ourselves again! Does n't that remind yer honor of the dark night on the Ottawa, when you sent the canoe, with the pine-torch burning in her bow, down the stream, and drew all the fire of the Indian fellows on her?"

"It was a grand sight," cried Daly, rapturously, "to see the dark river glittering with its torchlight, and the chiefs, as they stood rifle in hand, peering into the dense pine copse, and making the echoes ring with their war-cries."

"It was unco near at one time," said Sandy, as he took up the fold of the blanket with which his effigy in the canoe was costumed. "There 's the twa bullet-holes, and here the arrow-bead in the plank, where I had my bead! If ye had missed the Delaware chap wi' the yellow cloth on his forehead—"

"I soon changed its color for him," said Daly, savagely.

"Troth did ye; ye gied him a bonny war-paint. How he sprang into the air! I think I see him noo; many a night when I 'm lying awake, I think I can hear the dreadful screech he gave, as he plunged into the river."

"It was not a cry of pain, it was baffled vengeance," said Daly.

"He never forgave the day ye gripped him by the twa hands in yer ain one, and made the squaws laugh at him. Eh, how that auld deevil they cau'd Black Buffalo yelled! Her greasy cheeks shook and swelled over her dark eyes, till the face looked like nothing but a tar lake in Demerara when there 's a hurricane blowin' over it."

"You had rather a tenderness in that quarter, if I remember aright," said Daly, dryly.

"I 'll no deny she was a bra sauncie woman, and kenned weel to make a haggis wi' an ape's head and shoulders." Sandy smacked his lips, as if the thought had brought up pleasant memories.

"How I escaped that bullet is more than I can guess," said Daly, as he inspected the blanket where it was pierced by a shot; and as he spoke, he threw its wide folds over his shoulders, the better to judge of the position.

"Ye aye wore it more on this side," said Sandy, arranging the folds with tasteful pride; "an', troth, it becomes you well. Tak the bit tomahawk in your hand, noo. Ech! but yer like yoursel once more."

"We may have to don this gear again, and sooner than you think," said Daly, thoughtfully.

"Nae a bit sooner than I 'd like," said Sandy. "The salvages, as they ca' them, hae neither baillies nor policemen, they hae nae cranks about lawyers and 'tornies; a grip o' a man's hair and a sharp knife is even as mickle a reason as a hempen cord and a gallows tree! Ech, it warms my bluid again to see you stridin' up and doon, —if you had but a smudge o' yellow ochre, or a bit o' red round your eyes, ye 'd look awful well."

"What are you staring at?" said Daly, as Sandy opened a door stealthily, and gazed down the passage towards the kitchen.

"I 'm thinking that as there is naebody in the house but the twa lasses, maybe your honor would try a war-cry, —ye ken ye could do it bra'ly once."

"I may need the craft soon again," said Daly, thoughtfully.

"Mercy upon us! here 's the leddies!" cried Sandy. But before Daly could disencumber himself of his weapons and costume, Helen entered the hall.

If Lady Eleanor started at the strange apparition before her, and involuntarily turned her eye towards the canoe, to see that its occupant was still there, it is not much to be wondered at, so strongly did the real and the counterfeit man resemble each other. The first surprise over, he was welcomed with sincere pleasure. All the eccentricities of character which in former days were commented on so sharply were forgotten, or their memory replaced by the proofs of his ardent devotion.

"How well you are looking!" was his first exclamation, as he gazed at Lady Eleanor and Helen alternately, with that steady stare which is one of the prerogatives of age towards beauty.

"There is no such tonic as necessity," said Lady Eleanor, smiling, "and it would seem as if health were too jealous to visit us when we have every other blessing."

"It is worth them all, madam. I am an old man, and have seen much of the world, and I can safely aver that what are called its trials lie chiefly in our weaknesses. We can all of us carry a heavier load than fortune lays on us—" He suddenly checked himself, as if having unwittingly lapsed into something like rebuke, and then said, "I find you alone; is it not so?"

"Yes; Darcy has left us, suddenly and almost mysteriously, without you can help us to a clearer insight. A letter from the War Office arrived here on Tuesday, acknowledging, in most complimentary terms, the fairness of his claim for military employment, and requesting his presence in London. This was evidently in reply to an application, although the Knight made none such."

"But he has friends, mamma,—warm-hearted and affectionate ones,-who might have done so," said Helen, as she fixed her gaze steadily on Daly.

"And you, madam, have relatives of high and commanding influence," said he, avoiding to return Helen's glance,—"men of rank and station, who might well feel proud of such a *protégé* as Maurice Darcy. And what have they given him?"

"We can tell you nothing; the official letter may explain more to your clear-sightedness, and I will fetch it." So saying, Lady Eleanor arose and left the room. Scarcely had the door closed, when Daly stood up, and, walking over, leaned his arm on the back of Helen's chair.

"You received my letter, did you not?" said he, hurriedly. "You know the result of the trial?"

Helen nodded assent, while a secret emotion covered her face with crimson, as Daly resumed,—

"There was ill-luck everywhere: the case badly stated; Lionel absent; I myself detained in Dublin, by an unavoidable necessity,—everything unfortunate even to the last incident. Had I been there, matters would have taken another course. Still, Helen, Forester was right; and, depend upon it, there is no scanty store of generous warmth in a heart that can throb so strongly beneath the aiguiletted coat of an aide-de-camp. The holiday habits of that tinsel life teach few lessons of self-devotion, and the poor fellow has paid the penalty heavily."

"What has happened?" said Helen, in a voice scarcely audible.

"He is disinherited, I hear. All his prospects depended on his mother; she has cast him off, and, as the story goes, is about to marry. Marriage is always the last vengeance of a widow."

"Here is the letter," said Lady Eleanor, entering; "let us hope you can read its intentions better than we have."

"Flattering, certainly," muttered Daly, as he conned over the lines to himself. "It's quite plain they mean to do something generous. I trust I may learn it before I sail."

"Sail! you are not about to travel, are you?" asked Lady Eleanor, in a voice that betrayed her dread of being deprived of such support.

"Oh! I forgot I had n't told you. Yes, madam, another of those strange riddles which have beset my life compels me to take a long voyage—to America."

"To America!" echoed Helen; and her eye glanced as she spoke to the Indian war-cloak and the weapons that lay beside his chair.

"Not so, Helen," said Daly, smiling, as if replying to the insinuated remark; "I am too old for such follies now. Not in heart, indeed, but in limb," added he, sternly; "for I own I could ask nothing better than the prairie or the pine-forest. I know of no cruelty in savage life that has not its counterpart amid our civilization; and for the rude virtues that are nurtured there, they are never warmed into existence by the hotbed of selfishness."

"But why leave your friends,—your sister?"

"My sister!" He paused, and a tinge of red came to his cheek as he remembered how she had failed in all attention to the Darcys. "My sister, madam, is self-willed and headstrong as myself. She acknowledges none of the restraints or influence by which the social world consents to be bound and regulated; her path has ever been wild and erratic as my own. We sometimes cross, we never contradict, each other." He paused, and then muttered to himself, "Poor Molly! how different I knew you once! And so," added he, aloud, "I must leave without seeing Darcy! and there stands Sandy, admonishing me that my time is already up. Good-bye, Lady Eleanor; good-bye, Helen." He turned his head away for a second, and then, in a voice of unusual feeling, said: "Farewell is always a sad word, and doubly sad when spoken by one old as I am; but if my heart is heavy at this moment, it is the selfish sorrow of him who parts from those so near. As for you, madam, and your fortunes, I am full of good hope. When people talk of suffering virtue, believe me, the element of courage must be wanting; but where the stout heart unites with the good cause, success will come at last."

He pressed his lips to the hands he held within his own, and hurried, before they could reply, from the room.

"Our last friend gone!" exclaimed Lady Eleanor, as she sank into a chair.

Helen's heart was too full for utterance, and she sat down silently, and watched the retiring figure of Daly and his servant till they disappeared in the distance.

CHAPTER XI
THE DUKE OF YORK'S LEVEE

When Darcy arrived in London, he found a degree of political excitement for which he was little prepared. In Ireland the Union had absorbed all interest and anxiety, and with the fate of that measure were extinguished the hopes of those who had speculated on national independence. Not so in England; the real importance of the annexation was never thoroughly considered till the fact was accomplished, nor, until then, were the great advantages and the possible evils well and maturely weighed. Then, for the first time, came the anxious question, What next? Was the Union to be the compensation for large concessions to the Irish people, or was it rather the seal of their incorporation with a more powerful nation, who by this great stroke of policy would annihilate forever all dream of self-existence? Mr. Pitt inclined to the former opinion, and believed the moment propitious to award the Roman Catholic claims, and to a general remission of those laws which pressed so heavily upon them. To this opinion the King was firmly and, as it proved, insurmountably opposed; he regarded the Act of Union as the final settlement of all possible disagreements between the two countries, as the means of uniting the two Churches, and, finally, of excluding at once and forever the admission of Roman Catholics to Parliament. This wide difference led to the retirement of Mr. Pitt, and subsequently to the return of the dangerous indisposition of the King, an attack brought on by the anxiety and agitation this question induced.

The hopes of the Whig party stood high; the Prince's friends, as they were styled, again rallied around Carlton House, where, already, the possibility of a long Regency was discussed. Besides these causes of excitement were others of not less powerful interest,—the growing power of Bonaparte, the war in Egypt, and the possibility of open hostilities with Russia, who had now thrown herself so avowedly into the alliance of France.

Such were the stirring themes Darcy found agitating the public mind, and he could not help contrasting the mighty interests they involved with the narrow circle of consequences a purely local legislature could discuss or decide upon. He felt at once that he trod the soil of a more powerful and more ambitious people, and he remembered with a sigh his own anticipations, that in the English Parliament the Irish members would be but the camp-followers of the Crown or the Opposition.

If he was English in his pride of government and his sense of national power and greatness, he was Irish in his tastes, his habits, and his affections. If he gloried in the name of Briton as the type of national honor and truth throughout the globe, he was still more ardently attached to that land where, under the reflected grandeur of the monarchy, grew up the social affections of a poorer people. There is a sense of freedom and independence in the habits of semi-civilization very fascinating to certain minds, and all the advantages of more polished communities are deemed shallow compensation for the ready compliance and cordial impulses of the less cultivated.

With all his own high acquirements the Knight was of this mind; and if he did not love England less, he loved Ireland more.

Meditating on the great changes of fortune Ireland had undergone even within his own memory, he moved along through the crowded thoroughfares of the mighty city, when he heard his name called out, and at the same instant a carriage drew up close by him.

"How do you do, Knight?" said a friendly voice, as a hand was stretched forth to greet him. It was Lord Castle-reagh, who had only a few weeks previous exchanged his office of Irish Secretary for a post at the Board of Trade. The meeting was a cordial one on both sides, and ended in an invitation to dine on the following day, which Darcy accepted with willingness, as a gage of mutual good feeling and esteem.

"I was talking about you to Lord Netherby only yesterday," said Lord Castlereagh, "and, from some hints he dropped, I suspect the time is come that I may offer you any little influence I possess, without it taking the odious shape of a bargain; if so, pray remember that I have as much pride as yourself on such a score, and will be offended if you accept from another what might come equally well through *me*."

The Knight acknowledged this kind speech with a grateful smile and a pressure of the hand, and was about to move on, when Lord Castlereagh asked if he could not drop him in his carriage at his destination, and thus enjoy, a few moments longer, his society.

"I scarcely can tell you, my Lord," said Darcy, laughing, "which way I was bent on following. I came up to town to present myself at the Duke of York's levée, and it is only a few moments since I remembered that I was not provided with a uniform."

"Oh, step in then," cried Lord Castlereagh, hastily; "I think I can manage that difficulty for you. There is a levée this very morning; some pressing intelligence has arrived from Egypt, and his Royal Highness has issued a notice for a reception for eleven o'clock. You are not afraid," said Lord Castlereagh, laughing, as Darcy took his seat beside him,—"you are not afraid of being seen in such company now."

"If I am not, my Lord, set my courage down to my principle; for I never felt your kindness so dangerous," said the Knight, with something of emotion.

A few moments of rapid driving brought them in front of the Duke's residence, where several carriages and led horses were now standing, and officers in full dress were seen to pass in and out, with signs of haste and eagerness.

"I told you we should find them astir here," said Lord Castlereagh. "Holloa, Fane, have you heard anything new to-day?"

The officer thus addressed touched his hat respectfully, and approaching the window of the carriage, whispered a few words in Lord Castlereagh's ear.

"Is the news confirmed?" said his Lordship, calmly.

"I believe so, my Lord; at least, Edgecumbe says he heard it from Dundas, who got it from Pitt himself."

"Bad tidings these, Knight," said Lord Castlereagh, as the aide-de-camp moved away; "Pulteney's expedition against Ferrol has failed. These conjoint movements of army and navy seem to have a most unlucky fortune."

"What can you expect, my Lord, from an ill-assorted 'Union'?" said Darcy, slyly.

"They 'll work better after a time," said Lord Castlereagh, smiling good-humoredly at the hit; "for the present, I acknowledge the success is not flattering. The general always discovers that the land batteries can only be attacked in the very spot where the admiral pronounces the anchorage impossible; each feels compromised by the other; hence envy and every manner of uncharitableness."

"And what has been the result here? Is it a repulse?"

"You can scarcely call it that, since they never attacked. They looked at the place, sailed round it, and, like the King of France in the story, they marched away again. But here we are at length at the door; let us try if we cannot accomplish a landing better than Lord Keith and General Moore."

Through a crowd of anxious faces, whose troubled looks tallied with the evil tidings, Lord Castlereagh and Darcy ascended the stairs and reached the antechamber, now densely thronged by officers of every grade of the service. His Lordship was immediately recognized and surrounded by many of the company, eager to hear his opinion.

"You don't appear to credit the report, my Lord," said Darcy, who had watched with some interest the air of quiet incredulity which he assumed.

"It is all true, notwithstanding," said he, in a whisper; "I heard it early this morning at the Council, and came here to see how it would be received. They say that war will be soon as unpopular with the red-coats as with the no-coats; and really, to look at these sombre faces, one would say there was some truth in the rumor. But here comes Taylor." And so saying, Lord Castlereagh moved forward, and laid his hand on the arm of an officer in a staff uniform.

"I don't think so, my Lord," said he, in reply to some question from Lord Castlereagh; "I 'll endeavor to manage it, but I 'm afraid I shall not succeed. Have you heard of Elliot's death? The news has just arrived."

"Indeed! So then the government of Chelsea is to give away. Oh, that fact explains the presence of so many veteran generals! I really was puzzled to conceive what martial ardor stirred them."

"You are severe, my Lord," said Darcy; "I hope you are unjust."

"One is rarely so in attributing a selfish motive anywhere," said the young nobleman, sarcastically. "But, Taylor, can't you arrange this affair? Let me present my friend meanwhile: The Knight of Gwynne—Colonel Taylor."

Before Taylor could more than return the Knight's salutation he was summoned to attend his Royal Highness; and at the same moment the folding-doors at the end of the apartment were thrown open, and the reception began.

Whether the sarcasm of Lord Castlereagh was correct, or that a nobler motive was in operation, the number of officers was very great; and although the Duke rarely addressed more than a word or two to each, a considerable time elapsed before Lord Castlereagh, with the Knight following, had entered the room.

"It is against a positive order of his Royal Highness, my Lord," said an aide-de-camp, barring the passage; "none but field-officers, and in full uniform, are received by his Royal Highness."

Lord Castlereagh whispered something, and endeavored to move on; but again the other interposed, saying, "Indeed, my Lord, I'm deeply grieved at it, but I cannot—I dare not transgress my orders."

The Duke, who had been up to this moment engaged in conversing with a group, suddenly turned, and perceiving that the presentations were not followed up, said, "Well, gentlemen, I am waiting." Then recognizing Lord Castlereagh, he added, "Another time, my Lord, another time: this morning belongs to the service, and the color of your coat excludes you."

"I ask your Royal Highness's pardon," said Lord Castlereagh, in a tone of great deference, while he made the apology an excuse for advancing a step into the room. "I have but just left the Council, and was anxious to inform you that your Royal Highness's suggestions have been fully adopted."

"Indeed! is that the case?" said the Duke, with an elated look, while he drew his Lordship into the recess of a window. The intelligence, to judge from the Duke's expression, must have been both important and satisfactory, for he looked intensely eager and pleased by turns.

"And so," said he, aloud, "they really have determined on Egypt? Well, my Lord, you have brought me the best tidings I 've heard for many a day."

"And like all bearers of good despatches," said Lord Castlereagh, catching up the tone of the Duke, "I prefer a claim to your Royal Highness's patronage."

"If you look for Chelsea, my Lord, you are just five minutes too late. Old Sir Harry Belmore has this instant got it."

"I could have named as old and perhaps a not less distinguished soldier to your Royal Highness, with this additional claim,—a claim I must say, your Royal Highness never disregards"—

"That he has been unfortunate with the unlucky," said the Duke, laughing, and good-naturedly alluding to his own failure in the expedition to the Netherlands; "but who is your friend?"

"The Knight of Gwynne,—an Irish gentleman."

"One of your late supporters, eh, Castlereagh?" said the Duke, laughing. "How came he to be forgotten till this hour? Or did you pass him a bill of gratitude payable at nine months after date?"

"No, my Lord, he was an opponent; he was a man that I never could buy, when his influence and power were such as to make the price of his own dictating. Since that day, fortune has changed with him."

"And what do you want with him now?" said the Duke, while his eyes twinkled with a sly malice; "are you imitating the man that bowed down before statues of Hercules and Apollo at Rome, not knowing when the time of those fellows might come up again? Is that your game?"

"Not exactly, your Royal Highness; but I really feel some scruples of conscience that, having assisted so many unworthy candidates to pensions and peerages, I should have done nothing for the most upright man I met in Ireland."

"If we could make him a Commissary-General," said the Duke, laughing, "the qualities you speak of would be of service now: there never was such a set of rascals as we have got in that department! But come, what can we do with him? What's his rank in the army? Where did he serve?"

"If I dare present him to your Royal Highness without a uniform," said Lord Castlereagh, hesitatingly, "he could answer these queries better than I can."

"Oh, by Jove! it is too late for scruples now,—introduce him at once."

Lord Castlereagh waited for no more formal permission, but, hastening to the antechamber, took Darcy's hand, and led him forward.

"If I don't mistake, sir," said the Duke, as the old man raised his head after a deep and courteous salutation, "this is not the first time we have met. Am I correct in calling you Colonel Darcy?"

The Knight bowed low in acquiescence.

"The same officer who raised the Twenty-eighth Light Dragoons, known as Darcy's Light Horse?"

The Knight bowed once more.

"A very proud officer in command," said the Duke, turning to Lord Castlereagh with a stern expression on his features; "a colonel who threatened a prince of the blood with arrest for breach of duty."

"He had good reason, your Royal Highness, to be proud," said the Knight, firmly; "first, to have a prince to serve under his command; and, secondly, to have held that station and character in the service to have rendered so unbecoming a threat pardonable."

"And who said it was?" replied the Duke, hastily.

"Your Royal Highness has just done so."

"How do you mean?"

"I mean, my Lord Duke," said Darcy, with a calm and unmoved look, "that your Royal Highness would never have recurred to the theme to one humbled as I am, if you had not forgiven it."

"As freely as I trust you forgive me, Colonel Darcy," said the Duke, grasping his hand and shaking it with warmth. "Now for *my* part: what can I do for you?—what do you wish?"

"I can scarcely ask your Royal Highness; I find that some kind friend has already applied on my behalf. I could not have presumed, old and useless as I am, to prefer a claim myself."

"There's your own regiment vacant," said the Duke, musing. "No, by Jove! I remember Lord Netherby asking me for it the other day for some relative of his own. Taylor, is the colonelcy of the Twenty-eighth promised?"

"Your Royal Highness signed it yesterday."

"I feared as much. Who is it?—perhaps he'd exchange."

"Colonel Maurice Darcy, your Royal Highness, unattached."

"What! have I been doing good by stealth? Is this really so?"

"If it be, your Royal Highness," said Darcy, smiling, "I can only assure you that the officer promoted will not exchange."

"The depot is at Gosport, your Royal Highness," said Taylor, in reply to a question from the Duke.

"Well, station it in Ireland, Colonel Darcy may prefer it," said the duke; "for, as the regiment forms part of the expedition to Egypt, the depot need not be moved for some time to come."

"Your Royal Highness can increase the favor by only one concession—dare I ask it?—to permit me to take the command on service."

The Duke gazed with astonishment at the old man, and gradually his expression became one of deep interest, as he said,—

"Colonel Darcy could claim as a right what I feel so proud to accord him as a favor. Make a note of that, Taylor," said the Duke, raising his voice so as to be heard through the room: "'Colonel Darcy to take the command on service at his own special request.' Yes, gentlemen," added he, louder, "these are times when the exigencies of the service demand alike the energy of youth and the experience of age; it is, indeed, a happy conjuncture that finds them united. My Lord Castlereagh and Colonel Darcy, are you disengaged for Wednesday?"

They both bowed respectfully.

"Then on Wednesday I'll have some of your brother officers to meet you, Colonel. Now, Taylor, let us get through our list."

So saying, the Duke bowed graciously; and Lord Castlereagh and the Knight retired, each too full of pleasure to utter a word as he went.

CHAPTER XII
THE TWO SIDES OF A MEDAL

Although the Knight lost not an hour in writing to Lady Eleanor, informing her of his appointment, the letter, hastily written, and intrusted to a waiter to be posted, was never forwarded, and the first intelligence of the event reached her in a letter from her courtly relative, Lord Netherby.

So much depends upon the peculiar tact and skill of the writer, and so much upon our own frame of mind at the time of reading, that it is difficult to say whether we do not bear up better under the announcement of any sudden and sorrowful event from the hand of one less cared for than from those nearest and dearest to our hearts. The consolations that look like the special pleadings of affection become, as it were, the mere expressions of impartiality. The points of view, being so different, give a different aspect to the picture, and gleams of light fall where, seen from another quarter, all was shadow and gloom. So it was here. What, if the tidings had come from her husband, had been regarded in the one painful light of separation and long absence, assumed, under Lord Netherby's style, the semblance of a most gratifying event, with, of course, that alloy of discomfort from which no human felicity is altogether free: so very artfully was this done, that Lady Eleanor half felt as if, in indulging in her own sorrow, she were merely giving way to a selfish regret; and as Helen, the better to sustain her mother's courage, affected a degree of pleasure she was really far from feeling, this added to the conviction that she ought, if she could, to regard her husband's appointment as a happy event.

"Truly, mamma," said Helen, as she sat with the letter before her, "Me style c'est l'homme.' His Lordship is quite heroic when describing all the fêtes and dinners of London; all the honors showered on papa in visiting-cards and invitations; how excellencies called, and royal highnesses shook hands: he even chronicles the distinguishing favor of the gracious Prince, who took wine with him. But listen to him when the theme is really one that might evoke some trait, if not of enthusiasm, at least of national pride: 'As for the expedition, my dear cousin, though nobody knows exactly for what place it is destined, everybody is aware that it is not intended to be a fighting one. Demonstrations are now the vogue, and it is become just as bad taste for our army to shed blood as it would be for a well-bred man to mention a certain ill-conducted individual before ears polite. Modern war is like a game at whist between first-rate players; when either party has four by honors, he shows his hand, and saves the trouble of a contest. The Naval Service is, I grieve to say, rooted to its ancient prejudices, and continues its abominable pastime of broadsides and boardings; hence its mob popularity at this moment! The army will, however, always be the gentlemanlike cloth, and I thank my stars I don't believe we have a single relative afloat. Guy Herries was the last; he was shot or piked, I forget which, in boarding a Spanish galliot off Cape Verde. "Que diable allait-il faire dans cette galère?" Rest satisfied, therefore, if the gallant Knight has little glory, he will have no dangers; our expeditions never land. Jekyll says they are only intended to give the service an appetite for fresh meat and soft bread, after four months' biscuit and salt beef. At all events, my dear cousin, reckon on seeing my friend the Knight gazetted as major-general on the very next promotions. The Prince is delighted with him; and I carried a message from his Royal Highness yesterday to the War Office in his behalf. You would not come to see me, despite all the seductions I threw out, and now the season is nigh over. May I hope better things for the next year, when perhaps I can promise an inducement the more, and make your welcome more graceful by dividing its cares with one far more competent than myself to fulfil them.'—What does he mean, mamma?"

"Read on, my dear; I believe I can guess the riddle."

"'The person I allude to was, in former days, if not actually a friend, a favored intimate of yours; indeed, I say that this fact is but another claim to my regard.'—Is it possible, mamma, his Lordship thinks of marrying?"

"Even so, Helen," said Lady Eleanor, sighing, for she remembered how, in his very last interview with her at Gwynne Abbey, he spoke of his resolve on making Lionel his heir; but then, those were the days of their prosperous fortune, the time when, to all seeming, they needed no increase of wealth.

If Helen was disposed to laugh at the notion of Lord Netherby's marrying, a glance at the troubled expression of her mother's features would have checked the emotion. The heritage was a last hope, which was not the less cherished that she had never imparted it to another.

"Shall I read on?" said Helen, timidly; and at a signal from Lady Eleanor she resumed: "'I know how much "badinage" a man at my time of life must expect from his acquaintances, and how much of kind remonstrance from his friends, when he announces his determination to marry. A good deal of this must be set down to the score of envy, some of it proceeds from mere habit on these occasions, and lastly, one's bachelor friends very naturally are averse to the closure against them of a house "où on dîne." I have thought of all this, and, *per contra*, I have set down the isolation of one, if not deserted, at least somewhat neglected by his relatives, and fancied that if not exactly of that age when people marry for love, I am not yet quite so old but I may become the object of true and disinterested affection.

"'Lady———(I have pledged my honor not to write her name, even to you) is, in rank and fortune, fully my equal, in every other quality my superior. The idlers at "Boodle's" can neither sneer at a "mésalliance," nor hint at the "faiblesse" of an "elderly gentleman." It is a marriage founded on mutual esteem, and, so far as station is concerned, on equality; and when I say that his Royal Highness has expressed his unqualified approval of the step, I believe I can add no more. I owe you, my dear cousin, this early and full explanation of my motives on many accounts: if the result should change the dispositions I once believed unalterable, I beg it may be understood as proceeding far more from necessity than the sincere wish of your very affectionate relative,

"'Netherby.

"'My regret at not seeing Helen here this season is, in a measure, alleviated by Lady————- telling me that brunettes were more the rage; her Ladyship, who is no common arbiter, says that no "blonde" attracted any notice: even Lady Georgiana Maydew drew no admiration. My fair cousin is, happily, very young, *et les beaux jours viendront*, even before hers have lost their brilliancy.

"'I am sorry Lionel left the Coldstreams; with economy he could very well have managed to hold his ground, and we might have obtained something for him in the Household. As for India, the only influential person I know is my wine-merchant; he is, I am told, a Director of the Honorable Company, but he 'd certainly adulterate my Madeira if I condescended to ask him a favor.'"

"Well, Helen, I think you will agree with me, selfishness is the most candid of all the vices; how delightfully unembarrassed is his Lordship's style, how frank, honest, and straightforward!"

"After his verdict upon 'blondes', mamma," said Helen, laughing, "I dare not record my opinion of him,—I cannot come into court an impartial evidence. This, however, I will say, that if his Lordship be not an unhappy instance of the school, I am sincerely rejoiced that Lionel is not being trained up a courtier; better a soldier's life with all its hazards and its dangers, than a career so certain to kill every manly sentiment."

"I agree with you fully, Helen; life cannot be circumscribed within petty limits and occupied by petty cares without reducing the mind to the same miniature dimensions; until at last so immeasurably greater are our own passions and feelings than the miserable interests around us, we end by self-worship and egotism, and fancy ourselves leviathans because we swim in a fish-pond. But who can that be crossing the grass-plot yonder? I thought our neighbors of Port Ballintray had all left the coast?"

"It is the gentleman who dined here, mamma, the man that never spoke—I forget his name—"

Helen had not time to finish, when a modest tap was heard at the door, and the next moment Mr. Leonard presented himself. He was dressed with more than his wonted care, but the effort to make poverty respectable was everywhere apparent; the blue frock was brushed to the very verge of its frail existence, the gloves were drawn on at the hazard of their integrity, and his hat, long inured to every vicissitude of weather, had been cocked into a strange counterfeit of modish smartness. With all these signs of unusual attention to appearances, his manner was modest even to humility, and he took a chair with the diffidence of one who seemed to doubt the propriety of being seated in such a presence.

Notwithstanding Lady Eleanor's efforts at conversation, aided by Helen, who tried in many ways to relieve the embarrassment of their visitor, this difficulty seemed every moment greater, and he seemed, as he really felt, to have summoned up all his courage for an undertaking, and in the very nick of the enterprise, to have left himself beggared of his energy. A vague assent, a look of doubt and uncertainty, a half-muttered expression of acquiescence in whatever was said, was all that could be obtained from him; but still, while his embarrassment appeared each instant greater, he evinced no disposition to take his leave. Lady Eleanor, who, like many persons whose ordinary manner is deemed cold and haughty, could exert at will considerable powers of pleasing, did her utmost to put her visitor at his ease, and by changing her topics from time to time, detect, if possible, some clew to his coming. It was all in vain: he followed her, it is true, as well as he was able, and with a bewildered look of constrained attention, seemed endeavoring to interest himself in what she said, but it was perfectly apparent, all the while, that his mind was preoccupied, and by very different thoughts.

At length she remained silent, and resuming the work she was engaged on when he entered, sat for some time without uttering a word, or even looking up. Mr. Leonard coughed slightly, but, as if terrified at his own rashness, soon became mute and still. At last, after a long pause, so long that Lady Eleanor and Helen, forgetful of their visitor, had become deeply immersed in their own reflections, Mr. Leonard arose slowly, and with a voice not free from a certain tremor, said, "Well, madam, then I suppose I may venture to say that I saw you and Miss Darcy both well."

Lady Eleanor looked up with astonishment, for she could not conceive the meaning of the words, nor in what quarter they were to be reported.

"I mean, madam," said Leonard, "that when I present myself to the Colonel, I may take the liberty to mention having seen you."

"Do you speak of my husband, sir,—Colonel Darcy?" said Lady Eleanor, with a very different degree of interest in her look and accent.

"Yes, madam," said Leonard, with a kind of forced courage in his manner. "I hope to be under his command in a few days."

"Indeed, sir!" said Lady Eleanor, with animation; "I did not know that you had served, still less that you were about to join the army once more."

Leonard blushed deeply, and he suddenly grew deadly pale, while, in a voice scarcely louder than a mere whisper, he muttered, "So then, madam, Colonel Darcy has never spoken of me to you?"

Lady Eleanor, who misunderstood the meaning of the question, seemed slightly confused as she replied, "I have no recollection of it, sir,—I cannot call up at this moment having heard your name from my husband."

"I ought to have known it,—I ought to have been certain of it," said Leonard, in a voice bursting from emotion, while the tears gushed from his eyes; "he could not have asked me to his house to sit down at his table as a mere object of your pity and contempt; and yet I am nothing else."

The passionate vehemence in which he now spoke seemed so different from his recent manner, that both Lady Eleanor and Helen had some doubts as to his sanity, when he quickly resumed: "I was broke for cowardice,—dismissed the service with disgrace,—degraded! Well may I call it so, to be what I became. I would tell you that I was not guilty,—that Colonel Darcy knows,—but I dare not choose between the character of a coward and—a drunkard. I had no other prospect before me than a life of poverty and repining,—maybe of worse,—of shame and ignominy! when, last night, I received these letters; I scarcely thought they could be for me, even when I read my name on them. Yes, madam, this letter from the War Office permits me to serve as a volunteer with the Eighth Regiment of Foot; and this, which is without signature, encloses me fifty pounds to buy my outfit and join the regiment. It does not need a name; there is but one man living could stoop to help such as I am, and not feel dishonored by the contact; there is but one man brave enough to protect him branded as a coward."

"You are right, sir," cried Helen; "this must be my father's doing."

Leonard tried to speak, but could not; a trembling motion of his lips, and a faint sound issued, but nothing articulate. Lady Eleanor stopped him as he moved towards the door, and taking his hand pressed it cordially, while she said, "Be of good heart, sir; my husband is not less quick to perceive than he is ever ready to befriend. Be assured he would not now be your ally if he had not a well-grounded hope that you would merit it. Farewell, then; remember you have a double tie to duty, and that *his* credit as well as *your own* is on the issue."

Leonard muttered a faint "I will," and departed.

"How happily timed is this little incident, Helen," said Lady Eleanor, as she drew her daughter to her side; "how full of pleasant hope it fills the heart, at a moment when the worldly selfishness of the courtier's letter had left us low and sorrow-struck! These are indeed the sunny spots in life, that never look so brilliant as when seen amid lowering skies and darkening storms."

CHAPTER XIII
AN UNCEREMONIOUS VISIT

As winter drew near, with its dark and leaden skies, and days and nights of storm and hurricane, so did the worldly prospect of Lady Eleanor and her daughter grow hourly more gloomy. Bicknell's letters detailed new difficulties and embarrassments on every hand. Sums of money supposed to have been long since paid and acknowledged by Gleeson, were now demanded with all the accruing interest; rights hitherto unquestioned were now threatened with dispute, as Hickman O'Reilly's success emboldened others to try their fortune. Of the little property that still remained to them, the rents were withheld until their claim to them should be once more established by law. Disaster followed disaster, till at length the last drop filled up the measure of their misery, as they learned that the Knight's personal liberty was at stake, and more than one writ was issued for his arrest.

The same post that brought this dreadful intelligence brought also a few lines from Darcy, the first that had reached them since his departure.

His note was dated from the "'Hermione' frigate, off the Needles," and contained little more than an affectionate farewell. He wrote in health, and apparently in spirits, full of the assurance of a speedy and happy meeting; nor was there any allusion to their embarrassments, save in the vague mention of a letter he had written to Bicknell, and who would himself write to Lady Eleanor.

"It is not, dearest Eleanor," wrote he, "the time we would have selected for a separation, when troubles thicken around us; yet who knows if the incident may not fall happily, and turn our thoughts from the loss of fortune to the many blessings we enjoy in mutual affection and in our children's love, all to thicken around us at our meeting? I confess, too, I have a pride in being thought worthy to serve my country still, not in the tiresome monotony of a depot, but in the field,—among the young, the gallant, and the brave! Is it not enough to take off half this load of years, and make me fancy myself the gay colonel you may remember cantering beside your carriage in the Park—I shame to say how long ago! I wonder what the French will think of us, for nearly every officer in command might be superannuated, and Abercrombie is as venerable in white hairs as myself! There are, however, plenty of young and dashing fellows to replace us, and the spirit of the whole army is admirable.

"Whither we are destined, what will be our collective force, and what the nature of the expedition, are profound secrets, with which even the generals of brigades are not intrusted; so that all I can tell you is, that some seven hundred and fifty of us are now sailing southward, under a steady breeze from the north-northwest; that the land is each moment growing fainter to my eyes, while the pilot is eagerly pressing me to conclude this last expression of my love to yourself and dearest Helen. Adieu.

"Ever yours,

"Maurice Darcy."

As with eyes half dimmed by tears Lady Eleanor read these lines, she could not help muttering a thanksgiving that her husband was at least beyond the risk of that danger of which Bicknell spoke,—an indignity, she feared, he never could have survived.

"And better still," cried Helen, "if a season of struggle and privation awaits us, that we should bear it alone,' and not before *his* eyes, for whom such a prospect would be torture. Now let us see how to meet the evil." So saying, she once more opened Bicknell's letter, and began to peruse it carefully; while Lady Eleanor sat, pale and in silence, nor even by a gesture showing any consciousness of the scene.

"What miserable trifling do all these legal subtleties seem!" said the young girl, after she had read for some time; "how trying to patience to canvass the petty details by which a clear and honest cause must be asserted! Here are fees to counsel, briefs, statements, learned opinions, and wise consultations multiplied to show that we are the rightful owners of what our ancestors have held for centuries, while every step of usurpation by these Hickmans would appear almost unassailable. With what intensity of purpose, too, does that family persecute us! All these actions are instituted by them; these bonds are all in their hands. What means this hate?"

Lady Eleanor looked up; and as her eyes met Helen's, a faint flush colored her cheek, for she thought of her interview with the old doctor, and that proposal by which their conflicting interests were to be satisfied.

"We surely never injured them," resumed the young girl, eagerly; "they were always well and hospitably received by us. Lionel even liked Beecham, when they were boys together,-a mild and quiet youth he was."

"So I thought him, too," said Lady Eleanor, stealing a cautious glance at her daughter. "We saw them," continued she, more boldly, "under circumstances of no common difficulty,—struggling under the embarrassment of a false social position, with such a grandfather!"

"And such a father! Nay, mamma, of the two you must confess the doctor was our favorite. The old man's selfishness was not half so vulgar as his son's ambition."

"And yet, Helen," said Lady Eleanor, calmly, "such are the essential transitions by which families are formed; wealthy in one generation, aspiring in the next, recognized gentry—mayhap titled—in the third. It is but rarely that the whole series unfolds itself before our eyes at once, as in the present instance, and consequently it is but rarely that we detect so palpably all its incongruities and absurdities. A few years more," added she, with a deep sigh, "and these O'Reillys will be regarded as the rightful owners of Gwynne Abbey by centuries of descent; and if an antiquary detect the old leopards of the Darcys frowning from some sculptured keystone, it will be to weave an ingenious theory of intermarriage between the houses."

"An indignity they might well have spared us," said Helen, proudly.

"Such are the world's changes," continued Lady Eleanor, pursuing her own train of thought. "How very few remember the origin of our proudest houses, and how little does it matter whether the foundations have been laid by the rude courage of some lawless baron of the tenth century, or the crafty shrewdness of some Hickman O'Reilly of the nineteenth!"

If there was a tone of bitter mockery in Lady Eleanor's words, there was also a secret meaning which, even to her own heart, she would not have ventured to avow. By one of those strange and most inexplicable mysteries of our nature, she was endeavoring to elicit from her daughter some expression of dissent to her own recorded opinion of the O'Reillys and seeking for some chance word which might show that Helen regarded an alliance with that family with more tolerant feelings than she did herself.

Her intentions on this head were uot destined to be successful. Helen's prejudices on the score of birth and station were rather strengthened than shaken by the changes of fortune; she cherished the prestige of their good blood as a source of proud consolation that no adversity could detract from. Before, however, she could reply, the tramp of a horse's feet—a most unusual sound—was heard on the gravel without; and immediately after the heavy foot of some one, as if feeling his way in the dark towards the door. Without actual fear, but not without intense anxiety, both mother and daughter heard the heavy knocking of a loaded horsewhip on the door; nor was it until old Tate had twice repeated his question that a sign replied he might open the door.

"Look to the pony there!" cried a voice, as the old man peered out into the dark night. And before he could reply or resist, the speaker pushed past him and entered the room. "I crave your pardon, my Lady Eleanor," said she,—for it was Miss Daly, who, drenched with rain and all splashed with mud, now stood before them,—"I crave your pardon for this visit of so scant ceremony. Has the Knight returned yet?"

The strong resemblance to her brother Bagenal, increased by her gesture and the tones of her voice, at once proclaimed to Lady Eleanor who her visitor was; and as she rose graciously to receive her, she replied that "the Knight, so far from having returned, had already sailed with the expedition under General Abercrombie."

Miss Daly listened with breathless eagerness to the words, and as they concluded, she exclaimed aloud, "Thank God!" and threw herself into a chair. A pause, which, if brief, was not devoid of embarrassment, followed; and while Lady Eleanor was about to break it, Miss Daly again spoke, but with a voice and manner very different from before: "You will pardon, I am certain, the rudeness of my intrusion, Lady Eleanor, and you, too, Miss Darcy, when I tell you that my heart was too full of anxiety to leave any room for courtesy. It was only this afternoon that an accident informed me that a person had arrived in this neighborhood with a writ to arrest the Knight of Gwynne. I was five-and-twenty miles from this when I heard the news, and although I commissioned my informant to hasten thither with the tidings, I grew too full of dread, and had too many fears of a mischance, to await the result, so that I resolved to come myself."

"How full of kindness!" exclaimed Lady Eleanor, while Helen took Miss Daly's hand and pressed it to her lips. "Let our benefactress not suffer too much in our cause. Helen, dearest, assist Miss Daly to a change of dress. You are actually wet through."

"Nay, nay, Lady Eleanor, you must not teach me fastidiousness. It has been my custom for many a year not to care for weather, and in the kind of life I lead such training is indispensable." Miss Daly removed her hat as she spoke, and, pushing back her dripping hair, seemed really insensible to the discomforts which caused her hosts so much uneasiness.

"I see clearly," resumed she, laughing, "I was right in not making myself known to you before; for though you may forgive the eccentricities that come under the mask of good intentions, you 'd never pardon the thousand offences against good breeding and the world's prescription which spring from the wayward fancies of an old maid who has lived so much beyond the pale of affection she has forgotten all the arts that win it."

"If you are unjust to yourself, Miss Daly, pray be not so to us; nor think that we can be insensible to friendship like yours."

"Oh, as for this trifling service, you esteem it far too highly; besides, when you hear the story, you'll see how much more you have to thank your own hospitality than my promptitude."

"This is, indeed, puzzling me," exclaimed Lady Eleanor.

"Do you remember having met and received at your house a certain Mr. Dempsey?"

"Certainly, he dined with us on one occasion, and paid us some three or four visits. A tiresome little vulgar man, with a most intense curiosity devouring him to know everything of everybody."

"To this gift, or infirmity, whichever it be, we are now indebted. Since the breaking-up of the boarding-house at Port Ballintray, which this year was somewhat earlier than usual,"—here Miss Daly smiled slightly, as though there lay more in the words than they seemed to imply,—"Mr. Dempsey betook himself to a little village near Glenarm, where I have been staying, and where the chief recommendation as a residence lay possibly in the fact that the weekly mail-car to Derry changed horses there. Hence an opportunity of communing with the world he valued at its just price. It so chanced that the only traveller who came for three weeks, arrived the night before last, drenched to the skin, and so ill from cold, hunger, and exhaustion that, unable to prosecute his journey farther, he was carried from the car to his bed. Mr. Dempsey, whose heart is really as kind as inquisitive, at once tendered his services to the stranger, who after some brief intercourse commissioned him to open his portmanteau, and taking out writing-materials, to inform his friends in Dublin of his sudden indisposition, and his fears that his illness might delay, or perhaps render totally abortive, his mission to the north. Here was a most provoking mystery for Mr. Dempsey. The very allusion to a matter of importance, in this dubious half-light, was something more than human nature should be tried with; and if the patient burned with the fever of the body, Mr. Dempsey suffered under the less tolerable agony of mental torment,— imagining every possible contingency that should bring a stranger down into a lonely neighborhood, and canvassing every imaginable inducement, from seduction to highway robbery. Whether the sick man's sleep was merely the heavy debt of exhausted nature, or whether Mr. Dempsey aided his repose by adding a few drops to the laudanum prescribed by the doctor, true it is, he lay in a deep slumber, and never awoke till late the following day; meanwhile Mr. Dempsey recompensed his Samaritanism by a careful inspection of the stranger's trunk and its contents, and, in particular, made a patient examination of two parchment documents, which, fortunately for his curiosity, were not sealed, but simply tied with red tape.

Great was his surprise to discover that one of these was a writ to arrest a certain Paul Dempsey, and the other directed against the resident of 'The Corvy,' whom he now, for the first time, learned was the Knight of Gwynne.

"Self-interest, the very instinct of safety itself, weighed less with him than his old passion for gossip; and no sooner had he learned the important fact of who his neighbor was, than he set off straight to communicate the news to me. I must do him the justice to say, that when I proposed his hastening off to you with the tidings, the little man acceded with the utmost promptitude; but as his journey was to be performed on foot, and by certain mountain paths not always easily discovered in our misty climate, it is probable he could not reach this for some hours."

When Miss Daly concluded, Lady Eleanor and her daughter renewed their grateful acknowledgments for her thoughtful kindness. "These are sad themes by which to open our acquaintance," said Lady Eleanor; "but it is among the prerogatives of friendship to share the pressure of misfortune, and Mr. Daly's sister can be no stranger to ours."

"Nor how undeserved they were," added Miss Daly, gravely.

"Nay, which of us can dare say so much?" interrupted Lady Eleanor; "we may well have forgotten ourselves in that long career of prosperity we enjoyed,—for ours was, indeed, a happy lot! I need not speak of my husband to one who knew him once so well. Generous, frank, and noble-hearted as he always was,-his only failing the excessive confidence that would go on believing in the honesty of others, from the prompting of a spirit that stooped to nothing low or unworthy,—he never knew suspicion." "True," echoed Miss Daly, "he never did suspect!" There was such a plaintive sadness in her voice that it drew Helen's eyes towards her; nor could all her efforts conceal a tear that trickled along her cheek.

"And to what an alternative are we now reduced!" continued Lady Eleanor, who, with all the selfishness of sorrow, loved to linger on the painful theme,—"to rejoice at separation, and to feel relieved in thinking that he is gone to peril life itself rather than endure the lingering death of a broken heart!"

"Yes, young lady," said Miss Daly, turning towards Helen, "such are the recompenses of the most endearing affection, such the penalties of loving. Would you not almost say, 'It were better to be such as I am, unloved, uncared for, without one to share a joy or grief with?' I half think so myself," added she, suddenly rising from her chair. "I can almost persuade myself that this load of life is easier borne when all its pressure is one's own."

"You are not about to leave us?" said Lady Eleanor, taking her hand affectionately.

"Yes," replied she, smiling sadly, "when my heart has disburdened itself of an immediate care, I become but sorry company, and sometimes think aloud. How fortunate I have no secrets!—Bring my pony to the door," said she, as Tate answered the summons of the bell.

"But wait at least for daylight," said Helen, eagerly; "the storm is increasing, and the night is dark and starless. Remember what a road you 've come."

"I often ride at this hour and with no better weather," said she, adjusting the folds of her habit; "and as to the road, Puck knows it too well to wander from the track, daylight or dark."

"For our sakes, I entreat you not to venture till morning," cried Lady Eleanor.

"I could not if I would," said Miss Daly, steadily. "By to-morrow, at noon, I have an engagement at some distance hence, and much to arrange in the mean time. Pray do not ask me again. I cannot bear to refuse you, even in such a trifle; and as to me or my safety, waste not another thought about it. They who have so little to live for are wondrous secure from accident."

"When shall we see you? Soon, I hope and trust!" exclaimed both mother and daughter together.

Miss Daly shook her head; then added hastily, "I never promise anything. I was a great castle-builder once, but time has cured me of the habit, and I do not like, even by a pledge, to forestall the morrow. Farewell, Lady Eleanor. It is better to see but little of me, and think the better, than grow weary of my waywardness on nearer acquaintance. Adieu, Miss Darcy; I am glad to have seen you; don't forget me." So saying, she pressed Helen's hands to her lips; but ere she let them drop, she squeezed a letter into her grasp; the moment after, she was gone.

"Oh, then, I remember her the beauty wonst!" said Tate, as he closed the door, after peering out for some seconds into the dark night: "and proud she was too,—riding a white Arabian, with two servants in scarlet liveries after her! The world has quare changes; but hers is the greatest ever I knew!"

CHAPTER XIV
A TÊTE-À-TÊTE AND A LETTER

Long after Miss Daly's departure, Lady Eleanor continued to discuss the eccentricity of her manners and the wilful abruptness of her address; for although deeply sensible and grateful for her kindness, she dwelt on every' peculiarity of her appearance with a pertinacity that more than once surprised her daughter. Helen, indeed, was very far from being a patient listener, not only because she was more tolerant in her estimate of their visitor, but because she was eager to read the letter so secretly intrusted to her hands. A dread of some unknown calamity, some sad tidings of her father or Lionel, was ever uppermost in her thoughts, nor could she banish the impression that Miss Daly's visit had another and very different object than that which she alleged to Lady Eleanor.

It may be reckoned among the well-known contrarieties of life, that our friends are never more disposed to be long-winded and discursive than at the very time we would give the world to be alone and to ourselves. With a most malicious intensity they seem to select that moment for indulging in all those speculations by which people while away the weary hours. In such a mood was Lady Eleanor Darcy. Not only did she canvass and criticise Miss Daly, as she appeared before them, but went off into long rambling reminiscences of all she had formerly heard about her; for although they had never met before, Miss Daly had been the reigning Belle of the West before her own arrival in Ireland.

"She must have been handsome, Helen, don't you think so?" said she, at the end of a long enumeration of the various eccentricities imputed to her.

"I should say very handsome," replied Helen.

"Scarcely feminine enough, perhaps," resumed Lady Eleanor,—"the features too bold, the expression too decided; but this may have been the fault of a social tone, which required everything in exaggeration, and would tolerate nothing save in excess."

"Yes, mamma," said Helen, vaguely assenting to a remark she had not attended to.

"I never fancied that style, either in beauty or in manner," continued Lady Eleanor. "It wants, in the first place, the great element of pleasing; it is not natural."

"No, mamma!" rejoined Helen, mechanically as before.

"Besides," continued Lady Eleanor, gratified at her daughter's ready assent, "for one person to whom these mannerisms are becoming, there are at least a hundred slavish imitators ready to adopt without taste, and follow without discrimination. Now, Miss Daly was the fashion once. Who can say to what heresies she has given origin, to what absurdities in dress, in manner, and in bearing?"

Helen smiled, and nodded an acquiescence without knowing to what.

"There is one evil attendant on all this," said Lady Eleanor, who, with the merciless ingenuity of a thorough poser, went on ratiocinating from her own thoughts; "one can rarely rely upon even the kindest intentions of people of this sort, so often are their best offices but mere passing, fitful impulses; don't you think so?"

"Yes, mamma," said Helen, roused by this sudden appeal to a more than usual acquiescence, while totally ignorant as to what.

"Then, they have seldom any discretion, even when they mean well."

"No, mamma."

"While they expect the most implicit compliance on your part with every scheme they have devised for your benefit."

"Very true," chimed in Helen, who assented at random.

"Sad alternative," sighed Lady Eleanor, "between such rash friendship and the lukewarm kindness of our courtly cousin."

"I think not!" said Helen, who fancied she was still following the current of her mother's reflections.

"Indeed!" exclaimed Lady Eleanor, iu astonishment, while she looked at her daughter for an explanation.

"I quite agree with you, mamma," cried Helen, blushing as she spoke, for she was suddenly recalled to herself.

"The more fortunate is the acquiescence, my dear," said Lady Eleanor, dryly, "since it seems perfectly instinctive. I find, Helen, you have not been a very attentive listener, and as I conclude I must have been a very unamusing companion, I'll even say good-night; nay, my sweet child, it is late enough not to seek excuse for weariness—goodnight."

Helen blushed deeply; dissimulation was a very difficult task to her, and for a moment seemed more than her strength could bear. She had resolved to place the letter in her mother's hands, when the thought flashed across her, that if its contents might occasion any sudden or severe shock, she would never forgive herself. This mental struggle, brief as it was, brought the tears to her eyes,—an emotion Lady Eleanor attributed to a different cause, as she said,—

"You do not suppose, my dearest Helen, that I am angry because your thoughts took a pleasanter path than my owu."

"Oh, no,-no!" cried Helen, eagerly, "I know you are not. It is my own—" She stopped; another word would have revealed everything, and with an affectionate embrace she hurried from the room.

"Poor child!" exclaimed her mother; "the courage that sustained us both so long is beginning to fail her now; and yet I feel as if our trials were but commencing."

While Lady Eleanor dwelt on these sad thoughts, Helen sat beside her bed weeping bitterly.

"How shall I bear up," thought she, "if deprived of that confiding trust a mother's love has ever supplied,—without one to counsel or direct me?"

Half fearing to open the letter, lest all her resolves should be altered by its contents, she remained a long time balancing one difficulty against another. Wearied and undecided, she turned at last to the letter itself, as if for advice. It was a strange hand, and addressed to "Miss Daly." With trembling fingers she unfolded the paper, and read the writer's name,— "Richard Forester."

A flood of grateful tears burst forth as she read the words; a sense of relief from impending calamity stole over her mind, while she said, "Thank God! my father and Lionel—" She could say no more, for sobbing choked her utterance. The emotions, if violent, passed rapidly off; and as she wiped away her tears, a smile of hope lit up her features. At any other time she would have speculated long and carefully over the causes which made Forester correspond with Miss Daly, and by what right she herself should be intrusted with his letter. Now her thoughts were hurried along too rapidly for reflection. The vague dread of misfortune, so suddenly removed, suggested a sense of gratitude that thrilled through her heart like joy. In such a frame of mind she read the following lines:—

At Sea. My dear Miss Daly,-I cannot thank you enough for your letter, so full of kindness, of encouragement, and of hope. How much I stand in need of them! I have strictly followed every portion of your counsel,— would that I could tell you as successfully as implicitly! The address of this letter will, however, be the shortest reply to that question. I write these lines from the "Hermione" frigate. Yes, I am a volunteer in the expedition to the Mediterranean; and only think who is my commanding officer,—the Knight himself. I had enrolled myself under the name of Conway; but when called up on deck this morning for inspection, such was my surprise on seeing the Knight of Gwynne, or, as he is now called, Colonel Darcy, I almost betrayed myself. Fortunately, however, I escaped unnoticed,—a circumstance I believe I owe chiefly to the fact that several young men of family are also volunteers, so that my position attracted no unusual attention. It was a most anxious moment for me as the colonel came down the line, addressing a word here and there as he went; he stopped within one of me, and spoke for some seconds to a young fellow whose appearance indicated delicate health. How full of gentleness and benevolence were his words! But when he turned and fixed his eyes on me, my heart beat so quick, my head grew so dizzy, I thought I should have fainted. He remained at least half a minute in front of me, and then asked the orderly for my name—"Conway! Conway!" repeated he more than once. "A very old name. I hope you'll do it credit, sir," added he, and moved on,—how much to my relief I need not say. What a strange rencontre! Often as I wonder at the singular necessity that has made me a private soldier, all my astonishment is lost in thinking of the Knight of Gwynne's presence amongst us; and yet he looks the soldier even as much as he did the country gentleman when I first saw him, and, strangely too, seems younger and more active than before. To see him here, chatting with the officers under his command, moving about, taking interest in everything that goes on, who would suspect the change of fortune that has befallen him! Not a vestige of discontent, not even a passing look of impatience on his handsome features; and yet, with this example before me, and the consciousness that my altered condition is nothing in comparison with his, I am low-spirited and void of hope! But a few weeks ago I would have thought myself the luckiest fellow breathing, if told that I were to serve under Colonel Darcy, and now I feel ashamed and abashed, and dread a recognition every time I see him. In good truth, I cannot forget the presumption that led me first to his acquaintance. My mind dwells on that unhappy mission to the West, and its consequences. My foolish vanity in supposing that I, a mere boy, uninformed, and without reflection, should be able to influence a man so much my superior in every way! and this, bad as it is, is the most favorable view of my conduct, for I dare not recall the dishonorable means by which I was to buy his support. Then, I think of my heedless and disreputable quarrel. What motives and what actions in the eyes of her whose affection I sought! How worthily am I punished for my presumption!

I told you that I strictly followed the advice of your last letter. Immediately on receiving it I wrote a few lines to my mother, entreating her permission to see and speak with her, and expressing an earnest hope that our interview would end in restoring me to the place I so long enjoyed in her affection. A very formal note, appointing the following day, was all the reply.

On arriving at Berkeley Square, and entering the drawing-room, I found, to my great astonishment, I will not say more, that a gentleman, a stranger to me, was already there, seated at the fire, opposite my mother, and with that easy air that bespoke his visit was not merely accidental, but a matter of pre-arrangement.

Whatever my looks might have conveyed, I know not, but I was not given the opportunity for a more explicit inquiry, when my mother, in her stateliest of manners, arose and said,—

"Richard, I wish to present you to my esteemed friend, Lord Netherby; a gentleman to whose kindness you are indebted for any favorable construction I can put upon your folly, and who has induced me to receive you here to-day."

"If I knew, madam, that such influence had been necessary, I should have hesitated before I laid myself under so deep an obligation to his Lordship, to whose name and merits I confess myself a stranger."

"I am but too happy, Captain Forester," interposed the Earl, "if any little interest I possess in Lady Wallincourt's esteem enables me to contribute to your reconciliation. I know the great delicacy of an interference, in a case like the present, and how officious and impertinent the most respectful suggestions must appear, when offered by one who can lay no claim, at least to *your* good opinion."

A very significant emphasis on the word "your," a look towards my mother, and a very meaning smile from her in reply, at once revealed to me what, till then, I had not suspected,—that his Lordship meditated a deeper influence over her Ladyship's heart than the mere reconciliation of a truant son to her esteem.

"I believe, my Lord," said I, hastily, and I fear not without some anger,— "I believe I should not have dared to decline your kind influence in my behalf, had I suspected the terms on which you would exert it. I really was not aware before that you possessed, so fully, her Ladyship's confidence."

"If you read the morning papers, Captain Forester," said he, with the blandest smile, "you could scarcely avoid learning that my presence here is neither an intrusion nor an impertinence."

"My dear mother," cried I, forgetting all, save the long-continued grief by which my father's memory was hallowed, "is this really the case?"

"I can forgive your astonishment," replied she, with a look of anger, "that the qualities you hold so highly in your esteem should have met favor from one so placed and gifted as the Earl of Netherby."

"Nay, madam; on the contrary. My difficulty is to think how any new proffer of attachment could find reception in a heart I fondly thought closed against such appeals; too full of its own memories of the past to profane the recollection by—"

I hesitated and stopped. Another moment, and I would have uttered a word which for worlds I would not have spoken.

My mother became suddenly pale as marble, and lay back in her chair as if faint and sick. His Lordship adjusted his neckcloth and his watch-chain, and walked towards the window, with an air of as much awkwardness as so very courtly a personage could exhibit.

"You see, my Lord," said my mother,—and her voice trembled at every word,—"you see, I was right: I told you how much this interview would agitate and distress me."

"But it need not, madam," interposed I; "or, at all events, it may be rendered very brief. I sought an opportunity of speaking to you, in the hope that whatever impressions you may have received of my conduct in Ireland were either exaggerated or unjust; that I might convince you, however I may have erred in prudence or judgment, I have transgressed neither in honor nor good faith."

"Vindications," said my mother, "are very weak things in the face of direct facts. Did you, or did you not, resign your appointment on the viceroy's staff—I stop not to ask with what scant courtesy—that you might be free to rove over the country, on some knight-errant absurdity? Did you, after having one disreputable quarrel in the same neighborhood, again involve yourself and your name in an affair with a notorious mob-orator and disturber, and thus become the 'celebrity' of the newspapers for at least a fortnight? And lastly, when I hoped, by absence from England, and foreign service, to erase the memory of these follies—to give them no harsher name,—did you not refuse the appointment, and without advice or permission sell out of the army altogether?"

"Without adverting to the motives, madam, you have so kindly attributed to me, I beg to say 'yes' to all your questions. I am no longer an officer in his Majesty's service."

"Nor any longer a member of *my* family, sir," said my mother, passionately; "at least so far as the will rests with me. A gentleman so very independent in his principles is doubtless not less so in his circumstances. You are entitled to five thousand pounds only, by your father's will: this, if I mistake not, you have received and spent many a day ago. I will not advert to what my original intentions in your behalf were; they are recorded, however, in this paper, which you, my Lord, have read." Here her Ladyship drew forth a document, like a law-paper, while the Earl bowed a deep acquiescence, and muttered something like—"Very generous and noble-minded, indeed!"

"Yes, sir," resumed my mother, "I had no other thought or object, save in establishing you in a position suitable to your name and family; you have thought fit to oppose my wishes on every point, and here I end the vain struggle." So saying, she tore the paper in pieces, and threw the fragments into the fire.

A deep silence ensued, which I, for many reasons, had no inducement to break. The Earl coughed and hemmed three or four times, as though endeavoring to hit upon something that might relieve the general embarrassment, but my mother was again the first to speak.

"I have no doubt, sir, you have determined on some future career. I am not indiscreet enough to inquire what; but that you may not enter upon it quite unprovided, I have settled upon you the sum of four hundred pounds yearly. Do not mistake me, nor suppose that this act proceeds from any lingering hope on my part that you will attempt to retrace your false steps, and recover the lost place in my affection. I am too well acquainted with the family gift of determination, as it is flatteringly styled, to think so. You owe this consideration entirely to the kind interference of the Earl of Netherby. Nay, my Lord, it is but fair that you should have any merit the act confers, where you have incurred all the responsibility."

"I will relieve his Lordship of both," said I. "I beg to decline your Ladyship's generosity and his Lordship's kindness, with the self-same feeling of respect."

"My dear Captain Forester, wait one moment," said Lord Netherby, taking my arm. "Let me speak to you, even for a few moments."

"You mistake him, my Lord," said my mother, with a scornful smile, while she arose to leave the room,—"you mistake him much."

"Pray hear me out," said Lord Netherby, taking my hand in both his own. "It is no time, nor a case for any rash resolves," whispered he; "Lady Wallincourt has been misinformed,—her mind has been warped by stories of one kind or other. Go to her, explain fully and openly everything."

"Her Ladyship is gone, my Lord," exclaimed I, stopping him.

Yes, she had left the room while we were yet speaking. This was my last adieu from my mother! I remember little more, though Lord Netherby detained me still some time, and spoke with much kindness; indeed, throughout, his conduct was graceful and good-natured.

Why should I weary you longer? Why speak of the long dreary night, and the longer day that followed this scene,—swayed by different impulses,- now hoping and fearing alternately,—not daring to seek counsel from my friends, because I well knew what worldly advice would be given,—I was wretched. In the very depth of my despondency, like a ray of sunlight darting through some crevice of a prisoner's cell, came your own words to me, "Be a soldier in more than garb or name, be one in the generous ardor of a bold career. Let it be your boast that you started fairly in the race, and so distanced your competitors." I caught at the suggestion with avidity. I was no more depressed or down-hearted. I felt as if, throwing off my load of care, a better and a brighter day was about to break for me; the same evening I left London for Plymouth, and became a volunteer.

Before concluding these lines, I would ask why you tell me no more of Miss Darcy than that "she is well, and, the reverse of her fortune considered, in spirits." Am I to learn no more than that? Will you not say if my name is ever spoken by or before her? How am I remembered? Has time-have my changed fortunes softened her stern determination towards me? Would that I could know this,—would that I could divine what may lurk in her heart of compassionate pity for one who resigned all for her love, and lost! With all my gratitude for your kindness, when I well-nigh believed none remained in the world for me,

I am, yours in sincere affection,

Richard Forester.

I forgot to ask if you can read one strange mystery of this business, at least so the words seem to imply. Lord Netherby said, when endeavoring to dissuade me from leaving my mother's house, "Remember, Captain Forester, that Lady Wallincourt's prejudices regarding your Irish friends have something stronger than mere caprice to strengthen them. You must not ask her to forget as well as forgive, all at once." Can you interpret this riddle for me? for although at the time it made little impression, it recurs to my mind now twenty times a day.

Here concluded Forester's letter. A single line in pencil was written at the foot, and signed "M. D. ": "I am a bad prophet, or the volunteer will turn out better than the aide-de-camp."

CHAPTER XV
A DINNER AT COM HEFFERNAN'S

When the Union was carried, and the new order of affairs in Ireland assumed an appearance of permanence, a general feeling of discontent began to exhibit itself in every class in the capital. The patriots saw themselves neglected by the Government, without having reaped in popularity a recompense for their independence. The mercantile interest perceived, even already, the falling off in trade from the removal of a wealthy aristocracy; and the supporters of the Minister, or such few as still lingered in Dublin, began to suspect how much higher terms they might have exacted for their adhesion, had they only anticipated the immensity of the sacrifice to which they contributed.

Save that comparatively small number who had bargained for English peerages and English rank, and had thereby bartered their nationality, none were satisfied.

Even the moderate men—that intelligent fraction who believe that no changes are fraught with one half the good or evil their advocates or opponents imagine—even they were disappointed on finding that the incorporation of the Irish Parliament with that of England was the chief element of the new measure, and no more intimate or solid Union contemplated. The shrewd men of every party saw not only how difficult would be the future government of the country, but that the critical moment was come which should decide into whose hands the chief influence would fall. Among these speculators on the future, Mr. Heffernan held a prominent place. No man knew better the secret machinery of office, none had seen more of that game, half fair, half foul, by which an administration is sustained. He knew, moreover, the character and capability of every public man in Ireland, had been privy to their waverings and hesitations, and even their bargains with the Crown; he knew where gratified ambition had rendered a new peer indifferent to a future temptation, and also where abortive negotiations had sowed the seeds of a lingering disaffection.

To construct a new party from these scattered elements—a party which, possessing wealth and station, had not yet tasted any of the sweets of patronage—was the task he now proposed to himself. By this party, of whom he himself was to be the organ, he hoped to control the Minister, and support him by turns. Of those already purchased by the Government, few would care to involve themselves once more in the fatigues of a public life. Many would gladly repose on the rewards of their victory; many would shrink from the obloquy their reappearance would inevitably excite. Mr. Heffernan had then to choose his friends either from that moderate section of politicians whom scruples of conscience or inferiority of ability had left un-bought, or the more energetic faction, suddenly called into existence by the success of the French Revolution, and of which O'Halloran was the leader. For many reasons his choice fell on the former. Not only because they possessed that standing and influence which, derived from property, would be most regarded in England, but that their direction and guidance would be an easier task; whereas the others, more numerous and more needy, could only be purchased by actual place or pension, while in O'Halloran Heffernan would always have a dangerous rival, who, if he played subordinate for a while, it would only be at the price of absolute rule hereafter.

From the moment Lord Castlereagh withdrew from Ireland, Mr. Heffernan commenced his intrigue,—at first by a tour of visits through the country, in which he contrived to sound the opinions of a great number of persons, and subsequently by correspondence, so artfully sustained as to induce many to commit themselves to a direct line of action which, when discussing, they had never speculated on seeing realized.

With a subtlety of no common kind, and an indefatigable industry, Heffernan labored in the cause during the summer and autumn, and with such success that there was scarcely a county in Ireland where he had not secured some leading adherent, while for many of the boroughs he had already entered into plans for the support of new candidates of his own opinions.

The views he put forward were simply these: Ireland can no longer be governed by an oligarchy, however powerful. It must be ruled either by the weight and influence of the country gentlemen, or left to the mercy of the demagogue. The gentry must be rewarded for their adhesion, and enabled to maintain their pre-eminence, by handing over to them the patronage, not in part or in fractions, but wholly and solely. Every civil appointment must be filled up by them,—the Church, the law, the revenue, the police, must all be theirs. "The great aristocracy," said he, "have obtained the marquisates and earldoms; bishoprics and governments have rewarded their services. It is now *our* turn; and if our prizes be less splendid and showy, they are not devoid of some sterling qualities.

"To make Ireland ungovernable without us must be our aim and object, — to embarrass and confound every administration, to oppose the ministers, pervert their good objects, and exaggerate their bad. Pledged to no distinct line of acting, we can be patriotic when it suits us, and declaim on popular rights when nothing better offers. Acting in concert, and diffusing an influence in every county and town and corporation, what ministry can long resist us, or what government anxious for office would refuse to make terms with us? With station to influence society, wealth to buy the press, activity to watch and counteract our enemies, I see nothing which can arrest our progress. We must and will succeed."

Such was the conclusion of a letter he wrote to one of his most trusted allies, — a letter written to invite his presence in Dublin, where a meeting of the leading men of the new party was to be held, and their engagements for the future determined upon.

For this meeting Heffernan made the greatest exertions, not only that it might include a great portion of the wealth and influence of the land, but that a degree of *éclat* and splendor should attend it, the more likely to attract notice from the secrecy maintained as to its object and intention. Many were invited on the consideration of the display their presence would make in the capital; and not a few were tempted by the opportunity for exhibiting their equipages and their liveries at a season when the recognized leaders of fashion were absent.

It is no part of our object to dwell on this well-known intrigue, one which at the time occupied no small share of public attention, and even excited the curiosity and the fears of the Government. Enough when we say that Mr. Heffernan's disappointments were numerous and severe. Letters of apology, some couched in terms of ambiguous cordiality, others less equivocally cold, came pouring in for the last fortnight. The noble lord destined to fill the chair regretted deeply that domestic affairs of a most pressing nature would not permit of his presence. The baronet who should move the first resolution would be compelled to be absent from Ireland; the seconder was laid up with the gout. Scarcely a single person of influence had promised his attendance: the greater number had given vague and conditional replies, evidently to gain time and consult the feeling of their country neighbors.

These refusals and subterfuges were a sad damper to Mr. Heffernan's hopes. To any one less sanguine, they would have led to a total abandonment of the enterprise. He, however, was made of sterner stuff, and resolved, if the demonstration could effect no more, it could at least be used as a threat to the Government, — a threat of not less power because its terrors were involved in mystery. With all these disappointments time sped on, the important day arrived, and the great room of the Rotunda, hired specially for the occasion, was crowded by a numerous assemblage, to whose proceedings no member of the public press was admitted. Notice was given that in due time a declaration, drawn up by a committee, would be published; but until then the most profound secrecy wrapped their objects and intentions.

The meeting, convened for one o'clock, separated at five; and, save the unusual concourse of carriages, and the spectacle of some liveries new to the capital, there seemed nothing to excite the public attention. No loud-tongued orator was heard from without, nor did a single cheer mark the reception of any welcome sentiment; and as the members withdrew, the sarcastic allusions of the mob intimated that they were supposed to be a new sect of "Quakers." Heffernan's carriage was the last to leave the door; and it was remarked, as he entered it, that he looked agitated and ill,—signs which few had ever remarked in him before. He drove rapidly home, where a small and select party of friends had been invited by him to dinner.

He made a hasty toilet, and entered the drawing-room a few moments after the first knock at the street-door announced the earliest guest. It was an old and intimate friend, Sir Giles St. George, a south-country baronet of old family, but small fortune, who for many years had speculated on Heffernan's interest in his behalf. He was a shrewd, coarse man, who from eccentricity and age had obtained a species of moral "writ of ease," absolving him from all observance of the usages in common among all well-bred people,—a privilege he certainly did not seem disposed to let rust from disuse.

"Well, Con," said he, as he stood with his back to the fire, and his hands deeply thrust into his breeches-pockets,—"well, Con, your Convention has been a damnable failure. Where the devil did you get up such a rabble of briefless barristers, ungowned attorneys, dissenting ministers, and illegitimate sons? I'd swear, out of your seven hundred, there were not five-and-twenty possessed of a fifty-pound freehold,—not five who could defy the sheriff in their own county."

Heffernan made no reply, but with arms crossed, and his head leaned forward, walked slowly up and down the room, while the other resumed,—

"As for old Killowen, who filled the chair, that was enough to damn the whole thing. One of King James's lords, forsooth!—why, man, what country gentleman of any pretension could give precedence to a fellow like that, who neither reads, writes, nor speaks the King's English—and your great gun, Mr. Hickman O'Reilly—"

"False-hearted scoundrel!" muttered Heffernan, half aloud.

"Faith he may be, but he's the cleverest of the pack. I liked his speech well. There was good common sense in his asking for some explicit plan of proceeding,—what you meant to do, and how to do it. Eh, Con, that was to the point."

"To the point!" repeated Heffernan, scornfully; "yes, as the declaration of an informer, that he will betray his colleagues, is to the point."

"And then his motion to admit the reporters," said St. George, as with a malignant pleasure he continued to suggest matter of annoyance.

"He 's mistaken, however," said Heffernan, with a sarcastic bitterness that came from his heart. "The day for rewards is gone by. He 'll never get the baronetcy by supporting the Government in this way. It is the precarious, uncertain ally they look more after. There is consummate wisdom, Giles, in not saying one's last word. O'Reilly does not seem aware of that. Here come Godfrey and Hume," said he, as he looked out of the window. "Burton has sent an apology."

"And who is our sixth?"

"O'Reilly—and here's his carriage. See how the people stare admiringly at his green liveries; they scarcely guess that the owner is meditating a change of color. Well, Godfrey, in time for once. Why, Robert, you seem quite fagged with your day's exertion. Ah! Mr. O'Reilly, delighted to find you punctual. Let me present you to my old friend Sir Giles St. George. I believe, gentlemen, you need no introduction to each other. Burton has disappointed us; so we may order dinner at once."

As Mr. Heffernan took the head of the table, not a sign of his former chagrin remained to be seen. An air of easy conviviality had entirely replaced his previous look of irritation, and in his laughing eye and mellow voice there seemed the clearest evidence of a mind perfectly at ease, and a spirit well disposed to enjoy the pleasures of the board. Of his guests, Godfrey was a leading member of the Irish bar, a man of good private fortune and a large practice, who, out of whim rather than from any great principle, had placed himself in contiuual opposition to the Government, and felt grievously injured and affronted when the minister, affecting to overlook his enmity, offered him a silk gown. Hume was a Commissioner of Customs, and had been so for some thirty years; his only ambition in life being to retire on his full salary, having previously filled his department with his sons and grandsons. The gentle remonstrances of the Secretary against his plan had made him one of the disaffected, but without courage to avow or influence to direct his animosity. Of Mr. O'Reilly the reader needs no further mention. Such was the party who now sat at a table most luxuriously supplied; for although Heffeman was very far from a frequent inviter, yet his dinners were admirably arranged, and the excellence of his wine was actually a mystery among the *bons vivants* of the capital. The conversation turned of course upon the great event of the day; but so artfully was the subject managed by Heffeman that the discussion took rather the shape of criticism on the several speakers, and their styles of delivery, than on the matter of the meeting itself.

"How eager the Castle folks will be to know all about it!" said Godfrey. "Cooke is, I hear, in a sad taking to learn the meaning of the gathering."

"I fancy, sir," said St. George, "they are more indifferent than you suppose. A meeting held by individuals of a certain rank and property, and convened with a certain degree of ostentation, can scarcely ever be formidable to a government."

"You forget the Volunteers," said Heffernan.

"No, I remember their assembling well enough, and a very absurd business they made of it. The Bishop of Downe was the only man of nerve amongst them; and as for Lord Charlemont, the thought of an attainder was never out of his head till the whole association was disbanded."

"They were very formidable, indeed," said Heffernan, gravely. "I can assure you that the Government were far more afraid of their defenders than of the French."

"A government that is ungrateful enough to neglect its supporters," chimed in Hume, "men that have spent their best years in *its* service, can scarcely esteem itself very secure. In the department I belong to myself, for instance—"

"Yours is a very gross case," interrupted Heffernan, who from old experience knew what was coming, and wished to arrest it.

"Thirty-four years, come November next, have I toiled as a commissioner."

"Unpaid!" exclaimed St. George, with a well-simulated horror,— "unpaid!"

"No, sir; not without my salary, of course. I never heard of any man holding an office in the Revenue for the amusement it might afford him. Did you, Godfrey?"

"As for me," said the lawyer, "I spurn their patronage. I well know the price men pay for such favors."

"What object could it be to *you*," said Heffernan, "to be made Attorney-General or placed on the bench, a man independent in every seuse? So I said to Castlereagh, when he spoke on the subject: 'Never mind Godfrey,' said I, 'he'll refuse your offers; you'll only offend him by solicitation;' and when he mentioned the 'Rolls'—"

Here Heffernan paused, and filled his glass leisurely. An interruption contrived to stimulate Godfrey's curiosity, and which perfectly succeeded, as he asked in a voice of tremulous eagerness,—

"Well, what did you say?"

"Just as I replied before,—'he 'll refuse you.'"

"Quite right, perfectly right; you have my unbounded gratitude for the answer," said Godfrey, swallowing two bumpers as rapidly as he could fill them.

"Very different treatment from what I met,—an old and tried supporter of the party," said Hume, turning to O'Reilly and opening upon him the whole narrative of his long-suffering neglect.

"It's quite clear, then," said St. George, "that we are agreed,—the best thing for us would be a change of Ministry."

"I don't think so at all," interposed Heffernan.

"Why, Con," interrupted the baronet, "they should have *you* at any price,—however these fellows have learned the trick,—the others know nothing about it You 'd be in office before twenty-four hours."

"So I might to-morrow," said Heffernan. "There's scarcely a single post of high emolument and trust that I have not been offered and refused. The only things I ever stipulated for in all my connection with the Government were certain favors for my personal friends." Here he looked significantly towards O'Reilly; but the glance was intercepted by the commissioner, who cried out,—"Well, could they say I had no claim? Could they deny thirty-four years of toil and slavery?"

"And in the case for which I was most interested," resumed Heffernan, not heeding the interruption, "the favor I sought would have been more justly bestowed from the rank and merits of the party than as a recompense for any sen-ices of mine."

"I won't say that, Heffernan," said Hume, with a look of modesty, who with the most implicit good faith supposed he was the party alluded to; "I won't go that far; but I will and must say, that after four-and-thirty years as a commissioner—"

"A man must have laid by a devilish pretty thing for the rest of his life," said St. George, who felt all the bitterness of a narrow income augmented by the croaking complaints of the well-salaried official.

"Well, I hope better days are coming for all of us," said Heffernan, desirous of concluding the subject ere it should take an untoward turn.

"You have got a very magnificent seat in the west, sir," said St. George, addressing O'Reilly, who during the whole evening had done little more than assent or smile concurrence with the several speakers.

"The finest thing in Ireland," interrupted Heffernan.

"Nay, that is saying too much," said O'Reilly, with a look of half-real, half-affected bashfulness. "The abbey certainly stands well, and the timber is well grown."

"Are you able to see Clew Bay from the small drawing-room still?— for I remember remarking that the larches on the side of the glen would eventually intercept the prospect."

"You know the Abbey, then?" asked O'Reilly, forgetting to answer the question addressed to him.

"Oh, I knew it well. My family is connected-distantly, I believe—with the Darcys, and in former days we were intimate. A very sweet place it was; I am speaking of thirty years ago, and of course it must have improved since that."

"My friend here has given it every possible opportunity," said Heffernan, with a courteous inclination of the head.

"I've no doubt of it," said St. George; "but neither money nor bank securities will make trees grow sixty feet in a twelvemonth. The improvements I allude to were made by Maurice Darcy's father; he sunk forty thousand pounds in draining, planting, subsoiling, and what not. He left a rent-charge in his will to continue his plans; and Maurice and his son— what's the young fellow called?—Lionel, isn't it?—well, they are, or rather they were, bound to expend a very heavy sum annually on the property."

A theme less agreeable to O'Reilly's feelings could scarcely have been started; and though Heffernan saw as much, he did not dare to interrupt it suddenly, for fear of any unpalatable remark from St. George. Whether from feeling that the subject was a painful one, or that he liked to indulge his loquacity in detailing various particulars of the Darcys and their family circumstances, the old man went on without ceasing,—now narrating some strange caprice of an ancestor in one century, now some piece of good fortune that occurred to another. "You know the old prophecy in the family, I suppose, Mr. O'Reilly?" said he, "though, to be sure, you are not very likely to give it credence."

"I scarcely can say I remember what you allude to."

"By Jove, I thought every old woman in the west would have told it to you. How is this the doggerel runs—ay, here it is,—

'A new name in this house shall never begin
Till twenty-one Darcys have died in Gwynne.'

Now, they say that, taking into account all of the family who have fallen in battle, been lost at sea, and so on, only eleven of the stock died at the Abbey."

Although O'Reilly affected to smile at the old rhyme, his cheek became deadly pale, and his hand shook as he lifted the glass to his lips. It was no vulgar sense of fear, no superstitious dread that moved his cold and calculating spirit, but an emotion of suppressed anger that the ancient splendor of the Darcys should be thus placed side by side with his own unhonored and unknown family.

"I don't think I ever knew one of these good legends have even so much of truth,—though the credit is now at an end," said Heffernau, gayly.

"I'll engage old Darcy's butler wouldn't agree with you," replied St. George. "Ay, and Maurice himself had a great dash of old Irish superstition in him, for a clever, sensible fellow as he was."

"It only remains for my friend here, then, to fit up a room for the Darcys and invite them to die there at their several conveniences," said Con, laughing. "I see no other mode of fulfilling the destiny."

"There never was a man played his game worse," resumed St. George, who with a pertinacious persistence continued the topic. "He came of age with a large unencumbered estate, great family influence, and a very fair share of abilities. It was the fashion to say he had more, but I never thought so; and now, look at him!"

"He had very heavy losses at play," said Heffernan, "certainly."

"What if he had? They never could have materially affected a fortune like his. No, no. I believe 'Honest Tom' finished him,—raising money to pay off old debts, and then never clearing away the liabilities. What a stale trick, and how invariably it succeeds!"

"You do not seem, sir, to take into account an habitually expensive mode of living," insinuated O'Reilly, quietly.

"An item, of course, but only an item in the sum total," replied St. George. "No man can eat and drink above ten thousand a year, and Darcy had considerably more. No; he might have lived as he pleased, had he escaped the acquaintance of honest Tom Gleeson. By the by, Con, is there any truth in the story they tell about this fellow, and that he really was more actuated by a feeling of revenge towards Darcy than a desire for money?"

"I never heard the story. Did you, Mr. O'Reilly?" asked Heffernan.

"Never," said O'Reilly, affecting an air of unconcern, very ill consorting with his pale cheek and anxious eye.

"The tale is simply this: that, as Gleeson waxed wealthy, and began to assume a position in life, he one day called on the Knight to request him to put his name up for ballot at 'Daly's.' Darcy was thunderstruck, for it was in those days when the Club was respectable; but still the Knight had tact enough to dissemble his astonishment, and would doubtless have got through the difficulty had it not been for Bagenal Daly, who was present, and called out, 'Wait till Tuesday, Maurice, for I mean to propose M'Cleery, the breeches-maker, and then the thing won't seem so remarkable!' Gleeson smiled and slipped away, with an oath to his own heart, to be revenged on both of them. If there be any truth in the story, he did ruin Daly, by advising some money-lender to buy up all his liabilities."

"I must take the liberty to correct you, sir," said O'Reilly, actually trembling with anger. "If your agreeable anecdote has no better foundation than the concluding hypothesis, its veracity is inferior to its ingenuity. The gentleman you are pleased to call a money-lender is my father; the conduct you allude to was simply the advance of a large sum on mortgage."

"Foreclosed, like Darcy's, perhaps," said St. George, his irascible face becoming blood-red with passion.

"Come, come, Giles, you really can know nothing of the subject you are talking of; besides, to Mr. O'Reilly the matter is a personal one."

"So it is," muttered St. George; "and if report speaks truly, as unpleasant as personal."

This insulting remark was not heard by O'Reilly, who was deeply engaged in explaining to the lawyer beside him the minute legal details of the circumstance.

"Shrewd a fellow as Gleeson was," said St. George, interrupting O'Reilly, by addressing the lawyer, "they say he has left some flaw open in the matter, and that Darcy may recover a very large portion of the lost estate."

"Yes; if for instance this bond should be destroyed. He might move in Equity—"

"He 'd move heaven and earth, sir, if it's Bagenal Daly you mean," said St. George, who had stimulated his excitement by drinking freely. "Some will tell you that he is a steadfast, firm friend; but I 'll vouch for it, a more determined enemy never drew breath."

"Very happily for the world we live in, sir," said O'Reilly, "there are agencies more powerful than the revengeful and violent natures of such men as Mr. Daly."

"He's every jot as quick-sighted as he's determined; and when he wagered a hogshead of claret that Darcy would one day sit again at the head of his table in Gwynne Abbey—"

"Did he make such a bet?" asked O'Reilly, with a faint laugh.

"Yes; he walked down the club-room, and offered it to any one present, and none seemed to fancy it; but young Kelly, of Kildare, who, being a new member just come in, perhaps thought there might be some *éclat* in booking a bet with Bagenal Daly."

"Would you like to back his opinion, sir?" said O'Reilly, with a simulated softness of voice; "or although I rarely wager, I should have no objection to convenience you here, leaving the amount entirely at your option."

"Which means," said St. George, as his eyes sparkled with wine and passion, "that the weight of *your* purse is to tilt the beam against that of *my* opinion. Now, I beg leave to tell you—"

"Let me interrupt you, Giles; I never knew my Burgundy disagree with any man before, but I d smash every bottle of it to-morrow if I thought it could make so pleasant a fellow so wrong-headed and unreasonable. What say you if we qualify it with some cognac and water?"

"Maurice Darcy is my relative," said St. George, pushing his glass rudely from him, "and I have yet to learn the unreasonableness of wishing well to a member of one's own family. His father and mine were like brothers! Ay, by Jove! I wonder what either of them would think of the changes time has wrought in their sons' fortunes." His voice dropped into a low, muttering sound, while he mumbled on, "One a beggar and an exile, the other"— here his eye twinkled with a malicious intelligence as he glanced around the board—"the other the guest of Con Heffernan." He arose as he spoke, and fortunately the noise thus created prevented his words being overheard. "You 're right, Con," said he, "that Burgundy has been too much for me. The wine is unimpeachable, notwithstanding."

The others rose also; although pressed in all the customary hospitality of the period to have "one bottle more," they were resolute in taking leave, doubtless not sorry to escape the risk of any unpleasant termination to the evening's entertainment.

The lawyer and the commissioner agreed to see St. George home; for although long seasoned to excesses, age had begun to tell upon him, and his limbs were scarcely more under control than his tongue. O'Reilly had dropped his handkerchief, he was not sure whether in the drawing or the dinner room, and this delayed him a few moments behind the rest; and although he declared, at each moment, the loss of no consequence, and repeated his "good-night," Heffernan held his hand and would not suffer him to leave.

"Try under Mr. O'Reilly's chair, Thomas.—Singular specimen of a by-gone day, the worthy baronet!" said he, with a shrug of his shoulders. "Would you believe it, he and Darcy have not been on speaking terms for thirty years, and yet how irritable be showed himself in his behalf!"

"He seems to know something of the family affairs, however," said O'Reilly, cautiously.

"Not more than club gossip; all that about Daly and his wager is a week old."

"I hope my father may never hear it," said O'Reilly, compassionately; "he has all the irritability of age, and these reports invariably urge him on to harsh measures, which, by the least concession, he would never have pursued. The Darcys, indeed, have to thank themselves for any severity they have experienced at our hands. Teasing litigation and injurious reports of us have met all our efforts at conciliation."

"A compromise would have been much better, and more reputable for all parties," said Heffernan, as he turned to stir the fire, and thus purposely averted his face while making the remark.

"So it would," said O'Reilly, hurriedly; then stopping abruptly short, he stammered out, "I don't exactly know what you mean by the word, but if it implies a more amicable settlement of all disputed points between us, I perfectly agree with you."

Heffernan never spoke: a look of cool self-possession and significance was all his reply. It seemed to say, "Don't hope to cheat *me*; however, you may rely on my discretion."

"I declare my handkerchief is in my pocket all this while," said O'Reilly, trying to conceal his rising confusion with a laugh. "Good-night, once more—you 're thinking of going over to England to-morrow evening?"

"Yes, if the weather permits, I 'll sail at seven. Can I be of any service to you?"

"Perhaps so: I may trouble you with a commission. Good-night."

"So, Mr. Hickman, you begin to feel the hook! Now let us see if we cannot play the fish without letting him know the weakness of the tackle!" said Heffernan, as he looked after him, and then slowly retraced his steps to the now deserted drawing-room.

"How frequently will chance play the game more skilfully for us than all our cleverness!" said he, while he paced the room alone. "That old bear, St. George, who might have ruined everything, has done me good service. O'Reilly's suspicions are awakened, his fears are aroused; could I only find a clew to his terror, I could hold him as fast by his fears as by this same baronetcy. This baronetcy," added he, with a sneering laugh, "that I am to negotiate for, and—be refused!"

With this sentiment of honest intentions on his lips, Mr. Heffernan retired to rest, and, if this true history is to be credited, to sleep soundly till morning.

CHAPTER XVI
PAUL DEMPSEY'S WALK

With the most eager desire to accomplish his mission, Paul Dempsey did not succeed in reaching "The Corvy" until late on the day after Miss Daly's visit. He set out originally by paths so secret and circuitous that he lost his way, and was obliged to pass his night among the hills, where, warned by the deep thundering of the sea that the cliffs were near, he was fain to await daybreak ere he ventured farther. The trackless waste over which his way led was no bad emblem of poor Paul's mind, as, cowering beneath a sand-hill, he shivered through the long hours of night. Swayed by various impulses, he could determine on no definite line of action, and wavered and doubted and hesitated, till his very brain was addled by its operations.

At one moment he was disposed, like good Launcelot Gobbo, to "run for it," and, leaving Darcy and all belonging to him to their several fates, to provide for his own safety; when suddenly a dim vision of meeting Maria Daly in this world or the next, and being called to account for his delinquency, routed such determinations. Then he revelled in the glorious opportunity for gossip afforded by the whole adventure. How he should astonish Coleraine and its neighborhood by his revelations of the Knight and his family! Gossip in all its moods and tenses, from the vague indicative of mere innuendo, to the full subjunctive of open defamation! Not indeed that Mr. Dempsey loved slander for itself; on the contrary, his temperament was far more akin to kindliness than its opposite; but the passion for retailing one's neighbor's foibles or misfortunes is an impulse that admits no guidance; and as the gambler would ruin his best friend at play, so would the professed gossip calumniate the very nearest and dearest to him on earth. There are in the social as in the mercantile world characters who never deal in the honest article of commerce, but have a store of damaged, injured, or smuggled goods, to be hawked about surreptitiously, and always to be sold in the "strictest secrecy." Mr. Dempsey was a pedler in this wise, and, if truth must be told, he did not dislike his trade.

And yet, at moments, thoughts of another and more tender kind were wafted across Paul's mind, not resting indeed long enough to make any deep impression, but still leaving behind them, as pleasant thoughts always will, little twilights of happiness. Paul had been touched—a mere graze, skin deep, but still touched—by Helen Darcy's beauty and fascinations. She had accompanied him more than once on the piano while he sang, and whether the long-fringed eyelashes and the dimpled cheek had done the mischief, or that the thoughtful tact with which she displayed Paul's good notes and glossed over his false ones had won his gratitude, certain is it he had already felt a very sensible regard for the young lady, and more than once caught himself, when thinking about her, speculating on the speedy demise of Bob Dempsey, of Dempsey's Grove, and all the consequences that might ensue therefrom.

If the enjoyment Mr. Dempsey's various peculiarities afforded Helen suggested on her part the semblance of pleasure in his society, Paul took these indications all in his own favor, and even catechized himself how far he might be deemed culpable in winning the affections of a charming young lady, so long as his precarious condition forbid all thought of matrimony. Now, however, that he knew who the family really were, such doubts were much allayed; for, as he wisely remarked to himself, "Though they are ruined, there's always nice picking in the wreck of an Indiaman!" Such were the thoughts by which his way was beguiled, when late in the afternoon he reached "The Corvy."

Lady Eleanor and her daughter were out walking when Mr. Dempsey arrived, and, having cautiously reconnoitred the premises, ventured to approach the door. All was quiet and tranquil about the cottage; so, reassured by this, he peered through the window into the large hall, where a cheerful fire now blazed and shed a mellow glow over the strange decorations of the chamber. Mr. Dempsey had often desired an opportunity of examining these curiosities at his leisure. Not indeed prompted thereto by any antiquarian taste, but, from a casual glance at the inscriptions, he calculated on the amount of private history of the Dalys he should obtain. Stray and independent facts, it is true, but to be arranged by the hand of a competent and clever commentator.

With cautious hand he turned the handle of the door and entered.

There he stood, in the very midst of the coveted objects; and never did humble bookworm gaze on the rich titles of an ample library with more enthusiastic pleasure. He drew a long breath to relieve his overburdened heart, and glutted his eyes in ecstasy on every side. Enthusiasm takes its tone from individuality, and doubtless Mr. Dempsey felt at that moment something as Belzoni might, when, unexpectedly admitted within some tomb of the Pyramids, he found himself about to unravel some secret history of the Pharaohs.

"Now for it," said he, half aloud; "let us do the thing in order; and first of all, what have we here?" He stooped and read an inscription attached to a velvet coat embroidered with silver,—

"Coat worn by B. D. in his duel with Colonel Matthews,—62,—the puncture under the sword-arm being a tierce outside the guard; a very rare point, and which cost the giver seriously."

"He killed Matthews, of course," added Dempsey; "the passage can mean nothing else, so let us be accurate as to fact and date."

So saying, he proceeded to note down the circumstance in a little memorandum-book. "So!" added he, as he read his note over; "now for the next. What can this misshapen lump of metal mean?"

"A piece of brute gold, presented with twelve female slaves by the chiefs of Doolawochyeekeka on B. D.'s assuming the sovereignty of the island."

"Brute gold," said Mr. Dempsey; "devilish little of the real thing about it, I'll be sworn! I suppose the ladies were about equally refined and valuable."

"Glove dropped by the Infanta Donna Isidore within the arena at Madrid, a few moments after Ruy Peres da Castres was gored to death."

A prolonged low whistle from Mr. Dempsey was the only comment he made on this inscription; while he stooped to examine the fragment of a bull's horn, from which a rag of scarlet cloth was hanging. The inscription ran, "Portion of horn broken as the bull fell against the barrier of the circus. The cloth was part of Da Castres' vest."

A massive antique helmet, of immense size and weight, lay on the floor beside this. It was labelled, "Casque of Rudolf v. Hapsbourg, presented to B. D. after the tilt at Regensburg by Edric Conrad Wilhelm Kur Furst von Bavera, a.d. 1750."

A splendid goblet of silver gilt, beautifully chased and ornamented, was inscribed on the metal as being the gift of the Doge of Venice to his friend Bagenal Daly; and underneath was written on a card, "This cup was drained to the bottom at a draught by B. D. after a long and deep carouse, the liquor strong 'Vino di Cypro.' The Doge tried it and failed; the mark within shows how far he drank."

"By Jove! what a pull!" exclaimed Dempsey, who, as he peered into the capacious vessel, looked as if he would not object to try his own prowess at the feat.

Wonderment at this last achievement seemed completely to have taken possession of Mr. Dempsey; for while his eyes ranged over weapons of every strange form and shape,—armor, idols, stuffed beasts and birds,—they invariably came back to the huge goblet with an admiring wonder that showed that here at least there was an exploit whose merits he could thoroughly appreciate.

"A half-gallon can is nothing to it!" muttered he, as he replaced it on its bracket.

The reflection was scarcely uttered, when the quick tramp of a horse and the sound of wheels without startled him. He hastened to the window just in time to perceive a jaunting-car drive up to the wicket, from which three men descended. Two were common-looking fellows in dark upper coats and glazed hats; the third, better dressed, and with a half-gentlemanlike air, seemed the superior. He threw off a loose travelling-coat, and discovered, to Mr. Dempsey's horror, the features of his late patient at Larne, the sheriff's officer from Dublin. Yes, there was no doubt about it. That smart, conceited look, the sharp and turned-up nose, the scrubby whisker, proclaimed him as the terrible Anthony Nickie, of Jervas Street, a name which Mr. Dempsey had read on his portmanteau before guessing how its owner was concerned in his own interests.

What a multitude of terrors jostled each other in his mind as the men approached the door, and what resolves did he form and abandon in the same moment! To escape by the rear of the house while the enemy was assailing the front, to barricade the premises and stand a siege, to arm himself—and there was a choice of weapons—and give battle, were all rapid impulses no sooner conceived than given up. A loud summons of the door-bell announced his presence; and ere the sounds died away, Tate's creaking footstep and winter cough resounded along the corridor. Mr. Dempsey threw a last despairing glance around, and the thought flashed across him, how happily would he exchange his existence with any of the grim images and uncouth shapes that grinned and glared on every side, ay, even with that saw-mouthed crocodile that surmounted the chimney! Quick as his eye traversed the chamber, he fancied that the savage animals were actually enjoying his misery, and Sandy's counterpart appeared to show a diabolical glee at his wretched predicament. It was at this instant he caught sight of the loose folds of the Indian blanket, which enveloped Bagenal Daly's image. The danger was too pressing for hesitation; he stepped into the canoe, and cowering down under the warlike figure, awaited his destiny. Scarcely had the drapery closed around him when Tate admitted the new arrival.

"'The Corvy?'" said Mr. Nickie to the old butler, who with decorous ceremony bowed low before him. "'The Corvy,' ain't it?"

"Yes, sir," replied Tate.

"All right, Mac," resumed Nickie, turning to the elder of his two followers, who had closely dogged him to the door. "Bring that carpet-bag and the small box off the car, and tell the fellow he 'll have time to feed his horse at that cabin on the road-side."

He added something in a whisper, too low for Tate to hear, and then, taking the carpet-bag, he flung it carelessly in a corner, while he walked forward and deposited the box on the table before the fire.

"His honor is coming to dine, maybe?" asked Tate, respectfully; for old habit of his master's hospitality had made the question almost a matter of course, while age had so dimmed his eyesight that even Anthony Nickie passed with him for a gentleman.

"Coming to dine," repeated Nickie, with a coarse laugh; "that's a bargain there 's always two words to, my old boy. I suppose you 've heard it is manners to wait to be asked, eh?—without," added he, after a second's pause,—"without I 'm to take this as an invitation."

"I believe your honor might, then," said Tate, with a smile. "'Tis many a one I kept again the family came home for dinner, and sorrow word of it they knew till they seen them dressed in the drawing-room! And the dinner-table!" said Tate, with a sigh, half in regret over the past, half preparing himself with a sufficiency of breath for a lengthened oration,-"the dinner-table! it's wishing it I am still! After laying for ten, or maybe twelve, his honor would come in and say, 'Tate, we 'll be rather crowded here, for here 's Sir Gore Molony and his family. You 'll have to make room for five more.' Then Miss Helen would come springing in with, 'Tate, I forgot to say Colonel Martin and his officers are to be here at dinner.' After that it would be my lady herself, in her own quiet way, 'Mr. Sullivan,'-she nearly always called me that,—'could n't you contrive a little space here for Lady Burke and Miss MacDonnel? But the captain beat all, for he 'd come in after the soup was removed, with five or six gentlemen from the hunt, splashed and wet up to their necks; over he 'd go to the side-table, where I 'd have my knives and forks, all beautiful, and may I never but he 'd fling some here, others there, till he 'd clear a space away, and then he'd cry, 'Tate, bring back the soup, and set some sherry here.' Maybe that wasn't the table for noise, drinking wine with every one at the big table, and telling such wonderful stories that the servants did n't know what they were doing, listening to them. And the master—the heavens be about him!—sending me over to get the names of the gentlemen, that he might ask them to take wine with him. Oh, dear—oh, dear, I'm sure I used to think my heart was broke with it; but sure it's nigher breaking now that it's all past and over."

"You seem to have had very jolly times of it in those days," said Nickie.

"Faix, your honor might say so if you saw forty-eight sitting down to dinner every day in the parlor for seven weeks running; and Master Lionel— the captain that is—at the head of another table in the library, with twelve or fourteen more,—nice youths they wor!"

While Tate continued his retrospections, Mr. Nickie had unlocked his box, and cursorily throwing a glance over some papers, he muttered to himself a few words, and then added aloud,—"Now for business."

CHAPTER XVII
MR. ANTHONY NICKIE, ATTORNEY-AT-LAW

We have said that Mr. Dempsey had barely time to conceal himself when the door was opened,—so narrow indeed was his escape, that had the new arrival been a second sooner, discovery would have been inevitable; as it was, the pictorial Daly and Sandy rocked violently to and fro, making their natural ferocity and grimness something even more terrible than usual. Mr. Nickie remarked nothing of this. His first care was to divest himself of certain travelling encumbrances, like one who proposes to make a visit of some duration, and then, casting a searching look around the premises, he proceeded,—

"Now for Mr. Darcy—"

"If ye 'r maning the Knight of Gwynne, sir, his honor—"

"Well, is his honor at home?" said the other, interrupting with a saucy laugh.

"No, sir," said Tate, almost overpowered at the irreverence of his questioner.

"When do you expect him, then,—in an hour or two hours?"

"He 's in England," said Tate, drawing a long breath.

"In England! What do you mean, old fellow? He has surely not left this lately?"

"Yes, sir, 'twas the King sent for him, I heerd the mistress say."

A burst of downright laughter from the stranger stopped poor Tate's explanation.

"Why, it's *you* his Majesty ought to have invited," cried Mr. Nickie, wiping his eyes, "*you yourself*, man; devilish fit company for each other you 'd be."

Poor Tate had not the slightest idea of the grounds on which the stranger suggested his companionship for royalty, but he was not the less insulted at the disparagement of his master thus implied.

"'T is little I know about kings or queens," growled out the old man, "but they must be made of better clay than ever I seen yet, or they 're not too good company for the Knight of Gwynne."

After a stare for some seconds, half surprise, half insolence, Nickie said, "You can tell me, perhaps, if this cottage is called 'The Corvy'?"

"Ay, that's the name of it."

"The property of one Bagenal Daly, Esquire, isn't it?"

Tate nodded an assent.

"Maybe he is in England too," continued Nickie. "Perhaps it was the Queen sent for him,—he 's a handsome man, I suppose?"

"Faix, you can judge for yourself," said Tate, "for there he is, looking at you this minute."

Nickie turned about hastily, while a terrible fear shot through him that his remarks might have been heard by the individual himself; for, though a stranger to Daly personally, he was not so to his reputation for hare-brained daring and rashness, nor was it till he had stared at the wooden representative for some seconds that he could dispel his dread of the original.

"Is that like him?" asked he, affecting a sneer.

"As like as two pays," said Tate, "barring about the eyes; Mr. Daly's is brighter and more wild-looking. The Blessed Joseph be near us!" exclaimed the old man, crossing himself devoutly, "one would think the crayture knew what we were saying. Sorra lie in 't, there 's neither luck nor grace in talking about you!"

This last sentiment, uttered in a faint voice, was called forth by an involuntary shuddering of poor Mr. Dempsey, who, feeling that the whole scrutiny of the party was directed towards his hiding-place, trembled so violently that the plumes nodded, and the bone necklace jingled with the motion.

While Mr. Nickie attributed these signs to the wind, he at the same time conceived a very low estimate of poor Tate's understanding,—an impression not altogether un-warranted by the sidelong and stealthy looks which he threw at the canoe and its occupants.

"You seem rather afraid of Mr. Daly," said he, with a sneering laugh.

"And so would you be, too, if he was as near you as that chap is," replied Tate, sternly. "I 've known braver-looking men than either of us not like to stand before him. I mind the day—"

Tate-s reminiscences were brought to a sudden stop by perceiving his mistress and Miss Darcy approaching the cottage; and hastening forward, he threw open the door, while by way of introduction he said,—

"A gentleman for the master, my Lady."

Lady Eleanor flushed up, and as suddenly grew pale. She guessed at once the man and his errand.

"The Knight of Gwynne is from home, sir," said she, in a voice her efforts could not render firm.

"I understand as much, madam," said Nickie, who was struggling to recover the easy self-possession of his manner with the butler, but whose awkwardness increased at every instant. "I believe you expect him in a day or two?"

This was said to elicit if there might be some variance in the statement of Lady Eleanor and her servant.

"You are misinformed, sir. He is not in the kingdom, nor do I anticipate his speedy return."

"So I told him, my Lady," broke in the old butler. "I said the King wanted him—"

"You may leave the room, Tate," said Lady Eleanor, who perceived with annoyance the sneering expression old Tate's simplicity had called up in the stranger's face. "Now, sir," said she, turning towards him, "may I ask if your business with the Knight of Gwynne is of that nature that cannot be transacted in his absence or through his law agent?"

"Scarcely, madam," said Nickie, with a sententious gravity, who, in the vantage-ground his power gave him, seemed rather desirous of prolonging the interview. "Mr. Darcy's part can scarcely be performed by deputy, even if he found any one friendly enough to undertake it."

Lady Eleanor never spoke, but her hand grasped her daughter's more closely, and they both stood pale and trembling with agitation. Helen was the first to rally from this access of terror, and with an assured voice she said,—

"You have heard, sir, that the Knight of Gwynne is absent; and as you say your business is with him alone, is there any further reason for your presence here?"

Mr. Nickie seemed for a moment taken aback by this unexpected speech, and for a few seconds made no answer; his nature and his calling, however, soon supplied presence of mind, and with an air of almost insolent familiarity he answered,—

"Perhaps there may be, young lady." He turned, and opening the door, gave a sharp whistle, which was immediately responded to by a cry of "Here we are, sir," and the two followers already mentioned entered the cottage.

"You may have heard of such a thing as an execution, ma'am," said Nickie, addressing Lady Eleanor, in a voice of mock civility, "the attachment of property for debt. This is part of my business at the present moment."

"Do you mean here, sir—in this cottage?" asked Lady Eleanor, in an accent scarcely audible from terror.

"Yes, ma'am, just so. The law allows fourteen days for redemption, with payment of costs, until which time these men here will remain on the premises; and although these gimcracks will scarcely pay my client's costs, we must only make the best of it."

"But this property is not ours, sir. This cottage belongs to a friend."

"I am aware of that, ma'am. And that friend is about to answer for his own sins on the present occasion, and not yours. These chattels are attached as the property of Bagenal Daly, Esquire, at the suit of Peter Hickman, formerly of Loughrea, surgeon and apothecary."

"Is Mr. Daly aware-does he know of these proceedings?" gasped Lady Eleanor, faintly.

"In the multiplicity of similar affairs, ma'am, it is quite possible he may have let this one escape his memory; for if I don't mistake, he has two actions pending in the King's Bench, an answer in equity, three cases of common assault, and a contempt ol court,—all upon his hands for this present session, not to speak of what this may portend."

Here he took a newspaper from his pocket, and having doubled down a paragraph, handed it to Lady Eleanor.

Overwhelmed by grief and astonishment, she made no motion to take the paper, and Mr. Nickie, turning to Helen, read aloud,—

"'There is a rumor prevalent in the capital this morning, to which we cannot, in the present uncertainty as to fact, make any more than a guarded allusion. It is indeed one of those strange reports which we can neither credit nor reject,—the only less probable thing than its truth being that any one could deliberately fabricate so foul a calumny. The story in its details we forbear to repeat; the important point, however, is to connect the name of a well-known and eccentric late M. P. for an Irish borough with the malicious burning of Newgate, and the subsequent escape of the robber Freney.

"'The reasons alleged for this most extraordinary act are so marvellous, absurd, and contradictory that we will not trifle with our readers' patience by recounting them. The most generally believed one, however, is, that the senator and the highwayman had maintained, for years past, an intercourse of a very confidential nature, the threat to reveal which, on his trial, Freney used as compulsory means of procuring his escape.'

"Carrick goes further," added Mr. Nickie, as he restored the paper to his pocket, "and gives the name of Bagenal Daly, Esq., in full; stating, besides, that he sailed for Halifax on Sunday last."

Lady Eleanor and Helen exchanged looks of intelligent meaning, as he finished the paragraph. To them Daly's hurried departure had a most significant importance.

"This, ma'am, among other reasons," resumed Nickie, "was another hint to my client to press his claim; for Mr. Daly's departure once known, there would soon be a scramble for the little remnant of his property. With your leave, I 'll now put the keepers in possession. Perhaps you 'll not be offended," added he, in a lower tone, "if I remark that it's usual to offer the men some refreshment. Come here, M'Dermot," said he, aloud,-"a very respectable man, and married, too,—the ladies will make you comfortable, Mick, and I 'm sure you 'll be civil and obliging."

A grunt and a gesture with both hands was the answer.

"Falls, we'll station you in the kitchen; mind you behave yourself.

"I 'll just take a slight inventory of the principal things,—a mere matter of form, ma'am,—I know you 'll not remove one of them," said Mr. Nickie, who, like most coarsely minded people, was never more offensive than when seeking to be complimentary. He did not notice, however, the indignant look with which his speech was received, but proceeded regularly in his office.

There is something insupportably offensive and revolting in the business-like way of those who execute the severities of the law. Like the undertaker, they can sharpen the pangs of misfortune by vulgarizing its sorrows. Lady Eleanor gazed, in but half-consciousness, at the scene; the self-satisfied assurance of the chief, the ruffian contented-ness of his followers, grating on every prejudice of her mind. Not so Helen; more quick to reason on impressions, she took in, at a glance, their sad condition, and saw that, in a few days at furthest, they should be houseless as well as friendless in the world,—no one near to counsel or to succor them! Such were her thoughts as almost mechanically her eyes followed the sheriff's officer through the chamber.

"Not that, sir," cried she, hastily, as he stopped in front of a miniature of her father, and was noting it down in his list, among the objects of the apartment,—"not that, sir."

"And why not, miss?" said Nickie, with a leer of impudent familiarity.

"It is a portrait of the Knight of Gwynne, sir, and *our* property."

"Sorry for it, miss, but the law makes no distinction with regard to property on the premises. You can always recover by a replevin."

"Come, Helen, let us leave this," said Lady Eleanor, faintly; "come away, child."

"You said, sir," said Helen, turning hastily about,—"you said, sir, that these proceedings were taken at the suit of Dr. Hickman. Was it his desire that we should be treated thus?"

"Upon my word, young lady, he gave no special directions on the subject, nor, if he had, would it signify much. The law, once set in motion, must take its course; I suppose you know that."

Helen did not hear his speech out, for, yielding to her mother, she quitted the apartment.

Mr. Nickie stood for a few moments gazing at the door by which they had made their exit, and then, turning towards M'Dermot, with a knowing wink he said, "We'll be better friends before we part, I 'll engage, little as she likes me now."

"Faix, I never seen yer equal at getting round them," answered the sub, in a voice of fawning flattery, the very opposite of his former gruff tone.

"That's the way I always begin, when they take a saucy way with them," resumed Nickie, who felt evidently pleased at the other's admiration. "And when they 're brought down a bit to a sense of their situation, I can just be as kind as I was cruel."

"Never fear ye!" said M'Dermot, with a sententious shake of the head. "Devil a taste of her would lave the room, if it wasn't for the mother."

"I saw that plain enough," said Nickie, as he threw a self-approving look at himself in a tall mirror opposite.

"She's a fine young girl, there's no denying it," said M'Dermot, who anticipated, as the result of his chief's attention, a more liberal scale of treatment for himself. "But I don't know how ye 'll ever get round her, though to be sure if *you* can't, who can?"

"This inventory will keep me till night," said Nickie, changing the theme quite suddenly, "and I'll miss Dempsey, I 'm afraid."

"I hope not; sure you have his track,—haven't you?"

"Yes, and I have four fellows after him, along the shore here, but they say he 's cunning as a fox. Well, I 'll not give him up in a hurry, that's all. Is that rain I hear against the glass, Mick?"

"Ay, and dreadful rain too!" said the other, peeping through the window, which now rattled and shook with a sudden squall of wind. "You 'll not be able to leave this so late."

"So I 'm thinking, Mick," said Nickie, laying down his writing-materials, and turning his back to the fire; "I believe I must stay where I am."

"'T is yourself is the boy!" cried Mick, with a look of admiration at his master.

"You 're wrong, Mick," said he, with a scarce repressed smile, "all wrong; I wasn't thinking of her."

"Maybe not," said M'Dermot, shaking his head doubtfully; "maybe she's not thinking of you this minute! But, afther all, I don't know how ye 'll do it. Any one would say the vardic was again you."

"So it is, man, but can't we move for a new trial?" So saying, he turned suddenly about, and pulled the bell.

M'Dermot said nothing, but stood staring at his chief, with a well-feigned expression of wonderment, as though to say, "What is he going to do next?"

The summons was speedily answered by old Tate, who stood in respectful attention within the door. Not the slightest suspicion had crossed the butler's mind of Mr. Nickie's calling, or of his object with the Knight, or his manner would certainly have displayed a very different politeness. "Didn't you ring, sir?" said he, with a bow to Nickie, who now seemed vacillating, and uncertain how to proceed.

"Yes—I did—ring—the—bell," replied he, hesitating between each word of the sentence. "I was about to say that, as the night was so severe,—a perfect hurricane it seems,—I should remain here. Eh, did you speak?"

"No, sir," replied Tate, respectfully.

"You can inform your mistress, then, and say, with Mr. Nickie's respectful compliments,-mind that!—that if they have no objection, he would be happy to join them at supper."

Tate stood as if transfixed, not a sign of anger, not even of surprise in his features. The shock had actually stupefied him.

"Do ye hear what the gentleman 's saying to you?" asked Mick, in a stern voice.

"Sir?" said Tate, endeavoring to recover his routed faculties,—"sir?"

"Tell the old fool what I said," muttered Nickie, with angry impatience; and then, as if remembering that his message might possibly be not over-courteously worded by Mr. M'Dennot, he approached Tate, and said, "Give your mistress Mr. Nickie's compliments, and say that, not being able to return to Coleraine, he hopes he may be permitted to pass the evening with her and Miss Darcy." This message, uttered with great rapidity, as if the speaker dare not trust himself with more deliberation, was accompanied by a motion of the hand, which half pushed the old butler from the room.

Neither Mr. Nickie nor his subordinate exchanged a word during Tate's absence. The former, indeed, seemed far less confident of his success than at first, and M'Dermot waited the issue, for his cue what part to take in the transaction.

If Tate's countenance, when he left the room, exhibited nothing but confusion and bewilderment, when he reentered it his looks were composed and steadfast.

"Well?" said Nickie, as the old butler stood for a second without speaking,—"well?"

"Her Ladyship says that you and the other men, sir, may receive any accommodation the house affords." He paused for a moment or two, and then added, "Her Ladyship declines Mr. Nickie's society."

"Did she give you that message herself?" asked Nickie, hastily; "are those her own words?"

"Them's her words," said Tate, dryly.

"I never heerd the likes—"

"Stop, Mick, hold your tongue!" said Nickie, to his over-zealous follower; while he muttered to himself, "My name is n't Anthony Nickie, or I 'll make her repent that speech! Ay, faith," said he, aloud, as turning to the portrait of the Knight he appeared to address it, "you shall come to the hammer as the original did before you." If Tate had understood the purport of this sarcasm, it is more than probable the discussion would have taken another form; as it was, he listened to Mr. Nickie's orders about the supper with due decorum, and retired to make the requisite preparations. "I will make a night of it, by———-," exclaimed Nickie, as with clinched fist he struck the table before him. "I hope you know how to sing, Mick?"

"I can do a little that way, sir," grinned the ruffian, "when the company is pressin'. If it was n't too loud —"

"Too loud! you may drown the storm out there, if ye 're able. But wait till we have the supper and the liquor before us, as they might cut off the supplies." And with this prudent counsel, they suffered Tate to proceed in his arrangements, without uttering another word.

CHAPTER XVIII
A CONVIVIAL EVENING

While Tate busied himself in laying the table, Mr. Nickie, with bent brows and folded arms, passed up and down the apartments, still ruminating on the affront so openly passed upon him, and cogitating how best to avenge it. As passing and repassing he cast his eyes on the preparations, he halted suddenly, and said, "Lay another cover here." Tate stood, uncertain whether he had heard aright the words, when Nickie repeated, "Don't you hear me? I said lay another cover. The gentleman will sup here."

"Oh! indeed," exclaimed Tate, as, opening his eyes to the fullest extent, he appeared to admit a new light upon his brain; "I beg pardon, sir, I was thinking that this gentleman might like to sup with the other gentleman, out in the kitchen beyond!"

"I said he 'd sup here," said Nickie, vehemently, for he felt the taunt in all its bitterness.

"I say, old fellow," said M'Dermot in Tate's ear, "you needn't be sparin' of the liquor. Give us the best you have, and plenty of it. It is all the same to yer master, you know, in a few days. I was saying, sir," said he to Nickie, who, overhearing him, turned sharply round,-"I was saying, sir, that he might as well give up the ould bin with the cobweb over it. It's the creditors suffers now, and we've many a way of doin' a civil turn."

"His mistress has shut the door on that," said Nickie, savagely, "and she may take the consequences."

"Oh, never mind him," whispered M'Dermot to Tate; "he 's the best-hearted crayture that ever broke bread, but passionate, d' ye mind, passionate."

Poor Tate, who had suddenly become alive to the characters and objects of his quests, was now aware that his mistress's refusal to admit the chief might possibly be productive of very disastrous consequences; for, like all low Irishmen, he had a very ample notion of the elastic character of the law, and thought that its pains and penalties were entirely at the option of him who executed it.

"Her Ladyship never liked to see much company," said he, apologetically.

"Well, maybe so," rejoined M'Dennot, "but in a quiet homely sort of a way, sure she need n't have refused Mr. Anthony; little she knows, there 's not the like of him for stories about the Court of Conscience and the Sessions."

"I don't doubt it," exclaimed Tate, who, in assenting, felt pretty certain that his fascinations would scarcely have met appreciation in the society of his mistress and her daughter.

"And if ye heerd him sing 'Hobson's Choice,' with a new verse of his own at the end!"

Tate threw a full expression of wondering admiration into his features, and went on with his arrangements in silence.

"Does he know anything of Dempsey, do you think?" said Nickie, in a whisper to his follower.

"Not he," muttered the other, scornfully; "the crayture seems half a nat'ral." Then, in a voice pitched purposely loud, he said, "Do you happen to know one Dempsey in these parts?"

"Paul Dempsey?" added Nickie.

"A little, short man, with a turned-up nose, that walks with his shoulders far back and his hands spread out? Ay, I know him well; he dined here one day with the master, and sure enough he made the company laugh hearty!"

"I 'd be glad to meet him, if he 's as pleasant as you say," said Nickie, slyly.

"There's nothing easier, then," said Tate; "since the boarding-house is closed there at Ballintray, he's up in Coleraine for the winter. I hear he waits for the Dublin mail, at M'Grotty's door, every evening, to see the passengers, and that he has a peep at the way-bill before the agent himself."

"Has he so many acquaintances that he is always on the look out for one?"

"Faix, if they'd let him," cried Tate, laughing, "I believe he 'd know every man, woman, and child in Ireland. For curiosity, he beats all ever I seen."

As Tate spoke, a sudden draught of wind seemed to penetrate the chamber,—at least the canoe and its party shook perceptibly.

"We'll have a rare night of it," said Nickie, drawing nearer to the fire. Then resuming, added, "And you say I'll have no difficulty to find him?"

"Not the least, bedad! It would be far harder to escape him, from all I hear. He watches the coach, and never leaves it till he sees the fore boot and the hind one empty; not only looking the passengers in the face, but tumbling over the luggage, reading all the names, and where they 're going. Oh, he's a wonderful man for knowledge!"

"Indeed," said Nickie, with a look of attention to draw on the garrulity of the old man.

"I've reason to remember it well," said Tate, putting both hands to his loins. "It was the day he dined here I got the rheumatiz in the small of my back. When I went to open the gate without there for him, he kept me talking for three quarters of an hour in the teeth of an east wind that would shave a goat,—asking me about the master and the mistress and Miss Helen, ay, and even about myself at last,—if I had any brothers, and what their names was, and who was Mister Daly, and whether he did n't keep a club-house. By my conscience, it's well for him ould Bagenal did n't hear him!"

A clattering sound from the canoe suddenly interrupted Tate's narrative; he stopped short, and muttered, in a tone of unfeigned terror,—

"That's the way always,-may I never see glory! ye can't speak of him but he hears ye!"

A rude laugh from Nickie, chorused still more coarsely by M'Dermot, arrested Tate's loquacity, and he finished his arrangements without speaking, save in a few broken sentences.

If Mr. Nickie could have been conciliated by material enjoyments, he might decidedly have confessed that the preparations for his comfort were ample and hospitable. A hot supper diffused its savory steam on a table where decanters and flasks of wine of different sorts and sizes attested that the more convivial elements of a feast were not forgotten. Good humor was, however, not to be restored by such amends. He was wounded in his self-love, outraged in his vanity; and he sat down in a dogged silence to the meal, a perfect contrast in appearance to the coarse delight of his subordinate.

While Tate remained to wait on them, Nickie's manner and bearing were unchanged. A sullen, sulky expression sat on features which, even when at the best, conveyed little better than a look of shrewd keenness; nor could the appetite with which he eat suggest a passing ray of satisfaction to his face.

"I am glad we are rid of that old fellow at last," said he, as the door closed upon Tate. "Whether fool or knave, I saw what he was at; he would have been disrespectful if he dared."

"I did n't mind him much, sir," said M'Dermot, honestly confessing that the good cheer had absorbed his undivided attention.

"I did, then; I saw his eyes fixed effectually on us,—on you particularly. I thought he would have laughed outright when you helped yourself to the entire duck."

Nickie spoke this with an honest severity, meant to express his discontent with his companion fully as much as with the old butler.

"Well, it was an excellent supper, anyhow," said M'Dermot, taking the bottle which Nickie pushed towards him somewhat rudely; "and here 's wishing health and happiness and long life to ye, Mr. Anthony. May ye always have as plentiful a board, and better company round it."

There was a fawning humility in the fellow's manner that seemed to gratify the other, for he nodded a return to the sentiment, and, after a brief pause, said,—"The servants in these grand houses,—and that old fellow, you may remark, was with the Darcys when they were great people,— they give themselves airs to everybody they think below the rank of their master."

"Faix, they might behave better to *you*, Mr. Anthony," said M'Dermot.

"Well, they're run their course now," said Nickie, not heeding the remark. "Both master and man have had their day. I 've seen more executions on property in the last six months than ever I did in all my life before. Creditors won't wait now as they used to do. No influence now to make gaugers and tide-waiters and militia officers; no privilege of Parliament to save them from arrest!"

"My blessings on them for that, anyhow," said M'Dermot, finishing his glass. "The Union 's a fine thing."

"The fellows that got the bribes—and, to be sure, there was plenty of money going—won't stay to spend it in Ireland; devil a one will remain here, but those that are run out and ruined."

"Bad luck to it for a Bill!" said M'Dermot, who felt obliged to sacrifice his consistency in his desire to concur with each new sentiment of his chief.

"The very wine we're drinking, maybe, was given for a vote. Pitt knew well how to catch them."

"Success attend him!" chimed in M'Dermot.

"And just think of them now," continued Nickie, whose ruminations were never interrupted by the running commentary,—"just think of them! selling the country, trade, prosperity, everything, for a few hundred pounds."

"The blackguards!"

"Some, to be sure, made a fine thing out of it. Not like old Darcy here; they were early in the market, and got both rank and money too."

"Ay, that was doin' it in style!" exclaimed Mike, who expressed himself this time somewhat equivocally, for safety's sake.

"There 's no denying it, Castlereagh was a clever fellow!"

"The best man ever I seen—I don't care who the other is."

"He knew when to bid, and when to draw back; never became too pressing, but never let any one feel himself neglected; watched his opportunities slyly, and when the time came, pounced down like a hawk on his victim."

"Oh, the thieves' breed! What a hard heart he had!" muttered M'Dermot, perfectly regardless of whom he was speaking.

Thus did Mr. Nickie ramble on, in the popular cant, over the subject of the day; for although the Union was now carried, and its consequences—whatever they might be—so far inevitable, the men whose influence effected the measure were still before the bar of public opinion,—an ordeal not a whit more just and discriminating than it usually is. While the current of these reminiscences ran on, varied by some anecdote here or some observation there, both master and man drank deeply. So long as good liquor abounded, Mr. M'Dermot could have listened with pleasure, even to a less entertaining companion; and as for Nickie, he felt a vulgar pride in discussing, familiarly and by name, the men of rank and station who took a leading part in Irish politics. The pamphlets and newspapers of the day had made so many private histories public, had unveiled so many family circumstances before the eyes of the world, that his dissertations had all the seeming authenticity of personal knowledge.

It was at the close of a rather violent denunciation of the "Traitors"—as the Government party was ever called—that Nickie, striking the table with his fist, called on M'Dermot to sing.

"I say, Mac," cried he, with a faltering tongue, and eyes red and bleared from drink,—"the old lady—wouldn't accept my society—she did n't think—An-tho-ny Nickie, Esquire—good enough—to sit down—at her table. Let us show her what she has lost, my boy. Give her 'Bob Uniake's Boots' or 'The Major's Prayer.'"

"Or what d' ye think of the new ballad to Lord Castlereagh, sir?" suggested M'Dermot, modestly. "It was the last thing Rhoudlim had when I left town."

"Is it good?" hiccuped Nickie.

"If ye heerd Rhoudlim—"

"D——n Rhoudlim!—she used to sing that song Parsons made on the attorneys. Parsons never liked us, Mac. You know what he said to Holmes, who went to him for a subscription of five shillings, to help to bury Mat Costegan. 'Was n't he an attorney?' says Parsons. 'He was,' says the other. 'Well, here 's a pound,' says he; 'take it and bury four!'"

"Oh, by my conscience, that was mighty nate!" said M'Dermot, who completely forgot himself.

Nickie frowned savagely at his companion, and for a moment seemed about to express his anger more palpably, when he suddenly drank off his glass, and said, "Well, the song,-let us have it now."

"I 'm afraid—I don't know more than a verse here and there," said Mac, bashfully stroking down his hair, and mincing his words; "but with the help of a chorus—"

"Trust me for that," cried Nickie, who now drank glass after glass without stopping; "I'm always ready for a song." So saying he burst out into a half-lachryinose chant,—

> *"An old maid had a roguish eye!*
> *And she was call'd the great Kamshoodera!*
> *Rich was she and poor was I!*
> *Fol de dol de die do!*

"I forget the rest, Mickie, but it goes on about a Nabob and a bear, and—a—what's this ye call it, a pottle of green gooseberries that Lord Clangoff sold to Mrs. Kelfoyle."

"To be sure; I remember it well," said Mac, humoring the drunken lucubrations; "but my chant is twice as aisy to sing,—the air is the 'Black Joke;' and any one can chorus."

"Well, open the proceedings," hiccuped Nickie; "state the case."

And thus encouraged, Mr. M'Dermot cleared his throat, and in a voice loud and coarse enough to be heard above the howling din, began:—

> *"Though many a mile he's from Erin away,*
> *Here 's health and long life to my Lord Castlereagh,*
> *With his bag full of guineas so bright!*
> *'T was he that made Bishops and Deans by the score,*

And Peers, of the fashion of Lord Donoughmore!
And a Colonel of horse of our friend Billy Lake,
And Wallincourt a Lord,—t'other day but Joe Blake,
With his bag full of guineas so bright.

"Come Beresford, Bingham, Luke Fox, and Tyrone,
Come Kearney, Bob Johnston, and Arthur Malone,
With your bag full of guineas so bright;
Lord Charles Fitzgerald and Kit Fortescue,
And Henry Deane Grady,—we 'll not forget you,
Come Cuffe, Isaac Corry, and General Dunne,
And you Jemmy Vandeleur,—come every one,
With your bag full of guineas so bright.

Come Talbot and Townsend, Come Toler and Trench,
Tho' made for the gallows, ye 're now on the Bench,
With your bag full of guineas so bright
But if ever again this black list I 'll begin,
The first name I 'll take is the ould Knight of Gwynne,
Who, robb'd of his property, stripped of his pelf,
Would be glad to see Erin as poor as himself.
With no bag full of guineas so bright.

"If the Parliament 's gone, and the world it has scoffed us,
What a blessing to think that we 've Tottenham Loftus,
With his bag full of guineas so bright.
Oh, what consolation through every disaster,
To know that your Lordship is made our Postmaster,
And your uncle a Bishop, your aunt—but why mention,
Two thousand a year, 'of a long service pension'
Of a bag full of guineas so bright.

"But what is the change, since your Lordship appears!
You found us all Paupers, you left us all Peers,
With your bag full of guineas so bright.
Not a man in the island, however he boast,
But has a good reason to fill to the toast,—

From Cork to the Causeway, from Howth to Clue Bay,
A health and long life to my Lord Castlereagh,
With his bag full of guineas so bright."

The boisterous accompaniment by which Mr. Nickie testified his satisfaction at the early verses had gradually subsided into a low droning sound, which at length, towards the conclusion, lapsed into a prolonged heavy snore. "Fast!" exclaimed M'Dermot, holding the candle close to his eyes. "Fast!" Then taking up the decanter, he added, "And if ye had gone off before, it would have been no great harm. Ye never had the bottle out of yer grip for the last hour and half!" He heaped some wood on the grate, refilled his glass, and then disposing himself so as to usurp a very large share of the blazing fire, prepared to follow the good example of his chief. Long habit had made an arm-chair to the full as comfortable as a bed to the worthy functionary, and his arrangements were scarcely completed, when his nose announced by a deep sound that he was a wanderer in the land of dreams.

Poor Mr. Dempsey—for if the reader may have forgotten him all this while, we must not—listened long and watchfully to the heavy notes, nor was it without considerable fear that he ventured to unveil his head and take a peep under Daly's arm at the sleepers. Reassured by the seeming heaviness of the slumberers, he dared a step farther, and at last seated himself bolt upright in the canoe, glad to relieve his cramped-up legs, even by this momentary change of position. So cautious were all his movements, so still and noiseless every gesture, that had there been a waking eye to mark him, it would have been hard enough to distinguish between his figure and those of his inanimate neighbors.

The deep and heavy breathing of the sleepers was the only sound to be heard; they snored as if it were a contest between them; still it was long before Dempsey could summon courage enough to issue from his hiding-place, and with stealthy steps approach the table. Cautiously lifting the candle, he first held it to the face of one and then of the other of the sleepers. His next move was to inspect the supper-table, where, whatever the former abundance, nothing remained save the veriest fragments: the bottles too were empty, and poor Dempsey shook his head mournfully as he poured out and drank the last half-glass of sherry in a decanter. This done, he stood for a few minutes reflecting what step he should take next. A sudden change of position of Nickie startled him from these deliberations, and Dempsey cowered down beneath the table in terror. Scarcely daring to breathe, Paul waited while the sleeper moved from side to side, muttering some short and broken words; at length he seemed to have settled himself to his satisfaction, for so his prolonged respiration bespoke. Just as he had turned for the last time, a heavy roll of papers fell from his pocket to the floor. Dempsey eyed the packet with a greedy look, but did not dare to reach his hand towards it, till well assured that the step was safe.

Taking a candle from the table, Paul reseated himself on the floor, and opened a large roll of documents tied with red tape; the very first he unrolled seemed to arrest his attention strongly, and although passing on to the examination of the remainder, he more than once recurred to it, till at length creeping stealthily towards the fire, he placed it among the burning embers, and stirred and poked until it became a mere mass of blackened leaves.

"There," muttered he, "Paul Dempsey 's his own man again. And now what can he do for his friends? Ha, ha! 'Execution against Effects of Bagenal Daly, Esq.,'" said he, reading half aloud; "and this lengthy affair here, 'Instructions to A. N. relative to the enclosed'-let us see what that may be." And so saying, he opened the scroll; a bright flash of flame burst out from among the slumbering embers, and ere it died away Paul read a few lines of the paper. "What scoundrels!" muttered he, as he wiped the perspiration from his forehead, for already had honest Paul's feelings excited him to the utmost. The flame was again flickering, in another moment it would be out, when, stealing forth his hand, he placed an open sheet upon it, and then, as the blaze caught, he laid the entire bundle of papers on the top, and watched them till they were reduced to ashes.

"Maybe it's a felony—I'm sure it's a misdemeanor at least—what I 've done now," muttered he; "but there was no resisting it. I wish I thought it was no heavier crime to do the same by these worthy gentlemen here."

Indeed, for a second or two, Paul's hesitation seemed very considerable. Fear, or something higher in principle, got the victory at length, and after a long silence he said, —

"Well, I 'll not harm them." And with this benevolent sentiment he stood up, and detaching Darcy's portrait from the wall, thrust it into his capacious pocket. This done, he threw another glance over the table, lest some unseen decanter might still remain; but no, except a water-jug of pure element, nothing remained.

"Good-night, and pleasant dreams t'ye both," muttered Paul, as, blowing out one candle, he took the other, and slipped, without the slightest noise, from the room.

CHAPTER XIX
MR. DEMPSEY BEHIND THE SCENE

No very precise or determined purpose guided Mr. Dempsey's footsteps as he issued from the hall and gained the corridor, from which the various rooms of the cottage opened. Benevolent intentions of the vaguest kind towards Lady Eleanor were commingled with thoughts of his own safety, and perhaps more strongly than either, an intense curiosity to inspect the domestic arrangements of the family, not without the hope of finding something to eat.

He had now been about twenty-four hours without food, and to a man who habitually lived in a boarding-house, and felt it a point of honor to consume as much as he could for his weekly pay, the abstinence was far from agreeable. If then his best inspirations were blended with some selfishness, he was not quite unpardonable. Mr. Dempsey tried each door as he went along, and although they were all unlocked, the interiors responded to none of his anticipations. The apartments were plainly but comfortably furnished; in some books lay about, and an open piano told of recent habitation. In one, which he judged rightly to be the Knight's drawing-room, a table was covered over with letters and law papers,—documents which honest Paul beheld with some feeling akin to Aladdin, when he surveyed the inestimable treasures he had no means of carrying away with him from the mine. A faint gleam of light shone from beneath a door at the end of the corridor, and thither with silent footsteps he now turned. All was still: he listened as he drew near; but except the loud ticking of a clock, nothing was to be heard. Paul tried to reconnoitre by the keyhole, but it was closed. He waited for some time unable to decide on the most fitting course, and at length opened the door, and entered. Stopping short at the threshold, Paul raised the candle, to take a better view of the apartment. Perhaps any one save himself would have returned on discovering it was a bedroom. A large old-fashioned bed, with a deep and massive curtain closely drawn, stood against one wall; beside it, on the table, was a night-lamp, from which the faint glimmer he had first noticed proceeded. Some well-stuffed arm-chairs were disposed here and there, and on the tables lay articles of female dress. Mr. Dempsey stood for a few seconds, and perhaps some secret suspicion crept over him that this visit might be thought intrusive. It might be Lady Eleanor's, or perhaps Miss Darcy's chamber. Who was to say she was not actually that instant in bed asleep? Were the fact even so, Mr. Dempsey only calculated on a momentary shock of surprise at his appearance, well assured that his explanation would be admitted as perfectly satisfactory. Thus wrapped in his good intentions, and shrouding the light with one hand, he drew the curtain with the other. The bed was empty, the coverings were smooth, the pillows unpressed. The occupant, whoever it might be, had not yet taken possession. Mr. Dempsey's fatigue was only second to his hunger, and having failed to discover the larder, it is more than probable he would have contented himself with the gratification of a sleep, had he not just at that instant perceived a light flickering beside and beneath the folds of a heavy curtain which hung over a doorway at the farthest end of the room. His spirit of research once more encouraged, he moved towards it, and drawing it very gently, admitted his eye in the interspace. A glass door intervened between him and a small chamber, but permitted him to see without being heard by those within. Flattening his features on the glass, he stared at the scene; and truly one less inspired by the spirit of inquiry might have felt shocked at being thus placed. Lady Eleanor sat in her dressing-gown on a sofa, while, half kneeling, half lying at her feet, was Helen, her head concealed in her mother's lap, and her long hair loosely flowing over her neck and shoulders. Lady Eleanor was pale as death, and the marks of recent tears were ou her cheeks; but still her features wore the expression of deep tenderness and pity, rather than of selfish sorrow. Helen's face was hidden; but her attitude, and the low sobbing sounds that at intervals broke the stillness, told how her heart was suffering.

"My dear, dear child," said Lady Eleanor, as she laid her hand upon the young girl's head, "be comforted. Rest assured that in making me the partner in your sorrow, I will be the happier participator in your joy, whenever its day may come. Yes, Helen, and it will come."

"Had I told you earlier—"

"Had you done so," interrupted Lady Eleanor, "you had been spared much grief, for I could have assured you, as I now do, that you are not to blame,—that this young man's rashness, however we may deplore it, had no promptings from us."

Helen replied, but in so low a tone that Mr. Dempsey could not catch the words; he could hear, however, Lady Eleanor uttering at intervals words of comfort and encouragement, and at last she said,—

"Nay, Helen, no half-confidence, my child. Acknowledge it fairly, that your opinion of him is not what it was at first; or if you will not confess it, leave it to my own judgment And why should you not?" added she, in a stronger voice; "wiser heads may reprove his precipitancy, criticise what would be called his folly, but you may be forgiven for thinking that his Quixotism could deserve another and a fonder title. And I, Helen, grown old and chilly-hearted, each day more distrustful of the world, less sanguine in hope, more prone to suspect,—even I feel that devotion like his has a strong claim on your affection. And shall I own to you that on the very day he brought us that letter a kind of vague presentiment that I should one day like him stole across me. What was the noise? Did you not hear something stir?" Helen had heard it, but paid no further attention, for there was no token of any one being near.

Noise, however, there really was, occasioned by Mr. Dempsey, who, in his eagerness to hear, had pushed the door partly open. For some moments back, honest Paul had listened with as much embarrassment as curiosity, sorely puzzled to divine of whom the mother and daughter were speaking. The general tenor of the conversation left the subject no matter of difficulty. The individual was the only doubtful question. Lady Eleanor's allusion to a letter, and her own feelings at the moment, at once reminded him of her altered manner to himself on the evening he brought the epistle from Coleraine, and how she, who up to that time had treated him with unvarying distance and reserve, had as suddenly become all the reverse.

"Blood alive!" said he to himself, "I never as much as suspected it!" His eagerness to hear further was intense; and although he had contrived to keep the door ajar, his curiosity was doomed to disappointment, for it was Helen who spoke, and her words were uttered in a low, faint tone, utterly inaudible where he stood. Whatever pleasure Mr. Dempsey might have at first derived from his contraband curiosity, was more than repaid now by the tortures of anxiety. He suspected that Helen was making a full confession of her feelings towards him, and yet he could not catch a syllable. Lady Eleanor, too, when she spoke again, it was in an accent almost equally faint; and all that Paul could gather was that the mother was using expressions of cheerfulness and hope, ending with the words,—

"His own fortunes look now as darkly as ours; mayhap the same bright morning will dawn for both together, Helen. We have hope to cheer us, for him and for us."

"Ah! true enough," muttered Paul; "she's alluding to old Bob Dempsey, and if the Lord would take him, we 'd all come right again."

Helen now arose, and seated herself beside her mother, with her head leaning ou her shoulder; and Mr. Dempsey might have been pardoned if he thought she never looked more beautiful. The loose folds of her night-dress less concealed than delineated the perfect symmetry of her form; while through the heavy masses of the luxuriant hair that fell upon her neck and shoulders, her skin seemed more than ever delicately fair. If Paul's mind was a perfect whirl of astonishment, delight, and admiration, his doubts were no less puzzling. What was *he* to do? Should he at once discover himself, throw himself at Helen's feet in a rapture, confessing that he had heard her avowal, and declare that the passion was mutual? This, although with evident advantages on the score of dramatic effect, had also its drawback. Lady Eleanor, who scarcely looked as well in dishabille as her daughter, might feel offended. She might take it ill, also, that he had been a listener. Paul had heard of people who actually deemed eavesdropping unbecoming! Who knows, among her own eccentricities, if this one might not find place? Paul, therefore, resolved on a more cautious advance, and, for his guidance, applied his ear once more to the aperture. This time, however, without success, for they spoke still lower than before; nor, after a long and patient waiting, could he hear more than that the subject was their present embarrassment, and the necessity of immediately removing from "The Corvy," but where to, and how, they could not determine.

There was no time to ask Bicknell's advice; before an answer could arrive, they would be exposed to all the inconvenience, perhaps insult, which Mr. Nickie's procedure seemed to threaten. The subject appeared one to which all their canvassing had brought no solution, and at last Lady Eleanor said,—

"How thankful I am, Helen, that I never wrote to Lord Netherby; more than once, when our difficulties seemed to thicken, I half made up my mind to address him. How much would it add to my present distress of mind, if I had yielded to the impulse! The very thought is now intolerable."

"Pride! pride!" muttered Paul.

"And I was so near it," ejaculated Lady Eleanor.

"Yes," said Helen, sharply; "our noble cousin's kindness would be a sore aggravation of our troubles."

"Worse than the mother, by Jove!" exclaimed Paul. "Oh dear! if I had a cousin a lord, maybe he'd not hear of me."

Lady Eleanor spoke again; but Paul could only catch a stray word here and there, and again she reverted to the necessity of leaving the cottage at once.

"Could we even see this Mr. Dempsey," said she, "he knows the country well, and might be able to suggest some fitting place for the moment, at least till we could decide on better."

Paul scarcely breathed, that he might catch every syllable.

"Yes," said Helen, eagerly, "he would be the very person to assist us; but, poor little man! he has his own troubles, too, at this moment."

"She's a kind creature," muttered Paul; "how fond I'm growing of her!"

"It is no time for the indulgence of scruples; otherwise, Helen, I 'd not place much reliance on the gentleman's taste."

"Proud as Lucifer," thought Paul.

"His good-nature, mamma, is the quality we stand most in need of, and I have a strong trust that he is not deficient there."

"What a situation to be placed in!" sighed Lady Eleanor: "that we should turn with a shudder from seeking protection where it is our due, and yet ask counsel and assistance from a man like this!"

"I feel no repugnance whatever to accepting such a favor from Mr. Dempsey, while I should deem it a great humiliation to be suitor to the Earl of Netherby."

"And yet he is our nearest relative living,—with vast wealth and influence, and I believe not indisposed towards us. I go too fast, perhaps," said she, scornfully; "his obligations to my own father were too great and too manifold, that I should say so."

"What a Tartar!" murmured Paul.

"If the proud Earl could forget the services my dear father rendered him, when, a younger son, without fortune or position, he had no other refuge than our house,—if he could wipe away the memory of benefits once received,—he might perhaps be better minded towards us; but obligation is so suggestive of ill-will."

"Dearest mamma," said Helen, laughing, "if your hopes depend upon his Lordship's forgetfulness of kindness, I do think we may afford to be sanguine. I am well inclined to think that he is not weighed down by the load of gratitude that makes men enemies. Still," added she, more seriously, "I am very averse to seeking his aid, or even his counsel; I vote for Mr. Dempsey."

"How are we to endure the prying impertinence of his curiosity? Have you thought of that, Helen?"

Paul's cheek grew scarlet, and his very fingers' ends tingled.

"Easily enough, mamma. Nay, if our troubles were not so urgent, it would be rather amusing than otherwise; and with all his vulgarity—"

"The little vixen!" exclaimed Paul, so much off his guard that both mother and daughter started.

"Did you hear that, Helen? I surely heard some one speak."

"I almost thought so," replied Miss Darcy, taking up a candle from the table, and proceeding towards the door. Mr. Dempsey had but time to retreat behind the curtain of the bed, when she reached the spot where he had been standing. "No, all is quiet in the house," said she, opening the door into the corridor and listening. "Even our respectable guests would seem to be asleep." She waited for a few seconds, and then returned to her place on the sofa.

Mr. Dempsey had either heard enough to satisfy the immediate cravings of his curiosity, or, more probably, felt his present position too critical; for when he drew the curtain once more close over the glass door, he slipped noiselessly into the corridor, and entering the first room he could find, opened the window and sprang out.

"You shall not be disappointed in Paul Dempsey, anyhow," said he, as he buttoned up the collar of his coat, and pressed his hat more firmly on his head. "No, my Lady, he may be vulgar and inquisitive, though I confess it's the first time I ever heard of either; but he is not the man to turn his back on a good-natured action, when it lies full in front of him. What a climate, to be sure! it blows from the four quarters of the globe all at once, and the rain soaks in and deluges one's very heart's blood. Paul, Paul, you 'll have a smart twinge of rheumatism from this night's exploit."

It may be conjectured that Mr. Dempsey, like many other gifted people, had a habit of compensating for the want of society by holding little dialogues or discourses with himself,—a custom from which he derived no small gratification, for, while it lightened the weariness of a lonely way, it enabled him to say many more flattering and civil things to himself than he usually heard from an ungrateful world.

"They talk of Demerara," said he; "I back Antrim against the world for a hurricane. The rainy season here lasts all the year round; and if practice makes perfect—There, now I 'm wet through, I can't be worse. Ah! Helen, Helen, if you knew how unfit Paul Dempsey is to play Paris! By the way, who was the fellow that swam the Hellespont for love of a young lady? Not Laertes, no—that's not it-Leander, that's the name—Leander."

Paul muttered the name several times over, and by a train of thought which we will not attempt to follow or unravel, began humming to himself the well-known Irish ditty of—

> "Teddy, ye gander,
> Yer like a Highlander."

He soon came to a stop in the words, but continued to sing the air, till at last he broke out in the following version of his own:—

> "Paul Dempsey, ye gander,
> You 're like that Leander
> Who for somebody's daughter—for somebody's daughter
> Did not mind it one pin
> To be wet to the skin,
> With a dip in salt water—a dip in salt water.
>
> "Were you wiser, 'tis plain,
> You 'd be now in Coleraine,
> A nightcap on your head—a nightcap on your head,
> With a jorum of rum,
> Made by old Mother Fum,
> At the side of your bed—at the side of your bed.
>
> "For tho' love is divine,
> When the weather is fine,
> And a season of bliss—a season of bliss,
> 'Tis a different thing
> For a body to sing

On a night such as this—a night such as this.

"Paul Dempsey! remember,
On the ninth of December
You 'll be just forty-six—you 'll be just forty-six,
And the world will say
That at your time o' day
You 're too old for these tricks—you 're too old for these tricks.

"And tho' water may show
One's love, faith,
I know I 'd rather prove mine—I 'd rather prove mine
With my feet on the fender;
'T is then I grow tender,
O'er a bumper of wine—o'er a bumper of wine!

"A bumper of wine!" sighed he. "On my conscience, it would be an ugly toast I 'd refuse to drink this minute, if the liquor was near.

"Ah! when warm and snog,
With my legs on the rug,
By a turf fire red—a turf fire red—
But how can I rhyme it?
With this horrid climate,
Destroying my head—destroying my head?

"With a coat full of holes,
And my shoes without soles,
And my hat like a teapot—my hat like a teapot—

"Oh, murther, murther!" screamed he, aloud, as his shins came in contact with a piece of timber, and he fell full length to the ground, sorely bruised, and perfectly enveloped in snow. It was some minutes before he could rally sufficiently to get up; and although he still shouted for help, seeing a light in a window near, no one came to his assistance, leaving poor Paul to his own devices.

It was some consolation for his sufferings to discover that the object over which he had stumbled was the shaft of a jaunting-car, such a conveyance being at that moment what he most desired to meet with. The driver at last made his appearance, and informed him that he had brought Nickie and his two companions from Larne, and was now only waiting their summons to proceed to Coleraine.

Paul easily persuaded the man that he could earn a fare in the mean time, for that Nickie would probably not leave "The Corvy" till late on the following day, and that by a little exertion he could manage to drive to Coleraine and back before he was stirring. It is but fair to add that poor Mr. Dempsey supported his arguments by lavish promises of reward, to redeem which he speculated on mortgaging his silver watch, and probably his umbrella, when he reached Coleraine.

It was yet a full hour before daybreak, as Lady Eleanor, who had passed the night in her dressing-room, was startled by a sharp tapping noise at her window; Helen lay asleep on the sofa, and too soundly locked in slumber to hear the sounds. Lady Eleanor listened, and while half fearing to disturb the young girl, wearied and exhausted as she was, she drew near to the window. The indistinct shadow of a figure was all that she could detect through the gloom, but she fancied she could hear a weak effort to pronounce her name.

There could be little doubt of the intentions of the visitor; whoever he should prove, the frail barrier of a window could offer no resistance to any one disposed to enter by force, and, reasoning thus, Lady Eleanor unfastened the casement, and cried, "Who is there?"

A strange series of gestures, accompanied by a sound between a sneeze and the crowing of a cock, was all the reply; and when the question was repeated in a louder tone, a thin quivering voice muttered, "Pau-au-l De-de-dempsey, my La-dy."

"Mr. Dempsey, indeed!" exclaimed Lady Eleanor. "Oh! pray come round to the door at your left hand; it is only a few steps from where you are standing."

Short as the distance was, Mr. Dempsey's progress was of the slowest, and Lady Eleanor had already time to awaken Helen, ere the half-frozen Paul had crossed the threshold.

"He has passed the night in the snow," cried Lady Eleanor to her daughter, as she led him towards the fire.

"No, my Lady," stammered out Paul, "only the last hour and a half; before that I was snug under old Daly's blanket."

A very significant interchange of looks between mother and daughter seemed to imply that poor Mr. Dempsey's wits were wandering.

"Call Tate; let him bring some wine here at once, Helen."

"It's all drunk; not a glass in the decanter," murmured Paul, whose thoughts recurred to the supper-table.

"Poor creature, his mind is quite astray," whispered Lady Eleanor, her compassion not the less strongly moved, because she attributed his misfortune to the exertions he had made in their behalf. By this time the group was increased by the arrival of old Tate, who, in a flannel nightcap fastened under the chin, and a very ancient dressing-gown of undyed wool, presented a lively contrast to the shivering condition of Mr. Dempsey.

"It's only Mr. Dempsey!" said Lady Eleanor, sharply, as the old butler stood back, crossing himself and staring with sleepy terror at the white figure.

"May I never! But so it is," exclaimed Tate, in return to an attempt at a bow on Dempsey's part, which he accomplished with a brackling noise like creaking glass.

"Some warm wine at once," said Helen, while she heaped two or three logs upon the hearth.

"With a little ginger in it, miss," grinned Paul. But the polite attempt at a smile nearly cut his features, and ended in a most lamentable expression of suffering.

"This is the finest thing in life agin' the cowld," said Tate, as he threw over the shivering figure a Mexican mantle, all worked and embroidered with quills, that gave the gentle Mr. Dempsey the air of an enormous porcupine. The clothing, the fire, and the wine, of which he partook heartily, soon restored him, and erelong he had recounted to Lady Eleanor the whole narrative of his arrival at "The Corvy," his concealment in the canoe, the burning of the law papers, and even down to the discovery of the jaunting-car, omitting nothing, save the interview he had witnessed between the mother and daughter.

Lady Eleanor could not disguise her anxiety on the subject of the burned documents, but Paul's arguments were conclusive in reply,—

"Who's to tell of it? Not your Ladyship, not Miss Helen; and as to Paul, meaning myself, my discretion is quite Spanish. Yes, my Lady," said he, with a tragic gesture that threw back the loose folds of his costume, "there is an impression abroad, which I grieve to say is widespread, that the humble individual who addresses you is one of those unstable, fickle minds that accomplish nothing great; but I deny it, deny it indignantly. Let the occasion but arise, let some worthy object present itself, or herself,"—he gave a most melting look towards Helen, which cost all her efforts to sustain without laughter,—"and then, madam, Don Paulo Dempsey will come out in his true colors."

"Which I sincerely hope may not be of the snow tint," said Lady Eleanor, smiling. "But pray, Mr. Dempsey, to return to a theme more selfish. You are sufficiently aware of our unhappy circumstances here at this moment, to see that we must seek some other abode, at least for the present. Can you then say where we can find such?"

"Miss Daly's neighborhood, perhaps," broke in Helen.

"Never do,-not to be thought of," interrupted Paul; "there's nothing for it but the Panther—"

"The what, sir?" exclaimed Lady Eleanor, in no small surprise.

"The Panther, my Lady, Mother Fum's! snug, quiet, and respectable; social, if you like,—selfish, if you please it. Solitary or gregarious; just as you fancy."

"And where, sir, is the Panther?" said Lady Eleanor, who in her innocence supposed this to be the sign of some village inn.

"In the Diamond of Coleraine, my Lady, opposite M'Grotty's, next but one to Kitty Black's hardware, and two doors from the Post-Office; central and interesting. Mail-car from Newtown, Lim.,—takes up passengers, within view of the windows, at two every day. Letters given out at four,— see every one in the town without stirring from your window. Huston's, the apothecary, always full of people at post hour. Gibbin's tobacco-shop assembles all the Radicals at the same time to read the 'Patriot.' Plenty of life and movement."

"Is there nothing to be found more secluded, less—"

"Less fashionable, your Ladyship would observe. To be sure there is; but there 's objections,—at least I am sure you would dislike the prying, inquisitive spirit—Eh? Did you make an observation, miss?"

"No, Mr. Dempsey," said Helen, with some difficulty preserving a suitable gravity. "I would only remark that you are perfectly in the right, and that my mother seeks nothing more than a place where we can remain without obtrusiveness or curiosity directed towards us."

"There will always be the respectful admiration that beauty exacts," replied Paul, bowing courteously, "but I can answer for the delicacy of Coleraine as for my own."

If this assurance was not quite as satisfactory to the ladies as Mr. Dempsey might have fancied it ought to be, there was really no alternative; they knew nothing of the country, which side to direct their steps, or whither to seek shelter; besides, until they had communicated with Bicknell, they could not with safety leave the neighborhood to which all their letters were addressed.

It was then soon determined to accept Mr. Dempsey's suggestion and safe-conduct, and leaving Tate for the present to watch over such of their effects as they could not conveniently carry with them, to set out for Coleraine. The arrangements were made as speedily as the resolve, and day had scarcely dawned ere they quitted "The Corvy."

CHAPTER XX
MR. HEFFERNAN OUT-MANOEUVRED

It was on the very same evening that witnessed these events, that Lord Castlereagh was conducting Mr. Con Heffernan to his hotel, after a London dinner-party. The late Secretary for Ireland had himself volunteered the politeness, anxious to hear some tidings of people and events which, in the busy atmosphere of a crowded society, were unattainable. He speedily ran over a catalogue of former friends and acquaintances, learning, with that surprise with which successful men always regard their less fortunate contemporaries, that this one was still where he had left him, and that the other jogged on his daily road as before, when he suddenly asked, —

"And the Darcys, what of them?"

Heffernan shrugged his shoulders without speaking.

"I am sorry for it," resumed the other; "sorry for the gallant old Knight himself, and sorry for a state of society in which such changes are assumed as evidences of progress and prosperity. These upstart Hickmans are not the elements of which a gentry can be formed."

"O'Reilly still looks to you for the baronetcy, my Lord," replied Heffernan, with a half-sneer. "You have him with or against you on that condition, — at least, so I hear."

"Has he not had good fortune enough in this world to be satisfied? He has risen from nothing to be a man of eminence, wealth, and county influence; would it not be more reasonable in him to mature his position by a little patience, than endanger it by fresh shocks to public opinion? Even a boa, my dear Heffernan, when he swallows a goat, takes six months to digest his meal. No! no! such men must be taught reserve, if their own prudence does not suggest it!"

"I believe you are right, my Lord," said Heffernan, thoughtfully; "O'Reilly is the very man to forget himself in the sunshine of court favor, and mistake good luck for desert."

"With all his money, too," rejoined Lord Castlereagh, "his influence will just be proportioned to the degree of acceptance his constituents suppose him to possess with us here. He has never graduated as a Patriot, and his slight popularity is only 'special gratia.' His patent of Gentleman has not come to him by birth."

"For this reason the baronetcy—"

"Let us not discuss that," said Lord Castlereagh, quickly. "There is an objection in a high quarter to bestow honors, which would seem to ratify the downfall of an ancient house." He seemed to have said more than he was ready to admit, and to change the theme turned the conversation on the party they had just quitted.

"Sir George Hannaper always does these things well."

Mr. Heffernan assented blandly, but not over eagerly. London was not "*his* world," and the tone of a society so very different to what he was habituated had not made on him the most favorable impression.

"And after all," said Lord Castlereagh, musingly, "there is a great deal of tact—ability, if you will—essential to the success of such entertainments, to bring together men of different classes and shades of opinion, people who have never met before, perhaps are never to meet again, to hit upon the subjects of conversation that may prove generally interesting, without the risk of giving undue preponderance to any one individual's claims to superior knowledge. This demands considerable skill."

"Perhaps the difficulty is not so great *here*, my Lord," said Heffernan, half timidly, "each man understands his part so well; information and conversational power appear tolerably equally distributed; and when all the instruments are so well tuned, the leader of the orchestra has an easy task."

"Ah! I believe I comprehend you," said Lord Castlereagh, laughing; "you are covertly sneering at the easy and unexciting quietude of our London habits. Well, Heffernan, I admit we are not so fond of solo performances as you are in Dublin; few among us venture on those 'obligate passages' which are so charming to Irish ears; but don't you think the concerted pieces are better performed?"

"I believe, my Lord," said Heffernan, abandoning the figure in his anxiety to reply, "that we would call this dull in Ireland. I 'm afraid that we are barbarous enough to set more store by wit and pleasantry than on grave discussion and shrewd table-talk. It appears to me that these gentlemen carry an air of business into their conviviality."

"Scarcely so dangerous an error as to carry conviviality into business," said Lord Castlereagh, slyly.

"There's too much holding back," said Heffernan, not heeding the taunt; "each man seems bent on making what jockeys call 'a waiting race.'"

"Confess, however," said Lord Castlereagh, smiling, "there 's no struggle, no hustling at the winning-post: the best horse comes in first—-"

"Upon my soul, my Lord," said Heffernan, interrupting, "I have yet to learn that there is such a thing. I conclude from your Lordship's observation that the company we met to-day were above the ordinary run of agreeability."

"I should certainly say so."

"Well, then, I can only affirm that we should call this a failure in our less polished land. I listened with becoming attention; the whole thing was new to me, and I can safely aver I neither heard one remark above the level of commonplace, nor one observation evidencing acute perception of passing events or reflection on the past. As to wit or epigram—"

"Oh, we do not value these gifts at *your* price; we are too thrifty a nation, Heffernan, to expend all our powder on fireworks."

"Faith, I agree with you, my Lord; the man who would venture on a rocket would be treated as an incendiary."

"Come, come, Heffernan, I 'll not permit you to say so. Did you ever in any society see a man more appreciated than our friend Darcy was the last evening we met him, his pleasantry relished, his racy humor well taken, and his stores of anecdote enjoyed with a degree of zest I have never seen surpassed?"

"Darcy was always too smooth for our present taste," said Heffernan, caustically. "His school was antiquated years ago; there was a dash of the French courtier through the Irishmen of his day."

"That made the most polished gentlemen of Europe, I've been told," said Lord Castlereagh, interrupting. "I know your taste inclines to a less chastened and more adventurous pleasantry, shrewd insight into an antagonist's weak point, a quick perception of the ridiculous—-"

"Allied with deep knowledge of men and motives, my Lord," said Heffernan, catching up the sentence, "a practical acquaintance with the world in its widest sense; that cultivated keenness that smacks of reading intentions before they are avowed, and divining plans before they are more than conceived. These solid gifts are all essential to the man who would influence society, whether in a social circle or in the larger sphere of active life."

"Ah! but we were talking of merely social qualities," said Lord Castlereagh, stealing a cautious look of half malice, "the wit that sets the table in a roar."

"And which, like lightning, my Lord, must now and then prove dangerous, or men will cease to be dazzled by its brilliancy. Now, I rather incline to think that the Knight's pleasantry is like some of the claret we were drinking to-day, a little spoiled by age."

"I protest strongly against the judgment," said Lord Castlereagh, with energy; "the man who at his time of life consents to resume the toils and dangers of a soldier's career must not be accused of growing old."

"Perhaps your Lordship would rather shift the charge of senility against the Government which appoints such an officer," said Heffernan, maliciously.

"As to that," said Lord Castlereagh, laughingly, "I believe the whole thing was a mistake. Some jealous but indiscreet friend of Darcy's made an application in his behalf, and without his cognizance, pressing the claim of an old and meritorious officer, and directly asking for a restitution to his grade. This was backed by Lord Netherby, one of the lords in waiting, and without much inquiry—indeed, I fancy without any—he was named colonel, in exchange from the unattached list. The Knight was evidently flattered by so signal a mark of favor, and, if I read him aright, would not change his command for a brigade at home. In fact, he has already declined prospects not less certain of success."

"And is this really the mode in which officers are selected for an enterprise of hazard and importance?" said Heffernan, affecting a tone of startled indignation as he spoke.

"Upon my word, Heffernan," said Lord Castlereagh, subduing the rising tendency to laugh outright, "I fear it is too true. We live in days of backstairs and court favor. I saw an application for the office of Under Secretary for Ireland, so late as yesterday—"

"You did, my Lord!" interrupted Heffernan, with more warmth than he almost ever permitted himself to feel. "You did, from a man who has rendered more unrewarded services to the Government than any individual in the kingdom."

"The claim was a very suitable one," said Lord Castle-reagh, mildly. "The gentleman who preferred it could point to a long list of successful operations, whose conduct rested mainly or solely on his own consummate skill and address; he could even allege the vast benefit of his advice to young and not over-informed Chief Secretaries—-"

"I would beg to observe, my Lord—-"

"Pray allow me to continue," said Lord Castlereagh, laying his hand gently on the other's arm. "As one of that helpless class so feelingly alluded to, I am ready to evince the deepest sense of grateful acknowledgments. It may be that I would rather have been mentioned more flatteringly; that the applicant had spoken of me as an apter and more promising scholar—-"

"My Lord, I must and will interrupt you. The memorial, which was presented in my name, was sent forward under the solemn pledge that it should meet the eyes of Mr. Pitt alone; that whether its prayer was declined or accorded, none, save himself, should have cognizance of it. If, after this, it was submitted to your Lordship's critical examination, I leave it to your good taste and your sense of decorum how far you can avow or make use of the knowledge so obtained."

"I was no party in the compact you allege, nor. I dare to say, was Mr. Pitt," said Lord Castlereagh, proudly; but, momentarily resuming his former tone, he went on: "The Prime Minister, doubtless, knew how valuable the lesson might be to a young man entering on public life which should teach him not to lay too much store by his own powers of acuteness, not to trust too implicitly to his own qualities of shrewdness and perception; and that, by well reflecting on the aid he received from others, he might see how little the subtraction would leave for his own peculiar amount of skill. In this way I have to acknowledge myself greatly Mr. Heffernan's debtor, since, without the aid of this document, I should never have recognized how ignorant I was of every party and every public man in Ireland; how dependent on his good guidance; how I never failed save in rejecting, never succeeded save in profiting by his wise and politic counsels."

"Is your Lordship prepared to deny these assertions?" said Heffernan, with an imperturbable coolness.

"Am I not avowing my grateful sense of them?" said Lord Castlereagh, smiling blandly. "I feel only the more deeply your debtor, because, till now, I never knew the debt,—both principal and interest must be paid together; but seriously, Heffernan, if you wanted office, was I not the proper channel to have used in asking for it? Why disparage your pupil while extolling your system?"

"You did my system but little credit, my Lord," replied Heffernan, with an accent as unmoved as before; "you bought votes when you should have bought the voters themselves; you deemed the Bill of Union the consummation of Irish policy,—it is only the first act of the piece. You were not the first general who thought he beat the enemy when he drove in the pickets."

"Would my tactics have been better had I made one of my spies a major-general, Mr. Heffernan?" said Lord Castlereagh, sneeringly.

"Safer, my lord,—far safer," said Heffernan, "for he might not have exposed you afterwards. But I think this is my hotel; and I must say it is the first time in my life that I have closed an interview with your Lordship without regret."

"Am I to hope it will be the last?" said Lord Castle-reagh, laughing.

"The last interview, my Lord, or the last occasion of regretting its shortness?" said Heffernan, with a slight anxiety of voice.

"Whichever Mr. Heffernan opines most to his advantage," was the cool reply.

"The former, with your permission, my Lord," said Heffernan, as a flush suffused his cheek. "I wish your Lordship a very good night."

"Good-night, good-night! Stay, Thomas, Mr. Heffernan has forgotten his gloves."

"Thanks, my Lord; they were not left as a gage of battle, I assure you."

"I feel certain of it," said Lord Castlereagh, laughing. "Good-night, once more."

The carriage rolled on, and Mr. Heffernan stood for an instant gazing after it through the gloom.

"I might have known it," muttered he to himself; "these lords are the only people who do stick to each other nowadays." Then, after a pause, he added, "Drogheda is right, by Jove! there 's no playing against 'four by honors.'"

And with this reflection he slowly entered the hotel, and repaired to his chamber.

CHAPTER XXI
A BIT OF B Y-P L A Y

Reverses of fortune might be far more easily supported, if they did not entail, as their inevitable consequence, the association with those all of whose tastes, habits, and opinions run in a new and different channel. It is a terrible aggravation to the loss of those comforts which habit has rendered necessaries, to unlearn the usages of a certain condition, and adopt those of a class beneath us,—or, what is still worse, engage in the daily, hourly conflict between our means and our requirements.

Perhaps Lady Eleanor Darcy and her daughter never really felt the meaning of their changed condition, nor understood its poignancy, till they saw themselves as residents of Mrs. Fumbally's boarding-house, whither Mr. Dempsey's polite attentions had conducted them. It was to no want of respect on that lady's part that any portion of this feeling could be traced. "The Panther" had really behaved with the most dignified consideration; and while her new guests were presented as Mrs. and Miss Gwynne, intimated, by a hundred little adroit devices of manner, that their real rank and title were regarded by her as inviolable secrets,—not the less likely to be respected that she was herself ignorant of both. Heaven knows what secret anguish the retention of these facts cost poor Paul! secrecy being with him a quality something like Acres' courage, which "oozed out of his fingers' ends." Mr. Dempsey hated those miserly souls that can treasure up a fact for their own personal enjoyment, and yet never invite a neighbor to partake of it; and it was a very inefficient consolation to him, in this instance, to throw a mysterious cloak over the strangers, and, by an air of profound consciousness, seek to impose on the other boarders. He made less scruple about what he deemed his own share of the mystery; and scarcely had Mrs. Fumbally performed the honors of the two small chambers destined for Lady Eleanor and Helen, than Paul followed her to the little apartment familiarly termed her "den," and shutting the door, with an appearance of deep caution, took his place opposite to her at the fire.

"Well, Mr. Dempsey," said Mrs. Fumbally, "now that all is done and settled,—now that I have taken these ladies into the 'Establishment,'"—a very favorite designation of Mrs. Fum's when she meant to be imposing,—

"I hope I am not unreasonable iu expecting a full and complete account from you of who they are, whence they came, and, in fact, every particular necessary to satisfy me concerning them."

"Mrs. Gwynne! Miss Gwynne! mother and daughter—Captain Gwynne, the father, on the recruiting staff in the Isle of Skye, or, if you like it better, with his regiment at St. John's. Mrs. G———, a Miss Rickaby, one of the Rickabys of Pwhlmdlwmm, North Wales—ancient family—small estate—all spent—obliged to live retired—till—till—no matter what—a son comes of age—to sign something—or anything that way—"

"This is all fiddle-faddle, Mr. Dempsey," said Mrs. Fum, with an expression that seemed to say, "Take care how you trifle with me."

"To be sure it is," rejoined Paul; "all lies, every word of it. What do you say, then, if we have her the Widow Gwynne—husband shot at Bergen-op-Zoom—"

"I say, Mr. Dempsey, that if you wish me to keep your secret before the other boarders—"

"The best way is never to tell it to you—eh, Mrs. Fum? Well, come, I will be open. Name, Gwynne—place of abode unknown—family ditto—means supposed to be ample—daughter charming—so very much so, indeed, that if Paul Dempsey were only what he ought—the Dempsey of Dempsey's Grove—"

"Oh, is that it?" said Mrs. Fumbally, endeavoring to smile,-"is that it?"

"That's it," rejoined Paul, as he drew up his shirt-collar, and adjusted his cravat.

"Isn't she very young, Mr. Dempsey?" said Mrs. Fum, slyly.

"Twenty, or thereabouts, I take it," said Paul, carelessly,—"quite suitable as regards age."

"I never thought you 'd marry, Mr. Dempsey," said Mrs. Fum, with a languishing look, that contrasted strangely with the habitually shrewish expression of the "Pauther's" face.

"Can't help it, Mrs. Fum. The last of the Romans! No more Dempseys when I 'm gone, if I don't. Elder branch all dropped off,—last twig of the younger myself."

"Ah! these are considerations, indeed!" sighed the lady. "But don't you think that a person more like yourself in taste—more similar in opinion of the world? She looks proud, Mr. Dempsey; I should say, overbearingly proud."

"Rather proud myself, if that's all," said Dempsey, drawing himself up, and protruding his chin with a most comic imitation of dignity.

"Only becomingly so, Mr. Dempsey,—a proper sense of self-respect, a due feeling for your future position in life,—I never saw more than that, I must say. Now, I could n't help remarking the way that young lady threw herself into the chair, and the glance she gave at the room. It was number eight, Mr. Dempsey, with the chintz furniture, and the looking-glass over the chimney! Well, really you 'd say, it was poor Leonard's room, with the settee bed in the corner,—the look she gave it!"

"Indeed!" exclaimed Dempsey, who really felt horrified at this undervaluing judgment of what every boarder regarded as the very sanctum of the Fumbally Temple.

"Truth, every word of it!" resumed Mrs. Fum. "I thought my ears deceived me, as she said to her mother, 'Oh, it 's all very neat and clean!'—neat and clean, Mr. Dempsey! The elegant rug which I worked myself—the pointer—and the wild duck."

"Like life, by Jove, if it was n't that the dog has only three legs."

"Perspective, Mr. Dempsey, don't forget its perspective; and if the bird's wings are maroon, I could n't help it, it was the only color to be had in the town."

"The group is fine,—devilish fine!" said Paul, with the air of one whose word was final.

"'Neat and clean' were the expressions she used. I could have cried as I heard it." Here the lady, probably in consideration for the omission, wiped her eyes, and dropped her voice to a very sympathetic key. "She meant it well, depend upon it, Mrs. Fum, she meant it well."

"And the old lady," resumed Mrs. Fumbally, deaf to every consolation, "lay back in her chair this way, and said, 'Oh, it will all do very well,—you 'll not find us troublesome, Mrs. Flumary!' I haven't been the head of this establishment eight-and-twenty years to be called Flumary. How these airs are to be tolerated by the other boarders, I'm sure is more than I can say."

It appeared more than Mr. Dempsey could say also, if one might pronounce from the woe-begone expression of his face; for, up to this moment totally wrapped up in the mysterious portion of the affair, he had lost sight of all the conflicting interests this sudden advent would call into activity.

"That wasn't all," continued Mrs. Fumbally; "for when I told them the dinner-hour was five, the old lady interrupted me with, 'For the present, with your permission, we should prefer dining at six.' Did any one ever hear the like? I 'll have a pretty rebellion in the house, when it gets out! Mrs. Mackay will have her tea upstairs every night; Mr. Dunlop will always breakfast in bed. I would n't be surprised if Miss Boyle stood out for broth in the middle of the day."

"Oh!" exclaimed Paul, holding up both hands in horror.

"I vow and protest, I expect that next!" exclaimed Mrs. Fum, as folding her arms, and fixing her eyes rigidly on the grate, she sat, the ideal of abused and injured benevolence. "Indeed, Mr. Dempsey," said she, after a long silence on both sides, "it would be a great breach of the regard many years of intimacy with you has formed, if I did not say, that your affections are misplaced. Beauty is a perishable gift."

Paul looked at Mrs. Fumbally, and seemed struck with the truth of her remark.

"But the qualities of the miud, Mr. Dempsey, those rare endowments that make happy the home and hearth. You 're fond of beef hash with pickled onions," said she, smiling sweetly; "well, you shall have one to-day."

"Good creature!" muttered Paul, while he pressed her hand affectionately. "The best heart in the world!"

"Ah, yes," sighed the lady, half soliloquizing, "conformity of temper,— the pliancy of the reed,—the tender attachment of the ivy."

Paul coughed, and drew himself up proudly, and, as if a sudden thought occurred to him that he resembled the oak of the forest, he planted his feet firmly, and stood stiff and erect.

"You are not half careful enough about yourself, Mr. Dempsey,—never attend to changing your damp clothes,—and I assure you the climate here requires it; and when you come in cold and wet, you should always step in here, on your way upstairs, and take a little something warm and cordial. I don't know if you approve of this," suiting the action to the words. Mrs. Fum had opened a small cupboard in the wall, and taken out a quaint-looking flask, and a very diminutive glass.

"Nectar, by Jove,—downright nectar!"

"Made with some white currants and ginger," chimed in Mrs. Fum, simply, as if to imply, "See what skill can effect; behold the magic power of intelligence!"

"White currants and ginger!" echoed Paul, holding out the glass to be refilled.

"A trifle of spirits, of course."

"Of course! could n't be comforting without it."

"That's what poor dear Fumbally always called, 'Ye know, ye know!' It was his droll way of saying 'Noyau!'" Here Mrs. F. displayed a conflict of smiles and tears, a perfect April landscape on her features. "He had such spirits!"

"I don't wonder, if he primed himself with this often," said Dempsey, who at last relinquished his glass, but with evident unwillingness.

"He used to say that his was a happy home!" sobbed Mrs. Fum, while she pressed her handkerchief to her face.

Paul did not well know what he should say, or if, indeed, he was called upon to utter a sentiment at all; but he thought he could have drunk another glass to the late Fum's memory, if his widow had n't kept such a tight grip of the flask.

"Oh, Mr. Dempsey, who could have thought it would come to this?" The sorrowful drooping of her eyelids, as she spoke, seemed to intimate an allusion to the low state of the decanter, and Dempsey at once replied, —

"There's a very honest glass in it still."

"Kind—kind creature!" sobbed Mrs. Fum, as she poured out the last of the liquor. And Paul was sorely puzzled, whether the encomium applied to the defunct or himself. "Do you know, Mr. Dempsey," here she gave a kind of hysterical giggle, that might take any turn,—hilarious, or the reverse, as events should dictate,—"do you know that as I see you there, standing before the fire, looking so pleasant and cheerful, so much at home, as a body might say, I can't help fancying a great resemblance between you and my poor dear Fum. He was older than you," said she, rapidly, as a slight cloud passed over Paul's features;-"older and stouter, but he had the same jocose smile, the same merry voice, and even that little fidgety habit with the hands. I know you 'll forgive me,—even that was his."

This was in all probability strictly correct, inasmuch as for several years before his demise the gifted individual had labored under a perpetual "delirium tremens."

"He rather liked this kind of thing," said Paul, pantomiming the action of drinking with his now empty glass.

"In moderation,-only in moderation."

"I 've heard that it disagreed with him," rejoined Paul, who, not pleased with his counterpart, resolved on showing a knowledge of his habits.

"So it did," sighed Mrs. Fum; "and he gave it up in consequence."

"I heard that, too," said Paul; and then muttered to himself, "on the morning he died."

A gentle tap at the door now broke in upon the colloquy, and a very slatternly servant woman, with bare legs and feet, made her appearance.

"What d'ye want, Biddy?" asked her mistress, in an angry voice. "I 'm just settling accounts with Mr. Dempsey, and you bounce in as if the house was on fire."

"It 's just himsel 's wanted," replied the northern maiden; "the leddie canna get on ava without him, he maun come up to number 'eight,' as soon as he can."

"I 'm ready," quoth Paul, as he turned to arrange his cravat, and run his hand through his hair; "I 'm at their service."

"Remember, Mr. Dempsey, remember, that what I've spoken to you this day is in the strictest confidence. If matters have proceeded far with the young lady upstairs, if your heart, if hers be really engaged, forget everything,—forget *me*."

Mrs. Fumbally's emotion had so overpowered her towards the end of her speech, that she rushed into an adjoining closet and clapped-to the door, an obstacle that only acted as a sound-board to her sobs, and from which Paul hastened with equal rapidity to escape.

An entire hemisphere might have separated the small chamber where Mr. Dempsey's late interview took place from the apartment on the first floor, to which he now was summoned, and so, to do him justice, did Paul himself feel; and not all the stimulating properties of that pleasant cordial could allay certain tremors of the heart, as he turned the handle of the door.

Lady Eleanor was seated at a writing-table, and Helen beside her, working, as Mr. Dempsey entered, and, after a variety of salutations, took a chair, about the middle of the room, depositing his hat and umbrella beside him.

"It would seem, Mr. Dempsey," said Lady Eleanor, with a very benign smile, "it would seem that we have made a very silly mistake; one, I am bound to say, you are quite exonerated from any share in, and the confession of which will, doubtless, exhibit my own and my daughter's cleverness in a very questionable light before you. Do you know, Mr. Dempsey, we believed this to be an inn."

"An inn!" broke in Paul, with uplifted hands.

"Yes, and it was only by mere accident we have discovered our error, and that we are actually in a boarding-house. Pray now, Helen, do not laugh, the blunder is quite provoking enough already."

Why Miss Darcy should laugh, and what there could be to warrant the use of the epithet, "provoking," Paul might have been broken on the wheel without being able to guess, while Lady Eleanor went on, —

"Now, it would seem customary for the guests to adopt here certain hours in common, — breakfasting, dining together, and associating like the members of one family."

Paul nodded an assent, and she resumed.

"I need scarcely observe to *you*, Mr. Dempsey, how very unsuited either myself or Miss Darcy would be to such an assembly, if even present circumstances did not more than ever enjoin a life of strict retirement."

"Dear me!" exclaimed Paul in a tone of deprecation, "there never was anything more select than this. Mother Fum never admits without a reference; I can show you the advertisement in the Derry papers. We kept the Collector out for two months, till he brought us a regular bill of health, as a body might say."

"Could you persuade them to let us remain in 'Quarantine,' then, for a few days?" said Helen, smiling.

"Oh, no! Helen, nothing of the kind; Mr. Dempsey must not be put to any troublesome negotiations, on our account. There surely must be an hotel of some sort in the town."

"This is a nice mess!" muttered Paul, who began to anticipate some of the miseries his good nature might cost him.

"A few days, a week at furthest, I hope, will enable us to communicate with our law adviser, and decide upon some more suitable abode. Could you, then, for the meanwhile, suggest a comfortable inn, or if not, a lodging in the town?"

Paul wrung his hands in dismay, but uttered not a syllable.

"To be candid, Mr. Dempsey," said Helen, "my father has a horror of these kind of places, and you could recommend us no country inn, however humble, where he would not be better pleased to hear of our taking refuge."

"But, Fumbally's! the best-known boarding-house in the North."

"I should be sincerely grieved, to be understood as uttering one syllable in its disparagement," rejoined Lady Eleanor; "I could not ask for a more satisfactory voucher of its respectability; but ours are peculiar circumstances."

"Only a pound a week," struck in Paul, "with extras."

"Nothing could be more reasonable; but pray understand me, I speak of course in great ignorance, but it would appear to me that persons living together in this fashion have a kind of right to know something of those who present themselves for the first time amongst them. Now, there are many reasons why neither my daughter nor myself would like to submit to this species of inquiry."

"I 'll settle all that," broke in Paul; "leave that to me, and you 'll have no further trouble about it."

"You must excuse my reliance even on such discretion," said Lady Eleanor, with more hauteur than before.

"Are we to understand that there is neither inn nor lodging-house to be found?" said Helen.

"Plenty of both, but full of bagmen," ejaculated Paul, whose contrivances were all breaking down beneath him.

"What is to be done?" exclaimed Lady Eleanor to her daughter.

"Lord bless you!" cried Paul, in a whining voice, "if you only come down amongst them with that great frill round your neck you wore the first day I saw you at 'The Corvy,' you 'll scare them so, they 'll never have courage to utter a word. There was Miss Daly—when she was here—"

"Miss Daly,-Miss Maria Daly!" exclaimed both ladies together.

"Miss Maria Daly," repeated Dempsey, with an undue emphasis on every syllable. "She spent the summer with us on the coast."

"Where had she resided up to that time, may I ask?" said Lady Eleanor, hastily.

"At 'The Corvy' — always at 'The Corvy,' until your arrival."

"Oh, Helen, think of this!" whispered Lady Eleanor, in a voice tremulous with agitation. "Think what sacrifices we have exacted from our friends, — and now, to learn that while we stand hesitating about encountering the inconveniences of our lot, that we have been subjecting another to that very same difficulty from which we shrink." Then, turning to Mr. Dempsey, she added, —

"I need not observe, sir, that while I desire no mystery to be thrown around our arrival here, I will not be the less grateful for any restraint the good company may impose on themselves as to inquiries concerning us. We are really not worth the attention, and I should be sorry to impose upon kind credulity by any imaginary claim to distinction."

"You'll dine below, then?" asked Paul, far more eager to ascertain this fact than any reasons that induced it.

Lady Eleanor bowed; and Dempsey, with a face beaming with delight, arose to withdraw and communicate the happy news to Mrs. Fumbally.

CHAPTER XXII
A GLANCE AT MRS. FUMBALLY'S

Great as Lady Eleanor's objection was to subjecting herself or her daughter to the contact of a boarding-house party, when the resolve was once taken the matter cost her far less thought or anxiety than it occasioned to the other inmates of the "Establishment." It is only in such segments of the great world that curiosity reaches its true intensity, and the desire to know every circumstance of one's neighbor becomes an absorbing passion. A distrustful impression that nobody is playing on "the square "—that every one has some special cause of concealment, some hidden shame—seems the presiding tone of these places.

Mrs. Fumbally's was no exception to the rule, and now that the residents had been so long acquainted that the personal character and fortune of each was known to all, the announcement of a new arrival caused the most lively sensations of anxiety.

Directories were ransacked for the name of Gwynne, and every separate owner of the appellation canvassed and discussed. Army lists were interrogated and conned over. Dempsey himself was examined for two hours before a "Committee of the whole house;" and though his inventive powers were no mean gifts, certain discrepancies, certain unexplained difficulties, did not fail to strike the acute tribunal, and he was dismissed as unworthy of credit. Baffled, not beaten, each retired to dress for dinner,—a ceremony, be it remarked, only in use on great occasions,—fully impressed with the conviction that the Gwynne case was a legitimate object of search and discovery.

It is not necessary here to allude to the strange display of costume that day called forth, nor what singular extravagances in dress each drew from the armory of his fascinations. The collector closed the Custom-house an hour earlier, that he might be properly powdered for the occasion. Miss Boyle abandoned, "for the nonce," her accustomed walk on the Banside, where the officers used to lounge, and in the privacy of her chamber prepared for the event. There is a tradition of her being seen, with a formidable array of curl-papers, so late as four in the afternoon. Mr. Dunlop was in a perpetual trot all day, between his tailor and his bootmaker, sundry alterations being required at a moment's notice. Mrs. Fumbally herself, however, eclipsed all competitors, as, in a robe of yellow satin, spotted with red, she made her appearance in the drawing-room; her head-dress being a turban of the same prevailing colors, but ornamented by a drooping plume of feathers and spangles so very umbrageous and pendent, that she looked like a weeping-ash clad in tinsel. A crimson brooch of vast proportions—which, on near inspection, turned out to be a portrait of the departed Fumbally, but whose colors were, unhappily, not "fast ones"—confined a scarf of green velvet, from which envious time had worn off all the pile, and left a "sear and yellow" stubble everywhere perceptible.

Whether Mrs. Fum's robe had been devised at a period when dresses were worn much shorter, or that, from being very tall, a sufficiency of the material could not be obtained,—but true it is, her costume would have been almost national in certain Scotch regiments, and necessitated, for modesty's sake, a peculiar species of ducking trip, that, with the nodding motion of her head, gave her the gait of a kangaroo.

Scarcely had the various individuals time to give a cursory glance at their neighbors' finery, when Lady Eleanor appeared leaning on her daughter's arm. Mr. Dempsey had waited for above half an hour outside the door to offer his escort, which being coldly but civilly declined, the ladies entered.

Mrs. Fumbally rose to meet her guests, and was about to proceed in due form with a series of introducings, when Lady Eleanor cut her short by a very slight but courteous salutation to the company collectively, and then sat down.

The most insufferable assumption of superiority is never half so chilling in its effect upon underbred people as the calm quietude of good manners.

And thus the party were more repelled by Lady Eleanor and her daughter's easy bearing than they would have felt at any outrageous pretension. The elegant simplicity of their dress, too, seemed to rebuke the stage finery of the others, and very uneasy glances met and were interchanged at this new companionship. A few whispered words, an occasional courageous effort to talk aloud, suddenly ending in a cough, and an uneasy glance at the large silver watch over the chimney, were all that took place, when the uncombed head of a waiter, hired specially for the day, gave the announcement that dinner was served.

"Mr. Dempsey—Mr. Dunlop," said Mrs. Fumbally, with a gesture towards Lady Eleanor and her daughter. The gentlemen both advanced a step and then stood stock still, as Lady Eleanor, drawing her shawl around her with one hand, slipped the other within her daughter's arm. Every eye was now turned towards Mr. Dunlop, who was a kind of recognized type of high life; and he, feeling the urgency of the moment, made a step in advance, and with extended arm, said, "May I have the honor to offer my arm?"

"With your leave, I'll take my daughter's, sir," said Lady Eleanor, coldly; and without paying the least attention to the various significant glances around her, she walked forward to the dinner-room.

The chilling reserve produced by the new arrivals had given an air of decorous quietude to the dinner, which, if gratifying to Lady Eleanor and Helen, was very far from being so to the others, and as the meal proceeded, certain low mutterings—the ground swell of a coming storm—announced the growing feeling of displeasure amongst them. Lady Eleanor and Miss Darcy were too unconscious of having offered any umbrage to the party to notice these indications of discontent; nor did they remark that Mr.

Dempsey himself was becoming overwhelmed by the swelling waves of popular indignation.

A very curt monosyllable had met Lady Eleanor in the two efforts she had made at conversation with her neighbor, and she was perhaps not very sorry to find that table-talk was not a regulation of the "Establishment".

Had Lady Eleanor or Helen been disposed to care for it, they might have perceived that the dinner itself was not less anomalous than the company, and like them suffered sorely from being over-dressed. They, however, affected to eat, and seemed satisfied with everything, resolved that, having encountered the ordeal, they would go through with it to the last. The observances of the table had one merit in the Fumbally household; they were conducted with no unnecessary tediousness. The courses—if we dare so apply the name to an irregular skirmish of meats, hot, cold, and *réchauffé*—followed rapidly, the guests ate equally so, and the table presented a scene, if not of convivial enjoyment, at least of bustle and animation, that supplied its place. This movement, so to call it, was sufficiently new to amuse Helen Darcy, who, less pained than her mother at their companionship, could not help relishing many of the eccentric features of the scene; everything in the dress, manner, tone of voice, and bearing of the company presenting such a striking contrast to all she had been used to. This enjoyment on her part, although regulated by the strictest good-breeding, was perceived, or rather suspected, by some of the ladies present, and looks of very unmistakable anger were darted towards her from the end of the table, so that both mother and daughter felt the moment a very welcome one when a regiment of small decanters were set down on the board, and the ladies rose to withdraw.

If Lady Eleanor had consulted her own ardent wishes, she would at once have retired to her room, but she had resolved on the whole sacrifice, and took her place in the drawing-room, determined to follow in every respect the usages around her. Mrs. Fumbally addressed a few civil words to her, and then left the room to look after the cares of the household. The group of seven ladies who remained, formed themselves into a coterie apart, and producing from sundry bags and baskets little specimens of female handiwork, began arranging their cottons and worsteds with a most praiseworthy activity.

While Lady Eleanor sat with folded bands and half-closed lids, sunk in her own meditations, Helen arose and walked towards a book-shelf, where some well-thumbed volumes were lying. An odd volume of "Delphine," a "Treatise on Domestic Cookery," and "Moore's Zeluco" were not attractive, and she sauntered to the piano, on which were scattered some of the songs from the "Siege of Belgrade," the then popular piece; certain comic melodies lay also among them, inscribed with the name of Lawrence M'Farland, a gentleman whom they had heard addressed several times during dinner. While Helen turned over the music pages, the eyes of the others were riveted on her; and when she ran her fingers over the keys of the cracked old instrument, and burst into an involuntary laugh at its discordant tones, a burst of unequivocal indignation could no longer be restrained.

"I declare, Miss M'Corde," said an old lady with a paralytic shake in her head, and a most villanous expression in her one eye,—"I declare I would speak to her, if I was in your place."

"Unquestionably," exclaimed another, whose face was purple with excitement; and thus encouraged, a very thin and very tall personage, with a long, slender nose tipped with pink, and light red hair in ringlets, arose from her seat, and approached where Helen was standing.

"You are perhaps not aware, ma'am," said she, with a mincing, lisping accent, the very essence of gentility, "that this instrument is not a 'house piano.'"

Helen blushed slightly at the address, but could not for her life guess what the words meant. She had heard of grand pianos and square pianos, of cottage pianos, but never of "house pianos," and she answered in the most simple of voices, "Indeed."

"No, ma'am, it is not; it belongs to your very humble servant,"—here she courtesied to the ground,-"who regrets deeply that its tone should not have more of your approbation."

"And I, ma'am," said a fat old lady, waddling over, and wheezing as though she should choke, "I have to express my sorrow that the book-shelf, which you have just ransacked, should not present something worthy of your notice. The volumes are mine."

"And perhaps, ma'am," cried a third, a little meagre figure, with a voice like a nutmeg-grater, "you could persuade the old lady, who I presume is your mother, to take her feet off that worked stool. When I made it, I scarcely calculated on the honor it now enjoys!"

Lady Eleanor looked up at this instant, and although unconscious of what was passing, seeing Helen, whose face was now crimson, standing in the midst of a very excited group, she arose hastily, and said,—

"Helen, dearest, is there anything the matter?"

"I should say there was, ma'am," interposed the very fat lady,—"I should be disposed to say there was a great deal the matter. That to make use of private articles as if they were for house use, to thump one lady's piano, to toss another lady's books, to make oneself comfortable in a chair specially provided for the oldest boarder, with one's feet on another lady's footstool,—these are liberties, ma'am, which become something more than freedoms when taken by unknown individuals."

"I beg you will forgive my daughter and myself," said Lady Eleanor, with an air of real regret; "our total ignorance—"

"I thought as much, indeed," muttered she of the shaking head; "there is no other word for it."

"You are quite correct, ma'am," said Lady Eleanor, at once addressing her in the most apologetic of voices,-"I cannot but repeat the word; our very great ignorance of the usages observed here is our only excuse, and I beg you to believe us incapable of taking such liberties in future."

If anything could have disarmed the wrath of this Holy Alliance, the manner in which these words were uttered might have done so. Far from it, however. When the softer sex are deficient in breeding, mercy is scarcely one of their social attributes. Had Lady Eleanor assumed towards them the manner with which in other days she had repelled vulgar attempts at familiarity, they would in all probability have shrunk back, abashed and ashamed; but her yielding suggested boldness, and they advanced, with something like what in Cossack warfare is termed a "Hurra," an indiscriminate clang of voices being raised in reprobation of every supposed outrage the unhappy strangers had inflicted on the company. Amid this Babel of accusation Lady Eleanor could distinguish nothing, and while, overwhelmed by the torrent, she was preparing to take her daughter's arm and withdraw, the door which led into the dining-room was suddenly thrown open, and the convivial party entered *en masse*.

"Here's a shindy, by George!" cried Mr. M'Farland,—the Pickle, and the wit of the Establishment,—"I say, see how the new ones are getting it!"

While Mr. Dempsey hurried away to seek Mrs. Fumbally herself, the confusion and uproar increased; the loud, coarse laughter of the "Gentlemen" being added to the wrathful violence of the softer sex. Lady Eleanor, how-ever, had drawn her daughter to her side, and without uttering a word, proceeded to leave the room. To this course a considerable obstacle presented itself in the shape of the Collector, who, with expanded legs, and hands thrust deep into his side-pockets, stood against the door.

"Against the ninth general rule, ma'am, which you may read in the frame over the chimney!" exclaimed he, in a voice somewhat more faltering and thicker than became a respectable official. "No lady or gentleman can leave the room while any dispute in which they are concerned remains unsettled. Isn't that it, M'Farland?" cried he, as the young gentleman alluded to took down the law-table from its place.

"All right," replied M'Farland; "the very best rule in the house. Without it, all the rows would take place in private! Now for a court of inquiry. Mr. Dunlop, you are for the prosecution, and can't sit."

"May I beg, sir, you will permit us to pass out?" said Lady Eleanor, in a voice whose composure was slightly shaken.

"Can't be, ma'am; in contravention of all law," rejoined the Collector.

"Where is Mr. Dempsey?" whispered Helen, in her despair; and though the words were uttered in a low voice, one of the ladies overheard them. A general titter ran immediately around, only arrested by the fat lady exclaiming aloud, "Shameless minx!"

A very loud hubbub of voices outside now rivalled the tumult within, amid which one most welcome was distinguished by Helen.

"Oh, mamma, how fortunate! I hear Tate's voice."

"It's me,—it's Mrs. Fumbally," cried that lady, at the same moment tapping sharply at the door.

"No matter, can't open the door now. Court is about to sit," replied the Collector. "Mrs. Gwynne stands arraigned for—for what is't? There's no use in making that clatter; the door shall not be opened."

This speech was scarcely uttered, when a tremendous bang was heard, and the worthy Collector, with the door over him, was hurled on his face in the midst of the apartment, upsetting in his progress a round table and a lamp over the assembled group of ladies.

Screams of terror, rage, pain, and laughter were now commingled; and while some assisted the prostrate official to rise, and sprinkled his temples with water, others bestowed their attentions on the discomfited fair, whose lustre was sadly diminished by lamp-oil and bruises, while a third section, of which M'Farland was chief, lay back in their chairs and laughed vociferously. Meanwhile, how and when nobody could tell, Lady Eleanor and her daughter had escaped and gained their apartments in safety.

A more rueful scene than the room presented need not be imagined. The Collector, whose nose bled profusely, sat pale, half fainting, in one corner, while some kind friends labored to stop the bleeding, and restore him to animation. Lamentations of the most poignant grief were uttered over silks, satins, and tabinets irretrievably ruined; while the paralytic lady having broken the ribbon of her cap, her head rolled about fearfully, and even threatened to come clean off altogether. As for poor Mrs. Fumbally, she flew from place to place, in a perfect agony of affliction; now wringing her hands over the prostrate door, now over the fragments of the lamp, and now endeavoring to restore the table, which, despite all her efforts, would not stand upon two legs. But the most miserable figure of all was Paul Dempsey, who saw no footing for himself anywhere. Lady Eleanor and Helen must detest him to the day of his death. The boarders could never forgive him. Mrs. Fum would as certainly regard him as the author of all evil, and the Collector would inevitably begin dunning him for an unsettled balance of fourteen and ninepence, lost at "Spoiled five" two winters before.

Already, indeed, symptoms of his unpopularity began to show themselves. Angry looks and spiteful glances were directed towards him, amidst muttered expressions of displeasure. How far these manifestations might have proceeded there is no saying, had not the attention of the company been drawn to the sudden noise of a carriage stopping at the street door.

"Going, flitting, evacuating the territory!" exclaimed M'Farland, as from an open window he contemplated the process of packing a post-chaise with several heavy trunks and portmanteaus.

"The Gwynnes!" muttered the Collector, with his handkerchief to his face.

"Even so! flying with camp equipage and all. There stands your victor, that little old fellow with the broad shoulders. I say, come here a moment," called he aloud, making a sign for Tate to approach. "The Collector is not in the least angry for what's happened; he knew you did n't mean anything serious. Pray, who are these ladies, your mistresses I mean?"

"Lady Eleanor Darcy and Miss Darcy, of Gwynne Abbey," replied Tate, sturdily, as he gave the names with a most emphatic distinctness.

"The devil it was!" exclaimed M'Farland.

"By my conscience, ye may well wonder at being in such company, sir," said Tate, laughing, and resuming his place just in time to assist Lady Eleanor to ascend the steps. Helen quickly followed, the door was slammed to, and, Tate mounting with the alacrity of a town footman, the chaise set out at a brisk pace down the street.

CHAPTER XXIII
THE COAST IN WINTER

Although Tate Sullivan had arrived in Coleraine and provided himself with a chaise expressly to bring his mistress and her daughter back to "The Corvy,"—from which the sheriff's officers had retired in discomfiture, on discovering the loss of their warrants,—Lady Eleanor, dreading a renewal of the law proceedings, had determined never to return thither.

From the postilion they learned that a small but not uncomfortable lodging could be had near the little village of Port Ballintray, and to this spot they now directed their course. The transformation of a little summer watering-place into the dismal village of some poor fishermen in winter, is a sad spectacle; nor was the picture relieved by the presence of the fragments of a large vessel, which, lately lost with all its crew, hung on the rocks, thumping and clattering with every motion of the waves. By the faint moonlight Lady Eleanor and her daughter could mark the outlines of figures, as they waded in the tide or clambered along the rocks, stripping the last remains of the noble craft, and contending with each other for the spoils of the dead.

If the scene itself was a sorrowful one, it was no less painful to their eyes from feeling a terrible similitude between their own fortunes and that of the wrecked vessel; the gallant ship, meant to float in its pride over the ocean, now a broken and shattered wreck, falling asunder with each stroke of the sea!

"How like and yet how unlike!" sighed Lady Eleanor; "if these crushed and shattered timbers have no feeling in the hour of adversity, yet are they denied the glorious hopefulness that in the saddest moments clings to humanity. Ours is shipwreck, too, but, taken at its worst, is only temporary calamity!"

Helen pressed her mother's hands with fervor to her lips; perhaps never had she loved her with more intensity than at that instant.

The chaise drew up at the door of a little cabin, built at the foot of, and, as it actually seemed, against a steep rocky cliff of great height. In summer it was regarded as one of the best among the surrounding lodgings, but now it looked dreary enough. A fishing-boat, set up on one end, formed a kind of sheltering porch to the doorway; while spars, masts, and oars were lashed upon the thatch, to serve as a protection against the dreadful gales of winter.

A childless widow was the only occupant, whose scanty livelihood was eked out by letting lodgings to the summer visitors,—a precarious subsistence, which in bad seasons, and they were not unfrequent, failed altogether. It was with no small share of wonderment that Mary Spellan— or "old Molly," as the village more usually called her—saw a carriage draw up to the cabin door late of a dark night in winter; nor was this feeling unalloyed by a very strong tincture of suspicion, for Molly was an Antrim woman, and had her proportion of the qualities, good and bad, of the "Black North."

"They 'll no be makin' a stay on't," said she to the postboy, who, in his capacity of interpreter, had got down to explain to Molly the requirements of the strangers. "They 'll be here to-day and awa to-morrow, I 'm thenkin'," said she, with habitual and native distrust. "And what for wull I make a 'hottle'"—no greater indignity could be offered to the lodging-house keeper than to compare the accommodation in any respect with that of an hotel— "of my wee bit house, takin' out linen and a' the rest o' it for maybe a day or twa."

Lady Eleanor, who watched from the window of the chaise the course of the negotiations without hearing any part of the colloquy, was impatient at the slow progress events seemed to take, and supposing that the postboy's demands were made with more regard to their habits than to old Molly's means of accommodation, called out,—

"Tell the good woman that we are easily satisfied; and if the cabin be but clean and quiet—"

"What's the leddie sayin'?" said Molly, who heard only a stray word, and that not overpleasing to her.

"She 's saying it will do very well," said the postboy, conciliatingly, "and 'tis maybe a whole year she 'll stay with you."

"Ech, dearee me!" sighed Molly, "it's wearisome enough to hae' them a' the summer, without hae'ing them in the winter too. Tell her to come ben, and see if she likes the place." And with this not over-courteous proposal, Molly turned her back, and rolled, rather thau walked, into the cabin.

The three little rooms which comprised the whole suite destined for strangers, were, in all their poverty, scrupulously clean; and Molly, gradually thawed by the evident pretensions of her guests, volunteered little additions to the furniture, as she went along, concluding with the very characteristic remark,—

"But ye maun consider, that it's no my habit, or my likin' either, to hae lodgers in the winter; and af ye come, ye maun e'en pay for your whistle, like ither folk."

This was the arrangement that gave Lady Eleanor the least trouble; and though the terms demanded were in reality exorbitant, they were acceded to without hesitation by those who never had had occasion to make similar compacts, and believed that the sum was a most reasonable one.

As is ever the case, the many wants and inconveniences of a restricted dwelling were far more placidly endured by those long habituated to every luxury than by their followers; and so, while Lady Eleanor and Helen submitted cheerfully to daily privations of one kind or other, Tate lived a life of everlasting complaint and grumbling over the narrow accommodation of the cabin, continually irritating old Molly by demands impossible to comply with, and suggesting the necessity of changes perfectly out of her power to effect. It is but justice to the faithful old butler to state, that to this line of conduct he was prompted by what he deemed due to his mistress and her high station, rather than by any vain hope of ever succeeding, his complaints being less demands for improvement than after the fashion of those "protests" which dissentient members of a legislature think it necessary to make in cases where opposition is unavailing.

These half-heard mutterings of Tate were the only interruptions to a life of sad but tranquil monotony. Lady Eleanor and her daughter lived as though in a long dream; the realities around them so invested with sameness and uniformity that days, weeks, and months blended into each other, and became one commingled mass of time, undivided and unmarked. Of the world without they heard but little; of those dearest to them, absolutely nothing. The very newspapers maintained a silence on the subject of the expedition under Abercrombie, so that of the Knight himself they had no tidings whatever. Of Daly they only heard once, at the end of one of Bicknell's letters, one of those gloomy records of the law's delay; that he said, "You will be sorry to learn that Mr. Bagenal Daly, having omitted to appear personally or by counsel in a cause lately called on here, has been cast in heavy damages, and pronounced in contempt, neither of which inflictions will probably give him much uneasiness, if, as report speaks, he has gone to pass the remainder of his days in America. Miss Daly speaks of joining him, when she learns that he has fixed on any spot of future residence." The only particle of consolation extractable from the letter was in a paragraph at the end, which ran thus: "O'Reilly's solicitor has withdrawn all the proceedings lately commenced, and there is an evident desire to avoid further litigation. I hear that for the points now in dispute an arbitration will be proposed.

Would you feel disposed or free to accept such an offer, if made? Let me know this, as I should be prepared at all events."

Even this half-confession of a claim gave hope to the drooping spirits of Lady Eleanor, and she lost no time in acquainting Bicknell with her opinion that while they neither could nor would compromise the rights of their son, for any interests actually their own, and terminating with their lives, they would willingly adopt any arrangement that should remove the most pressing evils of poverty, and permit them to live united for the rest of their days.

The severe winter of northern Ireland closed in, with all its darkening skies and furious storms; scattered fragments of wrecked vessels, spars, and ship-gear strewed the rocky coast for miles. The few cottages here and there were closed and barricaded as if against an enemy, the roofs fastened down by ropes and heavy implements of husbandry, to keep safe the thatch; the boats of the fishermen drawn up on land, grouped round the shealings in sad but not unpicturesque confusion. The ever-restless sea beating like thunder upon that iron shore, the dark impending clouds lowering over cliff and precipice, were all that the eye could mark. No cattle were on the hills; the sheep nestling in the little glens and valleys were almost undistinguishable from the depth of gloom around; not a man was to be seen.

The little village of Port Ballintray, which a few months before abounded in all the sights and sounds of human intercourse, was now perfectly deserted. Most of the cottages were fastened on the inside; in some the doors, burst open by the storm, showed still more unquestionably that no dwellers remained; the little gardens, tended with such care, were now uprooted and devastated; fallen trellises and ruined porches were seen on every side; and even Mrs. Fumbally's, the pride and glory of the place, had not escaped the general wreck, and the flaunting archway, on which, in bright letters, her name was inscribed, hung pensively by one pillar, and waved like a sad pendulum, "counting the weary minutes over!"

While nothing could less resemble the signs of habitation than the aspect of matters without, within a fire burned on more than one hearth, and a serving-woman was seen moving from place to place occupied in making those arrangements which bespoke the speedy arrival of visitors.

It was long after nightfall that a travelling carriage and four—a rare sight in such a place, even in the palmiest days of summer—drew up at the front of the little garden, and after some delay a very old and feeble man was lifted out, and carried between two servants into the house; he was followed by another, whose firm step and erect figure indicated the prime of life; while after him again came a small man, most carefully protected by coats and comforters against the severity of the season. He walked lame, and in the shuddering look he gave around in the short transit from the carriage to the house-door, showed that such prospects, however grand and picturesque, had few charms for him.

A short interval elapsed after the luggage was removed from the carriage, and then one of the servants mounted the box, the horses' beads were turned, and the conveyance was seen retiring by the road to Coleraine.

The effective force of Mrs. Fum's furniture was never remarkable, in days of gala and parade; it was still less imposing now, when nothing remained save an invalided garrison of deal chairs and tables, a few curtainless beds, and a stray chest of drawers or two of the rudest fashion.

The ample turf fire on the hearth of the chief sitting-room, cheering and bright as was its aspect, after the dark and rainy scene without doors, could not gladden the air of these few and comfortless movables into a look of welcome; and so one of the newly arrived party seemed to feel, as he threw his glance over the meagre-looking chamber, and in a half-complaining, half-inquiring tone, said, —

"Don't you think, sir, they might have done this a little better? These windows are no defence against the wind or rain, the walls are actually soaked with wet; not a bit of carpet, not a chair to sit upon! I 'm greatly afraid for the old gentleman; if he were to be really ill in such a place—"

A heavy fit of coughing from the inner room now seemed to corroborate the suspicion.

"We must make the best of it, Nalty," said the other. "Remember, the plan was of your own devising; there was no time for much preparation here, if even it had been prudent or possible to make it; and as to my father, I warrant you his constitution is as good as yours or mine; anxiety about this business has preyed upon him; but let your plan only succeed, and I warrant him as able to undergo fatigue and privation as either of us."

"His cough is very troublesome," interposed Nalty, timidly.

"About the same I have known it every winter since I was a boy," said the other, carelessly. "I say, sir," added he, louder, while he tapped the door with his knuckles, —"I say, sir, Nalty is afraid you have caught fresh cold."

"Tell him his annuity is worth three years' purchase," said the old man from within, with a strange unearthly effort at a laugh. "Tell him, if he 'll pay five hundred pounds down, I 'll let him run his own life against mine in the deed."

"There, you hear that, Nalty! What say you to the proposal?"

"Wonderful old man! astonishing!" muttered Nalty, evidently not flattered at the doubts thus suggested as to his own longevity.

"He doesn't seem to like that, Bob, eh?" called out the old man, with another cackle.

"After that age they get a new lease, sir,—actually a new lease of life," whispered Nalty.

Mr. O'Reilly—for it was that gentleman, who, accompanied by his father and confidential lawyer, formed the party—gave a dry assent to the proposition, and drawing his chair closer to the fire, seemed to occupy himself with his own thoughts. Meanwhile the old doctor continued to maintain a low muttering conversation with his servant, until at length the sounds were exchanged for a deep snoring respiration, and he slept.

The appearance of a supper, which, if not very appetizing, was at least very welcome, partially restored the drooping spirits of Mr. Nalty, who now ate and talked with a degree of animation quite different from his former mood.

"The ham is excellent, sir, and the veal very commendable," said he, perceiving that O'Reilly sat with his untouched plate before him, "and a glass of sherry is very grateful after such a journey."

"A weary journey, indeed," said O'Reilly, sighing: "the roads in this part of the island would seem seldom travelled, and the inns never visited; however, if we succeed, Nalty—"

"So we shall, sir, I have not the slightest doubt of it; it is perfectly evident that they have no money to go on. 'The sinews of war' are expended, all Bicknell's late proceedings indicate a failing exchequer; that late record, for instance, at Westport, should never have been left to a common jury."

"All this may be true, and yet we may find them unwilling to adopt a compromise: there is a spirit in this class of men very difficult to deal with."

"But we have two expedients," interrupted Nalty.

"Say, rather, a choice between two; you forget that if we try my father's plan, the other can never be employed."

"I incline to the other mode of procedure," said Nalty, thoughtfully; "it has an appearance of frankness and candor very likely to influence people of this kind; besides, we have such a strong foundation to go upon,—the issue of two trials at bar, both adverse to them, O'Grady's opinion on the ejectment cases equally opposed to their views. The expense of a suit in equity to determine the validity of the entail, and show how far young Darcy can be a plaintiff: then the cases for a jury; all costly matters, sir!

Bicknell knows this well; indeed, if the truth were out, I suspect Sam is getting frightened about his own costs, he has sold out of the funds twice to pay fees."

"Yet the plan is a mere compromise, after all," said O'Reilly; "it is simply saying, relinquish your right, and accept so much money."

"Not exactly, sir; we deny the right, we totally reject the claim, we merely say, forego proceedings that are useless, spare yourselves and us the cost and publicity of legal measures, whose issue never can benefit you, and, in return for your compliance, receive an annuity or a sum, as may be agreed upon."

"But how is Lady Eleanor to decide upon a course so important, in the absence of her husband and her son? Is it likely, is it possible, she would venture on so bold a step?"

"I think so; Bicknell half acknowledged that the funds of the suit were her jointure, and that Darcy, out of delicacy towards her, had left it entirely at her option to continue or abandon the proceedings."

"Still," said O'Reilly, "a great difficulty remains; for supposing them to accept our terms, that they give up the claim and accept a sum in return, what if at some future day evidence should turn up to substantiate their views,—they may not, it is true, break the engagement—though I don't see why they should not—but let us imagine them to be faithful to the contract,- what will the world say? In what position shall we stand when the matter gains publicity?"

"How can it, sir?" interposed Nalty, quickly; "how is it possible, if there be no trial? The evidence, as you call it, is no evidence unless produced in court. You know, sir," said the little man, with twinkling eyes and pleased expression, "that a great authority at common law only declined the testimony of a ghost because the spirit was n't in court to be cross-examined. Now all they could bring would be rumor, newspaper allegations and paragraphs, asterisks and blanks."

"There may come a time when public opinion, thus expounded, will be as stringent as the judgments of the law courts," said O'Reilly, thoughtfully.

"I am not so certain of that, sir; the license of an unfettered press will always make its decisions inoperative; it is 'the chartered libertine' the poet speaks of."

"But what if, yielding to public impression, it begins to feel that its weight is in exact proportion to its truth, that well-founded opinions, just judgments, correct anticipations, obtain a higher praise and price than scandalous anecdotes and furious attacks? What if that day should arrive, Nalty? I am by no means convinced that such an era is distant."

"Let it come, sir," said the little man, rubbing his hands, "and when it does there will be enough employment on its hand without going back on our trangressions; the world will always be wicked enough to keep the moralist at his work of correction. But to return to our immediate object, I perceive you are inclined to Dr. Hickman's plan."

"I am so far in its favor," said O'Reilly, "that it solves the present difficulty, and prevents all future danger. Should my father succeed in persuading Lady Eleanor to this marriage, the interest of the two families is inseparably united. It is very unlikely that any circumstance, of what nature soever, would induce young Darcy to dispute his sister's claim, or endanger her position in society. This settlement of the question is satisfactory in itself, and shows a good face to the world, and I confess I am curious to know what peculiar objection you can see against it."

"It has but one fault, sir."

"And that?"

"Simply, it is impossible."

"Is it the presumption of a son of mine seeking an alliance with the daughter of Maurice Darcy that appears so very impossible?" said Hickman, with a hissing utterance of each word, that bespoke a fierce conflict of passion within him.

"Certainly not, sir," replied Nalty, hastily excusing himself. "I am well aware which party contributes most to such a compact. Mr. Beecham O'Reilly might look far higher—"

"Wherein lies the impossibility you speak of, then?" rejoined O'Reilly, sternly.

"I need scarcely remind *you*, sir," said Nalty, with an air of deep humility, "*you* that have seen so much more of life than I have, of what inveterate prejudices these old families, as they like to call themselves, are made up; that, creating a false standard of rank, they adhere to its distinctions with a tenacity far greater than what they exhibit towards the real attributes of fortune. They seem to adopt for their creed the words of the old song,—

> "The King may make a Baron bold,
> Or an Earl of any fool, sir,
> But with all his power, and all his gold
> He can never make an O'Toole, sir."

"These are very allowable feelings when sustained by wealth and fortune," said O'Reilly, quietly.

"I verily believe their influence is greater in adversity," said Nalty; "they seem to have a force of consolation that no misery can rob them of. Besides, in this case—for we should not lose sight of the matter that concerns us most—we must not forget that they regard your family in the light of oppressors. I am well aware that you have acted legally and safely throughout; but still—let us concede something to human prejudices and passions—is it unreasonable to suppose that they charge you and yours with their own downfall?"

"The more natural our desire to repair the apparent wrong."

"Very true on *your* part, but not perhaps the more necessary on theirs to accept the amende."

"That will very much depend, I think, on the way of its being proffered. Lady Eleanor, cold, haughty, and reserved as she is to the world, has always extended a degree of cordiality and kindness towards my father; his age, his infirmities, a seeming simplicity in his character, have had their influence. I trust greatly to this feeling, and to the effect of a request made by an old man, as if from his death-bed. My father is not deficient in the tact to make an appeal of this kind very powerful; at all events, his heart is in the scheme, and nothing short of that would have induced me to venture on this long and dreary journey at such a season. Should he only succeed in gaining an influence over Lady Eleanor, through pity or any other motive, we are certain to succeed. The Knight, I feel sure, would not oppose; and as for the young lady, a handsome young fellow with a large fortune can scarcely be deemed very objectionable."

"How was the proposition met before?" said Nalty, inquiringly; "was their refusal conveyed in any expression of delicacy? Was there any acknowledgment of the compliment intended them?"

"No, not exactly," said O'Reilly, blushing; for, while he hesitated about the danger of misleading his adviser, he could not bear to repeat the insolent rejection of the offer. "The false position in which the families stood towards each other made a great difficulty; but, more than all, the influence of Bagenal Daly increased the complexity; now he, fortunately for us, is not forthcoming, his debts have driven him abroad, they say."

"So, then, they merely declined the honor in cold and customary phrase?" said Nalty, carelessly.

"Something in that way," replied O'Reilly, affecting an equal unconcern; "but we need not discuss the point, it affords no light to guide us regarding the future."

If Nalty saw plainly that some concealment was practised towards him, he knew his client too well to venture on pushing his inquiries further; so he contented himself with asking when and in what manner O'Reilly proposed to open the siege.

"To-morrow morning," replied the other; "there's no time to be lost. A few lines from my father to Lady Eleanor will acquaint her with his arrival in the neighborhood, after a long and fatiguing search for her residence. We may rely upon him performing his part well; he will allude to his own breaking health in terms that will not fail to touch her, and ask permission to wait upon her. As for us, Nalty, we must not be foreground figures in the picture. You, if known to be here at all, must be supposed to be my father's medical friend. I must be strictly in the shade."

Nalty gave a grim smile at the notion of his new professional character, and begged O'Reilly to proceed.

"Our strategy goes no further; such will be the order of battle. We must trust to my father for the mode he will engage the enemy afterwards, for the reasons which have led him to take this step,—the approaching close of a long life, unburdened with any weighty retrospect, save that which concerns the Darcy family; for, while affecting to sorrow over their changed fortunes, he can attribute their worst evils to bad counsels and rash advice, and insinuate how different had been their lot had they only consented to regard us—as they might and ought to have done—in the light of friends. Hush! who is speaking there?"

They listened for a second or two, and then came the sound of the old man's voice, as he talked to himself in his sleep; his accents were low and complaining, as if he were suffering deeply from some mental affliction, and at intervals a heavy sob would break from him.

"He is ill, sir; the old gentleman is very ill!" said Nalty, in real alarm.

"Hush!" said O'Reilly, as, with one hand on the door, he motioned silence with the other.

"Yes, my Lady," muttered the sleeper, but in a voice every syllable of which was audible, "eighty-six years have crept to your feet, to utter this last wish and die. It is the last request of one that has already left the things of this world, and would carry from it nothing but the thought that will track him to the grave!" A burst of grief, too sudden and too natural to admit of a doubt of its sincerity, followed the words; and O'Reilly was about to enter the room, when a low dry laugh arrested his steps, and the old man said,—

"Ay! Bob Hickman, did n't I tell you that would do? I knew she 'd cry, and I told you, if she cried one tear, the day was ours!"

There was something so horrible in the baseness of a mind thus revelling in its own duplicity, that even Nalty seemed struck with dread. O'Reilly saw what was passing in the other's mind, and, affecting to laugh at these "effects of fatigue and exhaustion," half led, half pushed him from the room, and said "Good-night."

CHAPTER XXIV
THE DOCTOR'S LAST DEVICE

"Tell Mister Bob—Mr. O'Reilly I mean—to come to me," were the first words of old Dr. Hickman, as he awoke on the following morning.

"Well, sir, how have you slept?" said his son, approaching the bedside, and taking a chair; "have you rested well?"

"Middling,-only middling, Bob. The place is like a vault, and the rats have it all their own way. They were capering about the whole night, and made such a noise trying to steal off with one of my shoes." "Did they venture that far?"

"Ay, did they! but I couldn't let it go with them. I know you 're in a hurry to stand in them yourself, Bob, and leave me and the rats to settle it between us—ay!" "Really, sir, these are jests—-"

"Too like earnest to be funny, Bob; so I feel them myself. Ugh! ugh! The damp of this place is freezing the very heart's blood of me. How is Nalty this morning?" "Like a fellow taken off a wreck, sir, after a week's starvation. He is sitting at the fire there, with two blankets round him, and vows to heaven, every five minutes, that if he was once back in Old Dominick Street, a thousand guineas would n't tempt him to such another expedition."

The old doctor laughed till it made him cough, and when the fit was over, laughed again, wiping his weeping eyes, and chuckling in the most unearthly glee at the lawyer's discomfiture.

"Wrapped up in blankets, eh, Bob?" said he, that he might hear further of his fellow-traveller's misery.

O'Reilly saw that he had touched the right key, and expatiated for some minutes upon Nalty's sufferings, throwing out, from time to time, adroit hints that only certain strong and hale constitutions could endure privations like these. "Now, you, sir," continued he, "you look as much yourself as ever; in fact, I half doubt how you are to play the sick man, with all these signs of rude health about you."

"Leave that to me, Bob; I think I 've seen enough of them things to know them now. When I 've carried my point, and all's safe and secure, you 'll see me like the pope we read of, that looked all but dead till they elected him, and then stood up stout and hearty five minutes after,—we 'll have a miracle of this kind in our own family."

"I suspect, sir, we shall have difficulty in obtaining an interview," said O'Reilly.

"No!" rejoined the old man, with a scarcely perceptible twinkle of his fishy eyes.

"Nalty 's of my opinion, and thinks that Lady Eleanor will positively decline it."

"No," echoed he once more.

"And that, without any suspicion of our plan, she will yet refuse to receive you."

"I 'm not going to ask her, Bob," croaked the old doctor, with a species of chuckling crow in his voice.

"Then you have abandoned your intention," exclaimed O'Reilly, in dismay, "and the whole journey has been incurred for nothing."

"No!" said the doctor, whose grim old features were lit up with a most spiteful sense of his superior cunning.

"Then I don't understand you,—that's clear," exclaimed O'Reilly, testily. "You say that you do not intend to call upon her—"

"Because she's coming here to see me," cried the old man, in a scream of triumph; "read that, it's an answer to a note I sent off at eight o'clock. Joe waited and brought back this reply." As he spoke, he drew from beneath his pillow a small note, and handed it to his son. O'Reilly opened it with impatience, and read:—

"Lady Eleanor Darcy begs to acknowledge the receipt of Dr. Hickman's note, and, while greatly indisposed to accept of an interview which must be so painful to both parties without any reasonable prospect of rendering service to either, feels reluctant to refuse a request made under circumstances so trying. She will therefore comply with Dr. Hickman's entreaty, and, to spare him the necessity of venturing abroad in this severe weather, will call upon him at twelve o'clock, should she not learn in the meanwhile that the hour is inconvenient."

"Lady Eleanor Darcy come out to call upon you, sir!" said O'Reilly, with an amazement in part simulated to flatter the old man's skill, but far more really experienced. "This is indeed success."

"Ay, you may well say so," chimed in the old man; "for besides that I always look ten years older when I 'm in bed and unshaved, with my nightcap a little off,—this way,—the very sight of these miserable walls, green with damp and mould, this broken window, and the poverty-struck furniture, will all help, and I can get up a cough, if I only draw a long breath."

"I vow, sir, you beat us all; we are mere children compared to you. This is a master-stroke of policy."

"What will Nalty say now—eh, Bob?"

"Say, sir? What can any one say, but that the move showed a master's hand, as much above our skill to accomplish as it was beyond our wit to conceive? I should like greatly to hear how you intend to play the game out," said O'Reilly, throwing a most flattering expression of mingled curiosity and astonishment into his features.

"Wait till I see what trumps the adversary has in hand, Bob; time enough to determine the lead when the cards are dealt."

"I suppose I must keep out of sight, and perhaps Nalty also."

"Nalty ought to be in the house if we want him; as my medical friend, he could assist to draw any little memorandum we might determine upon; a mere note, Bob, between friends, not requiring the interference of lawyers, eh?" There was something fiendish in the low laugh which accompanied these words. "What brings that fellow into the room so often, putting turf on, and looking if the windows are fast? I don't like him, Bob." This was said in reference to a little chubby man, in a waiter's jacket, who really had taken every imaginable professional privilege to obtrude his presence.

"There, there, that will do," said O'Reilly, harshly; "you needn't come till we ring the bell."

"Leave the turf-basket where it is. Don't you think we can mind the fire for ourselves?"

"Let Joe wait, that will be better, sir," whispered O'Reilly; "we cannot be too cautious here." And with a motion of the hand he dismissed the waiter, who, true to his order, seemed never to hear "an aside."

"Leave me by myself, Bob, for half an hour; I 'd like to collect my thoughts,—to settle and think over this meeting. It's past eleven now, and she said twelve o'clock in the note."

"Well, I 'll take a stroll over the hills, and be back for dinner about three; you'll be up by that time."

"That will I, and very hungry too," muttered the old man. "This dying scene has cost me the loss of my breakfast; and, faith, I 'm so weak and low, my head is quite dizzy. There 's an old saying, Mocking is catching; and sure enough there may be some truth in it too."

O'Reilly affected not to hear the remark, and moved towards the door, when he turned about and said,—

"I should say, sir, that the wisest course would be to avoid anything like coercion, or the slightest approach to it. The more the appeal is made to her feelings of compassion and pity—"

"For great age and bodily infirmity," croaked the old man, while the filmy orbs shot forth a flash of malicious intelligence.

"Just so, sir. To others' eyes you do indeed seem weak and bowed down with years. It is only they who have opportunity to recognize the clearness of your intellect and the correctness of your judgment can see how little inroad time has made."

"Ay, but it has, though," interposed the old man, irritably. "My hand shakes more than it used to do; there 's many an operation I 'd not be able for as I once was."

"Well, well, sir," said his son, who found it difficult to repress the annoyance he suffered from his continual reference to the old craft; "remember that you are not called upon now to perform these things."

"Sorry I am it is so," rejoined the other. "I gave up seven hundred a year when I left Loughrea to turn gentleman with you at Gwynne Abbey; and faith, the new trade isn't so profitable as the old one! So it is," muttered he to himself; "and now there 's a set of young chaps come into the town, with their medical halls, and great bottles of pink and blue water in the windows! What chance would I have to go back again?"

O'Reilly heard these half-uttered regrets in silence; he well knew that the safest course was to let the feeble brain exhaust its scanty memories without impediment. At length, when the old doctor seemed to have wearied of the theme, he said,—

"If she make allusion to the Dalys, sir, take care not to confess our mistake about that cabin they called 'The Corvy,' and which you remember we discovered that Daly had settled upon his servant. Let Lady Eleanor suppose that we withdrew proceedings out of respect to her."

"I know, I know," said the old man, querulously, for his vanity was wounded by these reiterated instructions.

"It is possible, too, sir, she 'd stand upon the question of rank; if so, say that Heffernan—no, say that Lord Castlereagh will advise the king to confer the baronetcy on the marriage—don't forget that, sir—on the marriage."

"Indeed, then, I'll say nothing about it," said he, with an energy almost startling. "It's that weary baronetcy cost me the loan to Heffernan on his own bare bond; I 'm well sick of it! Seven thousand pounds at five and a half per cent, and no security!"

"I only thought, sir, it might be introduced incidentally," said O'Reilly, endeavoring to calm down this unexpected burst of irritation.

"I tell you I won't. If I'm bothered anymore about that same baronetcy, I 'll make a clause in my will against my heir accepting it How bad you are for the coronet with the two balls; faix, I remember when the family arms had three of them; ay, and we sported them over the door, too. Eh, Bob, shall I tell her that?"

"I don't suppose it would serve our cause much, sir," said O'Reilly, repressing with difficulty his swelling anger. Then, after a moment, he added, "I could never think of obtruding any advice of mine, sir, but that I half feared you might, in the course of the interview, forget many minor circumstances, not to speak of the danger that your natural kindliness might expose you to in any compact with a very artful woman of the world."

"Don't be afraid of that anyhow, Bob," said he, with a most hideous grin. "I keep a watchful eye over my natural kindliness, and, to say truth, it has done me mighty little mischief up to this. There, now, leave me quiet and to myself."

When the old man was left alone, his head fell slightly forward, and his hands, clasped together, rested on his breast. His eyes, half closed and downcast, and his scarcely heaving chest, seemed barely to denote life, or at most that species of life in which the senses are steeped in apathy. The grim, hard features, stiffened by years and a stern nature, never moved; the thin, close-drawn lips never once opened; and to any observer the figure might have seemed a lifeless counterfeit of old age. And yet within that brain, fast yielding to time and infirmity, where reason came and went like the flame of some flickering taper, and where memory brought up objects of dreamy fancy as often as bygone events, even there plot and intrigue held their ground, and all the machinery of deception was at work, suggesting, contriving, and devising wiles that in their complexity were too puzzling for the faculties that originated them. Is there a Nemesis in this, and do the passions by which we have swayed and controlled others rise up before us in our weak hours, and become the tyrants of our terror-stricken hearts?

It is not our task, were it even in our power, to trace the strange commingled web of reality and fiction that composed the old man's thoughts. At one time he believed he was supplicating the Knight to accord him some slight favor, as he had done more than once successfully. Then he suddenly remembered their relative stations, so strangely reversed; the colossal fortune he had himself accumulated; the hopes and ambitions of his son and grandson, whose only impediments to rank and favor lay in himself, the humble origin of all this wealth. How strange and novel did the conviction strike him that all the benefit of his vast riches lay in the pleasure of their accumulation, that for him fortune had no seductions to offer! Rank, power, munificence, what were they? He never cared for them.

No; it was the game he loved even more than the stake, that tortuous course of policy by which he had outwitted this man and doubled on that. The schemes skilfully conducted, the plots artfully accomplished, — these he loved to think over; and while he grieved to reflect upon the reckless waste he witnessed in the household of his sou, he felt a secret thrill of delight that he, and he alone, was capable of those rare devices and bold expedients by which such a fortune could be amassed. Once and only once did any expression of his features sympathize with these ponderings; and then a low, harsh laugh broke suddenly from him, so fleeting that it failed to arouse even himself. It came from the thought that if after his death his son or grandson would endeavor to forget his memory, and have it forgotten by others, that every effort of display, every new evidence of their gorgeous wealth, would as certainly evoke the criticism of the envious world, who, in spite of them, would bring up the "old doctor" once more, and, by the narrative of his life, humble them to the dust.

This desire to bring down to a level with himself those around him had been the passion of his existence. For this he had toiled and labored, and struggled through imaginary poverty when possessed of wealth; had endured scoffs and taunts, — had borne everything, — and to this desire could be traced his whole feeling towards the Darcys. It was no happiness to him to be the owner of their princely estate if he did not revel in the reflection that they were in poverty. And this envious feeling he extended to his very son. If now and then a vague thought of the object of his present journey crossed his mind, it was speedily forgotten in the all-absorbing delight of seeing the proud Lady Eleanor humbled before him, and the inevitable affliction the Knight would experience when he learned the success of this last device. That it would succeed he had little doubt; he had come too well prepared with arguments to dread failure. Nay, he thought, he believed he could compel compliance if such were to be needed.

It was in the very midst of these strangely confused musings that the doctor's servant announced to him the arrival of Lady Eleanor Darey. The old man looked around him on the miserable furniture, the damp, discolored walls, the patched and mended window-panes, and for a moment he could not imagine where he was; the repetition of the servant's announcement, however, cleared away the cloud from his faculties, and with a slight gesture of his hand he made a sign that she should be admitted. A momentary pause ensued, and he could hear his servant expressing a hope that her Ladyship might not catch cold, as the snow-drift was falling heavily, and the storm very severe. A delay of a few minutes was caused to remove her wet cloak. What a whole story did these two or three seconds reveal to old Hickman as he thought of that Lady Eleanor Darey of whose fastidious elegance the whole "West" was full, whose expensive habits and luxurious tastes had invested her with something like an Oriental reputation for magnificence,— of her coming on foot and alone, through storm and snow, to wait upon him!

He listened eagerly; her footstep was on the stairs, and he heard a low sigh she gave, as, reaching the landing-place, she stood for a moment to recover breath.

"Say Lady Eleanor Darey," said she, unaware that her coming had been already telegraphed to the sick man's chamber.

A faint complaining cry issued from the room as she spoke, and Lady Eleanor said: "Stay! Perhaps Dr. Hickman is too ill; if so, at another time. I 'll come this evening or to-morrow."

"My master is most impatient to see your Ladyship," said the man. "He has talked of nothing else all the morning, and is always asking if it is nigh twelve o'clock."

Lady Eleanor nodded as if to concede her permission, and the servant entered the half-darkened room. A weak, murmuring sound of voices followed; and the servant returned, saying, in a cautious whisper, "He is awake, my Lady, and wishes to see your Ladyship now."

Lady Eleanor's heart beat loudly and painfully; many a sharp pang shot through it, as, with a strong effort to seem calm, she entered.

CHAPTER XXV
A DARK CONSPIRACY

Dr. Hickman was so little prepared for the favorable change in Lady Eleanor's appearance since he had last seen her, as almost to doubt that she was the same, and it was with a slight tremor of voice he said,— "Is it age with me, my Lady, or altered health, that makes the difference, but you seem to me not what I remember you? You are fresher, pardon an old man's freedom, and I should say far handsomer too!"

"Really, Mr. Hickman, you make me think my excursion well repaid by such flatteries," said she, smiling pleasantly, and not sorry thus for a moment to say something that might relieve the awkward solemnity of the scene. "I hope sir, that this air, severe though it be, may prove as serviceable to yourself. Have you slept well?"

"No, my Lady, I scarcely dozed the whole night; this place is a very poor one. The rain comes in there,—where you see that green mark,—and the wind whistles through these broken panes,-and rats, bother them! they never ceased the night through. A poor, poor spot it is, sure enough!"

It never chanced to cross his mind, while bewailing these signs of indigence and discomfort, that she, to whom he addressed the complaint, had been reduced to as bad, even worse, hardships by his own contrivance. Perhaps, indeed, the memory of such had not occurred at that moment to Lady Eleanor, had not the persistence with which he dwelt on the theme somewhat ruffled her patience, and eventually reminded her of her own changed lot. It was then with a slightly irritated tone she remarked,—

"Such accommodation is a very unpleasant contrast to the comforts you are accustomed to, sir; and these sudden lessons in adversity are, now and then, very trying things."

"What does it signify?" sighed the old man, heavily; "a day sooner, a few hours less of sunshine, and the world can make little difference to one like me! Happy for me, if, in confronting them, I have done anything towards my great purpose, the only object between me and the grave!"

Lady Eleanor never broke the silence which followed these words; and though the old man looked as if he expected some observation or rejoinder, she said not a word. At length he resumed, with a faint moan,—"Ah, my Lady, you have much to forgive us for."

"I trust, sir, that our humble fortunes have not taught us to forget the duties of Christianity," was the calm reply.

"Much, indeed, to pardon," continued he, "but far less, my Lady, than is laid to our charge. Lawyers and attorneys make many a thing a cause of bitterness that a few words of kindness would have settled. And what two men of honest intentions could arrange amicably iu five minutes is often worked up into a tedious lawsuit, or a ruinous inquiry in Chancery. So it is!"

"I have no experience in these affairs, sir, but I conclude your remarks are quite correct."

"Faith you may believe them, my Lady, like the Bible; and yet, knowing these fellows so well, having dealings with them since—since—oh, God knows how long—upon my life, they beat me entirely after all. 'T is like taking a walk with a quarrelsome dog; devil a cur he sees but he sets on him, and gets you into a scrape at every step you go! That 's what an attorney does for you. Take out a writ against that fellow, process this one, distrain the other, get an injunction here, apply for a rule there. Oh dear! oh dear! I 'm weary of it for law! All the bitterness it has given me in my life long, all the sorrow and affliction it costs me now." He wiped his eyes as he concluded, and seemed as if overcome by grief.

"It must needs be a sorry source of reparation, sir," rejoined Lady Eleanor, with a calm, steady tone, "when even those so eminently successful can see nothing but affliction in their triumphs."

"Don't call them triumphs, my Lady; that's not the name to give them. I never thought them such."

"I 'm glad to hear it, sir,—glad to know that you have laid up such store of pleasant memories for seasons like the present."

"There was that proceeding, for instance, in December last. Now would you believe it, my Lady, Bob and I never knew a syllable about it till it was all over. You don't know what I 'm speaking of; I mean the writ against the Knight."

"Really, Dr. Hickman, I must interrupt you; however gratifying to me to hear that you stand exculpated for any ungenerous conduct towards my husband, the pleasure of knowing it is more than counterbalanced by the great pain the topic inflicts upon me."

"But I want to clear myself, my Lady; I want you to think of us a little more favorably than late events may have disposed you."

"There are few so humble, sir, as not to have opinions of more consequence than mine."

"Ay, but it's yours I want,—yours, that I'd rather have than the king's on his throne. 'T is in that hope I've come many a weary mile far away from my home, maybe never to see it again! and all that I may have your forgiveness, my Lady, and not only your forgiveness, but your approbation."

"If you set store by any sentiments of mine, sir, I warn you not to ask more than I have iu my power to bestow. I can forgive, I have forgiven, much; but ask me not to concur in acts which have robbed me of the companionship of my husband and my son."

"Wait a bit; don't be too hard, my Lady; I'm on the verge of the grave, a little more, and the dark sleep that never breaks will be on me, and if in this troubled hour I take a wrong word, or say a thing too strong,—forgive me for it. My thoughts are often before me, on the long journey I'm so soon to go."

"It were far better, Dr. Hickman, that we should speak of something less likely to be painful to us both, and if that cannot be, that you should rest satisfied with knowing that however many are the sources of sorrow an humble fortune has opened to us, the disposition to bear malice is not among their number."

"You forgive me, then, my Lady,—you forgive me all?"

"If your own conscience can only do so as freely as I do, believe me, sir, your heart will be tranquil."

The old man pressed his hands to his face, and appeared overcome by emotion. A dead silence ensued, which at length was broken by old Hickman muttering broken words to himself, at first indistinctly, and then more clearly.

"Yes, yes,—I made—the offer—I begged—I supplicated. I did all—all. But no, they refused me! There was no other way of restoring them to their own house and home—but they would n't accept it. I would have settled the whole estate—free of debt—every charge paid off, upon them. There's not a peer in the land could say he was at the head of such a property."

"I must beg, sir, that I may be spared the unpleasantness of overhearing what I doubt is only intended for your own reflection; and if you will permit me, to take my leave—"

"Oh, don't go—don't leave me yet, my Lady. What was it I said,—where was my poor brain rambling? Was I talking about Captain Darcy? Ah! that was the most painful part of all."

"My God! what is it you mean?" said Lady Eleanor, as a sickness like fainting crept over her. "Speak, sir,—tell me this instant!"

"The bills, my Lady,—the bills that he drew in Glee-son's name."

"In Gleeson's name! It is false, sir, a foul and infamous calumny; my son never did this thing,—do not dare to assert it before me, his mother."

"They are in that pocket-book, my Lady,-seven of them for a thousand pounds each. There are two more somewhere among my papers, and it was to meet the payment that the Captain did this." Here he took from beneath his pillow a parchment document, and held it towards Lady Eleanor, who, overwhelmed with terror and dismay, could not stretch her band to take it.

"Here—my Lady—somewhere here," said he, moving his finger vaguely along the lower margin of the document—"here you'll see Maurice Darcy written—not by himself, indeed, but by his son. This deed of sale includes part of Westport, and the town-lands of Cooldrennon and Shoughnakelly. Faith, and, my Lady, I paid my hard cash down on the nail for the same land, and have no better title than what you see! The Knight has only to prove the forgery; of course he could n't do so against his own son."

"Oh, sir, spare me,—I entreat of you to spare me!" sobbed Lady Eleanor, as, convulsed with grief, she hid her face.

A knocking was heard at this moment at the door, and on its being repeated louder, Hickman querulously demanded, "Who was there?"

"A note for Lady Eleanor Darcy," was the reply; "her Ladyship's servant waits for an answer."

Lady Eleanor, without knowing wherefore, seemed to feel that the tidings required prompt attention, and with an effort to subdue her emotion, she broke the seal, and read:—

"Lady Eleanor,—Be on your guard,—there is a dark plot against you. Take counsel in time,—and if you hear the words, 'T is eighty-six years have crept to your feet, to die,' you can credit the friendship of this warning."

"Who brought this note?" said she, in a voice that became full and strong, under the emergency of danger.

"Your butler, my Lady."

"Where is he? Send him to me." And as she spoke, Tate mounted the stairs.

"How came you by this note, Tate?"

"A fisherman, my Lady, left it this instant, with directions to be given to you at once and without a moment's delay."

"'Tis nothing bad, I hope and trust, my Lady," whispered the old man. "The darling young lady is not ill?"

"No, sir, she is perfectly well, nor are the tidings positively bad ones. There is no answer, Tate." So saying, she once more opened the paper and read it over.

Without seeing wherefore, Lady Eleanor felt a sudden sense of hardihood take possession of her; the accusation by which, a moment previous, she had been almost stunned, seemed already lighter to her eyes, and the suspicion that the whole interview was part of some dark design dawned suddenly on her mind. Nor was this feeling permanent; a glance at the miserable old man, who, with head beut down and half-closed eyes, lay before her, dispelling the doubts even more rapidly than they were formed. Indeed, now that the momentary excitement of speaking had passed away, he looked far more wan and wasted than before; his chest, too, heaved with a fluttering, irregular action, that seemed to denote severe and painful effort, while his fingers, with a restless and fidgety motion, wandered here and there, pinching the bed-clothes, and seeming to search for some stray object.

While the conflict continued in Lady Eleanor's mind, the old man's brain once more began to wander, and his lips murmured half inarticulately certain words. "I would give it all!" said he, with a sudden cry; "every shilling of it for that—but it cannot be—no, it cannot be."

"I must leave you, sir," said Lady Eleanor, rising; "and although I have heard much to agitate and afflict me, it is some comfort to my heart to think that I have poured some balm into yours; you have my forgiveness for everything."

"Wait a second, my Lady, wait one second!" gasped he, as with outstretched hands he tried to detain her. "I 'll have strength for it in a minute—I want—I want to ask you once more what you refused me once— and it is n't—it is n't that times are changed, and that you are in poverty now, makes me hope for better luck. It is because this is the request of one on his death-bed,—one that cannot turn his thoughts away from this world, till he has his mind at ease. There, my Lady, take that pocket-book and that deed, throw them into the fire there. They 're the only proofs against the Captain,—no eye but yours must ever see them. If I could see my own beautiful Miss Helen once more in the old house of her fathers—"

"I will not hear of this, sir," interposed Lady Eleanor, hastily. "No time or circumstances can make any change in the feelings with which I have already replied to this proposal."

"Heffernan tells me, my Lady, that the baronetcy is certain—don't go—don't go! It's the voice of one you 'll never hear again calls on you. 'Tis eighty-six years have crept to your feet, to die!"

A faint shriek burst from Lady Eleanor; she tottered, reeled, and fell fainting to the ground.

Terrified by the sudden shock, the old man rung his bell with violence, and screamed for help, in accents where there was no counterfeited anxiety; and in another moment his servant rushed iu, followed by Nalty, and in a few seconds later by O'Reilly himself, who, hearing the cries, believed that the effort to feign a death-bed bad *turned* into a dreadful reality.

"There—there—she is ill—she is dying! It was too much—the shock did it!" cried the old man, now horror-struck at the ruin he had caused.

"She is better,—her pulse is coming back," whispered O'Reilly; "a little water to her lips,-that will do."

"She is coming to—I see it now," said old Hickman; "leave the room, Bob; quick, before she sees you."

As O'Reilly gently disengaged his arm, which, in placing the fainting form on the sofa, was laid beneath her head, Lady Eleanor slowly opened her eyes, and fixed them upon him. O'Reilly suddenly became motionless; the calm and steady gaze seemed to have paralyzed him; he could not stir, he could not turn away his own eyes, but stood like one fascinated and spell-bound.

"Oh dear! oh dear!" muttered the old man; "she 'll know him now, and see it all."

"Yes," exclaimed Lady Eleanor, pushing back from her the officious bands that ministered about her. "Yes, sir, I do see it all! Oh, let me be thankful for the gleam of reason that has guided me in this dark hour. And you, too, do you be thankful that you have been spared from working such deep iniquity!"

As she spoke she arose, not a vestige of illness remaining, but a deep flush mantling in the cheek that, but a moment back, was deathly pale. "Farewell, sir. You had a brief triumph over the fears of a poor weak woman; but I forgive you, for you have armed her heart with a courage it never knew before."

With these words she moved calmly towards the door, which O'Reilly in respectful silence held open; and then, descending the stairs with a firm step, left the house.

"Is she gone, Bob?" said the old man, faintly, as the door clapped heavily. "Is she gone?"

O'Reilly made no reply, but leaned his head on the chimney, and seemed lost in thought.

"I knew it would fail," said Nalty in a whisper to O'Reilly.

"What 's that he 's saying, Bob?—what 's Nalty saying?"

"That he knew it would fail, sir," rejoined O'Reilly, with a bitterness that showed he was not sorry to say a disagreeable thing.

"Ay! but Nalty was frightened about his annuity; he thought, maybe, I 'd die in earnest. Well, we 've something left yet."

"What's that?" asked O'Reilly, almost sternly.

"The indictment for forgery," said Hickman, with a savage energy.

"Then you must look out for another lawyer, sir," said Nalty. "That I tell you frankly and fairly."

"What?—I didn't hear."

"He refuses to take the conduct of such a case," said O'Reilly; "and, indeed, I think on very sufficient grounds."

"Ay!" muttered the old doctor. "Then I suppose there 's no help for it! Here, Bob, put these papers in the fire."

So saying, he drew a thick roll of documents from beneath his pillow, and placed it in his son's hands. "Put them in the blaze, and let me see them burned."

O'Reilly did as he was told, stirring the red embers till the whole mass was consumed.

"I am glad of that, with all my heart," said he, as the flame died out. "That was a part of the matter I never felt easy about."

"Didn't you?" grunted the old man, with a leer of malice. "What was it you burned, d'ye think?"

"The bills,—the bonds with young Darcy's signature," replied O'Reilly, almost terrified by an unknown suspicion.

"Not a bit of it, Bob. The blaze you made was a costly fire to you, as you 'll know one day. That was my will."

CHAPTER XXVI
THE LANDING AT ABOUKIR

We must now ask our reader to leave for a season this scene of plot and intrigue, and turn with us to a very different picture. The same morning which on the iron-bound coast of Ireland broke in storm and hurricane, dawned fair and joyous over the shady shores of Egypt, and scarcely ruffled the long rolling waves as they swept into the deep bay of Aboukir. Here now a fleet of one hundred and seventy ships lay at anchor, the expedition sent forth by England to arrest the devouring ambition of Buonaparte, and rescue the land of the Pyramids from bondage.

While our concern here is less with the great event than with the fortune of one of its humble followers, we would fain linger a little over the memory of this glorious achievement of our country's arms. For above a week after the arrival of the fleet, the gale continued to blow with unabated fury; a sea mountains high rolled into the bay, accompanied by sudden squalls of such violence that the largest ships of the fleet could barely hold on by their moorings, while many smaller ones were compelled to slip their cables, and stand out to sea. If the damage and injury were not important enough to risk the success of the expedition, the casualties ever inseparable from such events threw a gloom over the whole force, a feeling grievously increased by the first tidings that met them,—the capture of one of the officers and a boat's crew, who were taken while examining the shore, and seeking out the fittest spot for a landing.

On the 7th of March the wind and sea subsided, the sky cleared, and a glorious sunset gave promise of a calm, so soon to be converted into a storm not less terrible than that of the elements.

As day closed, the outlying ships had all returned to their moorings, the accidents of the late gale were repaired, and the soaked sails hung flapping in the evening breeze to dry; while the decks swarmed with moving figures, all eagerly engaged in preparation for that event which each well knew could not now be distant. How many a heart throbbed high with ecstasy and hope, that soon was to be cold; how many an eye wandered over that strong line of defences along the shore, that never was to gaze upon another sunset!

And yet, to mark the proud step, the flashing look the eager speech of all around, the occasion might have been deemed one of triumphant pleasure rather than the approach of an enterprise full of hazard and danger. The disappointments which the storm had excited, by delaying the landing, were forgotten altogether, or only thought of to heighten the delight which now they felt.

The rapid exchange of signals between the line-of-battle ships showed that preparations were on foot; and many were the guesses and surmises current as to the meaning of this or that ensign, each reading the mystery by the light of his inward hopes. On one object, however, every eye was fixed with a most intense anxiety. This was an armed launch, which, shooting out from beneath the shadow of a three-decker, swept across the bay with muffled oars. Nothing louder than a whisper broke the silence on board of her, as they stole along the still water, and held on their course towards the shore. Through the gloom of the falling night, they were seen to track each indenture of the coast,—now lying on their oars to take soundings; now delaying, to note some spot of more than ordinary strength. It was already midnight before "the reconnoissance" was effected, and the party returned to the ship, well acquainted with the formidable preparations of the enemy, and all the hazard that awaited the hardy enterprise. The only part of the coast approachable by boats was a low line of beach, stretching away to the left, from the castle of Aboukir, and about a mile in extent; and this was commanded by a semicircular range of sand-hills, on which the French batteries were posted, and whose crest now glittered with the bivouac fires of a numerous army. From the circumstances of the ground, the guns were so placed as to be able to throw a cross-fire over the bay; while a lower range of batteries protected the shore, the terrible effect of whose practice might be seen on the torn and furrowed sands,—sad presage of what a landing party might expect! Besides these precautions, the whole breastwork bristled with cannon and mortars of various calibre, embedded in the sand; nor was a single position undefended, or one measure of resistance omitted, which might increase the hazard of an attacking force.

Time was an important object with the English general; reinforcements were daily looked for by the French; indeed it was rumored that tidings had come of their having sailed from Toulon, for, with an unparalleled audacity and fortune combined, a French frigate had sailed the preceding day through the midst of our fleet, and, amid the triumphant cheerings of the shore batteries, hoisted the tricolor in the face of our assembled ships. Scarcely had the launch reached the admiral's ship, when a signal ordered the presence of all officers in command to attend a council of war. The proceedings were quickly terminated, and in less than half an hour, the various boats were seen returning to their respective ships, the resolution having been taken to attack that very morning, or, in the words of the general order, "to bring the troops as soon as possible before the enemy." Never were tidings more welcomed; the delay, brief as it was, had stimulated the ardor of the men to the highest degree, and they actually burned with impatience to be engaged. The dispositions for attack were simple, and easily followed. A sloop of war, anchored just beyond the reach of cannon-shot, was named as a point of rendezvous. By a single blue light at her mizzen, the boats were to move towards her; three lights at the maintop would announce that they were all assembled; a single gun would then be the signal to make for the shore.

Strict orders were given that no unusual lights should be seen from the ships, nor any unwonted sight or sound betray extraordinary preparation. The men were mustered by the half-light in use on board, the ammunition distributed in silence, and every precaution taken that the attack should have the character of a surprise. These orders were well and closely followed; but so short was the interval, and so manifold the arrangements, it was already daylight before the rendezvous was accomplished.

If the plan of debarkation was easily comprehended, that of the attack was not less so. Nelson once summed up a "general order," by saying, "The captain will not make any mistake who lays his ship alongside of an enemy of heavier metal." So Abercrombie's last instructions were, "Whenever an officer may be in want of orders, let him assault an enemy's battery." These were to be carried by the bayonet alone, and, of the entire force, not one man landed with a loaded musket.

A few minutes after seven the signal was given, and the boats moved off. The sun was high, a light breeze fanned the water, the flags and streamers of the ships-of-war floated proudly out as the flotilla stood for the shore; in glorious rivalry they pulled through the surf, each eager to be first, and all the excitement of a race was imparted to this enterprise of peril.

Conspicuous among the leading boats were two, whose party, equipped in a brilliant uniform of blue and silver, formed part of the cavalry force. The inferiority of the horses supplied was such that only two hundred and fifty were mounted, and the remainder had asked and obtained permission to serve on foot. A considerable portion of this corps was made up of volunteers; and several young men of family and fortune were said to serve in the ranks, and from the circumstance of being commanded by the Knight of Gwynne, were called "Darcy's Volunteers." It was a glorious sight to see the first boat of this party, in the stern of which sat the old Knight himself, shoot out ahead, and amid the cheering of the whole flotilla, lead the way in shore.

Returning the various salutes which greeted him, the old man sat bareheaded, his silvery hair floating back in the breeze, and his manly face beaming with high enthusiasm.

"A grand spectacle for an unconcerned eyewitness," said an officer to his neighbor.

The words reached Darcy's ears, and he called out, "I differ with you, Captain. To enjoy all the thrilling ecstasy of this scene a man must have his stake on the venture. It is our personal hopes and fears are necessary ingredients in the exalted feeling. I would not stand on yonder cliff and look on, for millions; but such a moment as this is glorious." As he spoke, a long line of flame ran along the heights, and at the same instant the whole air trembled as the entire batteries opened their fire. The sea hissed and glittered with round shot and shell; while, in a perfect hurricane, they rained on every side.

The suddenness of the cannonade, and the confusion consequent on the casualties that followed, seemed for a moment to retard the advance, or, as it appeared to the French, to deter the invading force altogether; for as they perceived some of the boats to lie on their oars, and others withdrawn to the assistance of their comrades, a deafening cheer of triumph rang out from the batteries, and was heard over the bay. Scarcely had it been uttered when the British answered by another, whose hoarse roar bespoke the coming vengeance.

The flotilla had now advanced within a line of buoys laid down to direct the fire, and here grape and musketry mingled their clattering with the deeper thunder of cannon. "This is sharp work, gentlemen," said the Knight, as the spray twice splashed over the boat, from shot that fell close by. "They 'll have our range soon. Do you mark how accurately the shots fall over that line of surf?"

"That's a sand-bank, sir," said the coxswain who steered. "There 's barely draught of water there for heavy launches."

"I perceive there is some shelter yonder beneath that large battery."

"They can trust that spot," cried the coxswain, smiling. "There 's a heavy surf there, and no boat could live through it. But stay, there is a boat about to try it." Every eye was now turned towards a yawl which, with twelve oars, vigorously headed on through the very midst of a broken and foam-covered tract of water, where jets of sea sprang up from hidden rocks, and cross currents warred and contended against each other.

The hazardous venture was not alone watched by those iu the boats, but, from the crowning ridge of batteries, from every cliff and crag on shore, wondering enemies gazed on the hardihood of the daring.

"They'll do it yet, sir,—they 'll do it yet," cried the coxswain, wild with excitement. "There's deep water inside that reef."

The words were scarcely out, when a tremendous cannonade opened from the large battery. The balls fell on every side of the boat, and at length one struck her on the stem, rending her open from end to end, and scattering her shivered planks over the surfy sea.

A shout, a cheer, a drowning cry from the sinking crew, and all was over.

So sudden and so complete was this dreadful catastrophe, that they who witnessed it almost doubted the evidence of their senses, nor were the victors long to enjoy this triumph; the very discharge which sunk the boat having burst a mortar, and ignited a mass of powder near, a terrible explosion followed. A dense column of smoke and sand filled the air; and when this cleared away, the face of the battery was perceived to be rent in two.

"We can do it now, lads," cried Darcy. "They 'll never recover from the confusion yonder in time to see us." A cheer met his words, and the coxswain turned the boat's head in the direction of the reef.

Closely followed by their comrades in the second boat, they pulled along through the surf like men whose lives were on the venture; four arms to every oar, the craft bounded through the boiling tide; twice the keel was felt to graze the rocky bed, but the strong impulse of the boat's "way" carried her through, and soon they floated in the still water within the reef.

"It shoals fast here," cried the coxswain.

"What's the depth?" asked Darcy.

"Scarcely above three feet. If we throw over our six-pounder—"

"No, no. It's but wading, after all. Keep your muskets dry, move together, and we shall be the first to touch the shore."

As he said this, he sprang over the side of the boat into the sea, and waving his hat above his head, began his progress towards the land. "Come along, gentlemen, we 've often done as much when salmon-fishing in our own rivers." Thus, lightly jesting, and encouraging his party, he waded on, with all the seeming carelessness of one bent on some scheme of pleasure.

The large batteries had no longer the range; but a dreadful fire of musketry was poured in from the heights, and several brave fellows fell, mortally wounded, ere the strand was reached. Cheered by the approving shouts of thousands from the boats, they at length touched the beach; and wild and disorderly as had been their advance when breasting the waves, no sooner had they landed than discipline resumed its sway, and the words, "Fall in, men!" were obeyed with the prompt precision of a parade. A strong body of tirailleurs, scattered along the base of the sand-hills and through the irregularities of the ground, galled them with a dropping and destructive fire as they formed; nor was it till an advanced party had driven these back, that the dispositions could be well and properly taken. By this time several other boats had touched the shore, and already detachments from the Fortieth, Twenty-eighth, and Forty-second regiments were drawn up along the beach, and, from these, frequent cries and shouts were heard, encouraging and cheering the "Volunteers," who alone, of all the force, had yet come to close quarters with the enemy.

A brief but most dangerous interval now followed; for the boats, assailed by a murderous fire, had sustained severe losses, and a short delay inevitably followed, assisting the wounded, or rescuing those who had fallen into the sea. Had the French profited by this pause, to bear down upon the small force now drawn up inactive on the beach, the fate of that great achievement might have been perilled; as it happened, however, nothing was further from their thought than coming into immediate contact with the British, and they contented themselves with a distant but still destructive cannonade. It is not impossible that the audacity of those who first landed, and who—a mere handful—assumed the offensive, might have been the reason of this conduct, certain it is, the boats, for a time retarded, were permitted again to move forward and disembark then; men, with no other resistance than the fire from the batteries.

The three first regiments which gained the land were, strangely enough, representatives of the three different nationalities of the Empire; and scarcely were the words, "Forward! to the assault!" given, when an emulative struggle began, which should first reach the top and cross bayonets with the French. On the left, and nearest to the causeway that led up the heights, stood the Highlanders. These formed under an overwhelming shower of grape and musketry, and, with pibrochs playing, marched steadily forward. The Fortieth made an effort to pass them, which caused a momentary confusion, ending in an order for this regiment to halt, and support the Forty-second; and while this was taking place, the Twenty-eighth rushed to the ascent in broken parties, and, following the direction the "Volunteers" had taken in pursuit of the tirailleurs, they mounted the heights together.

So suddenly was the tirailleur force repelled, that they had scarcely time to give the alarm, when the Twenty-eighth passed the crest of the hill, and prepared to charge. The Irish regiment, glorying in being the first to reach the top, cheered madly, and bore down. The French poured in a single volley, and fell back; not to retreat, but to entice pursuit. The stratagem succeeded. The Twenty-eighth pursued them hotly, and almost at once found themselves engaged in a narrow gorge of the sand-hills, and exposed to a terrific cross-fire. To retreat was impossible; their own weight drove them on, and the deafening cheers of their comrades drowned every word of command. Grape at half-musket distance ploughed through their ranks, while one continuous crash of small-arms showed the number and closeness of their foes.

It was at this moment that Darcy, whose party was advancing by a smaller gorge, ascended a height, and beheld the perilous condition of his countrymen. There was but one way to liberate them, and that involved their own destruction: to throw themselves on the French flank, and while devoting themselves to death, enable the Twenty-eighth to retire or make head against the opposing force. While Darcy, in a few hurried words, made known his plan to those around him, the opportunity for its employment most strikingly presented itself. A momentary repulse of the French had driven a part of their column to the highroad leading to Alexandria, where already several baggage carts and ammunition wagons were gathered. This movement seemed so like retreat that Darcy's sanguine nature was deceived, and calling out, "Come along, lads,-they are running already!" he dashed onward, followed by his gallant band. His attack, if inefficient for want of numbers, was critical in point of time. The same instant that the French were assailed by him in flank, the Forty-second had gained the summit and attacked them in front: fresh battalions each moment arrived, and now along the entire crest of the ridge the fight raged fiercely. One after the other the batteries were stormed, and carried by our infantry at the bayonet's point; and in less than an hour from the time of landing, the British flag waved over seven of the nine heavy batteries.

The battle, severe as it was on the heights, was main-tained with even greater slaughter on the shore. The French, endeavoring too late to repair the error of not resisting the actual landing, had now thrown an immense force by a flank movement on the British battalions; and this attack of horse, foot, and artillery combined, was, for its duration, the great event of the day. For a brief space it appeared impossible for the few regiments to sustain the shock of such an encounter; and had it not been for the artillery of the gunboats stationed along the shore, they must have yielded. Their fire, however, was terribly destructive, sweeping through the columns as they came up, and actually cutting lanes in the dense squadrons.

Reinforcements poured in, besides, at every instant; and after a bloody and anxious struggle, the British were enabled to take the offensive, and advance against their foes. The French, already weakened by loss and dispirited by failure, did not await the conflict, but retired slowly, it is true, and in perfect order, on one of the roads leading into the great highway to Alexandria.

Victory had even more unequivocally pronounced for the British on the heights. By this time every battery was in their possession. The enemy were in full flight towards Alexandria, the tumultuous mass occasionally assailed by our light infantry, to whom, from our deficiency in cavalry, was assigned the duty of harassing the retreat. It was here that Darcy's Volunteers, now reduced to one third of their original number, highly distinguished themselves, not only attacking the flank of the retiring enemy, but seizing every opportunity of ground to assail them in front and retard their flight.

In one of these onslaughts, for such they were, the Volunteers became inextricably entangled with the enemy, and although fighting with the desperation of tigers, volley after volley tore through them; and the French, maddened by the loss they had already suffered at their hands, hastened to finish them by the bayonet. It was only by the intervention of the French officers, a measure in itself not devoid of peril, that any were spared; and those few, bleeding and mangled, were hurried along as prisoners, the only triumph of that day's battle! The strange spectacle of an affray in the very midst of a retiring column was seen by the British in pursuit, and the memory of this scene is preserved among the incidents of that day's achievements.

Many and desperate attempts were made to rescue the prisoners. The French, however, received the charges with deadly volleys, and as their flanks were now covered by a cloud of tirailleurs, they were enabled to continue their retreat on Alexandria, protected by the circumstances of the ground, every point of which they had favorably occupied. The battle was now over; guns, ammunition and stores were all landed; on the heights the English ensign waved triumphantly; and, far as the eye could reach, the French masses were seen in flight, to seek shelter within the lines of Alexandria.

It was a glorious moment as the last column ascended the cliffs, to find their gallant comrades masters of the French position in its entire extent. Here, now, two brigades reposed with piled arms, guns, mortars, camp equipage, and military chests strewed on every side, all attesting the completeness of a victory which even a French bulletin could hardly venture to disavow. It is perhaps fortunate that, at times like this, the feeling of high excitement subdues all sense of the regret so natural to scenes of suffering; and thus, amid many a sight and sound of woe, glad shouts of triumph were raised, and heartfelt bursts of joyous recognition broke forth as friends met, and clasped each other's hands. Incidents of the battle, traits of individual heroism, were recorded on every side: anecdotes then told for the first time, to be remembered, many a year after, among the annals of regimental glory!

It is but seldom, at such moments, that men can turn from the theme of triumph to think of the more disastrous events of the day; and yet a general feeling of sorrow prevailed on the subject of the brave Volunteers, of whose fate none could bring any tidings; some asserting that they had all fallen to a man on the road leading to Alexandria, others affirming that they were carried off prisoners by the French cavalry.

A party of light infantry, who had closely followed the enemy till nightfall, had despatched some of their wounded to the rear; and by these the news came, that in an open space beside the high-road the ground was covered with bodies in the well-known blue and silver of the Volunteers. One only of these exhibited signs of life; and him they had placed among the wounded in one of the carts, and brought back with them. As will often happen, single instances of suffering excite more of compassionate pity than wide-spread affliction; and so here. When death and agony were on every hand,—whole wagons filled with maimed and dying comrades,—a closely wedged group gathered around the dying Volunteer, their saddened faces betraying emotions that all the terrible scenes of the day had never evoked.

"It 's no use, sir," said the surgeon, to the field-officer who had called him to the spot. "There is internal bleeding, besides this ghastly sabre-cut."

"Who knows him?" said the officer, looking around; but none made answer. "Can no one tell his name?"

There was a silence for a few seconds; when the dying man lifted his failing eyes upwards, and turned them slowly around on the group. A slight tremor shook his lips, as if with an effort to speak; but no sound issued. Yet in the terrible eagerness of his features might be seen the working of a spirit fiercely struggling for utterance.

"Yes, my poor fellow," said the officer, stooping down beside him, and taking his hand. "I was asking for your name."

A faint smile and a slight nod of the head seemed to acknowledge the speech.

"He is speaking,—hush! I hear his voice," cried the officer.

An almost inaudible murmur moved his lips; then a shivering shook his frame, and his head fell heavily back.

"What is this?" said the officer..

"Death," said the surgeon, with the solemn calm of one habituated to such scenes. "His last words were strange-, did you hear them?"

"I thought he said 'Court-martial.'"

The surgeon nodded, and turned to move away.

"See here, sir," said a sergeant, as opening the dead man's coat he drew forth a white handkerchief, "the poor fellow was evidently trying to write his name with his own blood; here are some letters clear enough. L-e-o, and this is an n—or m—"

"I know him now," cried another. "This was the Volunteer who joined us at Malta; but Colonel Darcy got him exchanged into his own corps. His name was Leonard."

CHAPTER XXVII
THE FRENCH RETREAT

Let us now turn to the Knight of Gwynne, who, wounded and bleeding, was carried along in the torrent of the retreat. Poor fellow, he had witnessed the total slaughter or capture of the gallant band he had so bravely led into action but a few hours before, and now, with one arm powerless, and a sabre-cut in the side, could barely keep up with the hurried steps of the flying army.

From the few survivors among his followers, not one of whom was unwounded, he received every proof of affectionate devotion. If they were proud of the gallant old officer as their leader, they actually loved him like a father. The very last incident of their struggle was an effort to cut through the closing ranks of the French, and secure his escape; and although one of the Volunteers almost lifted him into the saddle, from which he had torn the rider, Darcy would not leave his comrades, but cried out, "What signifies a prisoner more or less, lads? The victory is ours; let that console us." The brave fellow who had perilled his life for his leader was cut down at the same instant. Darcy saw him bleeding and disarmed, and had but time to throw him his last pistol, when he was driven onward, and, in the mingled confusion of the movement, beheld him no more.

The exasperation of a defeat so totally unlooked for had made the French almost savage in their vindictiveness, and nothing but the greatest efforts on the part of the officers could have saved the prisoners from the cruel vengeance of the infuriated soldiery. As it was, insulting epithets, oaths, and obnoxious threats met them at every moment of the halt; and at each new success of the British their fury broke out afresh, accompanied by menacing gestures that seemed to dare and defy every fear of discipline.

Darcy, whom personal considerations were ever the last to influence, smiled at these brutal demonstrations, delighted at heart to witness such palpable evidence of insubordination in the enemy; nor could he, in the very midst of outrages which perilled his life, avoid comparing to his followers the French troops of former days with these soldiers of the Republic.

"I remember them at Quebec," said he, "under Montcalm. It may be too much to say that the spirit of a monarchy had imparted a sense of chivalry to its defenders, but certainly it is fair to think that the bloody orgies of a revolutionary capital have made a ruffian and ruthless soldiery."

Nor was this the only source of consolation open; for he beheld on every side of him, in the disorder of the force, the moral discouragement of the army, and the meagre preparations made for the defence of Alexandria. Wounded and weary, he took full note of these various circumstances, and made them the theme of encouragement to his companions in captivity. "There is little here, lads," said he, "to make us fear a long imprisonment. The gallant fellows, whose watch-fires crown yonder hills, will soon bivouac here. All these preparations denote haste and inefficiency. These stockades will offer faint resistance, their guns seem in many instances unserviceable, and from what we have seen of their infantry to-day, we need never fear the issue of a struggle with them."

In the brief intervals of an occasional halt, he lost no opportunity of remarking the appearance of the enemy's soldiery,—their bearing and their equipment,—and openly communicated to his comrades his opinion that the French army was no longer the formidable force it had been represented to be, and that the first heavy reverse would be its dismemberment. In all the confidence a foreign language suggests, he spoke his mind freely and without reserve, not sparing the officers in his criticisms, which now and then took a form of drollery that drew laughter from the other prisoners. It was at the close of some remark of this kind, and while the merriment had not yet subsided, that a French major, who had more than once shown interest for the venerable old soldier, rode close up to his side, and whispered a few words of friendly caution in his ear, while by an almost imperceptible gesture he pointed to a group of prisoners who accompanied the Knight's party, and persisted in pressing close to where he walked.— These were four dragoons of Hompesch's regiment, then serving with the British army, but a corps which had taken no part in the late action. Darcy could not help wondering at their capture,—a feeling not devoid of distrust, as he remarked that neither their dress nor accoutrements bore any trace of the fierce struggle, while their manner exhibited a degree of rude assurance and effrontery, rather than the regretful feelings of men taken prisoners.

Darcy's attention was not permitted to dwell much more on the circumstance, for at the same instant the column was halted, in order that the wounded might pass on; and in the sad spectacle that now presented itself, all memory of his own griefs was merged. The procession was a long one, and seemed even more so than it was, from the frequent halts in front, the road being choked up by tumbrels and wagons, all confusedly mixed up in the hurry of retreat. Night was now falling fast, but still there was light enough to descry the ghastly looks of the poor fellows, suffering in every variety of agony. Some sought vent to their tortures by shouts and cries of pain; others preserved a silence that seemed from their agonized features an effort as dreadful as the very wounds themselves; many were already mad with suffering, and sang and blasphemed, with shrieks of mingled recklessness and misery. What a terrible reverse to the glory of war, and how far deeper into the heart do such scenes penetrate than all the triumphs the most successful campaign has ever gathered! While Darcy still gazed on this sad sight, he was gently touched on the arm by the same officer who had addressed him before, saying, "There is an English soldier here among the wounded, who wishes to speak with you; it is against my orders to permit it, but be brief and cautious." With a motion to a litter some paces in the rear, the officer moved on to his place in the column, nor waited for any reply.

The Knight lost not a second in profiting by the kind suggestion, but in the now thickening, gloom it was some time before he could discover the object of his search. At length he caught sight of the well-known uniform of his corps,—the blue jacket slashed with silver,—as it was thrown loosely over the figure, and partly over the face of a wounded soldier. Gently removing it, he gazed with steadfastness at the pale and bloodless countenance of a young and handsome man, who with half-closed eyelids lay scarcely breathing before him. "Do you know me, my poor fellow?" whispered Darcy, bending down over him,—"do you know me? For I feel as if we should know each other well, and had met before this." The wounded man met his glance with a look of kind acknowledgment, but made no effort to speak; a faint sigh broke from him, as with a tremulous hand he pushed back the jacket and showed a terrible bayonet-stab in the chest, from which at each respiration the blood welled out in florid rivulets.

"Where is the surgeon?" said Darcy, to the soldier beside the litter.

"He is here, Monsieur," said a sharp-looking man, who, without coat and with shirt-sleeves tucked up, came hastily forward.

"Can you look to this poor fellow for me?" whispered Darcy, while he pressed into the not unwilling hand of the doctor a somewhat weighty purse.

"We can do little more thau put a pad on a wounded vessel just now," said the surgeon, as with practised coolness he split up with a scissors the portions of dress around the wound. "When we have them once housed in the hospital—Parbleu!" cried he, interrupting himself, "this is a severe affair."

Darcy turned away while the remorseless fingers of the surgeon probed the gaping incision, and then whispered low, "Can he recover?"

"Ah! *mon Dieu!* who knows? There is enough mischief here to kill half a squadron; but some fellows get through anything. If we had him in a quiet chamber of the Faubourg, with a good nurse, and all still and tranquil about him, there 's no saying; but here, with some seven hundred others,—many as bad, some worse than himself,—the chances are greatly against him. Come, however, we'll do our best for him." So saying, he proceeded to pass ligatures on some bleeding arteries; and although speaking rapidly all the while, his motions were even still more quick and hurried. "How old is he?" asked the surgeon, suddenly, as he gazed attentively at the youth.

"I can't tell you," said Darcy. "He belonged to my own corps, and by the lace on his jacket, I see, must have been a Volunteer; but I shame to say I don't remember even his name." "He knows *you*, then," replied the doctor, who, with the shrewd perception of his craft, watched the working of the sick man's features. "Is't not so?" said he, stooping down and speaking with marked distinctness. "You know your colonel?"

A gesture, too faint to be called a nod of the head, and a slight motion of the eyebrows, seemed to assent to this question; and Darcy, whose laboring faculties struggled to bring up some clew to the memory of a face he was convinced he had known before, was about to speak again, when a mounted orderly, with a led horse beside him, rode up to the spot, and looking round for a few seconds, as if in search of some one, said,—

"The English colonel, I believe?" The Knight nodded. "You are to mount this horse, sir," continued the orderly, "and proceed to the head-quarters at once."

The doctor whispered a few hasty sentences, and while promising to bestow his greatest care upon the sick man, assured Darcy that at the head-quarters he would soon obtain admission of the wounded Volunteer into the officers' hospital. Partly comforted by this, and partly yielding to what he knew was the inevitable course of fortune, the Knight took a farewell look of his follower, and mounted the horse provided for him.

Darcy was too much engrossed by the interest of the wounded soldier's case to think much on what might await himself; nor did he notice for some time that they had left the high-road by which the troops were marching for a narrower causeway, leading, as it seemed, not into, but at one side of Alexandria. It mattered so little to him, however, which way they followed, that he paid no further attention, nor was he aware of their progress, till they entered a little mud-built village, which swarmed with dogs, and miserable-looking half-clothed Arabs.

"How do they call this village?" said the Knight, speaking now for the first time to his guide.

"El Etscher," replied the soldier; "and here we halt" At the same moment he dismounted at the door of a low, mean-looking house; and having ushered Darcy into a small room dimly lighted by a lamp, departed.

The Knight listened to the sharp tramp of the horses' feet as they moved away; and when they had gone beyond hearing, the silence that followed fell heavily and drearily on his spirits. After sitting for some time in expectation of seeing some one sent after him, he arose and went to the door, but there now stood a sentry posted. He returned at once within the room, and partly overcome by fatigue, and partly from the confusion of his own harassed thoughts, he leaned his head on the table and slept soundly.

"Pardon, Monsieur le colonel," said a voice at his ear, as, some hours later in the night, he was awakened from his slumbers. "You will be pleased to follow me." Darcy looked up and beheld a young officer, who stood respectfully before him; and though for a second or so he could not remember where he was, the memory soon came back, and without a word he followed his conductor.

The officer led the way across a dirty, ill-paved courtyard, and entered a building beyond it of greater size, but apparently not less dilapidated than that they had quitted. From the hall, which was lighted with a large lamp, they could perceive through an open door a range of stables filled with horses; at the opposite side a door corresponding with this one, at which a dragoon stood with his carbine on his arm. At a word from the officer the soldier moved aside and permitted them to enter.

The room into which they proceeded was large, but almost destitute of furniture. A common deal table stood in the middle, littered with military cloaks, swords, and shakos. In one corner was a screen, from behind which the only light proceeded; and, with a gesture towards this, the officer motioned Darcy to advance, while with noiseless footsteps he himself withdrew.

Darcy moved forward, and soon came within the space enclosed by the screen, and in front of an officer in a plain uniform, who was busily engaged in writing. Maps, returns, printed orders, and letters lay strewed about him, and in the small brazier of burning wood beside him might be seen the charred remains of a great heap of papers. Darcy had full a minute to contemplate the figure before him ere he was noticed. The Frenchman was short and muscular, with a thick, bushy head of hair, bald in the centre of the head. His features were full of intelligence and quickness, but more unmistakably denoted violence of temper, and the coarse nature of one not born to his present rank, which seemed, at least, that of a field officer. His hands were covered with rings, but their shape and color scarcely denoted that such ornaments were native to them.

"Ha,—the English colonel,—sit down, sir," said he to Darcy, pointing to a chair without rising from his own. Darcy seated himself with the easy composure of one who felt that in any situation his birth and breeding made him unexceptionable company.

"I wished to see you, sir. I have received orders, that is," said he, speaking with the greatest rapidity, and a certain thickness of utterance very difficult to follow, "to send for you here, and make certain inquiries, your answers to which will entirely decide the conduct of the Commander-in-Chief in your behalf. You are not aware, perhaps, how completely you have put this in our power?"

"I suppose," said Darcy, smiling, "my condition as a prisoner of war makes me subject to the usual hardships of such a lot; but I am not aware of anything, peculiar to my case, that would warrant you in proposing even one question which a gentleman and a British officer could refuse to answer."

"There is exactly such an exception," replied the Frenchman, hastily. "The proofs are very easy, and nearer at hand than you think of."

"You have certainly excited my curiosity, sir," said the Knight, with composure; "you will excuse my saying that the feeling is unalloyed by any fear."

"We shall see that presently," said the French officer rising and moving towards the door of an apartment which Darcy had not noticed. "Auguste," cried he, "is that report ready?" The answer was not audible to the Knight. But the officer resumed, "No matter; it is sufficient for our purpose." And hastily taking a paper from the hands of a subaltern, he returned to his place within the screen. "A gentleman so conversant with our language, it would be absurd to suppose ignorant of our institutions. Now, sir, to make a very brief affair of this, you have, in contravention to a law passed in the second year of the Republic, ventured to apply opprobrious epithets to the forces of France, ridiculing the manner, bearing, and conduct of our troops, and instituting comparison between the free citizens of a free state and the miserable minions of a degraded monarchy. If a Frenchman, your accusation, trial, and sentence would have probably been nigh accomplished before this time. As a foreigner and a prisoner of war—"

"I conclude such remarks as I pleased to make were perfectly open to me," added Darcy, finishing the sentence.

"Then you admit the charge," said the Frenchman eagerly, as if he had succeeded in entrapping a confession.

"So far, sir, as the expressions of my poor judgment on the effectiveness of your army, and its chances against such a force as we have yonder, I am not only prepared to avow, but if you think the remarks worth the trouble of hearing, to repeat them."

"As a prisoner of war, sir, according to the eighty-fourth article of the Code Militaire, the offence must be tried by a court-martial, one-half of whose members shall have the same rank as the accused."

"I ask nothing better, sir, nor will I ever believe that any man who has carried a sword could deem the careless comments of a prisoner on what he sees around him a question of crime and punishment."

"I would advise you to reflect a little, sir, ere you suffer matters to proceed so far. The witnesses against you—"

"The witnesses!" exclaimed the Knight, in amazement.

"Yes, sir, four dragoons of a German regiment, thoroughly conversant with your language and ours, have deposed to the words—"

"I avow everything I have spoken, and am ready to abide by it."

"Take care, sir,—take care."

"Pardon me, sir," said Darcy, with a look of quiet irony, "but it strikes me that the exigencies of your army must be far greater than I deemed them, or you had never had recourse to a system of attempted intimidation."

"You are in error there," said the Frenchman. "It was the desire to serve, not to injure you, suggested my present course. It remains with yourself to show that my interest was not misplaced."

"Let me understand you more clearly. What is expected of me?"

"The answers to questions which doubtless every countryman of yours and mine could reply to from the public papers, but which, to us here, remote from intercourse and knowledge, are matters of slow acquirement." While the French officer spoke, he continued to search among the papers before him for some document, and at length, taking up a small slip of paper, resumed: "For instance, the 'Moniteur' asserts that you meditate sending a force from India to cross the Red Sea and the Desert, and menace us by an attack in the rear as well as in the front. This reads so like a fragment of an Oriental tale, that I can forgive the smile with which you hear it."

"Nay, sir; you have misinterpreted my meaning," said the Knight, calmly. "I am free to confess I thought this intelligence was no secret. The form of our Government, the public discussions of our Houses, the freedom of our press, are little favorable to mystery. If you have nothing to ask of me more difficult to answer than this—"

"And the expedition of Acre,—is this also correct?"

"Perfectly so. A combined movement, which shall compel you to evacuate the country, is in preparation."

"*Parbleu*, sir," said the Frenchman, stamping his foot with impatience, "these are somewhat bold words for a man in your situation to one in mine."

"I fancy, sir, that circumstance affects the issue I allude to very slightly indeed; even though the officer to whom I address myself should be General Menou, the Commander-in-Chief."

"And if I be, sir, and if you know it," said Menou,—for it was he,—his face suffused with anger, "is it consistent with the respect due to *my* position and to *your own* safety, to speak thus?"

"For the first, sir, although a mere surmise on my part, I humbly hope I have made no transgression; for the last, I have very little reason to feel any solicitude, knowing that if you hurt a hair of my head, a heavy reprisal will await such of your own officers as may be taken, and the events of yesterday may have told you that a contingency of this sort is neither improbable nor remote."

Menou made no answer to this threatening speech, but with folded arms paced the apartment for several minutes. At length he turned hastily round, and fixing his eyes on the Knight, said, with a rude oath, "You are a fortunate man, sir, that you did not hold this language to my predecessor in the command. General Kleber would have had you in front of a *peloton* of grenadiers within five minutes after you uttered it."

"I have heard as much," said the Knight, with a slight smile.

Menou rang a bell which stood beside him, and an aide-de-camp entered.

"Captain le Messurier," said he, in the ordinary tone of discipline, "this officer is under arrest. You will take the necessary steps for his safe keeping, and his due appearance when summoned before a military tribunal."

He bowed to Darcy as he spoke, and, reseating himself at the table, took up his pen to write.

"At the hazard of being thought very hardy, sir," said the Knight, as he moved towards the door, "I would humbly solicit a favor."

"A favor!" exclaimed Menou, staring in surprise.

"Yes, sir; it is that the services of a surgeon should be promptly rendered—"

"I have given orders on that score already. My own medical man shall attend to you."

"I speak not of myself, sir. It is of a Volunteer of my corps, a young man who now lies badly wounded; his case is not without hope, if speedily looked to."

"He must take his chance with others," said the general, gruffly, while he made a gesture of leave-taking; and Darcy, unable to prolong the interview, retired.

"I am sorry, sir," said the aide-de-camp, as he went along, "that my orders are peremptory, and you must, if the state of your health permit, at once leave this."

"Is it thus your prisoners of war are treated, sir?" said Darcy, scornfully, "or am I to hope—for hope I do—that the exception is created especially for me?"

The officer was silent; and although the flush of shame was on his cheek, the severe demands of duty overcame all personal feelings, and he did not dare to answer.

The Knight was not one of those on whom misfortune can press, without eliciting in return the force of resistance, and, if not forgetting, at least combating, the indignities to which he had been subjected; he resigned himself patiently to his destiny, and after a brief delay set forth for his journey to Akrish, which he now learned was to be the place of his confinement.

CHAPTER XXVIII
TIDINGS OF THE WOUNDED

The interests of our story do not require us to dwell minutely on the miserable system of intrigue by which the French authorities sought to compromise the life and honor of a British officer. The Knight of Gwynne was committed to the charge of a veteran officer of the Republic, who, though dignified with the title of the Governor of Akrish, was, in reality, invested with no higher functions than that of jailer over the few unhappy prisoners whom evil destiny had thrown into French hands.

By an alternate system of cruelty and concession, efforts were daily made to entrap Darcy either into some expression of violence or impatience at this outrage on all the custom of war, or induce him to join a plot for escape, submitted to him by those who, apparently prisoners like himself, were in reality the spies of the Republic. Sustained by a high sense of his own dignity, and not ignorant of the character under which revolutionized France accomplished her triumphs, the Knight resisted every temptation, and in all the gloom of this remote fortress, ominously secluded from the world, denied access to any knowledge of passing events, cut off from all communication with his country and his comrades, he never even for a moment forgot himself, nor became entangled in the perfidious schemes spread for his ruin. It was no common aggravation of the miseries of imprisonment to know that each day and hour had its own separate machinery of perfidy at work. At one moment he would be offered liberty on the condition of revealing the plans of the expedition; at another he would be suddenly summoned to appear before a tribunal of military law, when it was hinted he would be arraigned for having commanded a force of liberated felons,—for in this way were the Volunteers once designated,—in the hope that the insult would evoke some burst of passionate indignation. If the torment of these unceasing annoyances preyed upon his health and spirits, already harassed by sad thoughts of home, the length of time, to which the intrigues were protracted showed Darcy that the wiles of his enemies had not met success in their own eyes; and this gleam of hope, faint and slender as it was, sustained him through many a gloomy hour of captivity.

While the Knight continued thus to live in the long sleep of a prisoner's existence, events were hastening to their accomplishment by which his future liberty was to be secured. The victorious army of Abercrombie had already advanced and driven the French back beneath the lines of Alexandria. The action which ensued was terribly contested, but ended in the complete triumph of the British, whose glory was, however, dearly bought by the death of their gallant leader.

The Turkish forces now joined the English under General Hutchinson, and a series of combined movements commenced, by which the French saw themselves so closely hemmed in, that no course was open save a retreat upon Cairo.

Whether from the changed fortune of their arms,—for the French had now sustained one unbroken series of reverses,—or that the efforts to entrap the Knight had shown so little prospect of success, the manner of the governor had, for some time back, been altered much in his favor, and several petty concessions were permitted, which in the earlier days of his captivity were strictly denied. Occasionally, too, little hints of the campaign would be dropped, and acknowledgments made "that fortune had not been as uniformly favorable to the 'Great Nation' as was her wont." These significant confessions received a striking confirmation, when, at daybreak one morning, an order arrived for the garrison to abandon the fort of Akrish, and for the prisoners, under a strong escort, to fall back upon Damanhour.

The movements indicated haste and precipitancy; so much so, indeed, that ere the small garrison had got clear of the town, the head of a retreating column was seen entering it by the road from Alexandria; and now no longer doubt remained that the British had compelled them to fall back.

As the French retired, their forces continued to come up each day, and in the long convoy of wounded, as well as in the shattered condition of gun-carriages and wagons, it was easy to read the signs of a recent defeat. Nor was the matter long doubtful to Darcy; for, by some strange anomaly of human nature, the very men who would exaggerate the smallest accident of advantage into a victory and triumph, were now just as loud iu proclaiming that they had been dreadfully beaten. Perhaps the avowal was compensated for by the license it suggested to inveigh against the generals, and, in the true spirit of a republican army, to threaten them openly with the speedy judgments of the Home Government.

Among those who occasionally halted to exchange a few-words of greeting with the officer in conduct of the prisoners, the Knight recognized with satisfaction the same officer who, in the retreat from Aboukir, had so kindly suggested caution to him. At first he seemed half fearful of addressing him, to speak his gratitude, lest even so much might compromise the young captain in the eyes of his countrymen. The hesitation was speedily overcome, however, as the young Frenchman gayly saluted him, and said,—

"Ah, mon General, you had scarcely been here to-day if you had but listened to my counsels. I told you that the Republic, one and indivisible, did not admit criticism of its troops."

"I scarcely believed you could shrink from such an order," said the Knight, smiling.

"Not in the 'Moniteur,' perhaps," rejoined the Frenchman, laughing. "Yours, however, had an excess of candor, which, if only listened to at your own head-quarters, might have induced grave errors.

"I comprehend," interrupted Darcy, gayly catching up the ironical humor of the other,—"I comprehend, and you would spare an enemy such an injurious illusion."

"Just so; I wish your army had been equally generous, with all my heart," added he, as coolly as before; "here we are in full retreat on Cairo."

"On Damanhour, you mean," said Darcy.

"Not a bit of it; on Cairo, General. There's no need of mincing the matter; we need fear no eavesdropper here. Ah, by the by, your German friends were retaken, and by a detachment of their own regiment too. We saw the fellows shot the morning after the action."

"Now that you are kind enough to tell me what is going forward, perhaps you could let me know something of my poor comrades whom you took prisoners on the night of the 9th."

"Yes. They are with few exceptions dead of their wounds, two men exchanged about a week since; and then, what strange fellows your countrymen are! They sent us back a major of brigade in exchange for a wounded soldier who, when he left our camp, did not seem to have life enough to bring him across the lines!"

"Did you see him?" asked Darcy, eagerly.

"Yes; I commanded the escort. He was a young fellow of scarcely more than four-and-twenty, and must have been good-looking too."

"Of course you could not tell his name," said the Knight, despondingly.

"No; I heard it, however, but it has escaped me. There was a curious story brought back about him by our brigade-major, and one which, I assure you, furnished many a hearty laugh at your land of noble privileges and aristocratic forms'."

"Pray let me hear it."

"Oh, I cannot tell you one-half of it; the finale interested the major most, because it concerned himself, and this he repeated to us at least a dozen times. It would seem, then, that this youth—a rare thing, I believe, in your service—was a man of birth, but, according to your happy institutions, was a man of nothing more, for he was a younger son. Is not that your law?"

Darcy nodded, and the other resumed.

"Well, in some fit of spleen at not being born a year or two earlier, or for some love affair with one of your blond insensibles, or from weariness of your gloomy climate, or from any other true British cause of despair, our youth became a soldier. *Parbleu!* your English chivalry has its own queer notions, when it regards the service as a last resource of the desperate! No matter, he enlisted, came out here, fought bravely, and was taken prisoner in the very same attack with yourself; but while Fortune dealt heavily with one hand, she was caressing with the other, for, the same week she condemned him to a French prison, she made him a peer of England, having taken off the elder brother, an ambassador at some court, I believe, by a fever. So goes the world; good and ill luck battling against each, and one never getting uppermost without the other recruiting strength for a victory in turn."

"These are strange tidings, indeed," said the Knight, musing, "and would interest me deeply, if I knew the individual."

"That I am unfortunate enough to have forgotten," said the Frenchman, carelessly; "but I conclude he must be a person of some importance, for we heard that the vessel which was to sail with despatches was delayed several hours in the bay, to take him back to England."

Although the whole recital contained many circumstances which the Knight attributed to French misrepresentation of English habitudes, he was profoundly struck by it, and dwelt fondly on the hope that if the young peer should have served under his command, he would not neglect, on arriving in England, to inform his friends of his safety.

These thoughts, mingling with others of his home and of his son Lionel, far away in a distant quarter of the globe, filled his mind as he went, and made him ponder deeply over the strange accidents of a life that, opening with every promise, seemed about to close in sorrow and uncertainty. Full of movement and interest as was the scene around, he seldom bestowed on it even a passing glance; it was an hour of gloomy reverie, and he neither marked the long train of wagons with their wounded, the broken and shattered gun-carriages, or the miserable aspect of the cavalry, whose starved and galled animals could scarcely crawl.

The Knight's momentary indifference was interpreted in a very different sense by the officer who commanded the escort, and who seemed to suspect that this apathy concealed a shrewd insight into the real condition of the troops and the signs of distress and discomfiture so palpable on every side. As, impressed with this conviction, he watched the old man with prying curiosity, a smile, faint and fleeting enough, once crossed Darcy's features. The Frenchman's face flushed as he beheld it, and he quickly said,—

"They are the same troops that landed at the Arabs' Tower, and who carry such inscriptions on their standards as these." He snatched a flag from the sergeant beside him as he spoke, and pointed to the proud words embroidered there: "Le Passage de la Scrivia," "Le Passage de Tisonzo," "Le Pont de Lodi." Then, in a low, muttering voice, he added, "But Buonaparte was with us then."

Had he spoken for hours, the confession of their discontent with their generals could not have been more manifest; and a sudden gleam of hope shot through Darcy's breast, to think his captivity might soon be over.

There was every reason to indulge in this pleasing belief; disorganization had extended to every branch of the service. An angry correspondence, in which even personal chastisement was broadly hinted at, passed between the two officers highest in command; and this not secretly, but publicly known to the entire army. Peculation of the most gross and open kind was practised by the commissaries; and as the troops became distressed by want, they retaliated by daring breaches of discipline, so that at every parade men stood out from the ranks, boldly demanding their rations, and answering the orders of the officers by insulting cries of "Bread! bread!"

All this while the British were advancing steadily, overcoming each obstacle in turn, and with a force whose privations had made no inroad upon the strictest discipline; they felt confident of success. The few prisoners who occasionally fell into the hands of the French wore all the assurance of men who felt that their misfortunes could not be lasting, and in good-humored raillery bantered their captors on the British beef and pudding they would receive, instead of horseflesh, so soon as the capitulation was signed.

The French soldiers were, indeed, heartily tired of the war; they were tired of the country, of the leaders, whose incompetency, whether real or not, they believed; tired, above all, of absence from France, from which they felt exiled. Each step they retired from the coast seemed to them another day's journey from their native land, and they did not hesitate to avow to their prisoners that they had no wish or care save to return to their country.

Such was the spirit of the French army as it drew near Cairo, than which no greater contrast could exist than that presented by the advancing enemy.

Let us now return to the more immediate interests of our story; and while we beg to corroborate the brief narrative of the French officer, we hope it is unnecessary to add that the individual whose suddenly changed fortune had elevated him from the ranks of a simple volunteer to that of a peer of England was our old acquaintance Dick Forester.

From the moment when the tidings reached him, to that in which he lay, still suffering from his wounds, in the richly furnished chamber of a London hotel, the whole train of events through which he had so lately passed seemed like the incoherent fancies of a dream. The excited frame of mind in which he became a volunteer with the army had not time to subside ere came the spirit-stirring hour of the landing at Aboukir. The fight, in all its terrible but glorious vicissitudes; the struggle in which he perilled his own life to save his leader's; the moments that seemed those of ebbing life in which he lay upon a litter before Darcy's eyes, and yet unable to speak his name; and then the sudden news of his brother's death, overwhelming him at once with sorrow for his loss, and all the thousand fleeting thoughts of his own future, should life be spared him,—these were enough, and more than enough, to disturb and overbalance a mind already weakened by severe illness.

Had Forester known more of his only brother, it is certain that the predominance of the feeling of grief would have subdued the others, and given at least the calm of affliction to his troubled senses. But they were almost strangers to each other; the elder having passed his life almost exclusively abroad, and the younger, separated by distance and a long interval of years, being a complete stranger to his qualities and temper.

Dick Forester's grief, therefore, was no more than that which ties of so close kindred will ever call up, but unmixed with the tender attachment of a brother's love. His altered fortunes had not thus the strong alloy of heartfelt sorrow to make them distasteful; but still there was an unreality in everything,—a vague uncertainty in all his endeavors at close reasoning, which harassed and depressed him. And when he awoke from each short disturbed sleep, it took several minutes before he could bring back his memory to the last thought of his waking hours. The very title "my Lord," so scrupulously repeated at each instant, startled him afresh at each moment he heard it; and as he read over the names of the high and titled personages whose anxieties for his recovery had made them daily visitors at his hotel, his heart faltered between the pleasure of flattery and a deeper feeling of almost scorn for the sympathies of a world that could minister to the caprices of rank what it withheld from the real sufferings of the same man in obscurity. His mother he had not seen yet; for Lady Netherby, much attached to her eldest son, and vain of abilities by which she reckoned on his future distinction, was herself seriously indisposed. Lord Netherby, however, had been a frequent visitor, and had already seen Forester several times, although always very briefly, and only upon the terms of distant politeness.

Although in a state that precluded everything like active exertion, and which, indeed, made the slightest effort a matter of peril, Forester had already exchanged more than one communication with the Horse Guards on the subject of the Knight's safety, and received the most steady assurances that his exchange was an object on which the authorities were most anxious, and engaged at the very moment in negotiations for its accomplishment. There were two difficulties: one, that no officer of Darcy's precise rank was then a prisoner with the British; and secondly, that any very pressing desire expressed for his liberation would serve to weaken the force of that conviction they were so eager to impress, that the campaign was nearly ended, and that nothing but capitulation remained for the French.

Forester was not more gratified than surprised at the tone of obliging and almost deferential politeness which pervaded each answer to his applications. He had yet to learn how a vote in the "Lords" can make secretaries civil, and Under-Secretaries most courteous; and while his few uncertain lines were penned with diffidence and distrust, the replies gradually inducted him into that sense of confidence which a few months later he was to feel like a birthright.

How far these thoughts contributed to his recovery it would be difficult to say, nor does it exactly lie in our province to inquire. The likelihood is, that the inducements to live are strong aids to overcome sickness; for, as a witty observer has remarked, "There is no such *manque dre savoir vivre* as dying at four-and-twenty."

It is very probable Forester experienced all this, and that the dreams of the future in which he indulged were not only his greatest but his pleasantest aid to recovery. A brilliant position, invested with rank, title, fortune, and a character for enterprise, are all flattering adjuncts to youth; while in the hope of succeeding where his dearest wishes were concerned, lay a source of far higher happiness. How to approach this subject again most fittingly, was now the constant object of his thoughts. He sometimes resolved to address Lady Eleanor; but so long as he could convey no precise tidings of the Knight, this would be an ungracious task. Then he thought of Miss Daly, but he did not know her address; all these doubts and hesitations invariably ending in the resolve that as soon as his strength permitted he would go over to Ireland, and finding out Bicknell, obtain accurate information as to Lady Eleanor's present residence, and also learn if, without being discovered, he could in any way be made serviceable to the interests of the family.

Perhaps we cannot better convey the gradually dawning conviction of his altered fortune on his mind than by mentioning that while he canvassed these various chances, and speculated on their course, he never dwelt on the possibility of Lady Netherby's power to influence his determination. In the brief note he received from her each morning, the tone of affectionate solicitude for his health was always accompanied by some allusive hint of the "duties" recovery would impose, and each inquiry after his night's rest was linked with a not less anxious question as to how soon he might feel able to appear in public. Constitutionally susceptible of all attempts to control him, and from his childhood disposed to rebel against dictation, he limited his replies to brief accounts of his progress or inquiries after her own health, resolved in his heart that now that fortune was his own, to use the blessings it bestows according to the dictates of affection and a conscientious sense of right, and be neither the toy of a faction nor the tool of a party. In Darcy—could he but see him once more—he looked for a friend and adviser; and whatever the fortune of his suit, he felt that the Knight's counsels should be his guidance as to the future, reposing not even more trust on unswerving rectitude than the vast range of his knowledge of life, and the common-sense views he could take of the most complex as of the very simplest questions.

It was now some seven weeks after his return, and Forester, for we would still desire to call him by the name our reader has known him, was sitting upon a sofa, weak and nervous, as the first day of a convalescent's appearance in the drawing-room usually is, when his servant, having deposited on the table several visiting-cards of distinguished inquirers, mentioned that the Earl of Netherby wished to pay his respects. Forester moved his head in token of assent, and his Lordship soon after entered.

CHAPTER XXIX
THE DAWN OF CONVALESCENCE

Stepping noiselessly over the carpet, with an air at once animated and regardful of the sick man, Lord Netherby was at Forester's side before he could arise to receive him; and pressing him gently down with both hands, said, in a voice of most silvery cadence,—

"My dear Lord—you must not stir for the world—Halford has only permitted me to see you under the strict pledge of prudence; and now, how are you? Ah! I see—weak and low. Come, you must let me speak for you, or at least interpret your answers to my own liking. We have so much to talk over, it is difficult where to begin."

"How is Lady Netherby?" said Forester, with a slight hesitation between the words.

"Still very feeble and very nervous. The shock has been a dreadful one to her. You know that poor Augustus was coming home on leave—when—when this happened."

Here his Lordship sighed, but not too deeply, for he remembered that the law of primogeniture is the sworn enemy to grief.

"There was some talk, too, of his being sent on a special embassy to Paris,—a very high and important trust,—and so really the affliction is aggravated by thinking what a career was opening to him. But, as the Dean of Walworth beautifully expressed it, 'We are cut down like flowers of the field.' Ah!"

A sigh and a slight wave with a handkerchief, diffusing an odor of eau-de-Portugal through the chamber, closed this affecting sentiment.

"I trust in a day or two I shall be able to see my mother," said Forester, whose thoughts were following a far more natural channel. "I can walk a little to-day, and before the end of the week Halford promises me that I shall drive out."

"That's the very point we are most anxious about," said Lord Netherby, eagerly: "we want you, if possible, to take your seat in 'the Lords' next week. There is a special reason for it. Rumor runs that the Egyptian expedition will be brought on for discussion on Thursday next. Some malcontents are about to disparage the whole business, and, in particular, the affair at Alexandria. Ministers are strong enough to resist this attack, and even carry the war back into the enemy's camp; but we all think it would be a most fortunate moment for you, when making your first appearance in the House, to rise and say a few words on the subject of the campaign. The circumstances under which you joined—your very dangerous wound—have given you a kind of prerogative to speak, and the occasion is most opportune. Come, what say you? Would such an effort be too great?"

"Certainly not for my strength, my Lord, if not for my shame' sake; for really I should feel it somewhat presumptuous in me, a man who carried his musket in the ranks, to venture on a discussion, far more a defence, of the great operations in which he was a mere unit; one of those rank and file who figured, without other designation, in lists of killed and wounded."

"This is very creditable to your modesty, my dear Lord," said the old peer, smiling most blandly; "but pardon me if I say it displays a great forgetfulness of your present position. Remember that you now belong to the Upper House, and that the light of the peerage shines on the past as on the future."

"By which I am to understand," replied Forester, laughing, "that the events which would have met a merited oblivion in Dick Forester's life are to be remembered with honor to the Earl of Wallincourt."

"Of course they are," cried Lord Netherby, joining in the laugh. "If an unlikely scion of royalty ascends the throne, we look out for the evidences of his princely tastes in the sports of his boyhood. Nay, if a clever writer or painter wins distinction from the world, do we not 'try back' for his triumphs at school, or his chalk sketches on coach-house gates, to warrant the early development of genius?"

"Well, my Lord," said Forester, gayly, "I accept the augury; and as nothing more nearly concerns a man's life than the fate of those who have shown him friendship, let me inquire after some friends of mine, and some relations of yours,-the Darcys."

"Ah, those poor Darcys!" said Lord Netherby, wiping his eyes, and heaving a very profound sigh, as though to say that the theme was one far too painful to dwell upon, "theirs is a sad story, a very sad story indeed!"

"Anything more gloomy than the loss of fortune, my Lord?" asked Forester, with a trembling lip, and a cheek pale as death. Lord Netherby stared to see whether the patient's mind was not beginning to wander. That there could be anything worse than loss of fortune he had yet to learn; assuredly he had never heard of it. Forester repeated his question.

"No, no, perhaps not, if you understand by that phrase what I do," said Lord Netherby, almost pettishly. "If, like me, you take in all the long train of ruin and decay such loss implies,—pecuniary distress, moneyed difficulties, fallen condition in society, inferior association—"

"Nay, my Lord, in the present instance, I can venture to answer for it, such consequences have not ensued. You do your relatives scarcely justice to suppose it."

"It is very good and very graceful, both, in you," said Lord Netherby, with an almost angelic smile, "to say so. Unfortunately, these are not merely speculative opinions on my part. While I make this remark, understand me as by no means imputing any blame to them. What could they do?—that is the question,—what could they do?"

"I would rather ask of your Lordship, what have they done? When I know that, I shall be, perhaps, better enabled to reply to your question."

In all likelihood it was more the manner than the substance of this question which made Lord Netherby hesitate how to reply to it, and at last he said,—

"To say in so many words what they have done, is not so easy. It would, perhaps, give better insight into the circumstances were I to say what they have not done."

"Even as you please, my Lord. The negative charge, then," said Forester, impatiently.

"Lord Castlereagh, my Lord!" said a servant, throwing open the door; for he had already received orders to admit him when he called, though, had Forester guessed how inopportune the visit could have proved, he would never have said so.

In the very different expressions of Lord Netherby and the sick man's face, it might be seen how differently they welcomed the new arrival.

Lord Castlereagh saluted both with a courteous and cordial greeting, and although he could not avoid seeing that he had dropped in somewhat *mal-à-propos*, he resolved rather to shorten the limit of his stay than render it awkward by any expressions of apology. The conversation, therefore, took that easy, careless tone in which each could join with freedom. It was after a brief pause, when none exactly liked to be the first to speak, that Lord Netherby observed,—

"The very moment you were announced, my Lord, I was endeavoring to persuade my young friend here to a line of conduct in which, if I have your Lordship's co-operation, I feel I shall be successful."

"Pray let me hear it," said Lord Castlereagh, gayly, and half interrupting what he feared was but the opening of an over-lengthy exposition.

Lord Netherby was not to be defeated so easily, nor defrauded of a theme whereupon to expend many loyal sentiments; and so he opened a whole battery of arguments on the subject of the young peer's first appearance in the House, and the splendid opportunity, as he called it, of a maiden speech.

"I see but one objection," said Lord Castlereagh, with a well-affected gravity.

"I see one hundred," broke in Forester, impatiently.

"Perhaps *my* one will do," rejoined Lord Castlereagh.

"Which is—if I may take the liberty—" lisped out Lord Netherby.

"That there will be no debate on the subject. The motion is withdrawn."

"Motion withdrawn!—since when?"

"I see you have not heard the news this morning," said Lord Castlereagh, who really enjoyed the discomfiture of one very vain of possessing the earliest intelligence.

"I have heard nothing," exclaimed he, with a sigh of despondency.

"Well, then, I may inform you, that the 'Pike' has brought us very stirring intelligence. The war in Egypt is now over. The French have surrendered under the terms of a convention, and a treaty has been ratified that permits their return to France. Hostages for the guarantee of the treaty have been already interchanged, and"—here he turned towards Forester, and added—"it will doubtless interest you to hear that your old friend the Knight of Gwynne is one of them,—an evidence that he is not only alive, but in good health also."

"This is, indeed, good news you bring me," said Forester, with a flashing eye and a heightened complexion. "Has any one written? Do Colonel Darcy's friends know of this?"

"I have myself done so," said Lord Castlereagh. "Not that I may attribute the thoughtful attention to myself, for I received his Royal Highness's commands on the subject I need scarcely say that such a communication must be gratifying to any one."

"Where are they at present?" said Forester, eagerly.

"That was a question of some difficulty to me, and I accordingly called on my Lord Netherby to ascertain the point. I found he had left home, and now have the good fortune to catch him here." So saying, Lord Castlereagh took from the folds of a pocket-book a sealed but un-addressed letter, and dipping a pen in the ink before him, prepared to write.

There were, indeed, very few occurrences in life which made Lord Netherby feel ashamed. He had never been obliged to blush for any solecism in manner or any offence against high breeding, nor had the even tenor of his days subjected him to any occasion of actual shame, so that the confusion he now felt had the added poignancy of being a new as well as a painful sensation.

"It may seem very strange to you, my Lord," said he, in a broken and hesitating voice; "not but that, on a little reflection, the case will be easily accounted for; but—so it is—I—really must own—I must frankly acknowledge—that I am not at this moment aware of my dear cousin's address."

If his Lordship had not been too much occupied in watching Lord Castlereagh's countenance, he could not have failed to see, and be struck by, the indignant expression of Forester's features.

"How are we to reach them, then, that's the point?" said Lord Castlereagh, over whose handsome face not the slightest trace of passion was visible. "If I mistake not, Gwynne Abbey they have left many a day since."

"I think I can lay my hand on a letter. I am almost certain I had one from a law-agent, called—called—"

"Bicknell, perhaps," interrupted Forester, blushing between shame and impatience.

"Quite right,—you are quite right," replied Lord Netherby, with a significant glance at Lord Castlereagh, cunningly intended to draw off attention from himself. "Well, Mr. Bicknell wrote to me a very tiresome and complicated epistle about law affairs,—motions, rules, and so forth,—and mentioned at the end that Lady Eleanor and Helen were living in some remote village on the northern coast."

"A cottage called 'The Corvy,'" broke in Forester, "kindly lent to them by an old friend, Mr. Bagenal Daly."

"Will that address suffice," said Lord Castlereagh, "with the name of the nearest post-town?"

"If you will make me the postman, I'll vouch for the safe delivery," said Forester, with an animation that made him flushed and pale within the same instant.

"My dear young friend, my dear Lord Wallincourt!" exclaimed Lord Netherby, laying his hand upon his arm. He said no more; indeed he firmly believed the enunciation of his new title must be quite sufficient to recall him to a sense of due consideration for himself.

"You are scarcely strong enough, Dick," said Lord Castlereagh, coolly. "It is a somewhat long journey for an invalid; and Halford, I 'm sure, wouldn't agree to it."

"I 'm quite strong enough," said Forester, rising and pacing the room with an attempted vigor that made his debility seem still more remarkable: "if not to-day, I shall be to-morrow. The travelling, besides, will serve me,—change of air and scene. More than all, I am determined on doing it."

"Not if I refuse you the despatches, I suppose?" said Lord Castlereagh, laughing.

"You can scarcely do that," said Forester, fixing his eyes steadfastly on him. "Your memory is a bad one, or you must recollect sending me down once upon a time to that family on an errand of a different nature. Don't you think you owe an amende to them and to me?"

"Eh! what was that? I should like to know what you allude to," said Lord Netherby, whose curiosity became most painfully eager.

"A little secret between Dick and myself," said Lord Castlereagh, laughing. "To show I do not forget which, I 'll accede to his present request, always provided that he is equal to it."

"Oh, as to that—"

"It must be 'Halfordo non obstante,' or not at all," said Lord Castlereagh, rising. "Well," continued he, as he moved towards the door, "I 'll see the doctor on my way homeward, and if he incline to the safety of the exploit, you shall hear from me before four o'clock. I 'll send you some extracts, too, from the official papers, such as may interest your friends, and you may add, *bien des choses de ma part*, in the way of civil speeches and gratulation."

Lord Netherby had moved towards the window as Lord Castlereagh withdrew, and seemed more interested by the objects in the street than anxious to renew the interrupted conversation.

Forester—if one were to judge from his preoccupied expression—appeared equally indifferent on the subject, and both were silent. Lord Netherby at last looked at his watch, and, with an exclamation of astonishment at the lateness of the hour, took up his hat. Forester did not notice the gesture, for his mind had suddenly become awake to the indelicacy, to say no worse, of leaving London for a long journey without one effort to see his mother. A tingling feeling of shame burned in his cheek and made his heart beat faster, as he said, "I think you have your carriage below, my Lord?"

"Yes," replied Lord Netherby, not aware whether the question might portend something agreeable or the reverse.

"If you 'll permit me, I 'll ask you to drive me to Berkeley Square. I think the air and motion will benefit me; and perhaps Lady Netherby will see me."

"Delighted—charmed to see you—my dear young friend," said Lord Netherby, who having, in his own person, some experience of the sway and influence her Ladyship was habituated to exercise, calculated largely on the effect of an interview between her and her son. "I don't believe you could possibly propose anything more gratifying nor more likely to serve her. She is very weak and very nervous; but to see you will, I know, be of immense service. I 'm sure you 'll not agitate her," added he, after a pause. If the words had been "not contradict," they would have been nearer his meaning.

"You may trust me, for both our sakes," said Forester, smiling. "By the by, you mentioned a letter from a law-agent of the Darcys, Mr. Bicknell; was it expressive of any hope of a favorable termination to the suit, or did he opine that the case was a bad one?"

"If I remember aright, a very bad one,—bad, from the deficiency of evidence; worse, from the want of funds to carry it on. Of course I only speak from memory; and the epistle was so cramp, so complex, and with such a profusion of detail intermixed, that I could make little out of it, and retain even less. I must say that as it was written without my cousin's knowledge or consent, I paid no attention to it. It was, so to say, quite unauthorized."

"Indeed!" exclaimed Forester, in an accent whose scorn was mistaken by the hearer, as he resumed.

"Just so; a mere lawyer's *ruse*, to carry on a suit. He proposed, I own, a kind of security for any advance I should make, in the person of Miss Daly, whose property, amounting to some three or four thousand pounds, was to be given as security! There always is some person of this kind on these occasions—some tame elephant—to attract the rest; but I paid no attention to it. The only thing, indeed, I could learn of the lady was, that she had a fire-eating brother who paid bond debts with a pistol, and small ones with a horsewhip."

"I know Mr. Daly and his sister too. He is a most honorable and high-minded gentleman; of her I only needed to hear the trait your Lordship has just mentioned, to say that she is worthy to be his sister in every respect."

"I was not aware that they were acquaintances of yours."

"Friends, my Lord, would better express the relationship between us,— friends, firm and true, I sincerely believe them. Pray, if not indiscreet, may I ask the date of this letter?"

"Some day of June last, I think. The case was to come on for trial next November in Westport, and it was for funds to carry on the suit, it would seem, they were pressed."

"You did n't hear a second time?"

"No, I 've told you that I never answered this letter. I was quite willing, I am so at this hour, to be of any service to my dear cousin, Lady Eleanor Darcy, and to aid her to the fullest extent; but to prosecute a hopeless lawsuit, to throw away some thousands in an interminable Equity investigation,—to measure purses, too, against one of the richest men in Ireland, as I hear their antagonist is,—this, I could never think of."

"But who has pronounced this claim hopeless?" said Forester, impatiently.

A cold shrug of the shoulders was all Lord Netherby's reply.

"Not Miss Daly, certainly," rejoined Forester, "who was willing to peril everything she possessed in the world upon the issue."

The sarcasm intended by this speech was deeply felt by Lord Netherby, as with an unwonted concession to ill-humor, he replied,—

"There is nothing so courageous as indigence!"

"Better never be rich, then," cried Forester, "if cowardice be the first lesson it teaches. But I think better of affluence than this. I saw that same Knight of Gwynne when at the head of a princely fortune; and I never, in any rank of life, under any circumstances, saw the qualities which grace and adorn the humblest more eminently displayed."

"I quite agree with you; a more perfectly conducted household it is impossible to conceive."

"I speak not of his retinue, nor of his graceful hospitalities, my Lord, nor even of his generous munificence and benevolence; these are rich men's gifts everywhere. I speak of his trusting, confiding temper; the hopeful trust he entertained of something good in men's natures at the moment he was smarting from their perfidy and ingratitude; the forgiveness towards those that injured, the unvarying kindness towards those that forgot him."

"I declare," said Lord Netherby, smiling, "I must interdict a continuance of this panegyric, now that we have arrived, for you know Colonel Darcy was a first love of Lady Netherby."

Nothing but a courtier of Lord Netherby's stamp could have made such a speech; and while Forester became scarlet with shame and anger, a new light suddenly broke upon him, and the rancor of his mother respecting the Knight and his family was at once explained.

"Now to announce you," said Lord Netherby, gayly; "let that be my task." And so saying, he lightly tripped up the stairs before Forester.

CHAPTER XXX
A BOUDOIR

When, having passed through a suite of gorgeously furnished rooms, Forester entered the dimly lighted boudoir where his lady-mother reclined, his feelings were full of troubled emotion. The remembrance of the last time he had been there was present to his mind, mingled with anxious fears as to his approaching reception. Had he been more conversant with the "world," he needed not to have suffered these hesitations. There are few conditions in life between which so wide a gulf yawns as that of the titled heir of a house and the younger brother. He was, then, as little prepared for the affectionate greeting that met him as for the absence of all trace of illness in her Ladyship's appearance. Both were very grateful to his feelings as he drew his chair beside her sofa, and a soft remembrance of former days of happiness stole over his pleased senses. Lord Netherby, with a fitting consideration, had left them to enjoy this interview alone, and thus their emotions were unrestrained by the presence of the only one who had witnessed their parting. Perhaps the most distinguishing trait of the closest affection is that the interruptions to its course do not involve the misery of reconciliation to enable us to return to our own place in the heart; but that, the moment of grief or anger or doubt over, we feel that we have a right to resume our influence in the breast whose thoughts have so long mingled with our own. The close ties of filial and parental love are certainly of this nature, and it must be a stubborn heart whose instincts do not tend to that forgiveness which as much blots out as it pardons past errors. Such was not Lady Netherby's. Pride of station, the ambition of leadership in certain circles, had so incorporated themselves with the better dictates of her mind that she rarely, if ever, permitted mere feeling to influence her; but if for a moment it did get the ascendancy, her heart could feel as acutely as though it had been accustomed to such indulgence. In a word, she was as affectionate as the requirements of her rank permitted. Oh, this Rank, this Rank! how do its conventionalities twine and twist themselves round our natures till love and friendship are actually subject to the cold ordinance of a fashion! How many hide the dark spots of their heart behind the false screen they call their "Rank"! The rich man, in the Bible, clothed in his purple, and faring sumptuously, was but acting in conformity with his "Rank;" nay, more, he was charitable as became his "Rank," for the poor were fed with the crumbs from his table.

Forester was well calculated by natural advantages to attract a mother's pride. He was handsome and well-bred; had even more than a fair share of abilities, which gained credit for something higher from a native quickness of apprehension; and even already the adventurous circumstances of his first campaign had invested his character with a degree of interest that promised well for his success in the world. If her manner to him was then kind and affectionate, it was mingled also with something of admiration, which her woman's heart yielded to the romantic traits of the youth.

She listened with eager pleasure to the animated description he gave of the morning at Aboukir, and the brilliant panorama of the attack; nor was the enjoyment marred by the mention of the only name that could have pained her, the last words of Lord Netherby having sealed Forester's lips with respect to the Knight of Gwynne.

The changeful fortunes of his life as a prisoner were mingled with the recital of the news by which his exchange was effected; and this brought back once more the subject by which their interview was opened,—the death of his elder brother. Lady Netherby perhaps felt she had done enough for sorrow, for she dwelt but passingly on the theme, and rather addressed herself to the future which was now about to open before her remaining son, carefully avoiding, however, the slightest phrase that should imply dictation, and only seeming to express the natural expectation "the world" had formed of what his career should be. "Lord Netherby tells me," said she, "that the Duke of York will, in all likelihood, name you as an extra aide-decamp, in which case you probably would remain in the service. It is an honor that could not well be declined."

"I scarcely like to form fixed intentions which have no fixed foundations," said Forester; "but if I might give way to my own wishes, it would be to indulge in perfect liberty,—to have no master."

"Nor any mistress, either, to control you, for some time, I suppose," rejoined she, smiling, as if carelessly, but watching how her words were taken. Forester affected to partake in the laugh, but could not conceal a slight degree of confusion. Lady Netherby was too clever a tactician to let even a momentary awkwardness interrupt the interview, and resumed: "You will be dreadfully worried by all the 'lionizing' in store for you, I'm certain; you are to be feasted and feted to any extent, and will be fortunate if the gratulations on your recovery do not bring back your illness."

"I shall get away from it all at once," said Forester, rising, and walking up and down, as if the thought had suggested the impatient movement.

"You cannot avoid presenting yourself at the levee," said Lady Netherby, anxiously; for already a dread of her son's wilful temper came over her. "His Royal Highness's inquiries after you do not leave an option on this matter."

"What if I'm too ill?" said he, doggedly; "what if I should not be in town?"

"But where else could you be, Richard?" said she, with a resumption of her old imperiousness of tone and manner.

"In Ireland, madam," said Forester, coldly.

"In Ireland! And why, for any sake, in Ireland?"

Forester hesitated, and grew scarlet; he did not know whether to evade inquiry by a vague reply, or at once avow his secret determination. At length, with a faltering, uncertain voice, he said: "A matter of business will bring me to that country; I have already conversed with Lord Castlereagh on the subject. Lord Netherby was present."

"I'm sure he could never concur,-I'm certain." So far her Ladyship had proceeded, when a sudden fear came over her that she had ventured too far, and turning hastily, she rang the bell beside her. "Davenport," said she to the grave-looking groom of the chambers, who as instantaneously appeared, "is my Lord at home?"

"His Lordship is in the library, my Lady."

"Alone?"

"No, my Lady, a gentleman from Ireland is with his Lordship."

"A gentleman from Ireland!" repeated she, half aloud, as though the very mention of that country were destined to persecute her; then quickly added, "Say I wish to speak with him here."

The servant bowed and withdrew; and now a perfect silence reigned in the apartment. Forester felt that he had gone too far to retreat, even were he so disposed, and although dreading nothing more than a "scene," awaited, without speaking, the course of events. As much yielding to an involuntary impatience as to relieve the awkwardness of the interval, he arose and walked into the adjoining drawing-room, carelessly tossing over books and prints upon the tables, and trying to affect an ease he was very far from experiencing.

It was while he was thus engaged that Lord Netherby entered the boudoir, and seeing her Ladyship alone, was about to speak in his usual tone, when, at a gesture from her, he was made aware of Forester's vicinity, and hastily subdued his voice to a whisper. "Whatever the nature of the tidings which in a hurried and eager tone his Lordship retailed, her manner on hearing evinced a mingled astonishment and delight, if the word dare be applied to an emotion whose source was in anything rather than an amiable feeling.

"It seems too absurd, too monstrous in every way," exclaimed she, at the end of an explanation which took several minutes to recount. "And why address himself to you? That seems also inexplicable."

"This," rejoined Lord Netherby, aloud, —-"this was his own inspiration. He candidly acknowledges that no one either counselled or is even aware of the step he has taken."

"Perhaps the *à propos* may do us good service," whispered she, with a glance darted at the room where Forester was now endeavoring, by humming an air, to give token of his vicinity as well as assume an air of indifference.

"I thought of that," said Lord Netherby, in the same low voice. "Would you see him? A few moments would be enough."

Lady Netherby made no answer, but with closed eyes and compressed lips seemed to reflect deeply for several minutes. At last she said: "Yes, let him come. I'll detain Richard in the drawing-room; he shall hear everything that is said. If I know anything of him, the insult to his pride will do far more than all our arguments and entreaties."

"Don't chill my little friend by any coldness of manner," said his Lordship, smiling, as he moved towards the door; "I have only got him properly thawed within the last few minutes."

"My dear Richard," said she, as the door closed after Lord Netherby, "I must keep you prisoner in the drawing-room for a few minutes, while I receive a visitor of Lord Netherby's. Don't close the doors; I can't endure heat and this room becomes insupportable without a slight current of air. Besides, there is no secret, I fancy, in the communication. As well as I understand the matter, it does not concern us; but Netherby is always doing some piece of silly good-nature, for which no one thanks him!"

The last reflection was half soliloquy, but said so that Forester could and did hear every word of it. While her Ladyship, therefore, patiently awaited the arrival of her visitor in one room, Forester threw himself into a chair, and taking up a book at hazard, endeavored to pass the interval without further thought about the matter.

Sitting with his back towards the door of the boudoir. Forester accidentally had placed himself in such a position that a large mirror between the windows reflected to him a considerable portion of the scene within. It was then with an amount of astonishment far above ordinary that he beheld the strange-looking figure who followed Lord Netherby into the apartment of his mother. He was a short, dumpy man, with a bald head, over which the long hairs of either side were studiously combed into an ingenious kind of network, and meeting at an angle above the cranium, looked like the uncovered rafters of a new house. Two fierce-looking gray eyes that seemed ready for fun or malice, rolled and revolved unceasingly over the various decorations of the chamber, while a large thick-lipped mouth, slightly opened at either end, vouched for one who neglected no palpable occasion for self-indulgence or enjoyment. There was, indeed, throughout his appearance, a look of racy satisfaction and contentment, that consorted but ill with his costume, which was a suit of deep mourning; his clothes having all the gloss and shine of a recent domestic loss, and made, as seems something to be expected on these occasions, considerably too large for him, as though to imply that the defunct should not be defrauded in the full measure of sorrow. Deep crape weepers encircled his arms to the elbows, and a very banner of black hung mournfully from his hat.

"Mr. — — —-" Here Lord Netherby hesitated, forgetful of his name.

"Dempsey, Paul Dempsey, your Grace," said the little man, as, stepping forward, he performed the salutation before Lady Netherby, by which he was accustomed to precede an invitation to dance.

"Pray be seated, Mr. Dempsey. I have just briefly mentioned to her Ladyship the circumstances of our interesting conversation, and with your permission will proceed with my recital, begging that if I fall into any error you will kindly set me right. This will enable Lady Netherby, who is still an invalid, to support the fatigue of an interview wherein her advice and counsel will be of great benefit to us both."

Mr. Dempsey bowed several times, not sorry, perhaps, that in such an awful presence he was spared the office of chief orator.

"I told you, my dear," said Lord Netherby, turning towards her Ladyship, "that this gentleman had for a considerable time back enjoyed the pleasure of intimacy with our worthy relative Lady Eleanor Darcy—"

The fall of a heavy book in the adjoining room interrupted his Lordship, between whom and Lady Netherby a most significant interchange of glances took place. He resumed, however, without a pause,—

"Lady Eleanor and her accomplished daughter. If the more urgent question were uot now before us, it would gratify you to learn, as I have just done, the admirable patience she has exhibited under the severe trials she has met; the profound insight she obtained into the condition, hopeless as it proves to be, of their unhappy circumstances; and the resignation in which, submitting to changed fortune, she not only has at once abandoned the modes of living she was habituated to, but actually descended to what I can fancy must have been the hardest infliction of all,—vulgar companionship, and the society of a boarding-house."

"A most respectable establishment, though," broke in Paul; "Fumbally's is known all over Ulster—"

A very supercilious smile from Lady Netherby cut short a panegyric Mr. Dempsey would gladly have extended.

"No doubt, sir, it was the best thing of the kind," resumed his Lordship; "but remember who Lady Eleanor Darcy was,—ay, and is. Think of the station she had always held, and then fancy her in daily intercourse with those people—"

"Oh, it is very horrid, indeed!" broke in Lady Netherby, leaning back, and looking overcome even at the bare conception of the enormity.

"The little miserable notorieties of a fishing-village—"

"Coleraine, my Lord,—Coleraine," cried Dempsey.

"Well, be it so. What is Coleraine?"

"A very thriving town on the river Bann, with a smart trade in yarn, two breweries, three meeting-houses, a pound, and a Sunday-school," repeated Paul, as rapidly as though reading from a volume of a topographical dictionary.

"All very commendable and delightful institutions, on which I beg heartily to offer my congratulations, but, you will allow me to remark, scarcely enough to compensate for the accustomed appliances of a residence at Gwynne Abbey. But I see we are trespassing on Lady Netherby's strength. You seem faint, my dear."

"It's nothing,—it will pass over in a moment or so. This sad account of these poor people has distressed me greatly."

"Well, then, we must hasten on. Mr. Dempsey became acquainted with our poor friends in this their exile; and although from his delicacy and good taste he will not dwell on the circumstance, it is quite clear to me, has shown them many attentions; I might use a stronger word, and say kindnesses."

"Oh! by Jove, I did nothing. I could do nothing—"

"Nay, sir, you are unjust to yourself; the very intentions by which you set out on your present journey are the shortest answer to that question. It would appear, my dear, that my fair relative, Miss Darcy, has not forfeited the claim she possessed to great beauty and attraction; for here, in the gentleman before us, is an evidence of their existence. Mr. Dempsey, who 'never told his love,' as the poet says, waited in submission himself for the hour of his changing fortune; and until the death of his mother—"

"No, my Lord; my uncle, Bob Dempsey, of Dempsey's Grove."

"His uncle, I mean. Mr. Dempsey, of Dempsey's Hole."

"Grove,-Dempsey's Grove," interpolated Paul, reddening.

"Grove, I should say," repeated Lord Netherby, unmoved. "By which he has succeeded to a very comfortable independence, and is now in a position to make an offer of his hand and fortune."

"Under the conditions, my Lord,—under the conditions," whispered Paul.

"I have not forgotten them," resumed Lord Netherby, aloud. "It would be ungenerous not to remember them, even for your sake, Mr. Dempsey, seeing how much my poor, dear relative, Lady Eleanor, is beut on prosecuting this unhappy suit, void of all hope, as it seems to be, and not having any money of her owu—"

"Ready money,—cash," interposed Paul.

"So I mean—ready money to make the advances necessary—Mr. Dempsey wishes to raise a certain sum by loan, on the security of his property, which may enable the Darcys to proceed with their claim; this deed to be executed on his marriage with Miss Darcy. Am I correct, sir?"

"Quite correct, my Lord; you've only omitted that, to save expensive searches, lawyers' fees, and other devilments of the like nature, that your Lordship should advance the blunt yourself?"

"I was coming to that point. Mr. Dempsey opines that, taking the interest it is natural we should do in our poor friends, he has a kind of claim to make this proposition to us. He is aware of our relationship—mine, I mean—to Lady Eleanor. She spoke to you, I believe, on that subject, Mr. Dempsey?"

"Not exactly to *me*," said Paul, hesitating, and recalling the manner in which he became cognizant of the circumstance; "but I heard her say that your Lordship was under very deep obligation to her own father,—that you were, so to say, a little out at elbows once, very like myself before Bob died, and that then—"

"We all lived together like brothers and sisters," said his Lordship, reddening. "I 'm sure I can't forget how happily the time went over."

"Then Lady Eleanor, I presume, sir, did not advert to those circumstances as a reason for your addressing yourself to Lord Netherby?" said her Ladyship, with a look of stern severity.

"Why, my Lady, she knows nothing about my coming here. Lord bless us! I wouldn't have told her for a thousand pounds!"

"Nor Miss Darcy, either?"

"Not a bit of it! Oh, by Jove! if you think they 're not as proud as ever they were, you are much mistaken; and, indeed, on this very same subject I heard her say that nothing would induce her to accept a favor from your Lordship, if even so very improbable an event should occur as your offering one."

"So that we owe the honor of your visit to the most single-minded of motives, sir," said Lady Netherby, whose manner had now assumed all its stateliness.

"Yes, my Lady, I came as you see,—*Dempsius cum Dempsio*,—so that if I succeed, I can say like that fellow in the play, 'Alone, I did it.'"

Lord Netherby, who probably felt that the interview had lasted sufficiently long for the only purpose he had destined or endured it, was now becoming somewhat desirous of terminating the audience; nor was his impatience allayed by those sportive sallies of Mr. Dempsey in allusion to his own former condition as a dependant.

At length he said, "You must be aware, Mr. Dempsey, that this is a matter demanding much time and consideration. The Knight of Gwynne is absent."

"That's the reason there is not an hour to lose," interposed Paul.

"I am at a loss for your meaning."

"I mean that if he comes home before it's all settled, that the game is up. He would never consent, I'm certain."

"So you think that the ladies regard you with more favorable eyes?" said her Ladyship, smiling a mixture of superciliousness and amusement.

"I have my own reasons to think so," said Paul, with great composure.

"Perhaps you take too hopeless a view of your case, sir," resumed Lord Netherby, blandly. "I am, unhappily, very ignorant of Irish family rank; but I feel assured that Mr. Dempsey, of Dempsey's Hole—"

"Grove,—Dempsey's Grove," said Paul, with a look of anger.

"I ask your pardon, humbly,—I would say of Dempsey's Grove,-might be an accepted suitor in the very highest quarters. At all events, from news I have heard this morning it is more than likely that the Knight will be in London before many weeks, and I dare not assume either the responsibility of favoring your views, or incurring his displeasure by an act of interference. I think her Ladyship coucurs with me."

"Perfectly. The case is really one which, however we may and do feel the liveliest interest in, lies quite beyond our influence or control."

"Mr. Dempsey may rest assured that, even from so brief an acquaintance, we have learned to appreciate some of his many excellent qualities of head and heart."

Lady Netherby bowed an acquiescence cold and stately; and, his Lordship rising at the same time, Paul saw that the audience drew to a close. He arose then slowly, and with a faint sigh,—for he thought of his long and dreary journey, made to so little profit.

"So I may jog back again as I came," muttered he, as he drew on his gloves. "Well, well, Lady Eleanor knew him better than I did. Good-morning, my Lady. I hope you are about to enjoy better health. Good-bye, my Lord."

"Do you make any stay in town, Mr. Dempsey?" inquired his Lordship, in that bland voice that best became him. "Till I pack my portmanteau, my Lord, and pay my bill at the 'Tavistock,'—not an hour longer."

"I'm sorry for that. I had hoped, and Lady Netherby also expected, we should have the pleasure of seeing you again."

"Very grateful, my Lord; but I see how the land lies as well as if I was here a month."

And with this significant speech Mr. Dempsey repeated his salutations and withdrew.

"What presumption!" exclaimed Lady Netherby, as the door closed behind him. "But how needlessly Lady Eleanor Darcy must have lowered herself to incur such acquaintanceship!"

Lord Netherby made no reply, but gave a glance towards the still open door of the drawing-room. Her Ladyship understood it at once, and said,—

"Oh, let us release poor Richard from his bondage. Tell him to come in."

Lord Netherby walked forward; but scarcely had he entered the drawing-room, when he called out, "He's gone!"

"Gone! when?—how?" cried Lady Netherby, ringing the bell. "Did you see Lord Wall incourt when he was going, Davenport?" asked she, at once assuming her own calm deportment.

"Yes, my Lady."

"I hope he took the carriage."

"No, my Lady, his Lordship went on foot."

"That will do, Davenport. I don't receive to-day."

"I must hasten after him," said Lord Netherby, as the servant withdrew. "We have, perhaps, incurred the very hazard we hoped to obviate."

"I half feared it," exclaimed Lady Netherby, gravely. "Lose no time, however, and bring him to dinner; say that I feel very poorly, and that his society will cheer me greatly. If he is unfit to leave the house, stay with him; but above all things let him not be left alone."

Lord Netherby hastened from the room, and his carriage was soon heard at a rapid pace proceeding down the square.

Lady Netherby sat with her eyes fixed on the carpet, and her hands clasped closely, lost in thought. "Yes," said she, half aloud, "there is a fate in it! This Lady Eleanor may have her vengeance yet!"

It was about an hour after this, and while she was still revolving her own deep thoughts, that Lord Netherby re-entered the room.

"Well, is he here?" asked she, impatiently.

"No, he's off to Ireland; the very moment he reached the hotel he ordered four horses to his carriage, and while his servant packed some trunks he himself drove over to Lord Castlereagh's, but came back almost immediately. They must have used immense despatch, for Long told me that they would be nigh Barnet when I called."

"He's a true Wallincourt," said her Ladyship, bitterly. "Their family motto is 'Rash in danger,' and they have well deserved it."

CHAPTER XXXI
A LESSON FOR EAVES-DROPPING

Forester—for so to the end we must call him—but exemplified the old adage in his haste. The debility of long illness was successfully combated for some hours by the fever of excitement; but as that wore off, symptoms of severe malady again exhibited themselves, and when on the second evening of his journey he arrived at Bangor, he was dangerously ill. With a head throbbing, and a brain almost mad, he threw himself upon a bed, perhaps the thought of his abortive effort to reach Ireland the most agonizing feeling of his tortured mind. His first care was to inquire after the sailing of the packet; and learning that the vessel would leave within an hour, he avowed his resolve to go at every hazard. As the time drew nigh, however, more decided evidences of fever set in, and the medical man who had been called to his aid pronounced that his life would pay the penalty were he to persist in his rash resolve. His was not a temper to yield to persuasion on selfish grounds, and nothing short of his actual inability to endure moving from where he lay at last compelled him to cede; even then he ordered his only servant to take the despatches which Lord Castlereagh had given him, and proceed with them to Dublin, where he should seek out Mr. Bicknell, and place them in his hands, with strict injunctions to have them forwarded to Lady Eleanor Darcy at once. The burning anxiety of a mind weakened by a tedious and severe malady, the fever of travelling, and the impatient struggles be made to be clear and explicit in his directions, repeated as they were full twenty times over, all conspired to exaggerate the worst features of his case; and ere the packet sailed, his head was wandering in wild delirium.

Linwood knew his master too well to venture on a contradiction; and although with very grave doubts that he should ever see him again alive, he set out, resolving to spare no exertions to be back soon again in Bangor. The transit of the Channel forty-five years ago was, however, very different from that at present, and it was already the evening of the following day when he reached Dublin.

There was no difficulty in finding out Mr. Bicknell's residence; a very showy brass-plate on a door in a fashionable street proclaimed the house of the well-known man of law. He was not at home, however, nor would be for some hours; he had gone out on a matter of urgent business, and left orders that except for some most pressing reason, he was not to be sent for. Linwood did not hesitate to pronounce his business such, and at length obtained the guidance of a servant to the haunt in question.

It was in a street of a third or fourth-rate rank, called Stafford Street, that Bicknell's servant now stopped, and having made more than one inquiry as to name and number, at last knocked at the door of a sombre-looking, ruinous old house, whose windows, broken or patched with paper, bespoke an air of poverty and destitution. A child in a ragged and neglected dress opened the door, and answering to the question "If Mr. Bicknell were there," in the affirmative, led Linwood up stairs creaking as they went with rottenness and decay.

"You 're to rap there, and he 'll come to you," said the child, as they reached the landing, where two doors presented themselves; and so saying, she slipped noiselessly and stealthily down the stairs, leaving him alone in the gloomy lobby. Linwood was not without astonishment at the place in which he found himself; but there was no time for the indulgence of such a feeling, and he knocked, at first gently, and then, as no answer came, more loudly, and at last when several minutes elapsed, without any summons to enter, he tapped sharply at the panel with his cane. Still there was no reply; the deep silence of the old house seemed like that of a church at midnight; not a sound was heard to break it. There was a sense of dreariness and gloom over the ruinous spot and the fast-closing twilight that struck Linwood deeply; and it is probable, had the mission with which he was intrusted been one of less moment than his master seemed to think it, that Linwood would quietly have descended the stairs, and deferred his interview with Mr. Bicknell to a more suitable time and place. He had come, however, bent on fulfilling his charge; and so, after waiting what he believed to be half an hour, and which might possibly have been five or ten minutes, he applied his hand to the lock, and entered the room.

It was a large, low-ceilinged apartment, whose moth-eaten furniture seemed to rival with the building itself, and which, though once not without some pretension to respectability, was now crumbling to decay, or coarsely mended by some rude hand. A door, not quite shut, led into an inner apartment; and from this room the sound of voices proceeded, whose conversation in all probability had prevented Linwood's summons from being heard.

Whether the secret instincts of his calling were the prompter,—for Linwood was a valet,—or that the strange circumstances in which he found himself had suggested a spirit of curiosity, but Linwood approached the door and peeped in. The sin of eaves-dropping, like most other sins, would seem only difficult at the first step; the subsequent ones came easily, for, as the listener established himself in a position to hear what went forward, he speedily became interested in what he heard.

By the gray half-light three figures were seen. One was a lady; so at least her position and attitude bespoke her, although her shawl was of a coarse and humble stuff, and her straw bonnet showed signs of time and season. She sat back in a deep leather chair, with hands folded, and her head slightly thrown forward, as if intently listening to the person who at a distance of half the room addressed lier. He was a thick-set, powerful man, in a jockey-cut coat and top-boots; a white hat, somewhat crushed and travel-stained, was at his feet, and across it a heavy horsewhip; his collar was confined by a single fold of a spotted handkerchief that thus displayed a brawny throat and a deep beard of curly black hair that made the head appear unnaturally large. The third figure was of a little, dapper, smart-looking personage, with a neatly powdered head and a scrupulously white cravat, who, standing partly behind the lady's chair, bestowed an equal attention on the speaker.

The green-coated man, it was clear to see, was of an order in life far inferior to the others, and in the manner of his address, his attitude as he sat, and his whole bearing, exhibited a species of rude deference to the listeners.

"Well, Jack," cried the little man, in a sharp lively voice, "we knew all these facts before; what we were desirous of was something like proof,—something that might be brought out into open court and before a jury."

"I'm afraid then, sir," replied the other, "I can't help you there. I told Mr. Daly all I knew and all I suspected, when I was up in Newgate; and if he had n't been in such a hurry that night to leave Dublin for the north, I could have brought him to the very house this fellow Garret was living in."

"Who is Garret?" broke in the lady, in a deep, full voice.

"The late Mr. Gleeson's butler, ma'am," said the little man; "a person we have never been able to come at. To summon him as a witness would avail us nothing; it is his private testimony that might be of such use to us."

"Well, you see, sir," continued the green coat, or, as he was familiarly named by the other, Jack, whom, perhaps, our reader has already recognized as Freney, the others being Miss Daly and Bicknell,-"well, you see, sir, Mr.

Daly was angry at the way things was done that night,—and sure enough he had good cause,-and sorra bit of a word he 'd speak to me when I was standing with the tears in my eyes to thank him; no, nor he wouldn't take the mare that was ready saddled and bridled in Healey's stables waiting for him, but he turned on his heel with 'D——n you for a common highwayman; it's what a man of blood and birth ever gets by stretching a hand to save you.'"

"He should have thought of that before," remarked Miss Daly, solemnly.

"Faith, and if he did, ma'am, your humble servant would have had to dance upon nothing!" rejoined Freney, with a laugh that was very far from mirthful.

"And what was the circumstance which gave Mr. Daly so much displeasure, Jack?" asked Bicknell. "I thought that everything went on exactly as he had planned it."

"Quite the contrary, sir; nothing was the way it ought to be. The fire was never thought of—"

"Never thought of! Do you mean to say it was an accident?"

"No, I don't, sir; I mean that all we wanted was to make believe that the jail was on fire, which was easy enough with burning straw; the rest was all planned safe and sure. And when we saw the real flames shooting up, sorra one was more frightened than some of ourselves; each accusing the other, cursing and shouting, and crying like mad! Ay, indeed! there was an ould fellow in for sheep-stealing, and nothing would convince him but that it was 'the devil took us at our word,' and sent his own fire for us. Not one of them was more puzzled than myself. I turned it every way in my mind, and could make nothing of it; for although I knew well that Mr. Daly would burn down Dublin from Barrack Street to the North Wall if he had a good reason for it, I knew also he 'd not do it out of mere devilment. Besides, ma'am, the way matters was going, it was likely none of us would escape. There was I—saving your presence—with eight-pound fetters on my legs. Ay, faix! I went down the ladder with them afterwards."

"But the fire."

"I 'm coming to it, sir. I was sitting this way, with my chin on my hands, at the window of my cell, trying to get a taste of fresh air, for the place was thick of smoke, when I seen the flames darting out of the windows of a public-house at the corner, the sign of the 'Cracked Padlock,' and at the same minute out came the fire through the roof, a great red spike of flame higher than the chimney. 'That's no accident,' says I to myself, 'whatever them that's doing it means;' and sure enough, the blaze broke out in the other corner of the street just as I said the words. Well, ma'am, of all the terrible yells and cries that was ever heard, the prisoners set up then; for though there was eight lying for execution on Saturday, and twice as many more very sure of the same end after the sessions, none of us liked to face such a dreadful thing as fire. Just then, ma'am, at that very minute, there came, as it might be, under my window, a screech so loud and so piercing that it went above all the other cries, just the way the yellow fire darted through the middle of the thick lazy smoke. Sorra one could give such a screech but a throat I knew well, and so I called out at the top of my voice, 'Ah, ye limb of the devil, this is your work!' and as sure as I 'm here, there came a laugh in my ears; and whether it was the devil himself gave it or Jemmy, I often doubted since."

"And who is Jemmy?" asked Bicknell.

"A bit of a 'gossoon' I had to mind the horses, and meet me with a beast here and there, as I wanted. The greatest villain for wickedness that was ever pinioned!"

"And so he was really the cause of the fire?"

"Ay, was he! He not only hid the tinder and chips—"

Just as Freney had got thus far, he drew his legs up close beneath him, sunk down his head as if into his neck, and with a spring, such as a tiger might have given, cleared the space between himself and the door, and rolled over on the floor, with the trembling figure of Linwood under him. So terribly sudden was the leap, that Miss Daly and Bicknell scarcely saw the bound ere they beheld him with one hand upon the victim's throat, while with the other he drew forth a clasp-knife, and opened the blade with his teeth.

"Keep back, keep back!" said Freney, as Bicknell drew nigh; and the words came thick and guttural, like the deep growl of a mastiff.

"Who are you, and what brings you here?" said Freney, as, setting his knee on the other's chest, he relinquished the grasp by which he had almost choked him.

"I came to see Mr. Bicknell," muttered the nearly lifeless valet.

"What did you want with me?"

"Wait a bit," interposed Freney. "Who brought you here? How came you to be standing by that door?"

"Mr. Bicknell's servant showed me the house, and a child brought me to this room."

"There, sir," said Freney, turning his head towards

Bicknell, without releasing the strong pressure by which he pinned the other down,—"there, sir, so much for your caution. You told me if I came to this lady's lodgings here, that I was safe, and now here 's this fellow has heard us and everything we 've said, maybe these two hours."

"I only heard about Newgate," muttered the miserable Linwood; "I was but a few minutes at the door, and was going to knock. I came from Lord Wall incourt with papers of great importance for Mr. Bicknell. I have them, if you'll let me—"

"Let him get up," said Miss Daly, calmly.

Freney stood back, and retired between his victim and the door, where he stood, with folded arms and bent brows, watching him.

"He has almost broke in my ribs," said Linwood, as he pressed his hands to his side, with a grimace of true suffering.

"So much for eaves-dropping. You need expect no pity from me," said Miss Daly, sternly. "Where are these papers?"

"My Lord told me," said the man, as he took them from his breast, "that I was to give them into Mr. Bicknell's own hands, with strictest directions to have them forwarded at the instant But for that," added he, whining, "I had never come to this."

"Let it be a lesson to you about listening, sir," said Miss Daly. "Had my brother been here—"

"Oh, by the powers!" broke in Freney, "he 'd have pitched you neck and crop into the water-hogshead below, if your master was the Lord-Lieutenant."

By this time Bicknell was busy reading the several addresses on the packets, and the names inscribed in the corners of each.

"If I 'm not mistaken, madam," said he to Miss Daly, "this Lord Wallincourt is the new peer, whose brother died at Lisbon. The name is Forester."

"Yes, sir, you are right," muttered Linwood.

"The same Mr. Richard Forester my brother knew, the cousin of Lord Castlereagh?"

"Yes, ma'am," said Linwood.

"Where is he? Is he here?"

"No, ma'am, he's lying dangerously ill, if he be yet alive, at Bangor. He wanted to bring these papers over himself, but was only able to get so far when the fever came on him again."

"Is he alone?"

"Quite alone, ma'am, no one knows even his name. He would not let me say who he was."

Miss Daly turned towards Bicknell, and spoke for several minutes in a quick and eager voice. Meanwhile Freney, now convinced that he had not to deal with a spy or a thief-catcher, came near and addressed Linwood.

"I did n't mean to hurt ye till I was sure ye deserved it, but never play that game any more."

Linwood appeared to receive both apology and precept with equal discontent.

"Another thing," resumed Freney: "I 'm sure you are an agreeable young man in the housekeeper's room and the butler's parlor, very pleasant and conversable, with a great deal of anecdote and amusing stories; but, mind me, let nothing tempt ye to talk about what ye heard me say tonight.

It's not that I care about myself,—it's worse than jail-breaking they can tell of me,—but I won't have another name mentioned. D 'ye mind me?"

As if to enforce the caution, he seized the listener between his finger and thumb; and whether there was something magnetic in the touch, or that it somehow conveyed a foretaste of what disobedience might cost, but Linwood winced till the tears came, and stammered out,—

"You may depend on it, sir, I 'll never mention it."

"I believe you," said the robber, with a grin, and fell back to his place.

"I will not lose a post, rely upon it, madam," said Bick-nell; "and am I to suppose you have determined on this journey?"

"Yes," said Miss Daly, "the case admits of little hesitation; the young man is alone, friendless, and unknown. I 'll hasten over at once,—I am too old for slander, Mr. Bicknell. Besides, let me see who will dare to utter it."

There was a sternness in her features as she spoke that made her seem the actual image of her brother. Then, turning to Linwood, she continued,—

"I 'll go over this evening to Bangor in the packet, let me find you there."

"I 'll see him safe on board, ma'am," said Freney, with a leer, while, slipping his arm within the valet's, he half led, half drew him from the room.

CHAPTER XXXII
A LESSON IN POLITICS

In the deep bay-window of a long, gloomy-looking dinner-room of a Dublin mansion, sat a party of four persons around a table plentifully covered with decanters and bottles, and some stray remnants of a dessert which seemed to have been taken from the great table in the middle of the apartment. The night was falling fast, for it was past eight o'clock of an evening in autumn, and there was barely sufficient light to descry the few scrubby-looking ash and alder trees that studded the barren grass-plot between the house and the stables. There was nothing to cheer in the aspect without, nor, if one were to judge from the long pauses that ensued after each effort at conversation, the few and monotonous words of the speakers, were there any evidences of a more enlivening spirit within doors. The party consisted of Dr. Hickman and his son Mr. O'Reilly, Mr. Heffernan, and "Counsellor" O'Halloran.

At first, and by the dusky light in the chamber, it would seem as if but three persons were assembled; for the old doctor, whose debility had within the last few months made rapid strides, had sunk down into the recess of the deep chair, and save by a low quavering respiration, gave no token of his presence. As these sounds became louder and fuller, the conversation gradually dropped into a whisper, for the old man was asleep. In the subdued tone of the speakers, the noiseless gestures as they passed the bottle from hand to hand, it was easy to mark that they did not wish to disturb his slumbers. It is no part of our task to detail how these individuals came to be thus associated. The assumed object which at this moment drew them together was the approaching trial at Galway of a record brought against the Hickmans by Darcy. It was Bick-nell's last effort, and with it must end the long and wearisome litigation between the houses.

The case for trial had nothing which could suggest any fears as to the result. It was on a motion for a new trial that the cause was to come on. The plea was misdirection and want of time, so that, in itself, the matter was one of secondary importance. The great question was that a general election now drew nigh, and it was necessary for O'Reilly to determine on the line of political conduct he should adopt, and thus give O'Halloran the opportunity of a declaration of his client's sentiments in his address to the jury.

The conduct of the Hickmans since their accession to the estate of Gwynne Abbey had given universal dissatisfaction to the county gentry. Playing at first the game of popularity, they assembled at their parties people of every class and condition; and while affronting the better-bred by low association, dissatisfied the inferior order by contact with those who made their inferiority more glaring. The ancient hospitalities of the Abbey were remembered in contrast with the ostentatious splendor of receptions in which display and not kindness was intended. Vulgar presumption and purse-pride had usurped the place once occupied by easy good breeding and cordiality; and even they who had often smarted under the cold reserve of Lady Eleanor's manner, were now ready to confess that she was born to the rank she assumed, and not an upstart, affecting airs of superiority. The higher order of the county gentry accordingly held aloof, and at last discontinued their visits altogether; of the second-rate many who were flattered at first by invitations, became dissatisfied at seeing the same favors extended to others below them, and they, too, ceased to present themselves, until, at last, the society consisted of a few sycophantic followers, who swallowed the impertinence of the host with the aid of his claret, and buried their own self-respect, if they were troubled with such a quality, under the weight of good dinners.

Hickman O'Reilly for a length of time affected not to mark the change in the rank and condition of his guests, but as one by one the more respectable fell off, and the few left were of a station that the fine servants of the house regarded as little above their own, he indignantly declined to admit any company in future, reduced the establishment to the few merely necessary for the modest requirements of the family, and gave it to be known that the uncongenial tastes and habits of his neighbors made him prefer isolation and solitude to such association.

For some time he had looked to England as the means of establishing for himself and his son a social position. The refusal of the minister to accord the baronetcy was a death-blow to this hope, while he discovered that mere wealth, unassisted by the sponsorship of some one in repute, could not suffice to introduce Beeeham into the world of fashion. Although these things had preyed on him severely, there was no urgent necessity to act in respect of them till the time came, as it now had done, for a general election.

The strict retirement of his life must now give way before the requirements of an election candidate, and he must consent to take the field once more as a public man, or, by abandoning his seat in Parliament, accept a condition of what he knew to be complete obscurity. The old doctor was indeed favorable to the latter course,—the passion for hoarding had gone on increasing with age. Money was, in his estimation, the only species of power above the changes and caprice of the world. Bank-notes were the only things he never knew to deceive; and he took an almost fiendish delight in contrasting the success of his own penurious practices with all the disappointments his son O'Reilly had experienced in his attempts at what he called "high life." Every slight shown him, each new instance of coldness or aversion of the neighborhood, gave the old man a diabolical pleasure, and seemed to revive his youth in the exercise of a malignant spirit.

O'Reilly's only hope of reconciling his father to the cost of a new election was in the prospect held out that the seat might at last be secured in perpetuity for Beeeham, and the chance of a rich marriage in England thus provided. Even this view he was compelled to sustain by the assurance that the expense would be a mere trifle, and that, by the adoption of popular principles, he should come in almost for nothing. To make the old doctor a convert to these notions, he had called in Heffernau and O'Halloran, who both, during the dinner, had exerted themselves with their natural tact, and now that the doctor had dropped asleep, were reposing themselves, and recruiting the energies so generously expended.

Hence the party seemed to have a certain gloom and weight over it, as the shadow of coming night fell on the figures seated, almost in silence, around the table. None spoke save an occasional word or two, as they passed round the bottle. Each retreated into his own reflections, and communed with himself. Men who have exhibited themselves to each other, in a game of deceit and trick, seem to have a natural repugnance to any recurrence to the theme when the occasion is once over. Even they whose hearts have the least self-respect will avoid the topic if possible.

"How is the bottle?—with you, I believe," said O'Reilly to Heffernan, in the low tone to which they had all reduced the conversation.

"I have just filled my glass; it stands with the Counsellor."

O'Halloran poured out the wine and sipped it slowly. "A very remarkable man," said he, sententiously, with a slight gesture of his head to the chair where the old doctor lay coiled up asleep. "His faculties seem as clear, and his judgment as acute, as if he were only five-and-forty, and I suppose he must be nearly twice that age."

"Very nearly," replied O'Reilly; "he confesses commonly to eighty-six; but when he is weak or querulous, he often says ninety-one or two."

"His memory is the most singular thing about him," said Heffernan. "Now, the account of Swift's appearance in the pulpit with his gown thrust back, and his hands stuck in the belt of his cassock, brow-beating the lord mayor and aldermen for coming in late to church,—it came as fresh as if he were talking of an event of last week."

"How good the imitation of voice was, too," added Heffernan: "'Giving two hours to your dress, and twenty minutes to your devotions, you come into God's house looking more like mountebanks than Christian men!'"

"I 've seldom seen him so much inclined to talk and chat away as this evening," said O'Reilly; "but I think you chimed in so well with his humor, it drew him on."

"There was something of dexterity," said Heffernan, "in the way he kept bringing up these reminiscences and old stories, to avoid entering upon the subject of the election. I saw that he would n't approach that theme, no matter how skilfully you brought it forward."

"You ought not to have alluded to the Darcys, however," said O'Halloran. "I remarked that the mention of their name gave him evident displeasure; indeed, he soon after pushed his chair back from the table and became silent."

"He always sleeps after dinner," observed O'Reilly, carelessly. "It was about his usual time."

Another pause now succeeded, in which the only sounds heard were the deep-drawn breathings of the sleeper.

"You saw Lord Castlereagh, I think you told me?" said O'Reilly, anxious to lead Heffernan into something like a declaration of opinion.

"Oh, repeatedly; I dined either with him or in his company, three or four times every week of my stay in town."

"Well, is he satisfied with the success of his measure?" asked O'Halloran, caustically. "Is this Union working to his heart's content?"

"It is rather early to pass a judgment on that point, I think."

"I'm not of that mind," rejoined O'Halloran, hastily. "The fruits of the measure are showing themselves already. The men of fortune are flying the country; their town houses are to let; their horses are advertised for sale at Dycer's. Dublin is, even now, beginning to feel what it may become when the population has no other support than itself."

"Such will always be the fortune of a province. Influence will and must converge to the capital," rejoined Heffernan.

"But what if the great element of a province be wanting? What if we have not that inherent respect and reverence for the metropolis provincials always should feel? What if we know that our interests are misunderstood, our real wants unknown, our peculiar circumstances either undervalued or despised?"

"If the case be as you represent it—-"

"Can you deny it? Tell me that."

"I will not deny or admit it. I only say, if it be such, there is still a remedy, if men are shrewd enough to adopt it."

"And what may that remedy be?" said O'Reilly, calmly.

"An Irish party!"

"Oh, the old story; the same plot over again we had this year at the Rotunda?" said O'Reilly, contemptuously.

"Which only failed from our own faults," added Heffer-nan, angrily. "Some of us were lukewarm and would do nothing; some waited for others to come forward; and some again wanted to make their hard bargain with the minister before they made him feel the necessity of the compact."

O'Reilly bit his lip in silence, for he well understood at whom this reproof was levelled.

"The cause of failure was very different," said O'Hallo-ran, authoritatively. "It was one which has dissolved many an association, and rendered many a scheme abortive, and will continue to do so, as often as it occurs. You failed for want of a 'Principle.' You had rank and wealth, and influence more than enough to have made your weight felt and acknowledged, but you had no definite object or end. You were a party, and you had not a purpose."

"Come, come," said Heffernan, "you are evidently unaware of the nature of our association, and seem not to have read the resolutions we adopted."

"No,—-on the contrary, I read them carefully; there was more than sufficient in them to have made a dozen parties. Had you adopted one steadfast line of action, set out with one brief intelligible proposition,—I care not what,—Slave Emancipation, or Catholic Emancipation, Repeal of Tests Acts, or Parliamentary Reform, any of them,—taken your stand on that, and that alone, you must have succeeded. Of course, to do this is a work of time and labor; some men will grow weary and sink by the way, but others take up the burden, and the goal is reached at last There must be years long of writing and speaking, meeting, declaring, and plotting; you must consent to be thought vulgar and low-minded,—ay, and to become so, for active partisans are only to be found in low places. You will be laughed at and jeered, abused, mocked, and derided at first; later on, you will be assailed more powerfully and more coarsely; but, all this while, your strength is developing, your agencies are spreading. Persuasion will induce some, notoriety others, hopes of advantage many more, to join you. You will then have a press as well as a party, and the very men that sneered at your beginnings will have to respect the persistence and duration of your efforts. I don't care how trumpery the arguments used; I don't value one straw the fallacy of the statements put forward. Let one great question, one great demand for anything, be made for some five-and-twenty or thirty years,— let the Press discuss, and the Parliament debate it,—you are sure of its being accorded in the end. Now, it will be a party ambitious of power that will buy your alliance at any price; now, a tottering Government anxious to survive the session and reach the snug harbor of the long vacation. Now, it will be the high 'bid' of a popular administration; now, it will be the last hope of second-rate capacities, ready to supply their own deficiencies by incurring a hazard. However it come, you are equally certain of it."

There was a pause as O'Halloran concluded. Heffernan saw plainly to what the Counsellor pointed, and that he was endeavoring to recruit for that party of which he destined the future leadership for himself, and Con had no fancy to serve in the ranks of such an army. O'Reilly, who thought that the profession of a popular creed might be serviceable in the emergency of an election, looked with more favor on the exposition, and after a brief interval said,—

"Well, supposing I were to see this matter in your light, what support could you promise me? I mean at the hustings."

"Most of the small freeholders, now,-all of them, in time; the priests to a man, the best election agents that ever canvassed a constituency. By degrees the forces will grow stronger, according to the length and breadth of the principle you adopt,—make it emancipation, and I 'll insure you a lease of the county." Heffernan smiled dubiously. "Ah, never mind Mr. Heffernan's look; these notions don't suit him. He 's one of the petty traders in politics, who like small sales and quick returns."

"Such dealing makes fewest bankrupts," said Heffernan, coolly.

"I own to you," said O'Halloran, "the rewards are distant, but they 're worth waiting for. It is not the miserable bribe of a situation, or a title, both beneath what they would accord to some state apothecary; but power, actual power, and real patronage are in the vista."

A heavy sigh and a rustling sound in the deep armchair announced that the doctor was awaking, and after a few struggles to throw off the drowsy influence, he sat upright, and made a gesture that he wished for wine.

"We 've been talking about political matters, sir," said O'Reilly. "I hope we didn't disturb your doze?"

"No; I was sleeping sound," croaked the old man, in a feeble whine, "and I had a very singular dream! I dreamed I was sitting in a great kitchen of a big house, and there was a very large, hairy turnspit sitting opposite to me, in a nook beside the fire, turning a big spit with a joint of meat on it. 'Who's the meat for?' says I to him. 'For my Lord Castlereagh,' says he, 'devil a one else.' 'For himself alone?' says I. 'Just so,' says he; 'don't you know that's the Irish Parliament that we 're roasting and basting, and when it's done,' says he, 'we 'll sarve it up to be carved.' 'And who are you?' says I to the turnspit. 'I'm Con Heffernan,' says he; 'and the devil a bit of the same meat I 'm to get, after cooking it till my teeth 's watering.'"

A loud roar of laughter from O'Halloran, in which Heffernan endeavored to take a part, met this strange revelation of the doctor's sleep, nor was it for a considerable time after that the conversation could be resumed without some jesting allusion of the Counsellor to the turnspit and his office.

"Your dream tallies but ill, sir, with the rumors through Dublin," said O'Reilly, whose quick glance saw through the mask of indifference by which Heffernan concealed his irritation.

"I did n't hear it. What was it, Bob?"

"That the ministry had offered our friend here the secretaryship for Ireland."

"Sure, if they did—" He was about to add, "That he 'd have as certainly accepted it," when a sense of the impropriety of such a speech arrested the words.

"You are mistaken, sir," interposed Heffernan, answering the unspoken sentence. "I did refuse. The conditions on which I accorded my humble support to the bill of the Union have been shamefully violated, and I could not, if I even wished it, accept office from a Government that have been false to their pledges."

"You see my dream was right, after all," chuckled the old man. "I said they kept him working away in the kitchen, and gave him none of the meat afterwards."

"What if I had been stipulating for another, sir?" said Heffernan, with a forced smile. "What if the breach of faith I allude to had reference not to me, but to your son yonder, for whom, and no other, I asked—I will not say a favor, but a fair and reasonable acknowledgment of the station he occupies?"

"Ah, that weary title!" exclaimed the doctor, crankily. "What have we to do with these things?"

"You are right, sir," chimed in O'Halloran. "Your present position, self-acquired and independent, is a far prouder one than any to be obtained by ministerial favor."

"I 'd rather he'd help us to crush these Darcys," said the old man, as his eyes sparkled and glistened like the orbs of a serpent. "I 'd rather my Lord Castlereagh would put his heel upon *them* than stretch out the hand to *us*."

"What need to trouble your head about them?" said Heffernan, conciliatingly; "they are low enough in all conscience now."

"My father means," said O'Reilly, "that he is tired and sick of the incessant appeals to law this family persist in following; that these trials irritate and annoy him."

"Come sir," cried O'Halloran, encouragingly, "you shall see the last of them in a few weeks. I have reason to know that an old maiden sister of Bagenal Daly's has supplied Bicknell with the means of the present action. It's the last shot in the locker. We 'll take care to make the gun recoil on the hand that fires it."

"Darcy and Daly are both out of the country," observed the old man, cunningly.

"We 'll call them up for judgment, however," chimed in O'Halloran. "That same Daly is one of those men who infested our country in times past, and by the mere recklessness of their hold on life, bullied and oppressed all who came before them. I am rejoiced to have an opportunity of showing up such a character."

"I wish we had done with them all," sighed the doctor.

"So you shall, with this record. Will you pledge yourself not to object to the election expenses if I gain you the verdict?"

"Come, that's a fair offer," said Heffernan, laughing.

"Maybe, they 'll come to ten thousand," said the doctor, cautiously.

"Not above one half the sum, if Mr. O'Reilly will consent to take my advice."

"And why wouldn't he?" rejoined the old man, querulously. "What signifies which side he takes, if it saves the money?"

"Is it a bargain, then?"

"Will you secure me against more trials at law? Will you pledge yourself that I am not to be tormented by these anxieties and cares?"

"I can scarcely promise that much; but I feel so assured that your annoyance will end here, that I am willing to pledge myself to give you my own services without fee or reward in future, if any action follow this one."

"I think that is most generous," said Heffernan.

"It is as much as saying, he 'll enter into recognizances for an indefinite series of five-hundred-pound briefs," added O'Reilly.

"Done, then. I take you at your word," said the doctor; while stretching forth his lean and trembling hand, he grasped the nervous fingers of the Counsellor in token of ratification.

"And now woe to the Darcys!" muttered O'Halloran, as he arose to say good-night, Heffernan arose at the same time, resolved to accompany the Counsellor, and try what gentle persuasion could effect in the modification of views which he saw were far too explicit to be profitable.

CHAPTER XXXIII
THE CHANCES OF TRAVEL

Neither our space nor our inclination prompt us to dwell on Forester's illness; enough when we say that his recovery, slow at first, made at length good progress, and within a month after the commencement of the attack, he was once more on the road, bent on reaching the North, and presenting himself before Lady Eleanor and her daughter.

Miss Daly, who had been his kind and watchful nurse for many days and nights ere his wandering faculties could recognize her, contributed more than all else to his restoration. The impatient anxiety under which he suffered was met by her mild but steady counsels; and although she never ventured to bid him hope too sanguinely, she told him that his letter had reached Helen's hand, and that he himself must plead the cause he had opened.

"Your greatest difficulty," said she, in parting with him in Dublin, "will be in the very circumstance which, in ordinary cases, would be the guarantee of your success. Your own rise in fortune has widened the interval between you. This, to your mind, presents but the natural means of overcoming the obstacles I allude to; but remember there are others whose feelings are to be as intimately consulted,—nay, more so than your own. Think of those who never yet made an alliance without feeling that they were on a footing of perfect equality; and reflect that even if Helen's affections were all your own, Maurice Darcy's daughter can enter into no family, however high and proud it may be, save as the desired and sought-for by its chief members. Build upon anything lower than this, and you fail. More still," added she, almost sternly, "your failure will meet with no compassion from me. Think not, because I have gone through life a lone, uncared-for thing, that I undervalue the strength and power of deep affection, or that I could counsel you to make it subservient to views of worldliness and advantage. You know me little if you think so. But I would tell you this, that no love deserving of the name ever existed without those high promptings of the heart that made all difficulties easy to encounter,—ay, even those worst of difficulties that spring from false pride and prejudice. It is by no sudden outbreak of temper, no selfish threat of this or that insensate folly, that your lady-mother's consent should be obtained. It is by the manly dignity and consistency of a character that in the highest interests of a higher station give a security for sound judgment and honorable motives. Let it appear from your conduct that you are not swayed by passion or caprice. You have already won men's admiration for the gallantry of your daring. There is something better still than this, the esteem and regard that are never withheld from a course of honorable and independent action. With these on your side, rely upon it, a mother's heart will not be the last in England to acknowledge and glory in your fame. And now, good-bye; you have a better travelling-companion than me,-you have hope with you."

She returned the cordial pressure of his hand, and was turning away, when, after what had seemed a kind of struggle with her feelings, she added,—

"One word more, even at the hazard of wearying you. Above all and everything, be honest, be candid; not only with others, but with yourself! Examine well your heart, and let no sense of false shame, let no hopes of some chance or accident deceive you, by which your innermost feelings are to be guessed at, and not avowed. This is the blackest of calamities; this can even embitter every hour of a long life."

Her voice trembled at the last words; and as she concluded, she wrung his hand once more affectionately, and moved hurriedly away. Forester looked after her with a tender interest. For the first time in his life he heard her sob. "Yes," thought he, as he lay back and covered his eyes with his hand, "she, too, has loved, and loved unhappily."

There are few sympathies stronger, not even those of illness itself, than connect those whose hearts have struggled under unrequited affection; and so, for many an hour as he travelled, Forester's thoughts recurred to Miss Daly, and the last troubled accents of her parting speech. Perhaps he did not dwell the less on that theme because it carried him away from his own immediate hopes and fears,—emotions that rendered him almost irritable by their intensity.

While on the road, Forester travelled with all the speed he could accomplish. His weakness did not permit of his being many hours in a carriage, and he endeavored to compensate for this by rapid travelling at the time. His impatience to get forward was, however, such that he scarcely arrived at any halting-place without ordering horses to be at once got ready, so that, when able, he resumed the road without losing a moment.

In compliance with this custom, the carriage was standing all ready with its four posters at the door of the inn of Castle Blayney; while Forester, overcome by fatigue and exhaustion, had thrown himself on the bed and fallen asleep. The rattling crash of a mail-coach and its deep-toned horn suddenly awoke him: he started, and looked at his watch. Was it possible? It was nearly midnight; he must have slept more than three hours! Half gratified by the unaccustomed rest, half angry at the lapse of time, he arose to depart. The night was the reverse of inviting; a long-threatened storm had at last burst forth, and the rain was falling in torrents, while the wind, in short and fitful gusts, shook the house to its foundation, and scattered tiles and slates over the dreary street.

So terrible was the hurricane, many doubts were entertained that the mail could proceed further; and when it did at length set forth, gloomy prognostics of danger—dark pictures of precipices, swollen torrents, and broken bridges—were rife in the bar and the landlord's room. These arguments, if they could be so called, were all renewed when Forester called for his bill, as a preparation to depart, and all the perils that ever happened by land or by water recapitulated to deter him.

"The middle arch of the Slaney bridge was tottering when the up-mail passed three hours before. A horse and cart were just fished out of Mooney's pond, but no driver as yet discovered. The forge at the cross roads was blown down, and the rafters were lying across the highway." These, and a dozen other like calamities, were bandied about, and pitched like shuttlecocks from side to side, as the impatient traveller descended the stairs.

Had Forester cared for the amount of the reckoning, which he did not, he might have entertained grave fears of its total, on the principle well known to travellers, that the speed of its coming is always in the inverse ratio of the sum, and that every second's delay is sure to swell its proportions. Of this he never thought once; but he often reflected on the tardiness of waiters, and the lingering tediousness of the moments of parting.

"It's coming, sir; he's just adding it up," said the head waiter, for the sixth time within three minutes, while he moved to and fro, with the official alacrity that counterfeits despatch. "I'm afraid you'll have a bad night, sir. I'm sure the horses won't be able to face the storm over Grange Connel."

Forester made no reply, but walked up and down the hall in moody silence.

"The gentleman that got off the mail thought so too," added the waiter; "and now he's pleasanter at his supper, iu the coffee-room, than sitting out there, next to the guard, wet to the skin, and shivering with cold."

Less to inspect the stranger thus alluded to than to escape the impertinent loquacity of the waiter, Forester turned the handle of the door, and entered the coffee-room. It was a large, dingy-looking chamber, whose only bright spot seemed within the glow of a blazing turf-fire, where at a little table a gentleman was seated at supper. His back was turned to Forester; but even in the cursory glance the latter gave, he could perceive that he was an elderly personage, and one who had not abandoned the almost bygone custom of a queue.

The stranger, dividing his time between his meal and a newspaper, — which he devoured more eagerly than the viands before him, — paid no attention to Forester's entrance; nor did he once look round. As the waiter approached, he asked hastily, "What chance there was of getting forward?"

"Indeed, sir, to tell the truth," drawled out the man, "the storm seems getting worse, instead of better. Miles Finerty's new house, at the end of the street, is just blown down."

"Never mind Miles Finerty, my good friend, for the present," rejoined the old gentleman, mildly, "but just tell me, are horses to be had?"

"Faith! and to tell your honor no lie, I 'm afraid of it." Here he dropped to a whisper. "The sick-looking gentleman, yonder, has four waiting for him, since nine o'clock; and we 've only a lame mare and a pony in the stable."

"Am I never to get this bill?" cried out Forester, in a tone that illness had rendered peculiarly querulous. "I have asked, begged for it, for above an hour, and here I am still."

"He's bringing it now, sir," cried the waiter, stepping hastily out of the room, to avoid further questioning. Forester, whose impatience had now been carried beyond endurance, paced the room with hurried strides, muttering, between his teeth, every possible malediction on the whole race of innkeepers, barmaids, waiters, — even down to Boots himself. These imprecating expressions had gradually assumed a louder and more vehement tone, of which he was by no means aware, till the old gentleman, at the pause of a somewhat wordy denunciation, gravely added, —

"Insert a clause upon postboys, sir, and I 'll second the measure."

Forester wheeled abruptly round. He belonged to a class, a section of society, whose cherished prestige is neither to address nor be addressed by an unintroduced stranger; and had the speaker been younger, or of any age more nearly his own, it is more than likely a very vague stare of cool astonishment would have been his only acknowledgment of the speech. The advanced age, and something in the very accent of the stranger, were, however, guarantees against this conventional rudeness, and he remarked, with a smile, "I have no objection to extend the provisions of my bill in the way you propose, for perhaps half an hour's experience may teach me how much they deserve it."

"You are fortunate, however, to have secured horses. I perceive that the stables are empty."

"If you are pressed for time, sir," said Forester, on whom the quiet, well-bred manners of the stranger produced a strong impression, "it would be a very churlish thing of me to travel with four horses while I can spare a pair of them."

"I am really very grateful," said the old gentleman, rising, and bowing courteously; "if this be not a great inconvenience—"

"By no means; and if it were," rejoined Forester, "I have a debt to acquit to my own heart on this subject. I remember once, when travelling down to the west of Ireland, I reached a little miserable country town at nightfall, and, just as here, save that then there was no storm—" The entrance of the long-expected landlord, with his bill, here interrupted Forester's story. As he took it, and thus afforded time for the stranger to fix his eyes steadfastly upon him, unobserved, Forester quickly resumed: "I was remarking that, just as here, there were only four post-horses to be had, and that they had just been secured by another traveller a few moments before my arrival. I forget the name of the place—"

"Perhaps I can assist you," said the other, calmly. "It was Kilbeggan."

Had a miracle been performed before his eyes, Forester could not have been more stunned; and stunned he really was, and unable to speak for some seconds. At length, his surprise yielding to a vague glimmering of belief, he called out, "Great heavens! it cannot be—it surely is not—"

"Maurice Darcy, you would say, sir," said the Knight, advancing with an offered hand. "As surely as I believe you to be my son Lionel's brother officer and friend, Captain Forester."

"Oh, Colonel Darcy! this is, indeed, happiness," exclaimed the young man, as he grasped the Knight's hand in both of his, and shook it affectionately.

"What a strange rencontre," said the Knight, laughing; "quite the incident of a comedy! One would scarcely look for such meetings twice,— so like in every respect. Our parts are changed, however; it is your turn to be generous, if the generosity trench not too closely on your convenience."

Forester could but stammer out assurances of delight and pleasure, and so on, for his heart was too full to speak calmly or collectedly.

"And Lionel, sir, how is he,-when have you heard from him?" said the young man, anxious, by even the most remote path, to speak of the Knight's family.

"In excellent health. The boy has had the good fortune to be employed in a healthy station, and, from a letter which I found awaiting me at my army agent's, is as happy as can be. But to recur to our theme: will you forgive my selfishness if I say that you will add indescribably to the favor if you permit me to take these horses at once? I have not seen my family for some time back, and my impatience is too strong to yield to ceremony."

"Of course,—certainly; my carriage is, however, all ready, and at the door. Take it as it is, you 'll travel faster and safer."

"But you yourself," said Darcy, laughing,—"you were about to move forward when we met."

"It's no matter; I was merely travelling for the sake of change," said Forester, confusedly.

"I could not think of such a thing," said Darcy. "If our way led together, and you would accept of me as a travelling companion, I should be but too happy; but to take the long-boat, and leave you on the desolate rock, is not to be thought of." The Knight stopped; and although he made an effort to continue, the words faltered on his lips, and he was silent. At last, and with an exertion that brought a deep blush to his cheek, he said: "I am really ashamed, Captain Forester, to acknowledge a weakness which is as new to me as it is unmanly. The best amends I can make for feeling is to confess it. Since we met that same night, circumstances of fortune have considerably changed with me. I am not, as you then knew me, the owner of a good house and a good estate. Now, I really would wish to have been able to ask you to come and see me; but, in good truth, I cannot tell where or how I should lodge you if you said 'yes.' I believe my wife has a cabin on this northern shore, but, however it may accommodate us, I need not say I could not ask a friend to put up with it. There is my confession; and now that it is told, I am only ashamed that I should hesitate about it."

Forester once more endeavored, in broken, disjointed phrases, to express his acknowledgment, and was in the very midst of a mass of contradictory explanations, hopes, and wishes, when Linwood entered with, "The carriage is ready, my Lord."

The Knight heard the words with surprise, and as quickly remarked that the young man was dressed in deep mourning. "I have been unwittingly addressing you as Captain Forester," said he, gravely; "I believe I should have said—"

"Lord Wallincourt," answered Forester, with a slight tremor in his voice; "the death of my brother—" Here he hesitated, and at length was silent.

The Knight, who read in his nervous manner and sickly appearance the signs of broken health and spirits, resolved at once to sacrifice mere personal feeling in a cause of kindness, and said: "I see, my Lord, you are scarcely as strong as when I had the pleasure to meet you first, and I doubt not that you require a little repose and quietness. Come along with me then; and if even this cabin of ours be inhospitable enough not to afford you a room, we 'll find something near us on the coast, and I have no doubt we 'll set you on your legs again."

"It is a favor I would have asked, if I dared," said Forester, feebly. He then added: "Indeed, sir, I will confess it, my journey had no other object than to present myself to Lady Eleanor Darcy. Through the kindness of my relative, Lord Castlereagh, I was enabled to send her some tidings of yourself, of which my illness prevented my being the bearer, and I was desirous of adding my own testimony, so far as it could go." Here again he faltered.

"Pray continue," said the Knight, warmly; "I am never happier than when grateful, and I see that I have reason for the feeling here."

"I perceive, sir, you do not recognize me," said the young man, thoughtfully, while he fixed his deep, full eyes upon the Knight's countenance.

Darcy stared at him in turn, and, passing his hand across his brow, looked again. "There is some mystification here," said he, quickly, "but I cannot see through it."

"Come, Colonel Darcy," said Forester, with more animation than before. "I see that you forget me-, but perhaps you remember this." So saying, he walked over to a table where a number of cloaks and travelling-gear were lying, and taking up a pistol, placed it in Darcy's hand. "This you certainly recognize?"

"It is my own!" exclaimed the Knight; "the fellow of it is yonder. I had it with me the day we landed at Aboukir."

"And gave it to me when a French dragoon had his sabre at my throat," continued Forester.

"And is it to your gallantry that I owe my life, my brave boy?" cried the old man, as he threw his arm around him.

"Not one half so much as I owe my recovery to your kindness," said Forester. "Remember the wounded Volunteer you came to see on the march. The surgeon you employed never left me till the very day I quitted the camp; although I have had a struggle for life twice since then, I never could have lived through the first attack but for his aid."

"Is this all a dream," said the Knight, as he leaned his head upon his band, "or are these events real? Then you were the officer whose exchange was managed, and of which I heard soon after the battle?"

"Yes, I was exchanged under a cartel, and sailed for England the day after. And you, sir,—tell me of your fate."

"A slight wound and a somewhat tiresome imprisonment tells the whole story,—the latter a good deal enlivened by seeing that our troops were beating the French day after day, and the calculation that my durance could scarcely last till winter. I proved right, for last month came the capitulation, and here I am. But all these are topics for long evenings to chat over. Come with me; you can't refuse me any longer. Lady Eleanor has the right to speak *her* gratitude to you; I see you won't listen to *mine*."

The Knight seized the young man's arm, and led him along as he spoke. "Nay," said he, "there is another reason for it. If you suffered me to go off alone, nothing would make me believe that what I have now heard was not some strange trick of fancy. Here, with you beside me, feeling your arm within my own, and hearing your voice, it is all that I can do to believe it. Come, let me be convinced again. Where did you join us?"

Forester now went over the whole story of his late adventures, omitting nothing from the moment he had joined the frigate at Portsmouth to the last evening, when as a prisoner, he had sent for Darcy to speak to him before he died. "I thought then," said he, "I could scarcely have more than an hour or two to live; but when you came and stood beside me, I was not able to utter a word, I believe, at the time. It was rather a relief to me than otherwise that you did not know me."

"How strange is this all!" said the Knight, musing. "You have told me a most singular story; only one point remains yet unelucidated. How came you to volunteer,—you were in the Guards?"

"Yes," said Forester, blushing and faltering; "I had quitted the Guards, intending to leave the army, some short time previous; but—but—"

"The thought of active service brought you back again. Out with it, and never be ashamed. I remember now having heard from an old friend of mine, Miss Daly, how you had left the service; and, to say truth, I was sorry for it,—sorry for *your* sake, but sorrier because it always grieves me when men of gentle blood are not to be found where hard knocks are going. None ever distinguish themselves with more honor, and it is a pity that they should lose the occasion to show the world that birth and blood inherit higher privileges than stars and titles."

While the miles rolled over, they thus conversed; and as each became more intimately acquainted and more nearly interested in the other, they drew towards the journey's end. It was late on the following night when they reached Port Ballintray; and as the darkness threatened more than once to mislead them, the postilion halted at the door of a little cabin to procure a light for his lamps.

While the travellers sat patiently awaiting the necessary preparation, a voice from within the cottage struck Darcy's ear; he threw open the door as he heard it, and sprang out, and rushing forward, the moment afterwards pressed his wife and daughter in his arms.

Forester, who in a moment comprehended the discovery, hastened to withdraw from a scene where his presence could only prove a constraint, and leaving a message to say that he had gone to the little inn and would wait on the Knight next morning, he hurried from the spot, his heart bursting with many a conflicting emotion.

CHAPTER XXXIV
HOME

Perhaps in the course of a long and, till its very latter years, a most prosperous life, the Knight of Gwynne had never known more real unbroken happiness than now that he had laid his head beneath the lowly thatch of a fisherman's cottage, and found a home beside the humble hearth where daily toil had used to repose. It was not that he either felt, or assumed to feel, indifferent to the great reverse of his fortune, and to the loss of that station to which all his habits of life and thought had been conformed. Nor had he the innate sense that his misfortunes had been incurred without the culpability of, at least, neglect on his own part. No; he neither deceived nor exonerated himself. His present happiness sprang from discovering in those far dearer to him than himself powers of patient submission, traits of affectionate forbearance, signs of a hopeful, trusting spirit, that their trials were not sent without an aim and object,—all gifts of heart and mind, higher, nobler, and better than the palmiest days of prosperity had brought forth.

It was that short and fleeting season, the late autumn, a time in which the climate of Northern Ireland makes a brief but brilliant amende for the long dreary months of the year. The sea, at last calm and tranquil, rolled its long waves upon the shore in measured sweep, waking the echoes in a thousand caves, and resounding with hollow voice beneath the very cliffs. The wild and fanciful outlines of the Skerry Islands were marked, sharp and distinct, against the dark blue sky, and reflected not less so in the unruffled water at their base. The White Rocks, as they are called, shone with a lustre like dulled silver; and above them the ruined towers of old Dunluce hung balanced over the sea, and even in decay seemed to defy dissolution.

The most striking feature of the picture was, however, the myriad of small boats, amounting in some instances to several hundreds, which filled the little bay at sunset. These were the fishermen from Innisshowen, coming to gather the seaweed on the western shore their eastern aspect denied them,—a hardy and a daring race, who braved the terrible storms of that fearful coast without a thought of fear. Here were they now, their little skiffs crowded with every sail they could carry,—for it was a trial of speed who should be first up after the turn of the ebb-tide,—their taper masts bending and springing like whips, the white water curling at the bows and rustling over the gunwales; while the fishermen themselves, with long harpoon spears, contested for the prizes,—large masses of floating weed, which not unfrequently were seized upon by three or four rival parties at the same moment.

A more animated scene cannot be conceived than the bay thus presented: the boats tacking and beating in every direction, crossing each other so closely as to threaten collision,—sometimes, indeed, carrying off a bowsprit or a rudder; while, from the restless motion of those on board, the frail skiffs were at each instant endangered,—accidents that occurred continually, but whose peril may be judged by the hearty cheers and roars of laughter they excited. Here might be seen a wide-spreading surface of tangled seaweed, vigorously towed in two different directions by contending crews, whose exertions to secure it were accompanied by the wildest shouts and cries. There a party were hauling in the prey, while their comrades, with spars and spears, kept the enemy aloof; and here, on the upturned keel of a capsized boat, were a dripping group, whose heaviest penalty was the ridicule of their fellows.

Seated in front of the little cottage, the Darcys and Forester watched this strange scene with all the interest its moving, stirring life could excite; and while the ladies could enjoy the varying picture only for itself, to the Knight and the youth it brought back the memory of a more brilliant and a grander display, one to which heroism and danger had lent the most exciting of all interests.

"I see," said Darcy, as he watched his companion's countenance,—"I see whither your thoughts are wandering. They are off to the old castle of Aboukir, and the tall cliffs at Marmorica." Forester slightly nodded an assent, but never spoke, while the Knight resumed: "I told you it would never do to give up the service. The very glance of your eye at yonder picture tells me how the great original is before your miud. Come, a few weeks more of rest and quiet, you will be yourself again. Then must you present yourself before the gallant Duke, and ask for a restitution to your old grade. There will be sharp work erelong. Buonaparte is not the man to forgive Alexandria and Cairo. If I read you aright, you prefer such a career to all the ambition of a political life."

Forester was still silent; but his changing color told that the Knight's words had affected him deeply, but whether as they were intended, it was not so plain to see. The Knight went on: "I am not disposed to vain regrets; but if I were to give way to such, it would be that I am not young enough to enter upon the career I now see opening to our arms. Our insular position seems to have moulded our destiny in great part; but, rely on it, we are as much a nation of soldiers as of sailors." Warming with this theme, Darcy continued, while sketching out the possible turn of events, to depict the noble path open to a young man who to natural talents and acquirements added the high advantages of fortune, rank, and family influence.

"I told you," said he, smiling, "that I blamed you once unjustly, as it happened, because, as a Guardsman, you did not seize the occasion to exchange guard-mounting for the field; but now I shall be sorely grieved if you suffer yourself to be withdrawn from a path that has already opened so brightly, by any of the seductions of your station, or the fascinations of mere fashion."

"Are you certain," said Lady Eleanor, speaking in a voice shaken by agitation, — "are you certain, my dear, that these same counsels of yours would be in strict accordance with the wishes of Lord Wallincourt's friends, or is it not possible that *their* ambitions may point very differently for his future?"

"I can but give the advice I would offer to Lionel," said Darcy, "if my son were placed in similarly fortunate circumstances. A year or two, at least, of such training will be no bad discipline to a young man's mind, and help to fit him to discuss those terms which, if I see aright, will be rife in our assemblies for some years to come—" Darcy was about to continue, when Tate advanced with a letter, whose address bespoke Bicknell's hand. It was a long-expected communication, and, anxious to peruse it carefully, the Knight arose, and making his excuses, re-entered the cottage.

The party sat for some time in silence. Lady Eleanor's mind was in a state of unusual conflict, since, for the first time in her life, had she practised any concealment with her husband, having forborne to tell him of Forester's former addresses to Helen. To this course she had been impelled by various reasons, the most pressing among which were the evident change in the young man's demeanor since he last appeared amongst them, and, consequently, the possibility that he had outlived the passion he then professed; and secondly, by observing that nothing in Helen betrayed the slightest desire to encourage any renewal of those professions, or any chagrin at the change in his conduct. As a mother and as a woman, she hesitated to avow what should seem to represent her daughter as being deserted, while she argued that if Helen were as indifferent as she really seemed, there was no occasion whatever for the disclosure. Now, however, that the Knight had spoken his counsels so strongly, the thought occurred to her, that Forester might receive the advice in the light of a rejection of his former proposal, and suppose that these suggestions were only another mode of refusing his suit. Hence a struggle of doubt and uncertainty arose within her, whether she should at once make everything known to Darcy, or still keep silence, and leave events to their own development. The former course seemed the most fitting; and entirely forgetful of all else, she hastily arose, and followed her husband into the cabin.

Forester was now alone with Helen, and for the first time since that well-remembered night when he had offered his heart and been rejected. The game of dissimulating feelings is almost easiest before a numerous audience; it is rarely possible in a *tête-à-tête*. So Forester soon felt; and although he made several efforts to induce a conversation, they were all abrupt and disjointed, as were Helen's own replies to them. At length came a pause; and what a thing is a pause at such a moment! The long lingering seconds in which a duellist watches his adversary's pistol, wavering over the region of his heart or brain, is less torturing than such suspense. Forester arose twice, and again sat down, his face pale and flushed alternately. At length, with a thick and rapid utterance, he said,—

"I have been thinking over the Knight's counsels,—dare I ask if they have Miss Darcy's concurrence?"

"It would be a great, a very great presumption in me," said Helen, tremulously, "to offer an opinion on such a theme. I have neither the knowledge to distinguish between the opposite careers, nor have I any feeling for those sentiments which men alone understand in warfare."

"Nor, perhaps," added Forester, with a sudden irony, "sufficient interest in the subject to give it a thought."

Helen was silent; her slightly compressed lips and heightened color showed that she was offended at the speech, but she made no reply.

"I crave your pardon, Miss Darcy," said he, in a low, submissive accent, that told how heartfelt it was. "I most humbly ask you to forgive my rudeness. The very fact that I had no claim to that interest should have protected you from such a speech. But see what comes of kindness to those who are little used to it; they get soon spoiled, and forget themselves."

"Lord Wall incourt will have to guard himself well against flattery, if such humble attentions as ours disturb his judgment."

"I will get out of the region of it," said he, resolutely; "I will take the Knight's advice. It is but a plunge, and all is over."

"If I dare to say so, my Lord," said Helen, archly, "this is scarcely the spirit in which my father hoped his counsels would be accepted. His chivalry on the score of a military life may be overstrained, but it has no touch of that recklessness your Lordship seems to lend it."

"And why should not this be the spirit in which I join the army?" said he, passionately; "the career has not for me those fascinations which others feel. Danger I like, for its stimulus, as other men like it; but I would rather confront it when and where and how I please, than at the dictate of a colonel and by the ritual of a despatch."

"Rather be a letter of marque, in fact, than a ship-of-the-line,—more credit to your Lordship's love of danger than discipline."

Forester smiled, but not without anger, at the quiet persiflage of her manner. It took him some seconds ere he could resume.

"I perceive," said he, in a tone of deeper feeling, "that whatever my resolves, to discuss them must be an impertinence, when they excite no other emotion than ridicule—"

"Nay, my Lord," interposed Helen, eagerly; "I beg you to forgive my levity. Nothing was further from my thoughts than to hurt one to whom we owe our deepest debt of gratitude. I can never forget you saved my father's life; pray do not let me seem so base, to my heart, as to undervalue this."

"Oh, Miss Darcy," said he, passionately, "it is I who need forgiveness,—I, whose temper, rendered irritable by illness, suspect reproach and sarcasm in every word of those who are kindest to me."

"You are unjust to yourself," said Helen, gently,—"unjust, because you expect the same powers of mind and judgment that you enjoyed in health. Think how much better you are than when you came here. Think what a few days more may do. How changed—"

"Has Miss Darcy changed since last I met her?" asked he, in a tone that sank into the very depth of her heart.

Helen tried to smile; but emotions of a sadder shade spread over her pale features, as she said,—

"I hope so, my Lord; I trust that altered fortunes have not lost their teaching. I fervently hope that sorrow and suffering have left something behind them better than unavailing regrets and heart-repinings."

"Oh, believe me," cried Forester, passionately, "it is not of this change I would speak. I dared to ask with reference to another feeling."

"Be it so," said Helen, trembling, as if nerving herself for a strong and long-looked-for effort,-"be it so, my Lord, and is not my answer wide enough for both? Would not any change, short of a dishonorable one, make the decision I once came to a thousand times more necessary now?"

"Oh, Helen, these are cold and cruel words. Will you tell me that my rank and station are to be like a curse upon my happiness?"

"I spoke of *our* altered condition, my Lord. I spoke of the impossibility of your Lordship recurring to a theme which the sight of that thatched roof should have stifled. Nay, hear me out. It is not of *you* or *your* motives that is here the question; it is of *me* and *my* duties. They are there, my Lord,—they are with those whose hearts have been twined round mine from infancy,— mine when the world went well and proudly with us; doubly, trebly mine when affection can replace fortune, and the sympathies' of the humblest home make up for all the flatteries of the world. I have no reason to dwell longer on this to one who knows those of whom I speak, and can value them too."

"But is there no place in your heart, Helen, for other affections than these; or is that place already occupied?"

"My Lord, you have borne my frankness so well, I must even submit to yours with a good grace. Still, this is a question you have no right to ask, or I to answer. I have told you that whatever doubt there might be as to *your* road in life, *mine* offered no alternative. That ought surely to be enough."

"It shall be," said Forester, with a low sigh, as, trembling in every limb, he arose from the seat. "And yet, Helen," said he, in a voice barely above a whisper, "there might come a time when these duties, to which you cling with such attachment, should be rendered less needful by altered fortunes. I have heard that your father's prospects present more of hope than heretofore, have I not? Think that if the Knight should be restored to his own again, that then—"

"Nay,—it is scarcely worthy of your Lordship to exact a pledge which is to hang upon a decision like this. A verdict may give back my father's estate; it surely should not dispose of his daughter's hand?"

"I would exact nothing, Miss Darcy," said Forester, stung by the tone of this reply. "But I see you cannot feel for the difficulties which beset him who has staked his all upon a cast. I asked, what might your feelings be, were the circumstances which now surround you altered?"

Helen was silent for a second or two; and then, as if having collected all her energy, she said: "I would that you had spared me—had spared yourself—the pain I now must give us both; but to be silent longer would be to encourage deception." It was not till after another brief interval that she could continue: "Soon after you left this, my Lord, you wrote a letter to

Miss Daly. This letter-I stop not now to ask with what propriety towards either of us—she left in my hands. I read it carefully; and if many of the sentiments it contained served to elevate your character in my esteem, I saw enough to show me that your resolves were scarcely less instigated by outraged pride than what you fancied to be a tender feeling. This perhaps might have wounded me, had I felt differently towards you. As it was, I thought it for the best; I deemed it happier that your motives should be divided ones, even though you knew it not. But as I read on, my Lord,—as I perused the account of your interview with Lady Wallincourt,—then a new light broke suddenly upon me; I found what, had I known more of life, should not have surprised, but what in my ignorance did indeed astonish me, that my father's station was regarded as one which could be alleged as a reason against your feeling towards his daughter. Now, my Lord, we have our pride too; and had your influence over me been all that ever you wished it, I tell you freely that I never would permit my affection to be gratified at the price of an insult to my father's house. If I were to say that your sentiments towards me should not have suffered it, would it be too much?"

"But, dearest Helen, remember that I am no longer dependent on my mother's will,—remember that I stand in a position and a rank which only needs you to share with me to make it all that my loftiest ambition ever coveted."

"These are, forgive me if I tell you, very selfish reasonings, my Lord. They may apply to *you*; they hardly address themselves to *my* position. The pride which could not stoop to ally itself with our house in our days of prosperity, should not assuredly be wounded by suing us in our humbler fortunes."

"Your thoughts dwell on Lady Netherby, Miss Darcy," said Forester, irritably; "she is scarcely the person most to be considered here."

"Enough for me, if I think so," said Helen, haughtily. "The lady your Lordship's condescension would place in the position of a mother should at least be able to regard me with other feelings than those of compassionate endurance. In a word, sir, it cannot be. To discuss the topic longer is but to distress us both. Leave me to my gratitude to you, which is unbounded. Let me dwell upon the many traits of noble heroism I can think of in your character with enthusiasm, ay, and with pride,—pride that one so high and so gifted should have ever thought of one so little worthy of him. But do not weaken my principle by hoping that my affection can be won at the cost of my self-esteem."

Forester bowed with a deep, respectful reverence; and when he lifted up his head, the sad expression of his features was that of one who had heard an irrevocable doom pronounced upon his dearest, most cherished hopes. Lady Eleanor at the same moment came forward from the door of the cottage, so that he had barely time to utter a hasty good-bye ere she joined her daughter.

"Your father wishes to see Lord Wallincourt, Helen. Has he gone?" But before Helen could reply the Knight came up.

"I hope you have not forgotten to ask him to dinner, Eleanor?" said he. "We did so yesterday, and he never made his appearance the whole evening."

"Helen, did you?" But Helen was gone while they were speaking; so that Darcy, to repair the omission, hastened after his young friend with all the speed he could command.

"Have I found you?" cried Darcy, as, turning an angle of the rocky shore, he came behind Forester, who, with folded arms and bent-down head, stood like one sorrow-struck. "I just discovered that neither my wife nor my daughter had asked you to stop to dinner; and as you are punctilious, fully as much as they are forgetful, there was nothing for it but to run after you."

"You are too kind, my dear Knight,—but not to-day; I'm poorly,—a headache."

"Nay; a headache always means a mere excuse. Come back with me: you shall be as stupid a *convive* as you wish, only be a good listener, for I have got a great budget from my man of law, Mr. Bicknell, and am dying for somebody to inflict it upon."

"With the best grace he could muster,—which was still very far from a good one,—Forester suffered himself to be led back to the cottage, endeavoring, as he went, to feel or feign an interest in the intelligence the Knight was full of. It seemed that Bicknell was very anxious not only for the Knight's counsel on many points, but for his actual presence at the trial. He appeared to think that Darcy being there, would be a great check upon the line of conduct he was apprised O'Halloran would adopt. There was already a very strong reaction in the West in favor of the old gentry of the land, and it would be at least an evidence of willingness to confront the enemy, were the Knight to be present.

"He tells me," continued the Knight, "that Daly regretted deeply not having attended the former trial,—why, he does not exactly explain, but he uses the argument to press me now to do so."

Forester might, perhaps, have enlightened him on this score, had he so pleased, but he said nothing.

"Of course, I need not say, nothing like intimidation is meant by this advice. The days for such are, thank God, gone by in Ireland; and it was, besides, a game I never could have played at; but yet it might be what many would expect of me, and at all events it can scarcely do harm. What is your opinion?"

"I quite agree with Mr. Bicknell," said Forester, hastily; "there is a certain license these gentlemen of wig and gown enjoy, that is more protected by the bench than either good morals or good manners warrant."

"Nay, you are now making the very error I would guard against," said Darcy, laughing. "This legal sparring is rather good fun, even though they do not always keep the gloves on. Now, will you come with me?"

"Of course; I should have asked your leave to do so, had you not invited me."

"You 'll hear the great O'Halloran, and I suspect that is as much as I shall gain myself by this action. We have merely some points of law to go upon; but, as I understand, nothing new or material in evidence to adduce. You ask, then, why persist? I 'll own to you I cannot say; but there seems the same punctilio in legal matters as in military; and it is a point of honor to sustain the siege until the garrison have eaten their boots. I am not so far from that contingency now, that I should be impatient; but meanwhile I perceive the savor of something better, and here comes Tate to say it is on the table."

CHAPTER XXXV
AN AWKWARD DINNER-PARTY

When the reader is informed that Lady Eleanor had not found a fitting moment to communicate to the Knight respecting Forester, nor had Helen summoned courage to reveal the circumstances of their late interview, it may be imagined that the dinner itself was as awkward a thing as need be. It was, throughout, a game of cross purposes, in which Darcy alone was not a player, and therefore more puzzled than the rest, at the constraint and reserve of his companions, whose efforts at conversation were either mere unmeaning commonplaces, or half-concealed retorts to inferred allusions.

However quick to perceive, Darcy was too well versed in the tactics of society to seem conscious of this, and merely redoubled his efforts to interest and amuse. Never had his entertaining qualities less of success. He could scarcely obtain any acknowledgment from his hearers; and stores of pleasantry, poured out in rich profusion, were listened to with a coldness bordering upon apathy.

He tried to interest them by talking over the necessity of their speedy removal to the capital, where, for the advantage of daily consultation, Bicknell desired the Knight's presence. He spoke of the approaching journey to the West, for the trial itself; he talked of Lionel, of Daly, of their late campaigns; in fact, he touched on everything, hoping by some passing gleam of interest to detect a clew to their secret thoughts. To no avail. They listened with decorous attention, but no signs of eagerness or pleasure marked their features; and when Forester rose to take his leave, it was full an hour and a half before his usual time of going.

"Now for it, Eleanor," said the Knight, as Helen soon after quitted the room; "what's your secret, for all this mystery must mean something? Nay, don't look so in-penetrable, my dear; you'll never persuade any man who displayed all his agreeability to so little purpose, that his hearers had not a hidden source of preoccupation to account for their indifference. What is it, then?"

"I am really myself in the dark, without my conjectures have reason, and that Lord Wallincourt may have renewed to Helen the proposal he once made her, and with the same fortune."

"Renewed — proposal!"

"Yes, my dear Darcy, it was a secret I had intended to have told you this very day, and went for the very purpose of doing so, when I found you engaged with Bicknell's letters and advices, and scrupled to break in upon your occupied thoughts. Captain Forester did seek Helen's affections, and was refused; and I now suspect Lord Wallincourt may have had a similar reverse."

"This last is, however, mere guess," said Darcy.

"No more. Of the former Helen herself told me; she frankly acknowledged that her affections were disengaged, but that he had not touched them. It would seem that he was deeper in love than she gave him credit for. His whole adventure as a Volunteer sprang out of this rejected suit, and higher fortunes have not changed his purpose."

"Then Helen did not care for him?"

"That she did not once, I am quite certain; that she does not now, is not so sure. But I know that even if she were to do so, the disparity of condition would be an insurmountable barrier to her assent."

Darcy walked up and down with a troubled and anxious air, and at length said, —

"Thus is it that the pride we teach our children, as the defence against low motives and mean actions, displays its false and treacherous principles; and all our flimsy philosophy is based less on the affections of the human heart than on certain conventional usages we have invented for our own enslavement. There is but one code of right and wrong, Eleanor, and that one neither recognizes the artificial distinctions of grade, nor makes a virtue of the self-denial; that is a mere offering to worldly pride."

"You would scarcely have our daughter accept an alliance with a house that disdains our connection?" said Lady Eleanor, proudly.

"Not, certainly, when the consideration had been once brought before her mind. It would then be but a compromise with principle. But why should she have ever learned the lesson? Why need she have been taught to mingle notions of worldly position and aggrandizement with the emotions of her heart? It was enough — it should have been enough — that his rank and position were nearly her own, not to trifle with feelings immeasurably higher and holier than these distinctions suggest."

"But the world, my dear Darcy; the world would say—"

"The world would say, Eleanor, that her refusal was perfectly right; and if the world's judgments were purer, they might be a source of consolation against the year-long bitterness of a sinking heart. Well, well!" said he, with a sigh, "I would hope that her heart is free: go to her, Eleanor,—learn the truth, and if there be the least germ of affection there, I will speak to Wallincourt to-morrow, and tell him to leave us. These half-kindled embers are the slow poison of many a noble nature, and need but daily intercourse to make them deadly."

While Lady Eleanor retired to communicate with her daughter, the Knight paced the little chamber in moody reverie. As he passed and repassed before the window, he suddenly perceived the shadow of a man's figure as he stood beside a rock near the beach. Such an apparition was strange enough to excite curiosity in a quiet, remote spot, where the few inhabitants retired to rest at sunset. Darcy therefore opened the window, and moved towards him; but ere he had gone many paces, he was addressed by Forester's voice,—"I was about to pay you a visit, Knight, and only waited till I saw you alone."

"Let us stroll along the sands, then," said Darcy; "the night is delicious." And so saying, he drew his arm within Forester's, and walked along at his side.

"I have been thinking," said Forester, in a low, sad accent,—"I have been thinking over the advice you lately gave me; and although I own at the time it scarcely chimed in with my own notions, now the more I reflect upon it the more plausible does it seem. I have lived long enough out of fashionable life to make the return to it anything but a pleasure; for politics I have neither talent nor temper; and soldiering, if it does not satisfy every condition of my ambition, offers more to my capacity and my hopes than any other career."

"I would that you were more enthusiastic in the cause," said Darcy, who was struck by the deep depression of his manner; "I would that I saw you embrace the career more from a profound seuse of duty and devotion, than as a 'pis aller.'"

"Such it is," sighed Forester; and his arm trembled within Darcy's as he spoke. "I own it frankly, save in actual conflict itself, I have no military ardor in my nature. I accept the road in life, because one must take some path."

"Then, if this be so," said Darcy, "I recall my counsels. I love the service, and you also, too well to wish for such a *mésalliance*; no, campaigning will never do with a spirit that is merely not averse. Return to London, consult your relative, Lord Castlereagh,—I see you smile at my recommendation of him, but I have learned to read his character very differently from what I once did. I can see now, that however the tortuous course of a difficult policy may have condemned him to stratagems wherein he was an agent,—often an unwilling one,—that his nature is eminently chivalrous and noble. His education and his prejudices have made him less rash than we, in our nationality, like to pardon, but the honor of the empire lies next his heart Political profligacy, like any other, may be leniently dealt with while it is fashionable; but there are minds that never permit themselves to be enslaved by fashion, when once they have gained a consciousness of their own power: such is his. He is already beyond it; and ere many years roll over, he will be equally beyond his competitors too. And now to yourself. Let him be your guide. Once launched in public life, its interests will soon make themselves felt, and you are young enough to be plastic. I know that every man's early years, particularly those who are the most favored by fortune, have their clouds and dark shadows. You must not seek an exemption from the common lot; remember how much you have to be grateful for; think of the advantages for which others strive a life long, and never reach,-all yours, at the very outset; and then, if there be some sore spots, some secret sorrows under all, take my advice and keep them for your own heart. Confessions are admirable things for old ladies, who like the petty martyrdom of small sufferings, but men should be made of sterner stuff. There is a high pride in bearing one's load alone; don't forget that."

Forester felt that if the Knight had read his inmost feelings, his counsel could not have been more directly addressed to his condition; he had, indeed, a secret sorrow, and one which threw its gloom over all his prosperity. He listened attentively to Darcy's reasonings, and followed him, as in the full sincerity of his nature he opened up the history of his own life, now commenting on the circumstances of good fortune, now adverting to the mischances which had befallen him. Never had the genial kindness of the old man appeared more amiable. The just judgments, the high and honorable sentiments, not shaken by what he had seen of ingratitude and wrong, but hopefully maintained and upheld, the singular modesty of his character, were all charms that won more and more upon Forester; and when, after a *tête-à-tête* prolonged till late in the night, they parted, Forester's muttered ejaculation was, "Would that I were his son!"

"It is as I guessed," said Lady Eleanor, when the Knight re-entered the chamber; "Helen has refused him. I could not press her on the reasons, nor ask whether her heart approved all that her head determined. But she seemed calm and tranquil; and if I were to pronounce from appearance, I should say that the rejection has not cost her deeply."

"How happy you have made me, Eleanor!" exclaimed Darcy, joyfully; "for while, perhaps, there is nothing in this world I should like better than to see such a man my son-in-law, there is no misery I would not prefer to witnessing my child's affections engaged where any sense of duty or pride rendered the engagement hopeless. Now, the case is this: Helen can afford to be frank and sisterly towards the poor fellow, who really did love her, and after a few days he leaves us."

"I thought he would go to-morrow," said Lady Eleanor, somewhat anxiously.

"No; I half hinted to him something of the kind, but he seemed bent on accompanying me to the West, and really I did not know how to say nay."

Lady Eleanor appeared not quite satisfied with an arrangement that promised a continuation of restraint, if not of positive difficulty, but made no remark about it, and turned the conversation on their approaching removal to Dublin.

CHAPTER XXXVI
AN UNEXPECTED PROPOSAL

Our time is now brief with our reader, and we would not trespass on him longer by dwelling on the mere details of those struggles to which Helen and Forester were reduced by daily association and companionship.

One hears much of Platonism, and, occasionally, of those brother and sisterly affections which are adopted to compensate for dearer and tenderer ties. Do they ever really exist? Has the world ever presented one single successful instance of the compact? We are far, very far, from doubting that friendship, the truest and closest, can subsist between individuals of opposite sex. We only hazard the conjecture that such friendships must not spring out of "Unhappy Love." They must not be built out of the ruins of wrecked affection. No, no; when Cupid is bankrupt, there is no use in attempting to patch up his affairs by any composition with the creditors.

We are not quite so sure that this is exactly the illustration Forester would have used to convey his sense of our proposition; but that he was thoroughly of our opinion, there is no doubt. Whether Helen was one of the same mind or not, she performed her task more easily and more gracefully. We desire too sincerely to part with our fair readers on good terms, to venture on the inquiry whether there is not more frankness and candor in the character of men than women? There is certainly a greater difficulty in the exercise of this quality in the gentler sex, from the many restraints imposed by delicacy and womanly feeling; and the very habit of keeping within this artificial barrier of reserve gives an ease and tranquillity to female manner under circumstances where men would expose their troubled and warring emotions. So much, perhaps, for the reason that Miss Darcy displayed an equanimity of temper very different from the miserable Forester, and exerted powers of pleasing and fascination which, to him at least, had the singular effect of producing even more suffering than enjoyment. The intimacy hitherto subsisting between them was rather increased than otherwise. It seemed as if their relations to each other had been fixed by a treaty, and now that transgression or change was impossible. If this was slavery in its worst form to Forester, to Helen it was liberty unbounded. No longer restrained by any fear of misconception, absolved, in her own heart, of any designs upon his, she scrupled not to display her capacity for thinking and reflecting with all the openness she would have done to her brother Lionel; while, to relieve the deep melancholy that preyed upon him, she exerted herself by a thousand little stratagems of caprice or fancy, that, however successful at the time, were sure to increase his gloom when he quitted her presence. Such, then, with its varying vicissitudes of pleasure and pain, was the condition of their mutual feeling for the remainder of their stay on the northern coast Many a time had Forester resolved on leaving her forever, rather than perpetuate the lingering torture of an affection that increased with every hour; but the effort was more than his strength could compass, and he yielded, as it were, to a fate, until at last her companionship had become the whole aim and object of his existence.

As winter closed in, they removed to Dublin, and established themselves temporarily in an old-fashioned family hotel, selected by Bicknell, in a quiet, unpretending street. Neither their means nor inclination would have prompted them to select a more fashionable resting-place, while the object of strict seclusion was here secured. The ponderous gloom of the staid old house, where, from the heavy sideboard of almost black mahogany to the wrinkled visage of the grim waiter, all seemed of a bygone century, were rather made matters of mutual pleasantry among the party than sources of dissatisfaction; while the Knight assured them that this was in his younger days the noisy resort of the gay and fashionable of the capital.

"Indeed," added he, "I am not quite sure that this is not where the 'Townsends,' as the club was then called, used to meet in Swift's time. Bicknell will tell us all about it, for he's coming to dine with us."

Forester was the first to appear in the drawing-room before dinner. It is possible that he hurried his toilet in the hope of speaking a few words to Helen, who not un-frequently came down before her mother. If so, he was doomed to disappointment, as the room was empty when he entered; and there was nothing for it but to wait, impatiently indeed, and starting at every footstep on the stairs and every door that shut or opened.

At last he heard the sound of approaching steps, softened by the deep old carpet. They came,—he listened,—the door opened, and the waiter announced a name, what and whose Forester paid no attention to, in his annoyance that it was not hers he expected. The stranger-a very plump, joyous little personage in deep black—did not appear quite unknown to Forester; but as the recognition interested him very little, he merely returned a formal bow to the other's more cordial salute, and turned to the window where he was standing.

"The Knight, I believe, is dressing?" said the new arrival, advancing towards Forester.

"Yes; but I have no doubt he will be down in a few moments."

"Time enough,—no hurry in life. They told me below stairs that you were here, and so I came up at once. I thought that I might introduce myself. Paul Dempsey,—Dempsey's Grove. You've heard of me before, eh?"

"I have had that pleasure," said Forester, with more animation of manner; for now he remembered the face and figure of the worthy Paul, as he had seen both in the large mirror of his mother's drawing-room.

"Ha! I guessed as much," rejoined Paul, with a chuckling laugh; "the ladies are here, too, ain't they?"

Forester assented, and Paul went on.

"Only heard of it from Bicknell half an hour ago. Took a car, and came off at once. And when did *you* come?"

Forester stared with amazement at a question whose precise meaning he could not guess at, and to which he could only reply by a half-smile, expressive of his difficulty.

"You were away, weren't you?" asked Dempsey.

"Yes; I have been out of England," replied Forester, more than ever puzzled how this fact could or ought to have any interest for the other.

"Never be ashamed of it. Soldiering 's very well in its way, though I 'd never any taste for it myself,—none of that martial spirit that stirred the bumpkin as he sang,—

Perhaps a recruit
Might chance to shoot
Great General Buonaparte.

Well, well! it seems you soon got tired of glory, of which, from all I hear, a little goes very far with any man's stomach; and no wonder. Except a French bayonet, there 's nothing more indigestible than commissary bread."

"The service is not without some hardships," said Forester, blandly, and preferring to shelter himself under generality than invite further inquisitiveness.

"Cruelties you might call them," rejoined Dempsey, with energy. "The frightful stories we read in the papers!—and I suppose they are all true. Were you ever touched up a bit yourself?" This Paul said in his most insinuating manner; and as Forester's stare showed a total ignorance of his meaning, he added, "A little four-and-twenty, I mean," mimicking, as he spoke, the action of flogging.

"Sir!" exclaimed Forester, with an energy almost ferocious; and Dempsey made a spring backwards, and intrenched himself behind a sofa-table.

"Blood alive!" he exclaimed, "don't be angry. I wouldn't offend you for the world; but I thought—"

"Never mind, sir,-your apology is quite sufficient," said Forester, who had no small difficulty to repress laughing at the terrified face before him. "I am quite convinced there was no intention to give offence."

"Spoke like a man," said Dempsey, coming out from his ambush with an outstretched hand; and Forester, not usually very unbending in such cases, could not help accepting the salutation so heartily proffered.

"Ah, my excellent friend, Mr. Dempsey!" said the Knight, entering at the same moment, and gayly tapping him on the shoulder. "A man I have long wished to see, and thank for many kind offices in my absence.—I 'm glad to see you are acquainted with Mr. Dempsey.—Well, and how fares the world with you?"

"Better, rather better, Knight," said Paul, who had scarcely recovered the fright Forester had given him. "You've heard that old Bob's off? Didn't go till he could n't help it, though; and now your humble servant is the head of the house."

While the Knight expressed his warm congratulations, Lady Eleanor and Helen came in; and by their united invitation Paul was persuaded to remain for dinner,—an event which, it must be owned, Forester could not possibly comprehend.

Bicknell's arrival soon after completed the party, which, however discordant in some respects, soon exhibited signs of perfect accordance and mutual satisfaction. Mr. Dempsey's presence having banished all business topics for discussion, he was permitted to launch out into his own favorite themes, not the least amusing feature of which was the perfect amazement of Forester at the man and his intimacy.

As the ladies withdrew to the drawing-room, Paul became more moody and thoughtful, now and then interchanging glances with Bicknell, and seeming as if on the verge of something, and yet half doubting how to approach it. Two or three hastily swallowed bumpers, and a look, which he believed of encouragement, from Bicknell, at length rallied Mr. Dempsey, and after a slight hesitation, he said,—

"I believe, Knight, we are all friends here; it is, strictly speaking, a cabinet council?"

If Darcy did not fathom the meaning of the speech, he had that knowledge of the speaker which made his assent to it almost a matter of course.

"That's what I thought," resumed Paul; "and it is a moment I have been anxiously looking for. Has our friend here said anything?" added he, with a gesture towards Bicknell.

"I, sir? I said nothing, I protest!" exclaimed the man of law, with an air of deprecation. "I told you, Mr. Dempsey, that I would inform the Knight of the generous proposition you made about the loan; but, till the present moment, I have not had the opportunity."

"Pooh, pooh! a mere trifle," interrupted Paul. "It is not of that I was thinking: it is of a very different subject I would speak. Has Lady Eleanor or Miss Darcy—has she told you nothing of me?" said he, addressing the Knight.

"Indeed they have, Mr. Dempsey, both spoken of you repeatedly, and always in the same terms of grateful remembrance."

"It isn't that, either," said Paul, with a half-sigh of disappointment.

"You are unjust to yourself, Mr. Dempsey," said Darcy, good-humoredly, "to rest a claim to our gratitude on any single instance of kindness; trust me that we recognize the whole debt."

"But it's not that," rejoined Paul, with a shake of the head. "Lord bless us! how close women are about these things," muttered he to himself. "There is nothing for it but candor, I suppose, eh?"

This being put in the form of a direct question, and the Knight having as freely assented, Paul resumed,—"Well, here it is. Being now at the head of an ancient name, and very pretty independence,—Bicknell has seen the papers,—I have been thinking of that next step a man takes who would wish to—wish to-hand down a little race of Dempseys. You understand?" Darcy smiled approvingly, and Paul continued: "And as conformity of temper, taste, and habits are the surest pledges of such felicity, I have set the eyes of my affections upon—Miss Darcy."

So little prepared was the Knight for what was coming, that up to that moment he had been listening with a smile of easy enjoyment; but when the last word was spoken, he started as if he had been stung by a reptile, nor could all his habitual self-control master the momentary flush of irritation that covered his face.

"I know," said Paul, with a dim consciousness that his proposition was but half acceptable, "that we are not exactly, so to say, the same rank and class; but the Dempseys are looking up, and—"

"'The Darcys looking down,' you would add," said the Knight, with a gleam of his habitual humor in his eye.

"And, like the buckets in a well, the full and empty ones meet half-way," added Dempsey, laughing. "I know well, as I said before, we are not the same kind of people, and perhaps this would have deterred me from indulging any thoughts on the subject, but for a chance, a bit of an accident, as a body may call it, that gave me courage."

"This is the very temple of candor, Mr. Dempsey," said the Knight, smiling. "Pray proceed, and let us hear the source of your encouragement; what was it?"

"Say, who was it, rather," interposed Paul.

"Be it so, then. Who was it? You have only made my curiosity stronger."

"Lady Eleanor,—ay, and Miss Helen herself."

A start of anger and a half-spoken exclamation were as quickly interrupted by a fit of laughing; and the Knight leaned back in his chair, and shook with the emotion.

"You doubt it; you think it absurd," said Dempsey, himself laughing, and not exhibiting the slightest irritation. "What if they say it's true,—will that content you?"

"I'm afraid it would not," said Darcy, equivocally; "there's nothing less likely to do so. Still, I assure you, Mr. Dempsey, if the ladies are of the mind you attribute to them, I shall find it very difficult to disbelieve anything I ever hear hereafter."

"I'm satisfied to stand or fall by their verdict," said Paul, resolutely. "I'm not a fool, exactly; and do you think if I had not something stronger than mere suspicion to guide me, that I'd have gone that same journey to London? Oh, I forgot—I did not tell you about my going to Lord Netherby."

"You went to Lord Netherby, and on this subject?" said Darcy, whose face became suffused with shame, an emotion doubly painful from Forester's presence.

"That I did," rejoined the unabashed Paul, "and a long conversation we had over the matter. He introduced me to his wife too. Lord bless us, but that is a bit of pride!"

"You are aware that the lady is Lord Wallincourt's mother," interposed Darcy, sternly.

"Faith, so that she is n't mine," said the inexorable Paul, "I don't care! There she was, lying in state, with a greyhound with silver bells on his neck at her feet; and when I came into the room, she lifts up her head and gives me a look, as much as to say, 'Oh, that's him.'—'Mr. Dempsey, of Dempsey's Hole,'—for hole he would call it, in spite of me,—'Mr. Dempsey, my love,' said my Lord, bowing as ceremoniously as if he never saw her before; and so, taking the hint, I began a little course of salutations, when she called out, 'Tell him not to do that, Netherby,—tell him not to do that-'"

This was too much for Mr. Dempsey's hearers, who, however differently minded as to the narrative, now concurred in one outbreak of hearty laughter.

"Well, my Lord," said Darcy, turning to Forester, "you certainly have shown evidence of a most enviable good temper. Had your Lordship—"

"His Lordship!" exclaimed Paul, in amazement. "Is n't that your son,—Captain Darcy?"

"No, indeed, Mr. Dempsey," said the Knight; "I thought, as I came into the drawing-room, that you were acquainted, or I should have presented you to the Earl of Wallincourt."

"Oh, ain't I in for it now!" cried Paul, in an accent of grief most ludicrously natural. "Oh! by the powers, I 'm up to the knees in trouble! And that was your mother! oh dear! oh dear!"

"You see, my worthy friend," said Darcy, smiling, "how easy a thing deception is. Is it not possible that your misconceptions do not end here?"

"I 'll never get over it, I know I'll not!" exclaimed Paul, wringing his hands as he arose from the table. "Bad luck to it for grandeur!" muttered he between his teeth; "I never had a minute's happiness since I got the taste for it." And with this honest avowal he rushed out of the room.

It was some time before the party in the dining-room adjourned upstairs; but when they did, they found Mr. Dempsey seated at the fire, recounting to the ladies his late unhappy discomfiture,—a narrative which even Lady Eleanor's gravity was not enabled to withstand. A kind audience was always a boon of the first water to honest Paul; and very little pressing was needed to induce him to continue his revelations, for the Knight wisely felt that such pretensions as his could not be buried so satisfactorily as beneath the load of ridicule.

Mr. Dempsey's scruples soon vanished and thawed under the warmth of encouraging voices and smiles, and he began the narrative of his night at "The Corvy," his painful durance in the canoe, his escape, the burning of the law papers, and each step of his progress to the very moment that he stood a listener at Lady Eleanor's door. Then he halted abruptly and said, "Now I'm dumb! racks and thumbscrews wouldn't get more out of me."

"You cannot mean, sir," said Lady Eleanor, calmly but haughtily, "that you overheard the conversation that passed between my daughter and myself?"

"Every word of it!" replied Paul, bluntly.

"Oh, really, sir, I can scarcely compliment you on the spirit of your curiosity; for although the theme we talked on, if I remember aright, was the speedy necessity of removing,—the urgency of seeking some place of refuge—"

"If I had n't heard which, I could not have assisted you in your departure," rejoined the unabashed Paul: "the old Loyola maxim, 'Evil, that Good may come of it.'"

Helen sat pale and terrified all this time; for although Lady Eleanor had forgotten the discussion of any other topic on that night save that of their legal difficulties, she well remembered a theme nearer and dearer to her heart. Whether from the distress of these thoughts, or in the hope of propitiating Mr. Dempsey to silence, so it was, she fixed her eyes upon him with an expression Paul thought he could read, and he gave a look of such conscious intelligence in return as brought the blush to her cheek. "I 'm not going to say one word about it," said he, in a stage whisper that even the Knight himself overheard.

"Then I must myself insist upon Mr. Dempsey's revelations," said Darcy, not at all satisfied with the air of mystery Dempsey threw around his intercourse.

Another look from Helen here met Paul's, and he stood uncertain how to act.

"Really, sir," said Lady Eleanor, "however little the subject we discussed was intended for other ears than our own, I must beg of you now to repeat what you remember of it."

"Well, what can I do?" exclaimed Paul, looking at Helen with an expression of the most helpless misery; "I know you are angry, and I know that when you like it, you can blaze up like a Congreve rocket. Oh, faith! I don't forget the day I showed you the newspaper about the English officer thrashing O'Halloran!"

Helen grew scarlet, and turned away, but not before Forester had caught her eyes, and read in them more of hope than his heart had known for many a day before.

"These are more mysteries, Mr. Dempsey; and if you continue to scatter riddles as you go, we shall never get to the end of this affair."

"Perhaps," interposed Bicknell, hoping to close the unpleasant discussion,—"perhaps Mr. Dempsey, feeling that he had personally no interest in the conversation between Lady Eleanor and Miss Darcy—"

"Had n't he, then?" exclaimed Paul,—"maybe not. If I hadn't, then, who had?—tell me that. Wasn't it then and there I first heard of the kind intentions towards me?"

"Towards you, sir! Of what are you speaking?"

"Blood alive! will you tell me that I 'm not Paul Dempsey, of Dempsey's Grove?" exclaimed he, driven beyond all patience by what he deemed equivocation. "Will you tell me that your Ladyship didn't allude to the day I brought the letter from Coleraine, and say that you actually began to like me from that hour? Did n't you tell Miss Helen not to lie down-hearted, because there were better days in store for us? Miss Darcy remembers it, I see,— ay, and your Ladyship does now. Did n't you call me rash and headstrong and ambitious? I forgive it all; I believe it is true. And was n't I your bond-slave from that hour? Oh, mercy on me! the pleasant time I had of it at Mother Fum's! Then came the days and nights I was watching over you at Ballintray. Ay, faith, and money was very scarce with me when I gave old Denny Nolan five shillings for the loan of his nankeen jacket to perform the part of waiter at the little inn. Do you remember a little note, in the shape of a friendly warning? Eh, now, my Lady, I think your memory is something fresher."

If the confusion of Lady Eleanor and her daughter was extreme at this outpouring of Mr. Dempsey's confessions, the amazement of Darcy and the utter stupefaction of Forester were even greater; to throw discredit upon him would be to acknowledge the real bearing of the circumstances, which would be far worse than all his imputations; so there was no alternative but to lie under every suspicion his narrative might suggest.

Forester felt annoyed as much that such a person should have obtained this assumed intimacy as by the pretensions he well knew were only absurd, and took an early leave under the pretence of fatigue. Bicknell soon followed; and now the Knight, arresting Dempsey's preparations for departure, led him back towards the fire, and placing a chair for him between Lady Eleanor and himself, obliged him to recount his scattered reminiscences once more, and, what was a far less pleasing duty to him, to listen to Lady Eleanor while she circumstantially unravelled the web of his delusion, and, in order, explained on what unsubstantial grounds he had built the edifice of his hope. Perhaps honest Paul was not more afflicted at any portion of the disentanglement than that which, in disavowing his pretensions, yet confessed that some other held the favorable place, while that other's name was guarded as a secret. This was, indeed, a sore blow, and he could n't rally from it; and willingly would he have bartered all the gratitude they expressed for his many friendly offices to know his rival's name.

"Well," exclaimed he, as Lady Eleanor concluded, "it's clear I was n't the man. Only think of my precious journey to London, and the interview with that terrible old Countess,—all for nothing! No matter,—it's all past and over. As for the loan, I 've arranged it all; you shall have the money when you like."

"I must decline your generous offer, not without feeling your debtor for it; but I have determined to abandon these proceedings. The Government have promised me some staff appointment, quite sufficient for my wishes and wants; and I will neither burden my friends nor wear out myself by tiresome litigation."

"That's the worst of all," exclaimed Dempsey; "I thought you would not refuse me this."

"Nor would I, my dear Dempsey, but that I have no occasion for the sum. To-morrow I set out to witness the last suit I shall ever engage in; and as I believe there is little doubt of the issue, I have nothing of sanguine feeling to suffer by disappointment."

"Well, then, to-morrow I 'll start for Dempsey's Grove," said Paul, sorrowfully. "With very different expectations I quitted it a few days ago. Good-bye, Lady Eleanor; good-bye, Miss Helen. I suppose there 's no use in guessing?"

Mr. Dempsey's leave-taking was far more rueful than his wont, and woe seemed to have absorbed all other feeling; but when he reached the door, he turned round and said, —

"Now I am going, —never like to see him again; do tell me the name."

A shake of the head, and a merry burst of laughter, was all the answer; and Paul departed.

CHAPTER XXXVII
THE LAST STRUGGLE

That the age of chivalry is gone, we are reminded some twenty times in each day of our commonplace existence, Perhaps the changed tone of society exhibits nowhere a more practical but less picturesque advantage than in the fact that the "joust" of ancient times is now replaced by the combat of the law court. Some may regret—we will not say if we are not of the number—that the wigged Baron of the Exchequer is scarcely so pleasing an arbiter as the Queen of Love and Beauty. Others may deem the knotted subtleties of black-letter a sorry recompense for the "wild crash and tumult of the fray." The crier of the Common Pleas would figure to little advantage beside the gorgeously clad Herald of the Lists; nor are the artificial distinctions of service so imposing that a patent of precedency could vie with the white cross on the shield of a Crusader. Still, there are certain counterbalancing interests to be considered; and it is possible that the veriest décrier of the law's uncertainty "would rather stake life and fortune on the issue of a 'trial of law,' than on the thews and sinews of the doughtiest champion that ever figured in an 'ordeal of battle.'"

In one respect there is a strong similarity between the two institutions. Each, in its separate age, possessed the same sway and influence over men's minds, investing with the deepest interest events of which they were hitherto ignorant, and enlisting partisans of opinion in cases where, individually, there was nothing at stake.

An important trial has all the high interest of a most exciting narrative, whose catastrophe is yet to come, and where so many influential agencies are in operation to mould it. The proofs themselves, the veracity of witnesses, their self-possession and courage under the racking torture of cross-examination, the ability and skill of the advocate, the temper of the judge, his character of rashness or patience, of doubt or decisiveness; and then, more vague than all besides, the verdict of twelve perhaps rightly minded but as certainly very ordinarily endowed men, on questions sometimes of the greatest subtlety and obscurity. The sum of such conflicting currents makes up a "cross sea," where everything is possible, from the favoring tide that leads to safety, to the swell and storm of utter shipwreck.

At the winter assizes of Galway, in the year 1802, all the deep sympathies of a law-loving population were destined to be most heartily engaged by the record of Darcy *versus* Hickman, now removed by a change of *venue* for trial to that city. It needed not the unusual compliment of Galway being selected as a likely spot for the due administration of justice, to make the plaintiff somewhat popular on this occasion. The reaction which for some time back had taken place in favor of the "real gentry" had gone on gaining in strength, so that public opinion was already inclining to the side of those who had earned a sort of prescriptive right to public confidence. The claptraps of patriotism, associated as they were often found to be with cruel treatment of tenants and dependants, were contrasted with the independent bearing of men who, rejecting dictation and spurning mob popularity, devoted the best energies of mind and fortune to the interests of all belonging to them. All the vindictiveness and rancor of a party press could not obliterate these traits, and character sufficed to put down calumny.

Hickman O'Reilly, accompanied by the old doctor, had arrived in Galway the evening before the trial, in all the pomp of a splendid travelling-carriage, drawn by four posters. The whole of "Nolan's" Head Inn had been already engaged for them and their party, who formed a tolerably numerous suite of lawyers, solicitors, and clerks, together with some private friends, curious to witness the proceedings.

In a very quiet but comfortable old inn called the "Devil and the Bag of Nails,"—a corruption of the ancient Satyr and the Bacchanals,—Mr. Bicknell had pitched his camp, having taken rooms for the Knight and Forester, who were to arrive soon after him, but whose presence in Ireland was not even suspected by the enemy.

There was a third individual who repaired to the West on this occasion, but who studiously screened himself from observation, waiting patiently for the issue of the combat to see on which side he should carry his congratulation: need we say his name was Con Heffernan?

Bicknell had heard of certain threats of the opposite party, which, while he did not communicate them to Darcy, were sufficient to give him deep uneasiness, as they went so far as to menace a very severe reprisal for these continued proceedings by a criminal action against Lionel Darcy. Of what nature, and on what grounds sustained, he knew not; but he was given to understand that if his principal would even now submit to some final adjustment out of court, the Hickmans would treat liberally with him, and, while abandoning these threatened proceedings against young Darcy, show Bicknell all the grounds for such a procedure.

It was past midnight when Darcy and Forester arrived; but before the Knight retired to rest he had learned all Bicknell's doubts and scruples, and unhesitatingly decided on proceeding with his suit. He felt that a compromise would now involve the honor of his son, of which he had not the slightest dread of any investigation; and, however small the prospect of success, the trial must take place to evidence his utter disregard, his open defiance of this menace.

Morning came; and long before the judges took their seat, the court was crowded in every part. The town was thronged with the equipages of the neighboring gentry, all eager to witness the trial; while the country people, always desirous of an exciting scene, thronged every avenue and passage of the building, and even the wide area in front of it. Nothing short of that passion for law and its interests, so inherent in an Irish heart, could have held that vast multitude thus enchained; for the day was one of terrific storm, the rain beating, the wind howling, and the sea roaring as it swept into the bay and broke in showers of foam upon the rocky shore. Each moment ran the rumor of some new disaster in the town, —now it was a chimney fallen, now a roof blown in, now an entire house, with all its inmates destroyed; fires, too, the invariable accompaniment of hurricane, had broken out in various quarters, and cries for help and screams of wretchedness were mingled with the wilder uproar of the elements. Yet of that dense mob, few if any quitted their places for these sights and sounds of woe. The whole interest lay within that sombre building, and on the issue of an event of whose particulars they knew absolutely nothing, and the details of which it was impossible they could follow did they even hear them.

The ordinary precursors to the interest of these scenes are the chance appearances of those who are to figure prominently in them; and such, indeed, attracted far more of attention on this occasion than all the startling accidents by fire and storm then happening on every side. Each lawyer of celebrity on the circuit was speedily recognized, and greeted by tokens of welcome or expressions of disfavor, as politics or party inclined. The attorneys were treated with even greater familiarity, themselves not disdaining to exchange a repartee as they passed, in which combats, be it said, they were not always the victors. At last came old Dr. Hickman, feebly crawling along, leaning one arm on his son's, and the other on the stalwart support of Counsellor O'Halloran. The already begun cheer for the popular "Counsellor" was checked by the arrival of the sheriff, preceding and making way for the judges, whose presence ever imposed a respectful demeanor. The buzz and hum of voices, subdued for a moment, had again resumed its sway, when once more the police exerted themselves to make a passage through the throng, calling out, "Make way for the Attorney-General!" and a jovial, burly personage, with a face redolent of convivial humor and rough merriment, came up, rather dragging than linked with the thin, slight figure of Bicknell, who with unwonted eagerness was whispering something in his ear.

"I'll do it with pleasure, Bicknell," rejoined the full, mellow voice, loud enough to be heard by those on either side; "I know the sheriff very well, and he will take care to let him have a seat on the bench. What's the name?"

"The Earl of Wallincourt," whispered Bicknell, a little louder.

"That's enough; I'll not forget it" So saying, he released his grasp of the little man, and pursued his vigorous course. In a few moments after, Bicknell was seen accompanied by Forester alone; "the Knight" having determined not to present himself till towards the close of the proceedings, if even then.

The buzz and din incident to a tumultuous assembly had just subsided to the decorous quietude of a Court of Justice, by the judges entering and taking their seats, when, after a few words interchanged between the Attorney-General and the sheriff, the latter courteously addressed Lord Wallincourt, and made way for him to ascend the steps leading to the bench. The incident was in itself too slight and unimportant for mention, save that it speedily attracted the attention of O'Halloran, whose quick glance at once recognized his ancient enemy. So sudden was the shock, and so poignant did it seem, that he actually desisted from the occupation he was engaged in of turning over his brief, and sat down pale and trembling with passion.

"You are not ill?" asked O'Reilly, eagerly, for he had not remarked the incident.

"Not ill," rejoined O'Halloran, in a low, deep whisper; "but do you see who is sitting next Judge Wallace, on the left of the bench?"

"Forester, I really believe," exclaimed O'Reilly; for so separated were the two "United" countries at that period that his accession to rank and title was a circumstance of which neither O'Reilly nor his lawyer had ever heard.

"We 'll change the *venue* for him, too, before the day is over," said O'Halloran, with a savage leer. "Do not let him see that we notice him."

While these brief words were interchanged, the business of the court was opened, and, some routine matters over, the record of Darcy *versus* Hickman called on. After this, the names of the special jury list were recited, and the invariable scene of dispute and wrangling incident to their choice followed. In law, as in war, the combat opens by a skirmish; a single cannon-shot, or a leading question, if thrown out, is meant rather to ascertain "the range" than with any positive intention of damage; but gradually the light troops fall back, forces concentrate, and a mighty movement is made. In the present instance the preliminaries were unusually long, the plaintiff's counsel not only stating all the grounds of the present suit, but recapitulating, with painful accuracy, the reasons for the change of *venue*, and reviewing and of course rebutting by anticipation every possible or impossible objection that might be made by his learned friend on "the other side." For our purpose, it is enough if we condense the matter into a single statement, that the action was to show that Hickman, in purchasing portions of the Darcy estate, was and must have been aware that the Knight of Gwynne's signature appended to the deed of sale was a forgery, and that he never had concurred in, nor was even cognizant of, this disposal of his property. A single case was selected to establish this fact, on which, if proved, further proceedings in Equity would be founded.

The plaintiff's case opened by an examination of a number of witnesses, old tenants of the Darcy property. These were not only called to prove the value of their holdings, as being very far above the price alleged to have been paid by Hickman, but also that they themselves were in total ignorance that the estate had been conveyed away to another proprietor, and never knew till the flight and death of Gleeson took place, that for many years previous they had ceased to be tenants of Maurice Darcy, to become those of Dr. Hickman.

The examination and cross-examination of these witnesses presented all the varying and changeful fortunes ever observable in such scenes. At one moment some obdurate old farmer resisting, with ludicrous pertinacity, all the efforts of the examining counsel to elicit the very testimony he himself wished to give; at another, the native humor of the peasant was seen baffling and foiling all the trained skill and practised dexterity of the pleader. Many a merry burst of laughter, many a jest that set the court in a roar, were exchanged. It was in Ireland, remember; but still the business of the day advanced, and a great weight of evidence was adduced, which, however suggestive to common intelligence, went legally only so far as to show that the tenantry were, almost to a man, of an opinion which, whether well founded or not in reason, turned out to be incorrect.

Darcy's counsel, a man of quickness and intelligence, made a very able speech, summing up the evidence, and commenting on every leading portion of it. He dwelt powerfully on the fact that at the time of this alleged sale the Knight, so far from being a distressed and embarrassed man, and consequently likely to effect a sale at a great loss, was, in reality, in possession of a princely fortune, his debts few and insignificant, and his income far above any possible expenditure. If he studiously avoided adverting to Gleeson's perfidy, as solely in fault, he assumed to himself credit for the forbearance, alleging that less scrupulous advisers might have gone perhaps further, and inferred connivance in a case so dubious and dark. "My client, however," said he, "gave me but one instruction in this cause, and it was this: 'If the law of the land, justly administered, as I believe it will be, restores to me my own, I shall be grateful; but if the pursuit of what I feel my right involve the risk of reflecting on one honest man's fame, or imputing falsely aught of dishonor to an unblemished reputation, I tell you frankly, I don't think a verdict so obtained can carry with it anything but shame and disgrace.'"

With these words he sat down, amid a murmur of approving voices; for there were many there who knew the Knight by reputation, if not personally, and were aware how well such a speech accorded with every feature of his character.

There was a brief delay as he resumed his seat. It was already late, the court had been obliged to be lighted up a considerable time previous, and the question of an adjournmeut was now discussed. The probable length of O'Halloran's reply would best guide the decision, and the Chief Baron asked if the learned counsel's statement were likely to be long.

"Yes, my Lord," replied he; "it is not a case to be dismissed briefly, and I have many witnesses to call."

Another brief discussion took place on the bench, and the Chief Baron announced that as there were many important causes still standing over for trial, they should best consult public convenience by proceeding, and that, after a few moments devoted to refreshment, the case should go on.

The judges retired, and many of the leading counsel took the same opportunity to recruit strength exhausted by several hours of severe toil. The Hickmans and O'Halloran never quitted their places; a decanter of sherry and a sandwich from the hotel were served where they sat, but the old man took nothing. The interest of the scene appeared too absorbing to admit of even a sense of hunger or weariness, and he sat with his hands folded, and his eyes mechanically fixed upon the now empty jury-box; for there, the whole day, were his looks riveted, to read, if he might, the varying emotions in the faces of those who held so much of his fortune in their keeping.

While the noise and hubbub which characterize a court at such intervals was at its highest, a report was circulated that increased in no small degree the excitement of the scene, and gave a character of intense anxiety to an assemblage so lately broken up by varied and dissimilar passions. It was this: a large vessel had struck on a reef in the bay, and the sea was now breaking over her. She had been seen from an early hour endeavoring to beat to the southward; but the wind had drawn more to the westward as the storm increased, and a strong shore current had also drawn her on land. In a last endeavor to clear the headlands of Clare, she missed stays, and being struck by a heavy sea, her rudder was carried away. Totally unmanageable now, she was drifted along, till she struck on a most dangerous reef about a mile from shore. Signals of distress were seen at her masthead, but no boat could venture out. The storm was already a hurricane, and even in the very harbor two fishing-boats had sunk.

As the dreadful tidings flew from mouth to mouth, a terrible confirmation was heard in the booming of guns of distress, which at brief intervals sounded amid the crashing of the storm.

It was at this moment of intense excitement that the crier proclaimed silence for the approaching entry of the judges. If the din of human voices became hushed and low, the deafening thunder of the elements seemed to increase, and the roaring of the enraged sea appeared to fill the very atmosphere.

As the judges resumed their seats, and the vast crowd ceased to stir or speak, O'Halloran arose. His voice was singularly low and quiet; but yet every word he uttered was distinctly heard through all the clamor of the storm.

"My Lords," said he, "before entering upon my client's case, I would bespeak the kind indulgence of the court in respect to a matter purely personal to myself. Your Lordships are too well aware that I should insist upon it, that in a cause where the weightiest interests of property are engaged, the mind of the advocate should be disembarrassed and free,—not only free as regards the exercise of whatever knowledge and skill he may possess, not merely free from the supposition of any individual hazard the honest discharge of his duty might incur, but free from the greater thraldom of disturbed and irritated emotions, originating in the deepest sense of wounded honor.

"Far be it from me, my Lords, long used in the practice of these courts, and long intimate with the righteous principle on which the laws are administered in them, to utter a syllable that in the remotest degree might seem to impugn the justice of the bench; but, a mere frail and erring creature, with feelings common to all around me, I wish to protest against continuing my client's case while your Lordships' bench is occupied by one who, in my person, has grossly outraged the sanctity of the law. Yes, my Lords," said he, raising his voice, till the deep tones swelled and floated through the vast space, "as the humble advocate of a cause, I now proclaim that in addressing that bench, I am incapable to render justice to the case before me, so long as I see associated with your Lordships a man more worthy to figure in the dock than to take his seat among the ermined judges of the land. A moment more, my Lords. I am ready to make oath that the individual on your Lordships' left is Richard Forester, commonly called the Honorable Richard Forester;—how suitable the designation, your Lordships shall soon hear—"

"I beg to interrupt my learned friend," interposed the Attorney-General, rising. "He is totally in error; and I would wish to save him from the embarrassment of misdescription. The gentleman he alludes to is the Earl of Wallincourt, a peer of the realm."

"Proceed with your client's case, Mr. O'Halloran," said the Chief Baron, who saw that to discuss the question further was now irrelevant. O'Halloran sat down, overwhelmed with rage; a whispered communication from behind told him that the Attorney-General was correct, and that Forester was removed beyond the reach of his vengeance. After a few moments he rallied, and again rose. Turning slowly over the pages of a voluminous brief, he stood waiting, with practised art, till expectancy had hushed each murmur around, when suddenly the crier called, "Way, there,—make way for the High Sheriff!" and that functionary, with a manner of excessive agitation, leaned over the bar, and addressed the bench. "My Lords, I most humbly entreat your Lordships' forgiveness for thus interrupting the business of the court; but the extreme emergency will, I hope, pardon the indecorum. A large vessel has struck on the rocks in the bay: each moment it is expected she must go to pieces. A panic seems to prevail among even our hardy fishermen; and my humble request is, that if there be any individual in this crowded assembly possessing naval knowledge, or any experience in calamities of this nature, he will aid us by his advice and co-operation."

The senior judge warmly approved the humane suggestion of the sheriff; and several persons were seen now forcing their way through the dense mass,—the far greater part, be it owned, more excited by curiosity than stimulated by any hope of rendering efficient service. Notwithstanding Bicknell's repeated entreaties, and remembrances of his late severe illness, Forester also quitted the court, and accompanied the sheriff to the beach. And now O'Halloran, whose impatience during this interval displayed little sympathy with the sad occasion of the interruption, asked, in a manner almost querulous, if their Lordships were ready to hear him? The court assented, and he began. Without once adverting to the subject on which he so lately addressed them, he opened his case by a species of narrative of the whole legal contest which for some time back had been maintained between the opposite parties in the present suit. Nothing could be more calm or more dispassionate than the estimate he formed of such struggles; neither inclining the balance to one party nor the other, but weighing with impartiality all the reasons that might prompt men on one side to continue a course of legal investigations, and the painful necessity on the other to provide a series of defences, costly, onerous, and harassing. "I have only to point out to the court the defendant in this action, to show how severe such a duty may become. Here, my Lords, beside me, site the gentleman, bowed down with more years than are allotted to humanity generally. Look upon him, and say if it be not difficult to determine what course to follow,—the abandonment of a just right, or its maintenance, at the cost of rendering the few last years—why do I say years?—days, hours, of a life careworn, distracted, and miserable!"

Dwelling long enough on this theme to interest without wearying the jury, he adroitly addressed himself to the case of those who, by a system of litigious persecution, would seek to obtain by menace what they must despair of by law. Beginning by vague and wide generalities, he gradually accumulated a mass of allegations and inferences, which concentrating to a point, he suddenly checked himself, and said: "Now, my Lords, it may be supposed that I will imitate the delicate reserve of my learned friend opposite, and while filling your minds with dark and mysterious suspicions, profess a perfect ignorance of all intention to apply them. But I will not do this: I will be candid and free-spoken; nay, more, my Lords, I will finish what my learned friend has left incomplete; and I will proclaim to the court, and this jury, what he wished, but did not dare, to say,—that we, the defendants in this action, were not only cognizant of a forgery, but were associated in the act! There it is, my Lords; and I accept my learned friend's bland smile as the warm acknowledgment of the truth of my assertion. My learned friend is obliged to me. I see that he cannot conceal his joy at the inaptitude of my avowal. But we have a case, my Lords, that can happily dispense with the dexterity of an advocate, and make its truth felt, even through means as unskilful as mine. They disclaimed, it is true,—they disclaimed in words the wish to make this inference; but even take their disclaimer as such, and what is it? An avowal of their weakness, an open expression of the poverty of their proofs. Yes, my Lords, their disclaimers were like the ominous sounds which break from time to time upon our ear,—but signal-guns of distress. Like that fated vessel, whose sad destiny is perhaps this moment accomplishing, they have been storm-tossed and cast away,—their proud ensign torn, and their rudder gone, but, unlike her, they cannot brave their fate without seeking to involve others in the calamity."

A terrible gust of wind, so sudden and violent as to be like a thunderclap, now struck the building; and with one tremendous crash the great window of the court-house was driven in, and scattered in fragments of glass and timber throughout the court. A scene of the wildest confusion ensued, for almost immediately the lights became extinguished, and from the dark abyss arose a terrible chaos of voices in every agony of fear and suffering. Some announced that the roof was giving way and was about to crush them; others, in all the bodily torture of severe wounds, cried for help.

It was nearly an hour before the court could resume its sitting, which at length was done in one of the adjoining courts, the usual scene of the criminal trials. Here, now, lights were procured, and after a considerable delay the cause proceeded. If the various events of the night, added to the fatigue of the day, had impressed both the bench and the jury with signs of greatest exhaustion, O'Halloran showed no evidence of abated vigor. On the contrary, like one whose vengeance had been thwarted by opposing accident, he exhibited a species of impatient ardor to resume his work of defamation. With a brief apology for any want of due coherence in an argument so frequently interrupted, he launched out into the most ferocious attack upon the plaintiff in the suit; and while repudiating the affected reserve of the opposite counsel, boldly proclaimed that they would not imitate it; nay, further, that they were only awaiting the sure verdict in their favor, to commence a criminal action against the parties for the very crime they dared to insinuate against them.

"I shall now call my witnesses, my Lord; and if the Grand Cross of the Bath, which this day's paper tells me is to be conferred upon the plaintiff, be not meant, like the brand which foreign justice impresses on its felons, as a mark of ignominy, I am at a loss to understand how it has descended on this man. Call Nathaniel Leery."

The examination of the witnesses was in perfect keeping with the infamous scurrility of the speech, and the testimony elicited went to prove everything the advocate desired. Though exposed by cross-examination, and their perjury proved, O'Halloran kept a perpetual recapitulation of their assertions before the jury, and so artfully that few, save the practised minds of a legal auditory, could have distinguished in that confused web of truth and falsehood.

The business proceeded with difficulty; for, added to the uproar of the storm, was a continued tumult of voices in the outer hall of the court, and where now several sailors, saved from the wreck, had been brought for shelter. By frequent loud cries from this quarter the court was interrupted, and more than once its proceedings completely arrested,—inconveniences which the judges submitted to with the most tolerant patience,—when at length a loud murmur arose, which gradually swelling louder and louder, all respect for the sacred precincts of the judgment-seat seemed lost in the wild tumult. In a tone of sharp reproof the Chief Baron called on the sheriff to allay the uproar, and if necessary, to clear the hall. The order was scarcely given, when one deafening shout was raised from the street, and, soon caught up, echoed by a thousand voices, while shrill cries of "He has saved them! he has saved them!" rent the air.

"What means this, Mr. Sheriff?"

"It is my Lord Wallincourt, my Lord, who has just rescued from the wreck three men who persisted in being lost together rather than separate. Hitherto only one man was taken at each trip of the boat; but this young nobleman offered a thousand pounds to the crew who would accompany him, and it appears they have succeeded."

"Really, my Lords," said O'Halloran, who had heard the honorable mention of a hated name, "I must abandon my client's cause. These interruptions, which I conclude your influence is powerless to remove, have so interfered with the line of defence I had laid down for adoption, and have so confused the order of the proofs I had prepared, that I should but injure, and not serve, my respected client by continuing to represent his interests."

A bland assurance from the court that order should be rigidly enforced, and a pressing remonstrance from O'Reilly, overcame a resolve scarcely maturely taken, and he consented to go on.

"We will now, my Lords," said he, "call a very material witness,—a respectable tenant on the property,—who will prove that on a day in November, antecedent to Gleeson's death, he had a conversation with the Knight of Gwynne—Really, my Lords, I cannot proceed; this is no longer a court of justice."

The remainder of his words were lost in an uproar like that of the sea itself; and, like that element, the great mass swelled forward, and a rush of people from the outer hall bore into the court, till seats and barriers gave way before that overwhelming throng.

For some minutes the scene was one of almost personal conflict. The mob, driven forward by those behind, were obliged to endure a buffeting by the more recognized possessors of the place; nor was it till police and military had lent their aid that the court was again restored to quiet, while several of the rioters were led off in custody.

"Who are these men, and to what purpose are they here?" said the Chief Baron, as Bicknell officiously exerted himself to make way for some persons behind.

"I come to tender my evidence in this cause," said a deep, solemn voice, as a man advanced to the witness-table, displaying to the amazed assembly a bold, intrepid countenance, on which streaks of blue and yellow color were fantastically mingled, like the war-paint of a savage.

"Who are you, sir?" rejoined O'Halloran, with his habitual scowl.

"My name is Bagenal Daly. I believe their Lordships are not ignorant of my rank and station; and this gentleman at my side is also here to afford his testimony. This, my Lords, is Thomas Gleeson!"

One cry of amazement rang through the assembly, through which a wild shriek pierced with a clear and terrible distinctness; and now the attention was suddenly turned towards old Hickman, who had fallen forward senseless on the table.

"My client is very ill,—he is dangerously ill. My Lord, I beg to suggest an adjournment of the cause," said O'Halloran; while O'Reilly, with a face like death, continued to whisper eagerly in his ear. "I appeal to the plaintiff himself, if he be here, and is not devoid of the feelings attributed to him, and I ask that the cause may be adjourned."

"It is not a case in which the defendant's illness can be made use of to press such a demand," said one of the judges, mildly; "but if the opposite party consent—"

"He is worse, my Lord."

"I say, if the opposite party—"

"He is dead!" said O'Halloran, solemnly; and letting go the lifeless hand, it fell with a heavy bang upon the table.

"Take your verdict," said O'Halloran, with the look of a demon; and, bursting his way through the crowd, disappeared.

CHAPTER XXXVIII
CONCLUSION

When Forester entered the Knight's room in the inn, where, in calm quietude, he sat awaiting the verdict, he hesitated for a moment how he should break the joyful tidings of Daly's arrival.

"Speak out," said Darcy. "If not exactly without hope, I am well prepared for the worst."

"Can you say you are equally ready to hear the best?" asked Forester, eagerly.

"The best is a very strong word, my young friend," said Darcy, gravely.

"And yet, I speak advisedly,—the best."

"If so, perhaps I am not so prepared. My heart has dwelt so long on these troubles, recognizing them as I felt they must be, that I would, perhaps, ask a little time to think how I should hear tidings so remote from all expectation. Of course, I do not speak of the mere verdict here."

"Nor I," interposed Forester, impatiently. "I speak of what restores you to your ancient house and rank, your station and your fortune."

"Can this be true?"

"Ay, Maurice, every word of it," broke in Daly, who, having listened so far, could no longer restrain himself. The two old men fell into each other's arms with all the cordial affection with which they had embraced as schoolfellows sixty years before.

Great as was Darcy's amazement at seeing his oldest friend thus suddenly restored, it was nothing in comparison to what he felt as Daly narrated the event of the shipwreck, and his rescue from the sinking vessel by Forester.

"And your companions, who were they?" asked Darcy, eagerly.

"You shall hear."

"I guess one of them already," interposed the Knight "The trusty Sandy. Is it not so?"

"The other you will never hit upon," said Daly, nodding an assent.

"I 'm thinking over all our friends, and yet none seem likely."

"Come, Maurice, prepare yourself for surprise. What think you, if he to whose fate I had linked myself, resolving that, live or die, we should not separate,—if this man was—Gleeson—honest Tom Gleeson?"

The words seemed stunning in their effect; for Darey leaned back, and passing his hands over his closed lids, murmured, "I hope my poor faculties are not wandering,—I trust this may be no delusion."

"He is yonder," said Daly, taking the Knight's hand in his strong grasp; "Sandy mounts guard over him. Not that the poor devil thinks of or desires escape; he was too weary of a life of deception and sin when we caught him, to wish to prolong it. Now rouse yourself, and listen to me."

It would doubtless be a heavy tax on our kind reader's patience were we to relate, circumstantially, the conversation, that, now commencing, lasted during the entire night and till late in the following morning. Enough if we say that Daly, having, through Freney's instrumentality, discovered that Gleeson had not committed suicide, but only spread this rumor for concealment's sake, resolved to pursue him to America. Fearing that any suspicion of his object might escape, he did not even trust Bicknell with the secret; but by suffering him to continue law proceedings as before, totally blinded the Hickmans as to the possibility of the event.

It would in itself be a tale of marvel to recount the strange adventures which Daly encountered in his search and pursuit of Gleeson, who had originally taken up his residence in the States, was recognized there, and fled into Canada, where he wandered about from place to place, conscience-stricken and miserable. He was wretchedly poor, besides; for on the bills and securities he carried away, many being on eminent houses in America, payment was stopped, and being unable to risk proceedings, he was reduced to beggary.

It now appeared that at a very early period of life, when a clerk in the office of old Hickman's agent, he had committed a forgery. It was for a small sum, and only done in anticipation of meeting the bill by his salary due a few weeks later. So far the fraud was palliated by the intention. By some mischance the document fell into the possession of Dr. Hickman, whose name it falsely bore. He immediately took steps to trace its origin, and having succeeded, he sent for Gleeson. When the youth, pale and terror-stricken by suspicion, made his appearance, he was amazed that, instead of finding a prosecutor ready prepared for his ruin, he discovered a benevolent patron, who, having long watched the zeal and assiduity with which he discharged his duties, desired to be of use to him in life. Hickman told him that if he were disposed to make the venture on his own account, he would use his influence to procure him some small agencies, and even assist him with funds, to make advances to those landlords who might employ him. The interview lasted long. There was much excellent advice and wise admonition on one side, profuse expression of gratitude and lasting fidelity on the other. "Very well, very well," said old Hickman, at the close of a very devoted speech, in which Gleeson professed the most attached and the most honorable motives,—for he was not at all aware that his bill was known of,—"I am not ignorant of mankind; they are rarely, if ever, very bad or very good; they can be occasionally faithful to their friends; but there is one thing they are always—careful of themselves. See this,"—here he took from his pocket-book the forged paper, and held it before the almost sinking youth,—"there is what can bring you to the gallows any day! Is this the first time?"

"It is, so help me—" cried he, falling on his knees.

"Never mind swearing. I believe you. And the last also?"

"And the last!"

"I see it must be, by the date," rejoined Hickman.

"I can pay it, sir; I have the money ready—on Tuesday—"

"Never mind that," replied Hickman, folding it up, and replacing it in the pocket-book. "You shall pay me in something better than money,—in gratitude. Come and dine with me alone to-day, and we 'll talk over the future."

It has never been our taste to present pictures of depravity to our readers; we would more willingly turn from them, or, where that is impossible, make them as sketchy as may be. It will be sufficient, then, if we say that Gleeson's whole career was the plan and creation of Hickman. The rigid and scrupulous honor, the spotless decorum, the unshaken probity, were all devices to win public confidence and esteem. That they were eminently successful, the epithet of "honest Tom Gleeson," by which he was universally known, is the guarantee. The union of such qualities with consummate skill and the most unwearied zeal soon made him the most distinguished man in his walk, and made his services not only an evidence of success, but of a rectitude in obtaining success that men of character prized still more highly.

Possessed of the titles of immense estates, invested with unbounded confidence by the owners, cognizant of every legal flaw that could excite uneasiness, aware of every hitch and strait of their circumstances, he was less the servant than the master of those who employed him.

It was a period when habits of extravagance prevailed to the widest extent. The proprietors of estates deemed spending their incomes their only duty, and left its cares to the agents. The only reproach, then, ever laid to Gleeson's door was that when a question of a sale or a loan was agitated, honest Tom's scruples were often a most troublesome impediment to his less scrupulous employer. In fact, Gleeson stood before the public as a kind of guardian of estated property,—the providence of dowagers, widows, and younger children!

Such a man, with his neck in a halter, at any moment at the mercy of old Dr. Hickman, was an agent for ruin almost inconceivable. Through his instrumentality the old usurer laid out his immense stores of wealth at enormous interest, obtained possession of vast estates at a mere fraction of their worth, till at length, grown hardy by long impunity, and daring by the recognition of the world, bolder expedients were ventured on. Darcy's ruin was long the cherished dream of Hickman; and when, after many a wily scheme and long negotiation, he saw Gleeson engaged as his agent, he felt certain of victory. His first scheme was to make Gleeson encourage young Lionel in every project of extravagance, by putting his name to bills, assuring him that his father permitted him an almost unlimited expenditure. This course once entered upon, and well aware that the young man kept no record of such transactions, his name was forged to several acceptances of large amount, and, subsequently, to sales of property to meet them.

Meanwhile great loans were raised by Darcy to pay off incumbrances, and never so employed; till, at length, the Knight decided upon the negotiation which was to clear off Hickman's mortgage,—the debt, of all others, he hated most to think of. So quietly was this carried on, that Hickman heard nothing of it; for Gleeson, long wearied by a life of treachery and perfidy, and never knowing the day or the hour when disclosure might come, had resolved on escaping to America with this large sum of money, leaving his colleague in crime to carry on business alone.

"The Doctor" was not, however, to be thus duped. Secret and silent as the arrangements for flight were, he heard of them all; and hastening out to Gleeson's house, coolly told him that any attempt at escape would bring him to the gallows. Gleeson attempted a denial. He alleged that his intended going over to England was merely on account of this sum, which Darcy was negotiating for, to pay off the mortgage.

A new light broke on Hickman. He saw that his terrified confederate could not much longer be relied upon, and it was agreed between them that Gleeson should pay the money to redeem the mortgage, and, having obtained the release, show it to the Knight of Gwynne. This done, he was to carry it back to Hickman, and, for the sum of £10,000, replace it in his hands, thus enabling the doctor to deny the payment and foreclose the mortgage, while honest Tom, weary of perfidy, and seeking repose, should follow his original plan, and escape to America.

The money was paid, as Freney surmised and Daly believed; but Gleeson, still dreading some act of treachery, instead of returning the release and claiming the price, started a day earlier than he promised. The rest is known to the reader. Whether the Hickmans credited the story of the suicide or not, they were never quite free of the terror of a disclosure; and, in pressing the matrimonial arrangement, hoped forever to set at rest the disputed possession.

It would probably not interest our readers were we to dwell longer on Gleeson or his motives. That some vague intention existed of one day restoring to Darcy the release of his mortgage, is perhaps not unlikely. A latent spark of honor, long buried beneath the ashes of crime, often shines out brightly in the last hour of existence. There might be, too, a cherished project of vengeance against the man that tempted and destroyed him. Be it as it may, he guarded the document as though it had been his last hope; and when tracked, pursued, and overtaken near Fort Erie by a party of the Delawares, of whom the Howling Wind, alias Bagenal Daly, was chief, it was found stitched up in the breast of his waistcoat.

Our space does not permit us to dwell upon Bagenal Daly's adventures, though we may assure our readers that they were both wild and wonderful. One only regret darkened the happiness of his exploit. It was that he was compelled so soon to leave the pleasant society of the Red Skins, and the intellectual companionship of "Blue Fox" and "Hissing Lightning;" while Sandy, discovering himself to be a widower, would gladly have contracted new ties, to cement the alliance of the ancient house of M'Grane with that of the Royal Family of Hickinbooke, or the "Slimy Whip Snake," a fair princess of which had bid high for his affections. Indeed, the worthy Sandy had become romantic on the subject, and suggested that if the lady would condescend to adopt certain articles of attire, he would have no objection to take her back to "The Corvy." These were sacrifices, however, that not even love was called upon to make, and the project was abortive.

So far have we condensed Bagenal Daly's narrative, which, orally delivered, lasted till the sun was high and the morning fine and bright. He had only concluded, when a servant in O'Reilly's livery brought a letter, which he said was to be given to the Knight of Gwynne, but required no answer. Its contents were the following:—

Sir,—The melancholy catastrophe of yesterday evening might excuse me in your eyes from any attention to the claims of mere business. But the discovery of certain documents lately in the possession of my father demand at my hands the most prompt and complete reparation. I now know, sir, that we were unjustly possessed of an estate and property that were yours. I also know that severe wrongs have been inflicted upon you through the instrumentality of my family. I have only to make the best amende in my power, by immediately restoring the one, and asking forgiveness for the other. If you can and will accord me the pardon I seek, I shall, as soon as the sad duties which devolve upon me here are completed, leave this country for the Continent, never to return. I have already given directions to my legal adviser to confer with Mr Bicknell; and no step will be omitted to secure a safe and speedy restoration of your house and estate to its rightful owner. In deep humiliation, I remain

Your obedient servant,

H. O'Reilly.

"Poor fellow!" said Darcy, throwing down the letter before Daly; "he seems to have been no party to the fraud, and yet all the penalty falls upon him."

"Have no pity for the upstart rascal, Maurice; I'll wager a hundred—thank Heaven, Mr. Gleeson has put me in possession of a few—that he was as deep as his father. Give me this paper, and I'll ask honest Tom the question."

"Not so, Bagenal; I should be sorry to think worse of any man than I must do. Let him have at least the benefit of a doubt; and as to honest Tom, set him at liberty: we no longer want him; the papers he has given are quite sufficient,—more than we are ever like to need."

Daly had no fancy for relinquishing his hold of the game that cost him so much trouble to take; but the Knight's words were usually a law to him, and with a muttering remark of "I'll do it because I'll have my eye on him," he left the room to liberate his captive.

"There he goes," exclaimed Daly, as, re-entering the room, he saw a chaise rapidly drive from the door,—"there he goes, Maurice; and I own to you I have an easier conscience for having let loose Freney on the world than for liberating honest Tom Gleeson; but who have we here, with four smoking posters?—ladies too!"

A travelling-carriage drew up at the door of the little inn, and immediately three ladies descended. "That's Maria," cried Daly, rushing from the room, and at once returned with his sister, Lady Eleanor, and Miss Darcy.

Miss Daly had, three days before, received a letter from

Bagenal, detailing his capture of Gleeson, and informing her that he hoped to be back in Ireland almost as soon as his letter. With these tidings she hastened to Lady Eleanor, and concerted the journey which now brought them all together.

Story-tellers have but scant privilege to linger where all is happiness, unbroken and perfect. Like Mother Cary's chickens, their province is rather with menacing storm than the signs of fair weather. We have, then, but space to say that a more delighted party never met than those who now assembled in that little inn; but one face showed any signs of passing sorrow,—that was poor Forester's. The general joy, to which he had so much contributed by his exertions, rather threw a gloomier shade over his own unhappiness; and in secret he resolved to say "Good-bye" that same evening.

Amid a thousand plans for the future, all tinged with their own bright color, they sat round the fire at evening, when Miss Daly, whose affection for the youth was strengthened by what she had seen during his illness, remarked that he alone seemed exempt from the general happiness.

"To whom we owe so much," said Lady Eleanor, kindly. "My husband is indebted to him for his life."

"I can say as much, too," said Daly; "not to speak of Gleeson's gratitude."

"Nay!" exclaimed the young man, blushing, "I did not know the service I was rendering. I little guessed how grateful I should myself have reason to be for being its instrument."

"All this is very well," said Miss Daly, abruptly; "but it is not honest, — no, it is not honest. There are other feelings concerned here than such amiable generalities as Joy, Pity, and Gratitude. Don't frown, Helen, — that is better, love, — a smile becomes you to perfection."

"I must stop you," said Forester, blushing deeply. "It will be enough if I say that any observation you can make must give me the deepest pain, — not for myself—"

"But for Helen? I don't believe it. You may be a very sharp politician and a very brave soldier, but you know very little about young ladies. Yes, there 'a no denying it,-their game is all deceit."

"Oh! Colonel Darcy—Lady Eleanor, will you not speak a word?" exclaimed Forester, pale and agitated.

"A hundred, my dear boy," cried the Knight, "if they would serve you; but Helen's one is worth them all."

"Miss Darcy, dare I hope? Helen, dearest!" added he, in a whisper, as, taking her hand, he led her towards a window.

"My Lord, the carriage is ready," said his servant, throwing wide the door.

"You may order the horses back again," said Daly, dryly; "my Lord is not going this evening."

Has our reader ever made a long voyage? Has he ever experienced in himself the strange but most complete alteration in all his sentiments and feelings when far away from land, — on the wild, bleak waters, — and that same "himself," when in sight of shore, with seaweed around the prow, and land-breezes on his cheek? But a few hours back and that ship was his world; he knew her from "bow to taffrail;" he greeted the cook's galley as though it were the "restaurant" his heart delighted in; he even felt a kind of friendship for the pistons as they jerked up and down into a bowing acquaintance. But now how changed are his sentiments, how fixedly are his eyes turned to the pier of the harbor, and how impatient is he at those tacking zigzag approaches by which nautical skill and care approximate the goal!

Already landed in imagination, the cautious manouvres of the crew are an actual martyrdom; he has no bowels for anything save his own enfranchisement, and he cannot comprehend the tiresome detail of preparations, which, after all, perhaps, are scarcely five minutes in endurance. At last, the gangway launched, see him, how he elbows forward, fighting his way, carpet-bag in hand, regardless of passport-people, police, and porters; he'll scarce take time to mutter a "Good-bye, Captain," in the haste to leave a scene all whose interest is over, whose adventure is past.

Such is the end of a voyage; and such, or very nearly such, the end of a novel! You, most amiable reader, are the passenger, we the skipper. A few weeks ago you deemed us tolerable company, *faute de mieux*, perhaps. We 'll not ask why, at all events. We had you out on the wide, wild waters of uncertainty, free to sail where'er our fancy listed. In our very waywardness there was a mock semblance of power, for the creatures we presented to you were our own, their lives and fortunes in our hands. Now all that is over,— we have neared the shore, and all our hold on you is bygone.

How can we hope to excite interest in events already accomplished? Why linger over details which you have already filled up? Of course, say you, all ends happily now. Virtue is rewarded—as novelists understand rewarding—by matrimony, and vice punished in single blessedness. The hero marries the heroine; and if they don't live happy, etc.

But what became of Bagenal Daly? says some one who would compliment us by expressing so much of interest. Bagenal, then, only waited to see the Knight restored to his own, to retire with his sister to "The Corvy," where, attended by Sandy, he passed the remainder of his days in peace and quietude; his greatest enjoyment being to seize on a chance tourist to the Causeway, and make him listen to narratives of his early life, but which age had now so far commingled that the merely strange became actually marvellous.

Paul Dempsey grieved for a week, but consoled himself on hearing that his rival had been a "lord;" and subsequently, in a "moment of enthusiasm," he married Mrs. Fumbally. The Hickmans left Ireland for the Continent, where they are still to be found, rambling about from city to city, and expressing the utmost sympathy with their country's misfortunes, but, to avoid any admixture of meaner feeling, suffering no taint of lucre to mingle with their compassion.

As for Lionel Darcy, his name is to be found in the despatches from the East, and with a mention that shows that he has derogated in nothing from the proud character of his race.

Of all those who figured before our reader, but one remains on the stage where they all performed; and he, perhaps, has no claim to be especially remembered. There is always, however, somewhat of respectability attached to the oldest inhabitant, that chronicler of cold winters and warm summers, of rainy springs and stormy Octobers. Con Heffernan, then, lives, and still wields no inconsiderable share of his ancient influence. Each party has discovered his treachery, but neither can dispense with his services. He is the last link remaining between the men of Ireland's "great day" and the very different race who now usurp the direction of her destiny.

Of the period of which we have endeavored to picture some meagre resemblance, unhappily the few traces remaining are those most to be deplored. The poverty, the misery, and the anarchy survive; the genial hospitality, the warm attachment to country, the cordial generosity of Irish feeling, have sadly declined. Let us hope that from the depth of our present sufferings better days are about to dawn, and a period approaching when Ireland shall be "great" in the happiness of her people, "glorious" in the development of her inexhaustible resources, and "free" by that best of freedom,—free from the trammels of an unmeaning party warfare, which has ever subjected the welfare of the country to the miserable intrigues of a few adventurers.